T0148959

The Rebel's Mark

Also by S. W. Perry

The Angel's Mark

The Serpent's Mark

The Saracen's Mark

The Heretic's Mark

S. W. PERRY

First published in hardback in Great Britain in 2022 by Corvus,
an imprint of Atlantic Books Ltd.

This paperback edition published in 2023 by Corvus

10 9 8 7 6 5 4 3 2 1

A CIP catalogue record for this book is available from the British Library.

Hardback ISBN: 978 1 83895 398 0
Paperback ISBN: 978 1 83895 400 0
E-book ISBN: 978 1 83895 399 7

Printed in Great Britain.

Corvus
An imprint of Atlantic Books Ltd
Ormond House
26–27 Boswell Street
London
WC1N 3JZ

www.corvus-books.co.uk

For Jane.

Into Ireland I go. The Queen hath irrevocably decreed it…
And I am tied in my own reputation.

Robert Devereux, Earl of Essex, 1599

I'm off to the wars
For want of peace.
Oh, had I but money,
I'd show more sense.

Miguel de Cervantes, *Don Quixote*

PART 1

✠

The Death of Kings

1

The Atlantic Ocean, sixty leagues south-west of Ireland, September 1598

Since the sandglass was last turned, the storm has stalked the *San Juan de Berrocal* from behind the cover of a darkening sky. It has sniffed at her with its blustery breath, jostled her with watery claws, spat at her with a sudden icy blast of rain. Along the western horizon where the twilight is dying, flashes of lightning now ripple. Whenever the carrack rises on a wave crest, they seem brighter. Nearer. It is only a matter of time, thinks Don Rodriquez Calva de Sagrada, before the accompanying thunder is no longer drowned by the roaring of the sea and the screaming of the wind.

Drowned.

Don Rodriquez has faced death before in the service of Spain. He has made voyages longer and more uncertain even than this one. But to drown... that, he thinks, would be an ignominious death for a courtier of The Most Illustrious Philip, by the Grace of God, King of Spain, Aragon, Valencia, Mallorca, Naples, Sicily and Sardinia.

The deck cants alarmingly as the *San Juan* plunges down a vertiginous slope of black water. Don Rodriquez flails wildly for something to hang on to. His hands seize the wooden housing of the ship's lodestar, brightly painted red and gold – the colours of Castile. Beneath his numb fingers, the wet timber is as slippery as if the paint were blood. But to let go, he is sure, would result in him sliding off the deck and into the maelstrom surging mere feet below. He is beginning to wonder if the captain – fearful of interception by one of those sleek English sea-wolves bristling with cannon and possessed of Lucifer's luck – has made a fatal error of judgement.

As the deck soars upwards again, leaving Don Rodriquez's stomach somewhere in the depths of the ocean, the captain – a short, taciturn fellow with the darting eyes of a scavenging gull, and whose seaman's contempt for the landsman who chartered his ship has not abated since they left Coruña – pins his chart against the lid of the lodestar box. The corners thrash wildly in the gale like the wings of a bird trying to escape the hunter's net. 'Be not dismayed, my lord!' he says with an insulting smile as the index finger of his free hand, encased in the thick felt of his glove, makes landfall in the pool of dancing light cast by the helmsman's lantern. 'God, in his infinite mercy, has provided us with a safe anchorage – *here*.'

Don Rodriquez leans forward to study the map. It is a portolan chart, purchased in Seville for more *maravedís* than he had cared to pay. Everything on it – from the compass bearings to the harbours and inlets, promontories and coves – is based upon reports from Spanish fishermen who once plied these waters. But since the outbreak of the present war between the heretic English and God-fearing Spain there have been few enough of those in these waters. What if the map is out of date, and the English have built a castle where the captain's finger now rests? Besides, it will be utterly dark soon. Not even a lunatic would consider a night landfall on such a treacherous coast. And only a lunatic who was heartily tired of life would do so in the face of an approaching storm.

'Here' turns out to be some distance from Roaringwater Bay, where the captain had promised to put them ashore at first light.

'Is there nowhere closer? Every extra hour I am ashore is an hour given to the English to contrive our ruin.'

With an impertinence he would never dare risk on dry land, the captain says, 'We made a pact, my lord, did we not? I am not to ask why a grand courtier of our sovereign majesty wishes to interrupt his voyage to the Spanish Netherlands to spend a night in Ireland. In return, the same grand courtier shall leave *all* decisions of a maritime nature to me. Yes?'

'Yes,' admits Don Rodriquez despondently. 'We agreed.'

'Trust me – I know these waters,' the captain adds. 'I have sailed them before, with the Duke of Medina Sidonia.'

The man's familiarity with the coast of Ireland is why Don Rodriquez hired him in the first place. Now, thinking on the fate that befell the commander of the grand Armada, he is beginning to have second thoughts.

Another wave of watery malevolence sends the *San Juan* into a plunge even more sickening than the last. The sea breaks over the elegantly carved Castilian lion on her prow, and for a moment Don Rodriquez fears she will go on plunging into the deep, never to rise again. From beneath the deck planks, a shrill female scream carries clearly against the clamour of the gale.

'You had best go below and comfort the noble lady, your daughter, and leave me to my duties, my lord,' says the captain, fighting the wind for possession of the chart as he tries to tuck it back into his cape.

Don Rodriquez, being a man of honour, objects.

'You may think me a cosseted courtier, Señor, but I am also a soldier, and I have voyaged in His Majesty's service before. My arms are still strong. Let me stay here. Direct me as you will.'

The captain glances at his passenger's well-manicured hands, the fingers laden with bejewelled rings. He looks at the pretentiously styled black curls on his head, the conceit of a man just a little too old to carry them off. A landsman of the worst kind, he decides. A danger on a storm-tossed deck, not only to himself but to all around him.

'Voyaged where?' he asks. 'On the Sanabria, in a pleasure barge?'

'To New Spain. To Hispaniola.'

The captain looks Don Rodriquez up and down, wondering if this is little more than a courtier's boasting. 'You never told me that at Coruña. Was this recently?'

'Twenty years ago,' Don Rodriquez admits.

'Ah,' the captain says, barely bothering to keep the scorn out of his voice. 'In that case, your place is not here, my lord. I suggest you go below and leave me and my crew to our profession.' Then, with the sly smile of a Madrid street-trickster, he adds, 'I hope you and the women have strong stomachs. We're in for a tempestuous night.'

✠

Beyond the shuttered windows of the smaller of the two grand banqueting chambers at Greenwich Palace, on the southern bank of the Thames some five miles downriver from London Bridge, the early-September dusk is troubled by no more than a few high wisps of cloud, as insubstantial as an old man's breath on winter air. Inside, the candles have been lit, the dining boards and trestles cleared away, the covers of Flanders linen folded up and carted off to the wash-house, the plate and silverware removed. As for the diners, if indigestion is in danger of making its presence publicly known, they are doing their level best to suffer in silence. Elizabeth of England does not appreciate having her masques interrupted by vulgar noises off-stage.

Dr Nicholas Shelby and his wife Bianca have removed themselves to the gallery, amongst the other palace chaff who don't merit a place closer to the players. As a consequence, they have an uninterrupted view of the assembled courtiers bedecked in their late-summer plumage: satin peasecod doublets and venetians for the men, low-cut brocade gowns cascading richly over whalebone farthingales for the women – all striking languid poses around a raised dais covered in plush scarlet velvet. In the centre of the dais stands a gilded wooden chair emblazoned with the English lion and the Welsh dragon. Upon the chair lies a plump cushion covered in the finest cloth of gold. And upon the cushion, like a petite pharaoh perched on a ziggurat, sits a woman with the whitest face Bianca has ever seen.

'She's smaller than I expected,' Bianca whispers into her husband's ear.

'Smaller?' Nicholas answers. 'What did you expect – an Amazon?'

The court has assembled tonight to enjoy a recital of excerpts from Master Edmund Spenser's *The Faerie Queene*, performed by the best actors the Master of the Revels has contrived to drag out of the Southwark taverns and transport – standing fare only – on the ferry from Blackfriars.

On the assumption that mirth at the expense of royalty is probably treasonous, Bianca stifles a giggle. 'Has she let you see what she hides behind all that white ceruse yet?'

'Of course not. I'm not allowed to actually touch the sacred personage of the sovereign.'

'Then how can you treat her if she falls ill?'

'That's only half the problem,' Nicholas replies. 'What if I have to cast a horoscope before making a diagnosis? If it turns out to be inauspicious and I say so out loud, or write it down, I could be sent to the Tower for imagining her demise. At the moment, that's treason.'

'But you don't believe in casting horoscopes before making a diagnosis, Nicholas. You never have.'

'But the College of Physicians will insist on it. Otherwise they'll accuse me of not doing my job properly. Remember what happened to poor old Dr Lopez? Being the queen's doctor didn't save *him* from his enemies.'

'How can I forget?' Bianca says, rolling her eyes. 'I see his head on the parapet of the gatehouse every time I cross London Bridge. It's been up there since before we went away.' She pulls a face. 'Except for the jaw, of course. That must have dropped off and fallen into the river while we were in Padua.'

Nicholas rests his elbows on the balustrade and turns his face very close to hers. 'If you want the truth, I don't believe she ordered Sir Robert Cecil to call us back to England because she wanted *me* to be her physician. She can call on any number of the senior fellows from the College. They'd stab each other with a lancet to get the summons.'

Bianca pushes a rebellious strand of dark hair back under the rim of her lace caul. Holding his gaze, she whispers mischievously, 'Well, it wasn't because she was in need of a good dancing partner, was it, Husband?'

Nicholas feigns hurt feelings. 'It's not *my* fault I can't dance a decent pavane or a volta. My feet spent their formative years wading through good Suffolk clay.'

'Are you telling me that we subjected ourselves and our infant son to several uncomfortable weeks aboard an English barque all the way from Venice just to satisfy the passing fancy of an old woman who wears whitewash on her skin?' Bianca asks. Then, as an afterthought, 'And if that's her own hair, then I'm Lucrezia Borgia.'

Given his wife's known skills as an apothecary – and the long line of Italian women on her mother's side whose art in mixing poisons is still infamous throughout the Veneto – Nicholas winces at her choice of comparison.

'She likes to hear reports from foreign lands,' he says, 'particularly concerning the new sciences. She was very interested to hear about my studies with Professor Fabricius at the Palazzo Bo. She understood everything I told her about the professor's views on the mechanisms in the human eye.'

'Mercy! Who could possibly have imagined such a thing: a woman – a queen – understanding the musings of a learned professor?'

Nicholas has learned not to rise to the bait. 'Besides, I believe she's grown weary of being nagged by her old physicians,' he says. 'It is my diagnosis that she has chosen to discomfort them by favouring someone they all hold to be a dangerous rebel – someone young; someone who still has all his teeth.'

'You're her *plaything*,' Bianca announces with sly enjoyment. 'My husband – an old woman's sugar comfit.'

'It hasn't done the noble Earl of Essex any harm, has it?' Nicholas counters, nodding in the direction of Robert Devereux, lying like a favoured greyhound at the foot of the dais. At thirty-two – four years younger than Nicholas – he makes an elegant sight, only slightly less pearled and bejewelled than the queen herself.

'No, too thin in the calf for me,' Bianca says, surreptitiously running the instep of her right foot along the back of Nicholas's leg. 'And *far* too primped.'

On the floor below, two slender youths in gleaming breastplates are striking heroic postures. One declaims as loudly as his adenoidal voice will permit, "Upon a great adventure he was bound, that greatest Gloriana to him gave, that greatest Glorious Queen of Faerie land—"

'Tell me again, Husband: which one is the Gentle Knight?'

'Him – the one with the broken nose.'

'Why does he have that silly painted horse's head between his legs?'

'Didn't you catch the line about his angry steed chiding at the foaming bit?'

'Foaming bit? It looks to me as though someone's stuck a giant painted wooden pizzle onto his codpiece. It's the sort of thing I expect to see on a Bankside May Day, not at Greenwich Palace,' Bianca says, making a play of fanning the embarrassment from her cheeks.

'Just try to imagine it's an angry steed, *please*.'

'So, the other one – the one with the superior look on his face – that's Gloriana.'

'Correct.'

'And Gloriana is really Elizabeth.'

'You have it in one.'

'And this fairy land they're in – that's really England.'

'It's an *allegory*,' Nicholas says slowly, a hint of weariness in his voice.

'It's a delusion, that's what it is – a woman in her sixties being played by a boy who's barely plucked his first whisker.'

'Edmund Spenser is our finest poet,' Nicholas protests, not altogether convincingly.

'I'll take Italian comedy – Arlecchino and Pantalone – over your Master Spenser's allegory today and every day, thank you, Husband.'

A portly factotum from the Revel's office, lounging unnoticed against the wainscoting, leans forward. '*Some* people prefer to listen to quality verse,' he mutters, 'rather than the bickering of *other* people who are clearly devoid of any artistic appreciation whatsoever.'

'Sorry,' says Nicholas.

'How long will this go on?' Bianca whispers.

'It's a *very* long poem.'

'Do you think anyone will notice if we sit down against the wall and take a nap?'

'Don't worry,' Nicholas tells her. 'Gloriana herself will have nodded off long before the end.'

'Then we can all go to bed?'

'Bed?'

'That painted pizzle has given me an idea.'

'The players will all pretend she's wide awake. So will the court. You can't escape Edmund Spenser that easily,' Nicholas says despondently. 'I fear we're in for a long night.'

✠

Aboard the *San Juan de Berrocal*, Don Rodriquez huddles in the tiny cabin afforded by his status as a courtier and longs himself back in the Escorial in Madrid with his dying monarch. Anywhere but here, where the world seems as if it is trying to disassemble itself in a shrieking, plunging, battering paroxysm. Clasped in a terrified trinity with his daughter Constanza and her Carib maid Cachorra – calm, stately, brave Cachorra – his only comfort is that if tonight he must die, he will not die alone.

'Is it to be thus, Father?' Constanza asks in a moment when the howling of the wind, the crashing of the sea and the tortured groaning of the vessel subside just long enough for her voice to be heard. 'Am I not to know the blessings of marriage and motherhood? Am I to perish in the company of common mariners? Is this the pass you have brought me to, my lord Father?'

To the mind of Don Rodriquez, common mariners are all that now stand between his daughter and a watery grave. But Constanza is made in the mould of her late mother, choosy about the company she keeps ever since she was old enough to distinguish one face from another. She is a plump, haughty girl, whose fingernails have been sunk in his skin almost from the moment he entered the cabin to warn her of the approaching storm. He cannot see her face in the darkness, but he knows the look she is wearing well enough: the full lips turned down at the edges; the eternal crease between eyebrows stiffened to the texture of a brush with kohl, charcoal and grease (Constanza cannot come down to breakfast each morning until Cachorra has properly applied it); the air of permanent dissatisfaction, despite never knowing a moment without luxury until she boarded this ship.

At least the storm has taken away her hunger, he thinks. Every day since leaving Coruña she has turned up her nose at the food, utterly unaware that the very mariners she so disdains are on hard rations because half the St *Juan*'s hold is packed with crates containing her trousseau.

'God grant His torment will soon be over,' Don Rodriquez tells her with more certainty than he has any right to feel. 'And when we are done with Ireland, which will be no more than a day or two, we shall continue on our way to Antwerp and the joyous occasion of your wedding.'

Unobserved in the heaving darkness, he allows himself a shallow smile. A joyous occasion indeed, if only for the fact that Constanza will become someone else's worry. She is to marry a preposterously mannered cousin, currently in the service of King Philip's commander in the Spanish Netherlands, Archduke Ernst of Austria. By all accounts they will be well suited. They can look down their noses at the Flemings, the Brabantians and the Dutch to their hearts' content. He will stay for the ceremony, of course, but not a moment longer. With God's grace and favour, he will be back at the Escorial in time to mourn his dying king.

Don Rodriquez feels his daughter's chest heaving against his. He takes this as evidence of her mounting terror. Then the stomach-churning stench of vomit permeates the closed air of the cabin and he senses an uncomfortable warmth spreading into the weave of his expensively brocaded jerkin. God's punishment, he thinks, for his lack of charity.

From above the deckhead – though at this moment if they were capsized and upside-down Don Rodriquez is certain he would be none the wiser – comes a rapid series of crashes, loud enough to beat down even the frenzied screaming of the wind. He has grown uncomfortably familiar with the booming of the sea hammering against the *San Juan*'s planks. But these sounds are different. One of the masts must have gone, carrying heavy spars and tangled cordage with it. This is it, then, he thinks: the end. The sacred mission entrusted to him is ruined, stillborn, smothered even before it has left the cradle.

And then Don Rodriquez feels the fingers of another female hand, less frantic than his daughter's. They are seeking out the profile of his face in the darkness, as though the owner of them is trying to fix a last memory of him in her mind before the sea breaks in. He knows at once they are Cachorra's fingers. They have a strength in them, a resolve that he knows well, though no physical intimacy has ever existed between himself and his daughter's Carib maid. Freeing one hand from his daughter's frantic grasp, Don Rodriquez places it over the other woman's fingers and presses them against the side of his face. There is no light to see by, because the cabin lantern has long ago spun itself off its hook and now lies shattered somewhere amongst all the other debris that slides around in the darkness. So it is in his imagination that Don Rodriquez looks into Cachorra's astoundingly large brown eyes – eyes that every Spanish woman who has ever seen them says can only be the result of taking a measure of belladonna, because no one is ever born with eyes like those – and, for the first time since the storm struck, he knows comfort.

At Greenwich Palace the performance of *The Faerie Queene* is drawing towards its ponderous and impenetrable close. Several of the players, Bianca has noticed, are regulars at the Jackdaw on Bankside. She knows them well. She can see their hearts aren't in their work. She feels for them. It cannot be rewarding when the one person you have come to entertain has spent most of the evening in conversation with the Earl of Essex and several serious-looking members of the Privy Council, taking little notice of your performance.

Nicholas is almost asleep on his feet. Every few moments his head pitches forward and his close-cut beard rasps on the starched ruff that Rose Monkton insisted on laundering for him. Dear Rose. She still cannot quite comprehend that she is no longer Bianca's maid but the legal tenant of the Jackdaw, along with her husband, Ned.

It was Ned Monkton who had made it safe for them to return to England. It was Ned who had killed the lie that Nicholas was old Dr Lopez's co-conspirator in a plot to poison the queen, a slander that had forced Bianca to accompany her husband across the Narrow Sea, eventually seeking refuge in her birthplace, Padua, until his innocence could be proved. That acquittal had taken more than a year. By the time word reached them, Bianca was pregnant with little Bruno. Nicholas, too, was fully occupied studying anatomy under Professor Fabricius at the Palazzo Bo. Returning at once was out of the question. Besides, Robert Cecil valued having proxy eyes and ears in the Veneto and had wanted Nicholas to stay.

Then, last Twelfth Night, one of Cecil's enciphered messages had arrived at their house. The queen, apparently, had found time to enquire what had happened to that fetching young physician, the one with the tousled black hair and the frame of a ploughman, the Suffolk yeoman's son with the country burr in his voice, the one guaranteed to discomfort the grey, hidebound ranks of her royal stool-inspectors, urine-watchers and medical astrologers.

There had been no argument from Bianca about leaving. She had no family left in Italy, and before fleeing England with Nicholas had made a good life for herself on Bankside. Her sojourn in Padua, while pleasing enough, had merely reinforced her conviction that England was her home now. Besides, had Nicholas elected to stay in Padua, he would have announced himself a traitor to his sovereign and the country of his birth.

But which one of us is the worm in the apple's flesh – me or my husband? she asks herself as she watches the players end the performance with a lively jig played on sackbut and tambour. Does Robert Cecil not wonder if Nicholas might have warmed a little to the Catholic heresy while he was away in Italy? All those papist professors at the Palazzo Bo whose intellect Nicholas so admired... all those provocative altar paintings he was exposed to in the churches she took him to, the forbidden Masses he attended...

She can see Cecil now, from her vantage point in the gallery. There he is – almost directly below her – a crooked little thing in a lawyerly black gown, casting furtive daggers from his eyes at the perfection that is Robert Devereux, Earl of Essex.

Cecil has known of Bianca's heresy long enough. He has always tolerated it because Nicholas is one of his most trusted intelligencers. But how, she wonders as she looks down with the faintest trace of a wry smile, can the queen's principal secretary be certain that the man who answered his summons is – upon his return – in *all* regards the same man who left?

2

The dawn has arrived – and, with it, God's mercy. Like a disappointed matador faced with a cowardly bull, the storm has departed without bothering to stay around for the final, fatal thrust. The black night of terror they have endured was nothing but an *auto-da-fé*, a test of faith. It is a test Don Rodriquez believes he has passed. His abiding memory of the trial is not the raging of the tempest, the fear, the stench of his daughter's vomit on his doublet, but of Cachorra's touch against his cheek.

Beneath the cabin door a pale, narrow blade of grey light sweeps back and forth, as if searching for survivors within. We're here! he wants to shout at the sliver of probing dawn. We're alive! Instructing Constanza and Cachorra to offer prayers for their deliverance, he unbolts the door and goes out into morning to assess the damage.

What he sees astounds him. The wave tops are as high as the sides of the ship, rolling the *San Juan* like dice cupped in the hand of a desperate gambler on a losing streak. As the waves break, sheets of dazzling white foam stream across the deck, borne on the still-wicked wind. As the first low rays of sunlight pierce the fleeing black clouds, he braces himself against a tangled thicket of cordage, the ropes icy wet to his grasp, and shakes his head in wonder.

Only the lower part of the mainmast still stands, the noble Galician pine shredded at the break as if it were nothing but common kindling. The quarterdeck rail on the leeward side has been torn away, the posts – crowned with finely carved Castilian lions' heads – now so much driftwood lost somewhere in the night behind them. Not a single lantern has survived. Several of the deck cannon have gone, their rope tackles sheared. Many of the others are jumbled and overturned like nursery toys. If the English come across the *San Juan* now, Don Rodriquez thinks, they would have nothing in their hearts but pity. But not even the English would be so foolish as to venture out in seas like this.

On the main deck the sailors whom the sea has not taken in the night ignore the courtier's sudden appearance. They are too busy wielding axes and knives, trying to cut away the tangle of ropes that coil across the deck like the snakes on a gorgon's head. Their bodies seem bound by invisible bands of exhaustion, their movements laboured and dispirited. They remind Don Rodriquez of the native slaves who toil in the gold and silver mines of New Spain, barely human at all.

Turning to look up at the poop-deck, he sees the captain leaning over the side, observing the huge mat of tangled rigging and shattered yards that clings to the *San Juan de Berrocal* like a beard, rising and falling as the sea breaks against her. Noticing the newcomer on deck, the captain turns his head. Gaunt and red-eyed, he wears the expression of a man who has already stared into the burning eyes of far too many demons to care much about what awaits him in hell.

Don Rodriquez climbs what is left of the ladder to the poop-deck. From here he can see – between the surging wave crests – two small, jagged islands on the horizon. The captain points to a pair of inverted Vs on the portolan chart, about a finger's width from the Irish coast.

'We call the larger one Isla Santa,' he says, his voice a mere croak after a night of bellowing commands against the noise of the storm. 'There's a monastery on the peak. In their own language the heathens call it *Sceilg Mhichíl*. Ireland is but two leagues on. We won't see it yet, because of the waves.'

'Perhaps the monks will offer us sanctuary,' Don Rodriquez says. Even a tiny rock two leagues out into the ocean would be preferable to a minute more of this, he thinks.

'There *are* no monks,' the captain tells him with a disturbingly wild laugh. 'It's deserted. And even if there were, we cannot make a safe landfall there.'

'What hope do we have of reaching Roaringwater Bay?' Don Rodriquez asks.

The captain stares at him as though he's speaking Cachorra's native Carib.

'I understand you are used to the comforts of court, Señor, and therefore unaccustomed to my firmament,' he says. 'But even *you* must have realized by now that we're drifting at the mercy of wind and current.'

Señor. Don Rodriquez cannot help but notice this is the first time the master has called him anything less deferential than 'my lord'.

The captain looks out towards the rolling, pitching horizon. 'I'll order the anchors dropped when we reach shallower water,' he says. 'You'd best pray to Almighty God they hold.'

'And if God doesn't hear me?'

The captain looks at Don Rodriquez with something bordering on contempt.

'Then pray to the Devil instead. All will depend on where we get blown ashore.'

✠

I'll order the anchors dropped... You'd best pray to Almighty God they hold.

But the anchors have not held.

Now that the last of the ripped canvas had gone overboard, a fatal lassitude has fallen upon the *San Juan*. Isla Santa has long since disappeared astern. Now the only sounds to be heard are the funereal drumbeats of the waves pounding against the hull, the keening of the wind and the murmured praying of the crew. Everyone is praying now. Prayers are all they have left.

Don Rodriquez kneels on the quarterdeck and claps his hands together as though making a last confession before going into battle.

'Holy Father, have mercy on a poor sinner. Make your eyes to shine upon us and your grace to bear us up above these trials... You've done it once. You can do it again. Spain needs me...'

He knows the chances are slim. Most of the coastline here is unforgiving rock that towers above the breaking surf. He can see it drawing relentlessly nearer every time a wave crest breaks. It will smash to pieces what is left of the *San Juan*. Human flesh and bone won't last a minute. Better to drown than be flayed alive.

But if, by God's great fortune, they do survive the inevitable wreck, what then? wonders Don Rodriquez. Can a way be found to the meeting place? Will the Englishman wait for him? Can the enterprise upon which he is embarked be rescued, even in the face of disaster? All will depend upon whose hands – besides God's – are waiting to catch them.

If they find themselves amongst the Irish who have risen in revolt against the heretical English queen, then all will be well. Spain is a long-standing ally of all who would see the Protestant heretics chased out of the island ahead. He will be feted by their chieftains, perhaps even by the rebel leader himself, the Earl of Tyrone. It will take a while, but there is every reason to expect that these good Catholics will help him find another vessel to carry his daughter and Cachorra on to Antwerp, though with the trousseau and the dowry at the bottom of the sea, her exquisitely noble groom might think somewhat less of the match and tear up the contract. So be it. Constanza will sulk for a month or two, but he's used to that.

But what if there are other hands waiting to catch him? If he falls amongst the English settlers who think they hold this island for their ageing queen, what then?

In that event, Constanza herself will be his cover. A Spanish nobleman and his daughter shipwrecked on a voyage to her marriage is a tale that should play well enough with a nation that loves the frivolity of the playhouse. Constanza will speak for him. She has good English, taught to her by Padre Robert of the Jesuit seminary at Valladolid. It was Robert Persons himself who, on the quay at Coruña the day they departed, had wished them God's fair winds.

There is bound to be a period of confinement and interrogation in some draughty castle. But why should any minister of the English queen consider his appearance in Ireland to be anything more than what he will say it is: an unfortunate shipwreck on the way to a wedding? The food is likely to be unbearable and the company vulgar. A little of the family plate and jewels back in Castile may have to be sold to raise a ransom. But it has happened before. Who knows, in Antwerp the lucky groom may even wait, poor sap. Yes, Don Rodriquez thinks, if we fall into English hands, Constanza will be the saving of us.

The rocky cliffs are much closer now. The roar of the ocean breaking against them grows louder with every passing moment. The end cannot be long in coming. Don Rodriquez is not afraid. He has faced danger often in the service of Spain. He wonders if the dying King Philip will learn of his fate before his reign ends.

A king's prayers should count for something in the ledger of a man's life.

Sensing movement at his shoulder, he turns – to find himself staring at a plump Madonna in a green satin gown, a black lace mantilla covering her features. For a moment he is speechless. His exhaustion must be playing tricks on his mind. Then the Madonna speaks, her voice muffled by the folds of the mantilla.

'If I am to die, Father, I shall die as the bride of José de Vallfogona y Figaro-Madroñera!'

Constanza pulls aside the black lace veil. The full lips that have never quite decided if poise or petulance should be their lodestar are trembling. Her eyes dart from the rocks ahead to her father's face, accusing both. Behind her, Cachorra gives a resigned shrug, as if to say, *She ordered me to dress her. If she wants to drown in her trousseau, who am I to disobey her command?*

Before he finds his voice, Don Rodriquez can do little but stare. 'Christ's most holy wounds, Daughter! What nonsense is this?'

Constanza begins to wail.

He considers telling his daughter sternly to accept what must be accepted. Face it like a true daughter of Spain. Bear it the way your late mother bore the illness that carried her off. Show the same fortitude as your dying king. But he is not an uncaring father, so he remains silent. He puts an arm around Constanza's shoulders. Her little button-nose puckers at the smell of the vomit she left on his doublet all those hours ago.

It is Cachorra – the leopard cub that has grown to strength and beauty since that day in Hispaniola when he first set eyes upon her – who now shows more courage than any of them. She stands watching the oncoming cliffs as though they hold not the slightest danger for her. What right did I have to pluck such a flower from the edge of the known world, Don Rodriquez asks himself, only to bring it to a terrible end on a rocky Irish coast?

But it is too late now for remorse. Besides, Holy Spain has plucked whole meadows of such flowers from the golden lands across the ocean. What is one amongst so many?

The *San Juan* is now almost upon the rocks. Don Rodriquez can see in clear detail a jagged promontory jutting out towards the vessel, the sea breaking over its base in wild detonations of white foam that shine in the morning sunlight like clouds of jewels scattered from a giant's hand.

As if to a silent command, several of the praying sailors rise from their knees, pointing, laughing, waving. Even cheering.

Now Don Rodriquez can make out, either side of the sharp promontory, the entrances to two sheltered coves, each with a curved strand of shingle at the foot of steep, craggy bluffs. He allows himself a brief feeling of relief. God has not forsaken Spain. God never would.

Facing the shore, he has his back to the wave that comes in from the ocean like a thousand horsemen charging flank-to-flank. It breaks against the windward side of the *San Juan* in an explosion of white foaming water. She rolls almost onto her beam ends, toppling crew and passengers, scattering them about and mixing them with the debris that the storm has not already washed overboard. Don Rodriquez himself fetches up against a tangle of heavy pulley blocks and cordage, breathless from the impact, the icy brine burning his eyes, soaked and bruised, but still alive.

As though reflected in an imperfect mirror glass, he sees the distorted figure of Constanza some distance away across the deck. She is lying on her back, the expensive gown he bought her for her marriage transformed into a sodden winding sheet, her arms and legs flailing wildly. He can hear her shrieking in protest at this final humiliation. And he sees Cachorra – who has served her mistress with such quiet forbearance since the day the infant Constanza was able to issue her first unreasonable demand – running towards her across what looks to him like a fast-flowing ford, kicking up water as she goes.

It is barely an instant before he sees what Cachorra has seen: Constanza's left foot has become entangled in some rope netting that is already sliding over the side, dragging his daughter with it.

Exhausted by the storm and the sleepless hours spent in anticipation of his life's violent end, Don Rodriquez can barely find the strength to climb to his feet, let alone follow Cachorra across the deck. He stumbles after her, his eyes brimming with salt spray. As though viewed from behind a waterfall, he sees Cachorra reach his daughter, squat down and deftly free her from the jumble of cordage.

And then a second wave bursts over the deck.

It spins him around, slamming him up against the wooden bulwark, folding him over the painted rail like someone peering over the parapet of a bridge. He stares down in stunned confusion at the seething holly-green water.

Across his sight – carried on a sudden churn of the current – sweep the upturned faces of Constanza and Cachorra. They stare up at him, as though they have yet to register the shock of being swept overboard.

And then they are gone – lost in the tumbling spume.

Don Rodriquez Calva de Sagrada lifts his head to the sky in anguish, a sky now so clear and blue that it might never have known a single storm since its very creation. A howl of despair escapes from his mouth, heard clearly even against the crash of the waves.

The tossing back of his head takes his gaze up the jagged promontory to the very top of the cliff. He searches for God's face in the sky, wanting to demand of Him the reason for such arbitrary cruelty. But all he sees is a line of horsemen drawn up along the precipice, looking down at the drama playing out beneath them.

✠

Bianca lets her tired eyes wander around the sparse whitewashed interior of the guest chamber. She had expected that a royal palace might have guaranteed a more comfortable night's sleep. Beside her in the bed, which no one has thought to hang with curtains, Nicholas is sleeping the sleep of the not-quite-innocent. She is about to lean across and kiss the wiry black strands of hair where it breaks at the nape of his neck and curls back towards his ears, when she hears footsteps on the floorboards outside. An instant later, the chamber door shakes to a presumptive hammering.

Nicholas sits up beside her with a start. He stares about him, still half-snared in sleep. 'Who calls?' he demands. 'Is Her Majesty sick?'

No reply comes. But the hammering goes on.

Bianca is first out of bed. She throws back the coverlet that smells as though it's been kept in a leaky chest since Elizabeth's coronation. When she lifts the door latch, she comes eye-to-forehead with little Robert Cecil, the queen's principal Secretary of State.

'So *this* is where they put you,' he says, taking note of the spartan interior. 'If you're called again, I shall have a word with the Lord Chamberlain. You deserve better.'

'Why the alarm, Sir Robert?' Nicholas asks, now standing at Bianca's shoulder. 'Does Her Grace require a doctor?'

Cecil gives a tight smile that dies half-formed. 'Not the queen, Nicholas. Someone at Cecil House. My barge is being made ready as we speak. Mistress Bianca may travel with us as far as Bankside if she chooses. Either way, be at the water-stairs in ten minutes.'

Still sleepy, Nicholas is about to ask if Cecil's father, Lord Burghley, has taken a turn for the worse. Then he remembers: old Burghley died in August.

'May I ask who is sick? And the nature of the malady?' he enquires as Bianca hurries to fetch his shirt and hose. 'Not one of your children, I hope.'

'No,' says Robert Cecil curtly, turning on his heels. 'Ten minutes. No longer.'

The gilded Cecil barge is already approaching the royal dockyard at Woolwich before either Nicholas or Bianca gets round to wondering why a man of Robert Cecil's standing felt the need to deliver his summons in person.

3

'And another thing—Nicholas! Are you listening to me?'

The slapping of the water against the hull of the Cecil barge brings Nicholas out of a semi-slumber. To his right the gardens of the Inner Temple run down to the riverbank, with black-gowned students studying their law books in the shade of the trees. To his left lie the open fields between Southwark and Lambeth. Ahead, the Thames swings sharply south towards Westminster. He wonders if he's been dozing ever since they stopped at Blackfriars to let Bianca go ashore.

'Yes, Sir Robert. Of course I am,' he says brightly, trying to imply he's been wide awake all the while.

'That wife of yours—'

Nicholas feels a jab of disquiet in his stomach. Mr Secretary Cecil has tolerated Bianca's perceived heresy – her Catholic faith – for as long as Nicholas has been in his service, first as an intelligencer, latterly as his children's physician. More than once he has used it to coerce Nicholas into accepting a difficult commission. Nicholas wonders if, now that he's frequently in the queen's presence, Robert Cecil has decided it's time to reconsider his forbearance.

'What of her, Sir Robert?'

'Her name,' Cecil says, the irritation evident in his tone. 'Her *name*.'

'Bianca?'

'You're being obtuse, sirrah. Not Bianca – *Merton.*'

'What's amiss with it? It's an English name. It's her father's. Would you rather she called herself Caporetti, after her Paduan mother?'

Cecil gives him the sort of look a weary schoolmaster might give a pupil who simply will not grasp simple Latin declension. 'I'd rather she called herself Shelby. Goodwife Shelby.'

'Oh, *now* I understand,' says Nicholas, resisting a smile.

Cecil raises a cautionary finger. 'It is an abomination to go around refusing to acknowledge her own married name. It implies her husband has no governance over his household.'

Now there's no holding back a grin. 'Sir Robert, I regret to inform you that a husband could have no more governance over Bianca' – a glance up at the dark clouds gathering in the western sky – 'than you have over that approaching storm.'

A look of resigned bewilderment sweeps across Cecil's face. 'For a yeoman's son, you have a very odd understanding of tradition and propriety,' he says, shaking his head. Then, apparently defeated, he adds, 'You dwell now in Southwark, I think, yes?'

'At the Paris Garden, yes.'

'Then I recommend your attendance when next Master Shakespeare has his *Shrew* playing at the Rose. You might learn something.'

It is as close to humour as Nicholas has seen Cecil get. He says tentatively, not wanting to disappoint, 'Master Shakespeare is often at the Jackdaw. I suspect he used Bianca as a muse for his Kate.'

A sudden gust of wind ruffles the dense black frizado weave of Cecil's gown. 'You may jest at my expense, Nicholas. But be warned: Her Majesty has a habit of taking it badly when young men she favours have the temerity to wed without her approval.

She never forgave the Earl of Leicester for marrying that Knollys woman in secret. I suggest that you refer to your wife – within her hearing at least – as Goodwife Shelby. It would be best for *all* of us.'

'I shall tell her, Sir Robert,' Nicholas says, bringing his smile under control. 'In all civil company, Goodwife Shelby it shall be. But I cannot promise I will be able to persuade Bankside to think of her as anything other than Bianca Merton.'

'*That* I could abide to suffer,' Cecil says with a sigh of resignation, 'given that Her Majesty is unlikely to express a sudden desire to visit a tavern or a bawdy-house.' He turns his head to watch a pair of swans glide past. 'While we're on the subject of names, I have one other for you to keep in the back of your mind: Robert Devereux.'

'Why should I have a care for the Earl of Essex?'

'Because he has a long memory.'

'He's shown no sign that he even recalls who I am.'

When Cecil turns his face towards him again, Nicholas can see a parental concern in his eyes, even though the two men are of similar ages.

'Nevertheless, you would do well not to rouse him,' Cecil tells him. 'Even though you were exonerated of that false charge of seeking to harm the queen, he will not have forgotten the matter. You may well find yourself in his company at court. So I would advise against expressing any ludicrous and unworthy ideas about religious toleration that *Goodwife* Shelby – or her husband, for that matter – may have picked up while they were away in Padua.'

'You have my word on it, Sir Robert.'

'I'm relieved to hear it.'

The two men fall into a contrived silence. Up ahead, a grand house with sloping gardens is coming into sight, a jetty thrusting out into the river. As the bargemen port their oars, Cecil glances up at the darkening sky. 'Another storm on its way – out of Ireland, by the look of it. It will not be the first the Devil has sent us out of that place.' As he stands, gathering his gown about his crooked body as if to hide it, he adds, 'What you see here, let it remain in your memory – never on your tongue. Understand?'

Now, thinks Nicholas, I am to discover why the queen's principal Secretary of State has called me away from Greenwich in such a hurry. Because up until now, he has steadfastly refused to utter a single word on the matter.

For all he can tell, the warren of passages below Cecil House have been dug out of the ground by a race of ancient creatures, half-man, half-mole. The walls are only partly bricked. The floor is cold and moist. Nicholas is not overly tall, but even he feels the compulsion to duck. Ahead of him three servants form a human wall in front of a small door. They are big fellows, too well built for serving at table. Like him, they have adopted an uncomfortable stoop. Robert Cecil is the only one walking with his head up.

'Is the brute restrained?' he asks, his voice echoing in the confined space.

'He is, Sir Robert. With ankle irons.'

'Then open up.'

One of the servants wields a heavy key. The others set themselves ready to prevent whatever ferocious animal is caged inside from springing free. With a tortured groan of its old hinges, the door is opened. The three servants enter at a crouch, one after the other; there is no space to do otherwise. When whatever lies beyond is no longer deemed a danger, one of them signals to Robert Cecil that it is safe to go inside. Nicholas is the last in.

The chamber is even plainer than the one at Greenwich Palace. It has the furtive smell of human sweat and unwashed clothes, and the same oppressively low ceiling as the corridor that serves it. The sole source of light comes from a tiny semicircular window set into the apex of the vaulted outside wall.

Nicholas has long known that great men like Cecil keep such chambers in their grand houses. They are the useful antechambers to the Tower, where men with ill will in their hearts towards the realm and its queen can make a full and frank confession of their sins, without recourse to the hot irons and engines of agony they will surely face later – if they fail to seize the opportunity so generously on offer here. Nicholas himself has spent a few uncomfortable hours in such a chamber, at Essex House. It was four years ago, when an enemy falsely denounced him to Devereux for plotting to poison the queen.

Not that Robert Cecil looks much like a man who keeps company with torturers. The queen's principal Secretary of State has a tapering, scholarly face tipped by a little stab of beard. There are lines etched around the wide, full-lidded eyes that were not there when Nicholas left for Padua four years ago, and the skin beneath has started to sag a little, even though Cecil is the younger of the two by a year. There is a melancholy in the face, now. Nicholas attributes it to two bereavements: the death of Sir Robert's young wife, Elizabeth, and that of his father, Lord Burghley, the queen's oldest and most trusted advisor.

'Does he have a name?' Nicholas asks as he regards the figure lying before him on an unfurnished wooden cot set directly below the skylight. The pale light illuminates the man's pallid face like a martyr in an altar painting.

'Not to you, Nicholas,' Cecil says pleasantly.

Nicholas nods in understanding. If he does not know his patient's name, how can he later swear before an inquiry that any particular man was ever in Cecil House?

The man on the cot is younger than Nicholas by a decade, around his middle twenties. He is naked, the sinewy limbs suggesting a rural origin not dissimilar to Nicholas's own, a childhood in the fresh air, honest labour in the field. Like Nicholas, he is dark-haired, though instead of Nicholas's wiry curls this man has long, soft locks that might gently curtain his face if they were not matted and tangled with what Nicholas takes to be river weed. He is conscious but unmoving, save for the occasional shiver of the puckered white skin. Only the eyes are mobile. Nicholas can see no obvious sign of injury.

'What ails him?' he asks.

'He's a traitorous Irish papist rebel – that's what ails him,' Cecil tells him, as though he was describing a particularly untrainable deerhound.

'Am I permitted to make a closer observation?'

'That *is* why we are here.'

Chained by one ankle to the bed frame, the man remains as still as a corpse as Nicholas approaches. His head is tilted slightly, the long hair swept underneath and providing the only pillow. Now Nicholas can see dark bruises around the neck, raw weals around the wrists. Through cracked and slightly parted lips, the breath comes and goes in a slow, feeble tide, at odds with the muscular limbs. The man's darting eyes are the only other sign of animation in the whole body. They show how he despises himself for his weakness – but not nearly as greatly as he despises those who have weakened him.

'How did he come to be like this?'

The largest of the Cecil servants gives Nicholas a sheepish look. 'He went for a swim, sir.'

'He threw himself off my water-stairs,' Sir Robert explains, glancing at the servant for confirmation. 'Isn't that so, Latham?'

'He was bound at the wrists,' Latham says defensively. 'But he's a strong fellow and the rope was wringing wet. When he jumped, he took me by surprise.' He opens his big hands to show the red rope-marks on his palms.

Cecil raises one hand to lay a reassuring slap on Latham's shoulder, accentuating the imbalance of the principal secretary's crooked shoulders. 'Perhaps it would be best if you explain to Dr Shelby what passed.'

Latham does his best to look consoled. 'When we was on the water-stairs the prisoner asked where we was taking him. I told him 'twas the Tower, on account of how he's proving somewhat constipated of tongue. Next we know, he throws hisself head-first into the river. When we fished him out again, he was palsied.'

'Palsied?'

'At first it were just his legs,' Latham says. 'I thought he was playing us for fools, so I gave him several stout kicks to bring him to his feet. But he couldn't raise hisself. By the time we'd carried him back to the house, his arms had gone, too. Now it's only those eyes what move. I reckon they'll only stop their filthy jigging when the axe falls.' A glance at his fellows to see if they appreciate his wit. 'An' even then I wouldn't put money on it.'

'Did you see him strike anything when he went into the water?' Nicholas asks.

Latham shakes his head. 'That part of the river is as thick as my wife's pottage, sir. But I knows for a fact the masons left some old stones there when they rebuilt Lord Burghley's chapel. You can sees them when the tide is out.'

'So he could have struck his head against them when he dived in?'

'It's possible, sir.'

Nicholas stands over the cot. He reaches out and asks the man to grasp his hand. He gets no response. No movement – except the eyes, which fix on Nicholas's with a loathing that takes his breath away.

And then he speaks – a short, guttural snarl in a language Nicholas has never heard before.

'It's his heathen Irish tongue,' Robert Cecil says. 'I'm told he hasn't spoken any other since he was taken.'

'When was that? And where?'

'A fortnight since – in Ireland. He was caught trying to sneak into Dublin. He's one of the Earl of Tyrone's traitorous rogues. It is my belief he intended to assassinate the Lieutenant-General, the Earl of Ormonde.'

Nicholas asks to borrow Latham's dagger.

'What do you intend, Nicholas?' Cecil says with a doubting lift of an eyebrow. 'I have fellows properly trained for hard questioning.'

Without answering, Nicholas kneels at the patient's feet. He inspects the arches for signs of beating. The skin, though hard and yellowed, shows no bruising. Whatever inducement to talk Latham and his colleagues have already extended, it hasn't been made to the feet. Levelling the dagger, he presses the tip of the blade gently against the flesh of the right sole. The foot does not move. He presses again, more firmly than before. A small globule of blood blooms around the tip of the blade and trickles down over the calloused heel. Still the foot does not move.

'May we speak privily, Sir Robert?' Nicholas says, returning the dagger to Latham. Outside in the corridor he says, 'What exactly is it you want of me?'

'I would have thought that obvious, Nicholas. I want you to restore our friend to a better resemblance of health.'

'So that you can have him tortured more efficiently?'

Cecil gives him a patronizing frown. 'Well, there isn't much point in torturing him if he's dead, is there?'

For a moment Nicholas says nothing. He waits until his temper is under control before speaking again. 'I am a physician, Mr Secretary. I have sworn an oath to do no harm.'

'Very laudable. But that doesn't apply to papist rebels, does it?'

Nicholas cannot prevent a sharp, cynical laugh escaping his lips. 'Sir Robert, if I may speak bluntly—'

'I've come to expect nothing less.'

'You know full well that I gained my doctor's gown at Cambridge. I've spent three years at the Palazzo Bo, one of the most liberal universities in Italy, studying anatomy under Professor Fabricius. I am a good friend of Signor Galileo Galilei, the eminent mathematician. The queen herself seeks my opinions on matters of physic and seems approving of them—'

'Does this have *any* bearing on our friend downstairs?'

'I am not beyond understanding matters of state,' Nicholas protests. 'Indeed, you would not have made me one of your intelligencers if I was. But I'm sorry – I cannot treat a man merely in order to deliver him to a greater harm. I refuse to be an executioner's lackey.'

Cecil holds his gaze for a moment without replying. Then he beckons Nicholas to follow him up the steep stone stairs, his crooked little body bounding upwards with surprising agility.

They emerge into an oak-panelled hallway, fresh rushes strewn on the floor. An open door gives onto a terrace bordered by high privet hedges. The late-morning air is cool and smells of wood-smoke from a fire the gardeners have lit somewhere down towards the river. Cecil studies Nicholas like a father trying to gauge if an errant son is worth redeeming.

'I think it's time you and I had a little talk,' he says.

✠

Like everything about Mr Secretary Cecil, his pace around the terrace is urgent, driven. His gown ripples over his uneven back like black water burbling over rocks. Lengthening his stride to keep pace, Nicholas notices the wind is picking up, the clouds gathering. The storm is coming closer.

'There isn't time for me to summon the Bishop of London to give you a personal sermon on the duties we owe to our sovereign,' Cecil tells him. 'But now that Her Majesty is – apparently – favouring your continued presence, there are some things you must understand.'

'Things? What manner of things?'

'For a start, your oath to her takes precedence over all others. The queen *is* England. Your responsibility now is not solely to her as a patient. It is also to the health of her realm. And at this moment that health is in peril.'

Nicholas falters in his stride. Is Cecil suggesting the queen is stricken with a secret malady? Is that what this is about?

And then Cecil says something that in any tavern in England would stop the conversation dead.

'We must accept the fact, Nicholas, that the queen cannot live for ever.'

Hearing a man of Robert Cecil's position utter such words brings Nicholas to an involuntary halt. To speak of the succession – let alone Elizabeth's demise – is forbidden. Men have had their tongues branded for it.

'Don't look so shocked, Nicholas,' Cecil says, almost laughing at his expression. 'If I cannot state a simple medical fact to a physician, then to whom may I state it?'

'Is the queen sickening?' Nicholas asks. 'She seemed in good health—'

Cecil's pale, inverted teardrop of a face turns towards him. There is an intensity in his eyes that seems too great to be constrained by such a little body. 'She is well, as far as the Privy Council knows. But she is almost sixty-five. We have to look to the future. If the Spanish come at us again, will Her Majesty have the fortitude, the capacity, to stand against them as she has in the past?'

'You think they'll hazard another invasion?'

'Of course.'

Cecil leads Nicholas through a neat gap in the hedge and down towards the riverbank, speaking in a low, contemplative tone. The Spanish king is dying, he explains as they walk. Philip could be dead already, given the torturous precautions that Cecil's man in Madrid must take with his dispatches. And when kings are dying, sometimes they are inclined to make a last attempt at the great matters that have so far eluded them. And if they don't, their successors might feel the compulsion to pick up their legacy with even greater zeal.

'While you were listening to papist lecturers and drinking papist wine in Padua, Nicholas,' Cecil goes on, 'Philip of Spain sent another armada against us. Admittedly it was not as great an enterprise as the one a decade ago, and again by God's mercy it was scattered. A great storm sent them all scurrying back to Coruña. But it shows the enduring determination of that servant of the Antichrist in Madrid.'

'Where did they attempt to land?'

'Ireland,' Cecil says. 'It is the rebellion in Ireland that is the crack in our armour. Now that the traitorous Earl of Tyrone has raised the peasants there against our settlers, we cannot rely solely upon the weather to save us. So *now* do you see why it is imperative that we put any rebel we take to the hard press?'

Nicholas considers this as he stands looking out across the river. He finds Cecil's words persuasive. But not convincing.

'A man might say anything when the pain becomes unbearable, Mr Secretary. You have your intelligencers in Madrid. No doubt you have them in Coruña, Lisbon or Cádiz, too. Surely they will give you warning of another attempt.'

'I rely upon it.'

'Then my assisting you to torture a single palsied Irish rebel is of no consequence to England, is it? But it is of consequence to my conscience.'

Cecil's restless eyes have a sharpness in them that cuts into Nicholas's inner thoughts.

'Has your time living amongst the papists dulled your mettle, Nicholas?'

'Of course not. But there's another reason why I think it would be pointless.'

'And what, pray, is that?'

'This palsy he's suffering – I've seen it before, on the battlefield when I was a physician to Sir Joshua Wylde's company in the Low Countries. A blow to the neck or the back, or a shot received from a firing piece... these things can cause a loss of faculty in the limbs, such as your rebel is suffering. Sometimes it is instantaneous, sometimes gradual. It is caused by a fracture of the vertebrae. It appears that the nerves are unable to transmit their impulses either from the brain or the heart, depending upon which one you hold to be the source of the body's animation. The most modern thinking is that it is the brain.'

'You're saying he won't feel pain, even if we rack him?'

'Very likely not.'

'Nicholas, the Privy Council needs me to keep this wretch alive, at least until we have loosened his tongue. And you are the most practical physician I have yet encountered.'

'I rather fear he's cheated you out of your satisfaction, Sir Robert. He has no sensation in his limbs. If that holds true for the rest of his body, then thumb-irons or the rack will be as naught to him. Besides, I think this palsy will lead to his death, probably quite soon. Perhaps within hours.'

'There must be *something* you can do?'

Nicholas considers telling him that the late Ambroise Paré, the French surgeon, recommended removing tissue around the spinal column to relieve pressure from the fractured vertebrae. But to the best of his knowledge, Paré never agreed to treat a patient in order that someone else might do him even more harm than the original hurt. Cecil, he decides, can find *that* out from some other physician.

'I'll do what I can, on one condition,' he says.

'Name it.'

'That you find a Catholic priest to give him the Viaticum.'

Cecil stares at him. 'What wild fancy is this?'

'I'm guessing you must have at least one priest incarcerated somewhere, some Jesuit you've caught sneaking into the realm – if they've not all been sent to the scaffold already.'

'Do you think a traitorous rebel from the bogs of Ireland – a rogue who cannot even bring himself to speak English – is going to understand Latin?'

'He may not understand it, but he will know he's dying in a state of grace.'

'Why do you care whether he dies in God's grace or not? He's a heretic, a rebel. He has set his face against God's order.'

'He's a man. He has a soul.'

Robert Cecil shakes his head. 'Have I called home a different Dr Shelby?' He sets off back towards the house at his usual brisk scuttle. Nicholas hurries to catch up, unsure whether he's been dismissed. 'And the priest?'

Cecil waves his arms over his head in defeat. The flapping sleeves of his gown make him look like an angry raven about to launch itself into the sky. '*Yes, yes*, your rebel can have his priest. But I warn you, in this fight with the Antichrist a man must sometimes set aside his finer feelings. You should remember that, if you're going to be of any use to Her Majesty – or *me*, for that matter.'

'Yes, Sir Robert,' Nicholas says obediently.

'There is one other thing I need from you.'

I thought there might be, thinks Nicholas. There usually is.

'I desire you to speak to Master Edmund Spenser for me.'

'Spenser – the poet?'

'I know of no other Edmund Spenser. Do you?'

It seems a paltry commission, better suited to a clerk or a secretary. Nicholas wonders why Cecil has chosen him for the task.

'Am I to pass on Her Majesty's opinion of *The Faery Queene?*' he asks. 'Surely someone from the Office of the Revels can do that for you.'

'Spenser has written to me, insisting that we speak. He says it's urgent. I invited him to come and see me, but he declined.'

'You're the queen's Secretary of State – summon him.'

'He cites his present circumstances as preventing his travelling. He will, however, agree to talk to someone in whom I have complete confidence. He was most particular about that. "Complete and unshakeable confidence" – his very words. I'd tell him to go hang, but he happens to be Her Majesty's favourite English poet.'

As they regain the terrace it begins to rain – spiteful drops, like little balls of molten mercury spraying from an alchemist's furnace. Cecil hurries inside. Nicholas follows.

'When do you wish me to go?' he asks.

'As soon as you may find it convenient,' Cecil says, pausing at the top of the steps that lead down to the chamber Nicholas would rather not revisit. 'When you are ready, see one of my secretaries and have him send to the stables for a palfrey.'

'A horse? Is Master Spenser not then in London?'

A sudden gust of cold wind drives a spray of rain into the hallway. 'Mercy, no,' says Robert Cecil. 'Whatever gave you that impression?'

'I thought, with the Stationers' Office and the playhouses being in London—'

'No, Master Spenser does not dwell here in London,' Cecil says impatiently. 'He owns Kilcolman Castle – in the shire of Munster. He's in Ireland.'

4

On Bankside the storm has been merciful. A few open drains still overflow with filth, a few ankles still ache from stumbling into submerged potholes, a course of damaged thatch hangs forlornly askew on the occasional roof. But the only vessel to be wrecked on this shore is a public tilt-boat broken free from its mooring at the Mutton Lane water-stairs because the waterman spent too long drinking in the nearby Jackdaw tavern.

By the time the Lord Mayor crosses London Bridge at the head of his procession – all on horseback and wearing their plumed hats and aldermanic capes – the sky is once again clear and almost summery.

The mayor, accompanied by his aldermen and sheriffs, has come across the river to parade through the liberty of Southwark, as far as the painted stones that mark its ancient limits. Every year on this day – the seventh of September – the grand mayoral progress opens the great Southwark Fair, established under gracious charter by the fourth Edward. By tradition, it marks the end of harvest time, though for four years in a row the harvest has been poor. Nevertheless, for Bianca Merton it heralds the most profitable time of year for the Jackdaw, above even the staging of a new play at the Rose theatre.

There has been a Jackdaw tavern longer than there has been a fair. Only once in all that time has it not thrown open its doors to welcome a throng of happy fair-goers. When Bianca followed Nicholas out of England four years ago, for the first time in three centuries there had been no Jackdaw. The lopsided timber-framed building that had stood since the time of the first Richard, or the second Edward, or the third Henry – no one on Bankside is quite sure – was little more than ashes. The tavern Bianca Merton had bought on her arrival in England, the business she had made almost as profitable as the Tabard on Long Southwark, had been burned almost to the ground.

But now a new Jackdaw stands in its place. And Bianca knows that she has Rose and Ned Monkton to thank for it – *and* the sultan's bejewelled ring that Nicholas brought back from Marrakech. The ring paid for it; the Monktons oversaw the tavern's resurrection. Looking around the taproom now, she can only admire the result of their stewardship. The new brickwork of the chimney hearth is laid *almost* straight, *nearly* vertical. The mantel no longer looks as though it has been recovered from the black depths of some petrified forest. The benches, stools and tables are new. The ceiling beams – now as honeyed as when they were first cut from the tree, rather than blackened and smoothed with age – have been lifted just enough to save careless customers of even middling height from braining themselves. You can even see the carpenter's marks on the posts that hold them up. New flagstones – level for the first time in a couple of centuries – no longer trip the inebriated. The casks smell more of the cooper's workshop than of ale. Sometimes, when she gazes with unsettling unfamiliarity at this startling resurrection, Bianca has to remind herself that this really is *her* Jackdaw.

In the taproom a three-year-old boy with locks almost as dark and lustrous as his mother's is protesting as volubly as his little lungs will allow.

'But I want see Mord Lair! Let me see Mord Lair!'

Bianca caresses his cheek to soothe his disappointment. She does not subscribe to the prevailing notion that children should remain as still and silent as the furniture, animating themselves only with prayer and obedience. It was never that way in her family home in Padua and she doesn't see why it should be so on Bankside.

'The crowd will be too rough, sweet, and there'll be quarrels occasioned by drink,' she tells him. 'When you're older, I promise. But today Rose will hold you up to the window, so that you may see Mord Lair and all his horses. And his aldermenys. And his shurrufs.'

Bruno giggles his acquiescence.

'Come with me, Master Bruno,' Rose Monkton says, taking the lad by the hand. She is a plump buttered bun of black curls and shiny cheeks. With no child of her own, she dotes on little Bruno. 'While your mother and Master Nicholas are at the fair, what say we blow soap bubbles from Uncle Ned's tobacco pipe?'

Bruno excitedly puffs up his cheeks like bellows – the Lord Mayor and all his dignified splendour instantly forgotten.

'There's occasions when I could think ill of Mistress Bianca for bringing that slippery soap stuff back from Italy,' Ned Monkton says wearily. He leans over the boy like a brown bear inspecting a beehive for honey. 'Does *you* think, young gallant, that Sir Walter Raleigh likes to take his tobacco flavoured with *soap?*' he asks gruffly.

Bruno, the only male in Southwark utterly unintimidated by Ned Monkton's size and fiery auburn beard, stares up at him and nods vigorously.

'Better Bruno blowing bubbles than you fogging up the taproom with them awful fumes,' Rose chides.

Ned rolls his eyes. 'Least 'ave my pipe washed for when I get back. If word gets 'round that Ned Monkton blows bubbles out 'is nose when 'e takes 'is tobacca, there's some on Bankside will think I've gone soft.'

'Soft, Ned Monkton?' Rose says. 'You's been soft since swaddling.'

Bianca marvels at the change that has come over her former maid. There was a time when Rose's propensity for daydreaming led Bianca to nickname her 'Mistress Moonbeam'. But her stewardship of the Jackdaw's rebirth has been everything Bianca could have hoped for. The responsibility seems to have tamed Rose's wilder flights of fancy. Or perhaps, she thinks, it's simply that Rose has grown to full womanhood.

Nicholas ties off the points of his doublet and offers Bianca his arm. 'Is my lady ready to parade down Long Southwark, like the queen on her summer progress?' he asks archly.

'Ready, good husband,' she replies, her amber eyes gleaming. The day might not have the colour and warmth of Padua in September, but it is good to be home.

There is only one cloud darkening her thoughts as she steps out onto the muddy lane, barely having to dip her head to avoid the new, higher lintel.

When is her husband going to get round to telling her the truth about Ireland?

✠

Bianca Merton puts on a brave face as she, Nicholas and Ned battle the crowd on Long Southwark. The fair is in full cry: jugglers, tumblers, rope-walkers, fire-breathers, quacks selling cures for everything from piles to the pox, old women offering charms to chase away sprites and witches. In the yard at the Tabard a bearward is handing round his cap while his beast dances a fancy pavane to the accompaniment of a flute. Outside Bridge House, where later the Lord Mayor and his aldermen will enjoy a banquet of more dishes than most Banksiders will see in a year, a strongman is lifting giggling maids in pairs. Once hoisted aloft, they perch on each bicep like puffed-up hen harriers.

Now that it's common knowledge on Bankside that Dr Shelby is sometimes called upon to attend the queen, people treat him differently. The shouts of greeting he receives are occasionally accompanied by a formal bending of a knee, even a bow or two. But although it's nice to know her husband has come up in the world, Bianca is minded to call out, 'It's alright for you – Robert Cecil doesn't manoeuvre you into acting against your wiser inner counsel' or, 'You can bow when my husband is free of the Crab's malign influence.'

It cannot be ambition that makes Nicholas such easy prey, she has decided. If it were, they wouldn't still be renting lodgings in the Paris Garden. They would have built themselves a nice house on Kentish Street, where it runs into open countryside. Nicholas would not still be offering his skills to St Thomas's hospital for the poor every Tuesday, which he does for a paltry shilling a session because that's the sort of man he is.

Since their return from Padua, Bianca has become used to the summons that arrive from Cecil House, commanding Nicholas to drop everything and rush off to Greenwich, or Richmond, or Nonsuch, or Whitehall, or wherever else that appalling, cantankerous old battleaxe with the whitewashed face and the fake hair has mentioned in a moment of distraction that she's bored, and rather fancies spending an hour or two discussing the latest advances in physic with a handsome fellow half the age of her usual doctors. And now this:

Sweet Bianca, Robert Cecil wants me to go to Ireland...

Sweet Bianca, it is only a small matter – a discreet message to collect...

Sweet Bianca, I will be back inside three weeks, given a following wind...

If wealth was measured in sweetness, she'd be the richest woman in Christendom!

Of one thing she is sure: Nicholas is not going to Ireland alone. She has heard enough talk in the Jackdaw's taproom to know it's a wild and dangerous place, even without the presence of full-blown insurrection. She has made up her mind. Her place is beside her husband. Little Bruno can stay with Rose and blow soap bubbles through Ned's tobacco pipe. Three weeks, Nicholas has told her. Just three weeks. Bruno won't even realize she's been away.

Does that mean I am a bad mother?

She tries to push the self-recrimination out of her mind, like all the other times since she decided she couldn't let Nicholas go to Ireland alone. She has come to the conclusion that, to reconcile herself, she must employ the English Bianca Merton and not the Italian one. In England, she reminds herself, children of all ages are farmed out to relatives, benefactors or patrons, sometimes to almost total strangers. It's normal for an English child to be banished at the earliest opportunity. It's the only way for them to rise – an indentured apprenticeship, or an education in a richer man's household. She could believe that half the children now alive in England would be hard pressed to recognize their parents in a parade. Leaving Bruno with Rose and Ned Monkton for three weeks is nothing to trouble her conscience with. Even so, she cannot prevent herself imagining Robert Cecil as a child's cloth doll, and Bruno gleefully pulling his arms and legs off. Yes, she thinks, the Devil take Robert Cecil and all his works.

As they walk three abreast – Nicholas on one side of her, Ned Monkton on the other, arm-in-arm – down Long Southwark, the wind ruffling the feather in Nicholas's new cap of black sarcenet, Bianca's thoughts turn from her husband and her son to the man whose courage allowed them all to return to England in the first place.

She admires how Ned carries himself these days. When he nods courteously to acknowledge a greeting, she wants to smile. She can see the wariness in their faces, even as they bid him good morrow. She knows what they're thinking: can this really be the same poulterer's son from Scrope Alley whose readiness for a jug of knock-down, customarily followed by an explosion of raw violence, was once the stuff of Bankside legend? What happened to the old Ned Monkton?

It had been Nicholas who first realized the cause of Ned's ill-suppressed rage. Underneath that fiery, terrifying carapace lay a soul in despair. Trapped for most of the working day in the mortuary crypt at St Tom's, his only company the vagrant and impoverished dead, Ned had been trying to drown his despair in quarts of knock-down and aggression. But that life is behind him now. Ned Monkton is reborn, and halleluiah for it. And though Bianca may feel a measure of pride that she and Nicholas have played their part in this resurrection, there is no question that it is Rose who can rightly claim most of the credit. Rose has given Ned back his soul.

Bianca glances at him now. She notes how he walks with a new confidence. Only his right hand shows any tension. It is clenched. Perhaps it is the sight of those huge fingers balled into a fist that makes those who acknowledge him in the street seem a little unconvinced by his apparent transformation. But Bianca knows that Ned does not keep his fist clenched for fear of being unable to control it. He does so because he doesn't want anyone to see the M of scar tissue that disfigures his right thumb – the brand that shows he has taken another man's life.

No matter that it was taken in self-defence, while trying to clear Nicholas of the false accusation of attempting to poison the queen, Ned carries that mark with no little shame. And no one – not Rose, Bianca or indeed Nicholas himself – can convince him that he should not.

Bianca tightens her arms a little, to draw these two very different men closer. A precious gift indeed, she thinks, to have such a husband, to have such a friend.

✠

At the bottom of Long Southwark, on a patch of grass made sodden and muddy by the recent rain, a ceremonial muster is under way. The Lord Mayor is inspecting a score of young country lads who could almost pass for soldiers. Not one of them can boast a full suit of equipment. One has a steel tasset around his hips and thighs, the next is wearing a pauldron to protect his shoulders, a third has only greaves covering his shin. As for the rest: nothing but leather surcoats and breeches. Thank heaven, Nicholas thinks, that the rebels have no artillery to speak of.

With a sudden tattoo, a drummer brings the aspiring warriors to some semblance of attention. The muster ensign and his corporal, the only ones wearing breastplates, march up to greet the Lord Mayor and a brace of magistrates assembled for the purpose. The ensign signs the offered muster roll to confirm he has recruited the correct number of levies, as required by the Privy Council and the Lord Lieutenant of Surrey. In return, he receives a large purse for the future feeding, equipping, transporting and – if they're lucky – the paying of his men. The Lord Mayor makes a brief but stirring speech about God's fist smiting the papist rebels, doffs his hat to the recruits and rides off on the next leg of his progress through Southwark.

'Where are you bound?' Nicholas asks the nearest recruit, a gangly lad who looks as though he should be attending petty school rather than pike-drill classes.

'To Ireland, if it please Your Honour,' the boy says, 'to kill the papist rebels.'

Nicholas smiles and wishes him God's protection, relieved that at least these fellows are not destined for the Low Countries and a professional, well-drilled Spanish enemy.

Close by, an enterprising vendor of coney pies has chosen the muster as a likely spot to make a sale or two from his wicker basket. Ned, who has a fondness for coney, makes straight for him. Nicholas and Bianca follow. Ned has no sooner taken his first bite of pie when the muster ensign swaggers over. To Nicholas, he looks as unlikely a soldier as the others, a cadaverous fellow in his late forties with the gaunt, sallow face of a fallen priest. Beneath a shiny dome of forehead dressed with lank grey locks, a single functioning eye looks out on a world that it seems to be assessing for potential profit.

'May I enquire, who is *this* bold fellow?' the man says, making an exaggerated bend of the knee to Ned. When he straightens up again, he pauses in the moment before his knee locks, so that he looks like a dog flinching in expectation of a kick.

'Ned Monkton' – a glance at Bianca for approval – 'steward of the Jackdaw tavern, owned by Mistress Merton 'ere,' Ned replies proudly. 'And who are you?'

'Barnabas Vyves, gentles all,' the ensign says elaborately, his gaze dancing from Ned to Bianca and Nicholas like a thrown stone skipping on water. It comes to rest on Nicholas, who is making a professional assessment of the missing eyeball.

'An honest wound,' the ensign says, raising a grubby finger to the empty socket, 'earned in the storming of the breach at Cádiz in '96 – shoulder-to-shoulder with the Earl of Essex.'

A likely story, thinks Nicholas. There's no scarring. The missing eye is a deformity of birth, or lost in infancy through disease. He doubts that Barnabas Vyves has been anywhere near a contested breach, least of all with Robert Devereux standing at his shoulder.

Returning his attention to Ned, Vyves announces, 'We could use a doughty fellow like you in the ranks of Sir Oliver Henshawe's company. Sixpence a day, all found. Glory by the cartload. Will you step forward and help Her Majesty wrest back Ireland from the heathen rebel? Will you be the man to pitch the Earl of Tyrone on his traitorous pate and earn Sir Oliver's enduring gratitude, payable in a lump sum on the day of victory?'

Oliver Henshawe.

The name jolts Bianca out of a passing daydream – Nicholas in full jousting armour, sweaty and victorious as he rides out of the lists to claim her favour.

'Would that be the Oliver Henshawe whose family owns land out at Walworth?' she asks, the image of a persistent young gallant with dark eyes and a fragile swagger prising its way free from the recesses of her memory.

'Aye, that's Sir Oliver.'

'Is he here?' Bianca asks, looking about.

'Mercy, no, Mistress,' Vyves assures her. 'He's out in Ireland, at the head of his fine fellows, smiting the queen's enemies. I'm here to muster more of them to his banner.' He looks at Ned again. 'Stalwart fellows like this one.'

'No, thanks,' growls Ned. 'I've got a tobacco pipe to get clean of soap.'

'I've not heard *that* excuse before,' says Vyves. 'What if I say sixpence ha'penny?'

'You can say the King of Spain wears a farthingale in 'is spare time, Ensign Vyves,' Ned says. 'The answer is still no.'

'Pity,' says Vyves. 'We might have come to an agreement. You'd have found it worth your while.'

Nicholas decides to have a little sport with the man who stormed the breach at Cádiz.

'Is it sixpence ha'penny before or *after* deductions for butter and cheese, blanket, bread and transport?' he asks. 'I think Ned here would be lucky to see fourpence. What do you say, Ensign Vyves?'

Vyves gives him a startled glance. 'How do you know about pay an' victuals? Have you been a-soldiering?'

'A summer in the Low Countries, with Sir Joshua Wylde's company. I was his surgeon.'

'Oh,' says Vyves.

'Pity I wasn't at Cádiz. I would have valued a word or two with the physician who tended to your eye, Ensign Vyves. I might have learned something. It's been stitched neater than a maid-of-honour's kerchief.'

Vyves gives a huff of discomfort. 'Well, I can't stand here passing pleasantries while Ireland hangs in the balance,' he says hurriedly. He makes another knee, though only to Bianca, and marches off to the head of his file.

'Well, *they're* going to put the fear of God into the Earl of Tyrone, and no mistake,' she says, watching him lope up and down the file of recruits as he berates them for their unsoldierly appearance. 'We can surely expect his capitulation by this Michaelmas at the latest.'

'You know of this Sir Oliver Henshawe?' Nicholas enquires, with a narrowing of the eyes that Bianca could swear might be the first stirring of jealousy.

'It was a long time ago, Husband – before I met you.'

'Is that so? You've never mentioned him.'

'I never saw the need.'

'Was it serious?'

'He seemed to think so. He paid court to me with much boasting and poetry. The boasting was ludicrous: he was going to fight his way to Madrid and bring back Philip of Spain's wedding ring to place on my finger. And the poetry wasn't much better: mostly embarrassing doggerel.'

'Was this wooing a drawn-out affair?' Nicholas asks, implying by his voice that whatever the answer might be, he could scarcely care less.

'He began his suit in the July, I recall. By August he'd lost interest. I suspect he rather took offence at finding a mere tavern-mistress so resistant to his significant charms.'

'How did it end?'

'Uncomfortably. He stormed off in a huff. No matter. I'm sure there was a whole legion of foolish maids only too happy to flutter at his pretty plumage and his empty song.'

'Oh, good. I mean—'

Bianca takes pity on him. Laughing, she says, 'He never stood a chance. You may ask Rose, if you care to.'

'No, no, it is of no matter...' Nicholas's voice tails off as the file of men marches away to a merry rhythm beaten out on a tambour and a smattering of cheers from the crowd. 'I'm sure they'll be fine,' he says, 'with the bold Sir Oliver at their head.'

Bianca doesn't indulge him. Inside, she's thinking: my husband is going to Ireland for Robert Cecil, and all he'll have around him to keep him safe are a band of spotty farm boys and an ensign with only one eye.

✠

It is late afternoon. Ned has returned to the Jackdaw. Bianca has brought Nicholas to the one place on Bankside where speaking freely always seems that much easier. It is her secret physic garden. Near the bottom of Black Bull Alley and close to the riverbank, it lies hidden from view behind a sagging brick wall with single door in it that looks as though it's never been opened in a hundred years. In her absence in Padua, Rose tended it with thought and diligence. Her stewardship of this fragrant little paradise has allowed Bianca, on her return, to reopen her apothecary's shop on Dice Lane. It has always proved a place where, if you sow and tend with honesty in your heart, good things will inevitably grow.

'Must you forever dance to Robert Cecil's tune, Nicholas?' she asks when they are safely behind the door.

'I made a compact with him. I would be his intelligencer, and he would not hang you for a papist and a witch. It seemed a sensible bargain.'

'It was a pact with the Devil. I should never have let you make it.'

'Cecil has kept his side of the bargain. I can hardly deny mine.'

'I'm starting to think you actually admire him.'

Bianca plucks a sprig of hedge-mustard, remembering a promise to make up a syrup for Alice Nangle's sciatica. She pops one of the little yellow seeds into her mouth. When speaking of the Crab, it seems to her sensible to chew on something efficacious in warding off poisons. The bitter taste makes her pull a face.

'His mind is much consumed with thoughts for the safety of the realm and the queen,' Nicholas says. 'And with good reason – even more so now that his father, Lord Burghley, is dead.'

'When you returned from Cecil House, after we came back from Greenwich, I could swear that he had asked you to do something troubling to your conscience. Has he?'

A slight hesitation tells her all she needs to know.

'We have *both* had our consciences troubled in the service of Robert Cecil,' he says.

She waves the sprig of hedge-mustard at him. 'Anything I may have done was to protect *you*, Husband.'

'I know.'

'Then leave his service,' she says defiantly. 'Cast off the grip he has over you.'

'How can I?'

'Return to Barnthorpe if you must. Become a country physician.'

'Most people around Barnthorpe would rather trust old Mother Cotton, the wise woman, than a fellow with a doctorate in medicine from Cambridge. They think physicians are mostly charlatans. Besides, there's not one in fifty who could afford to pay me. We'd likely starve.'

'Then help your father on the land. I'm sure he and your brother Jack could do with the extra hands.'

'Me – a farmer?'

'Don't worry, I'll come with you. I promise I'll try to behave as a good yeoman's wife should, and not scandalize the labourers and the local parson.'

Nicholas stifles a smile at the thought of Bianca Merton setting the inhabitants of the wild Suffolk marshes on their ears. 'You know that I cannot.'

'You *will* not, more like.'

'First, there is the stipend Robert Cecil pays me to be his children's physician. And now that the queen, too, calls upon me I may command a goodly fee, if I choose to take patients from amongst the court.'

'But you despise that manner of physic,' Bianca tells him insistently. 'You've told me before – you would rather give up altogether than waste your time prescribing purges for rich men who don't know when to stop gorging themselves.'

'I *need* the money.'

Bianca rolls her eyes. 'The Jackdaw is turning a profit. My apothecary shop is prospering. Is this a matter of pride? Are you discomforted by the idea that a wife should maintain the household and not her husband?'

'It has nothing to do with pride.'

'Ambition, then. That must be it. The man I married – the man who would rather earn a shilling treating the poor at St Tom's than a gold angel listening to a gentleman complain about his gout – has become ambitious.'

'It has nothing to do with ambition – *Kate*.'

Bianca's amber eyes narrow. Her head tilts slightly, which is never – as Nicholas knows to his cost – a good sign.

'Kate? Why Kate?'

'Sir Robert seems to think I've married Master Shakespeare's *Shrew*.'

'Is that a fact?' Bianca says, ramming her fists into her waist. 'You've married a shrew?'

'I didn't *agree* with him.'

She turns towards a clump of sow-fennel, addressing it directly. 'Did you hear that? My husband doesn't agree with the Crab that his wife is a shrew. Marry! I must dance for joy.' She spreads her arms wide to encompass all the contents of the physic garden, calling out, 'Come, ladies all, we must sing hosannahs – to husbands bold and brave.'

And then she begins to sing.

'So happy I... no shrew am I... not mouse, nor vole, but vixen sly...'

Nicholas, taken aback as much by the beauty of her voice as by her sudden flight of wild fancy, sits down on an upturned pail. 'Alright, alright. I wish I'd kept my mouth shut. Be serious for a moment.'

Bianca turns towards him. The afternoon sun gives her hair the sheen of burnished mahogany. 'Very well, Nicholas, I shall be the very model of seriousness. If it's not pride, and it's not ambition, then *what* is it?'

He chooses his words carefully.

'I learn more from Robert Cecil than merely how to fill the queen's occasional moments of boredom. I learn things most people do not.'

'Such as?'

'The country we have returned to is not the one we left.'

'What do you mean, Nicholas?' Bianca asks, her face suddenly made serious by his tone.

'Although Cecil hasn't admitted it, I think the cost of this war with Spain is weighing very heavily on the Privy Council and the Treasury. And that cost cannot be borne purely by invoking the subsidy rolls and dipping into men's purses. While we've been away there have been four years of bad harvests. I didn't need Robert Cecil to tell me that; I've heard it from my father. Not enough feed for the cattle; not enough grain for the bread; vagrants flocking into the city and sleeping under hedges. People starving. Look at the fair today. The produce on the stalls was as meagre as we've ever seen it. And the prices – well, there'll be plenty of Banksiders who can only look on and wish. How long before there is real famine? And if the Spanish come again, I reckon the realm will collapse like a house made of rotten timbers.'

Bianca hurries to him and takes his hands in hers. 'Nicholas, I've never seen you like this before.'

He looks up into her eyes and she sees the yeoman's son in them, the country boy before he went to Cambridge and discovered he might have found a way into the world of those clever, successful men who would never need to face an empty larder.

'I need the money, Bianca,' he says, almost with embarrassment, 'so that I can ensure my father doesn't lose Barnthorpe.'

For a moment she says nothing. Then, still holding his hands in hers, 'I had no notion it was that troublesome.'

'He mortgaged the land so that I could study medicine. I won't stand idly and let him and the family face penury.'

She leans forward and kisses the black curling of his hairline. 'I understand.'

'There's something else.'

Stepping back, she says, 'Should I be worried?'

'Not at all. Before I left Cecil House, Sir Robert made me – *us* – a proposition.'

Despite his assurance, the news goes through her like a needle. Her hands tighten on his. 'A proposition? What manner of proposition? Does he want us to sell him our souls, too?'

'Little Bruno is to join Sir Robert's own children in the Cecil household.'

For a moment Bianca can do nothing but stare at him.

'The Crab is going to steal away our son?'

'No! Not steal – *advance*.' Nicholas's face brightens with enthusiasm. 'Think of it: our son schooled by the Cecil tutors, raised by the ladies of the queen's principal Secretary of State. Imagine what a future that will open up for him.'

'But he's *my* son. He's only three!'

'Yes, at the moment. But he won't be three for ever. He will go when he's ten.'

'Into a stranger's household?'

'Robert Cecil isn't a stranger, he's Lord Burghley's heir and successor. He's the queen's principal minister.'

'He's a scheming dissembler, that's what Robert Cecil is.'

Nicholas stares at her in puzzlement. 'Why are you so resistant to the notion?'

'Because Bruno is our *son*, Nicholas. Is that so hard to understand?'

'But it's what happens to all children, if they have the opportunity – which precious few on Bankside will ever have. It will give him more than I ever could, even as a successful physician. When Bruno goes to Cambridge, he won't be a sizar – little better than a servant to the gentlemen students. He'll go as their equal. He won't have to get his fists bloodied trying to prove he's their match. He'll be *one* of them.'

'Judging by some of the English gentlemen I've encountered, I'm not sure I want that. Better that he grows up with people like Rose and Ned about him – people who can teach him what true loyalty is.'

But in Nicholas's imagination, the scenes in Bruno's life are already flashing by, bright and clear.

'As a companion to the Cecil heir, he'll be welcome at court... There will be a good marriage, to a bride from a great family, the prospect of a knighthood...'

The shine in her husband's eyes puts a check on Bianca's anger. She will not chide him for wanting the best for their son. She says, as evenly as she can manage, 'I'd rather our son be his own man, like the cousin we named him after.'

She gets nothing but a harsh laugh for her efforts.

'That cousin spent his life always one step ahead of his creditors, ever on the search for the next wild enterprise. Is that what you want for our boy – a precarious existence, buffeted by the fickle winds of fortune?'

'Of course not,' Bianca says, pulling her hands from his rather more sharply than she had intended. 'But I'd take that over the alternative: every man or woman he meets valued solely by how much they may assist his advance.'

'But Bruno isn't like that.'

'Nicholas, Cecil House will *make* him like that.'

To break free from the argument before it gets out of hand, Bianca plucks at the flowers on a row of marjoram, picking those she thinks will make a good solution for the ringing in the ears that so troubles Henry Coxon, the farrier from the Tabard's stables. From out on the river comes raucous laughter, revellers in a tilt-boat heading towards the Paris Garden.

She is comfortable on Bankside, though she misses the colour and the heat of a Paduan summer. She has made a life here, though God knows the place has its dark side: the stews and the dice-houses, the bear-pits and the haunts of purse-divers. And heaven forbid that Bruno should grow up and desire to become a player at the Rose, like the ones who drink in the Jackdaw, strutting about like an earl while he borrows a ha'penny for another quart of knock-down and gets into a brawl over whose portrayal of mad Titus Andronicus is the most affecting.

But she cannot escape the truth in what Nicholas has said. Preferment by the Cecils will give Bruno vastly more opportunity in life than a Bankside tavern-mistress could ever hope for her son. Yet if she has learned one thing in all the while she has known Robert Cecil, it is that he gives nothing away for free. Nothing is forgotten. Every little favour goes down in the ledger. So what can be so important to him that he would offer Nicholas this bright future for her son?

'I'm coming with you,' she calls out, turning away from the marjoram.

'Take your ease,' he calls back, misunderstanding her. 'We've plenty of time.'

'No, I mean to Ireland.'

'That's impossible.'

'No, it isn't.'

'There's a rebellion—'

'There'll be a worse one here on Bankside if you object.'

'What about Bruno?'

'Oh, *now* you want him to be with his mother!'

'But—'

'Bruno will be fine with Rose and Ned. I'm coming with you.'

'Will there be a rage if I say no?'

Bianca's hands fly above her head, then apart, imitating the sudden breaking of a thundercloud. 'More than a rage, Husband – a tempest. A storm that will bring down spires and scatter ships onto the rocks.'

Nicholas sighs in defeat. 'Very well, for the sake of tranquillity... It's only three weeks or so, I suppose. After all, all I have to do is fetch a message from Edmund Spenser.'

Bianca runs over and kisses his cheek in reconciliation. 'Three weeks,' she says soothingly. 'Though if Master Spenser's company is as exciting as his poetry, it will probably feel like three years.'

5

Noon on a blustery day in late September, and beneath Dublin's city walls the Liffey has almost reached its flood, dashing the occasional surge of spray over the capstones along Wood Quay.

'Ten days, if the weather holds and the wind is in your favour,' Robert Cecil had told them. 'Take ship at Bristol, rather than Chester. Bristol is quieter. Fewer curious eyes.'

He hadn't bothered to explain why the number of eyes was important.

And he had been wrong on both counts. The Vale of Evesham had been much flooded by the sharp storm that had swept over London in the days before the Southwark Fair. Nicholas and Bianca had found the road west still inundated in several places. At Bristol every ship was crammed with troops bound for Waterford, most of them with little to do but stare in boredom at their surroundings and gamble away the pay they hadn't yet earned. And for every three soldiers, or so it seemed, there was at least one camp-follower – altogether, more eyes than you'd find gazing from the packed benches at the Rose theatre. In the end, they had made the journey from Bankside in twelve days.

'State your business, Master, if you please,' says the port searcher in the quilted surcoat and crested morion helmet, a broadsword at his belt long enough to hang washing from.

Nicholas drops his pack onto the quayside while the man's eyes linger on him. He can feel the inspection as though it's being done by touch rather than by sight. The searcher is taking note of the close-cut nature of Nicholas's beard, the style of stitching on his tan doublet, the weave of his venetians, the buckles on his leather shoes. He's looking for that tiny lapse in attention to detail that might tell him the man standing before him hasn't really come from Bristol at all, but from Douai, or Rome, or Valladolid, or any other of those foreign nests of Jesuit vipers where they prepare Catholic Englishmen to return home and foment sedition.

'I believe you'll find I do not need to state anything in present company,' Nicholas says as pleasantly as he can manage, handing the man a folded sheet of parchment about the size of a small book. It introduces Nicholas as a functionary of the Stationers' Company in London, come to discuss with Master Edmund Spenser his pamphlet *A View of the Present State of Ireland*, which is currently the subject of a dispute with the Stationers' Register, and as yet without a printer. It is as close to an official passport as Robert Cecil's clever secretaries can contrive. It bears the Stationers' Company wax seal. There is a grand signature upon it, too, executed in broad strokes of the nib. The president of the guild, were he to be asked, would undoubtedly recognize it as his own – as long as he didn't look too closely. Nowhere does it bear the name of Mr Secretary Cecil.

'But I know nothing about printing or publishing,' Nicholas had protested on the eve of his departure.

'Don't worry,' Cecil had assured him. 'Spenser is a poet. He'll be too busy talking about himself to notice any ignorance on your part.'

'Can you not just provide me with a letter of commission under your seal?' Nicholas had persisted.

'I'd rather not. There are certain people I would prefer didn't learn that I have a new man in Ireland. If you go around flashing a letter of commission with my name on it...'

'I take by *certain people* you refer to the Earl of Essex.'

Cecil had given him only a tight smile in reply. Then he'd said, 'When you meet Spenser, wait a while before you tell him that it was I who sent you. Get under his skin. Talk about his pamphlet. Get the measure of him.'

'To what purpose?' Nicholas had asked, perplexed.

'Spenser says he has something vital to tell me, but he won't say what. I mistrust his reticence. He might be trying to manoeuvre me into an indiscretion.'

'Why would he seek to play you false?'

'He's a poet,' Cecil had said. 'You could thatch Essex House with all the poets the noble earl likes to keep there. Essex promotes them, encourages them, indulges them – probably lasciviously. He could be planning to entrap me in some enterprise he can use to my disadvantage with Her Majesty, employing Spenser as bait.'

Bianca leans over the rail of the pinnace and hands her pack down to Nicholas. He sets it beside his own and reaches out to help her down. As she lands, a gust of wind blows her dark waves of hair into a tangled halo.

'There's nothing in there about a woman,' the searcher says, handing back the letter. 'Who is she – a mermaid you fished out of the sea?'

'She's my wife.'

'Ah,' says the searcher, giving Bianca a similar scrutiny to the one he's just this moment given Nicholas, but for a quite different reason. 'Well then, you're one less body who'll be needing precious firewood to keep himself warm at night.'

'Do you perchance know if Master Spenser is in the city?' Nicholas asks.

'The fellow named in that letter?'

'Yes, Edmund Spenser – the poet.'

'Is he any good?'

'Ask my wife.'

The searcher shakes his head. 'You could try the castle. I've seen some fine verse scratched on the walls of the jakes up there.'

'I don't think that's Master Spenser's sort of poetry.'

'Then ask at the Tholsel.'

'What's that?'

'It's where the sheriff's clerks keep the register of strangers. You'll have to go there to give your name, and where you're lodging, anyway.'

'Is that necessary? We won't be staying long.'

'The Council of Munster likes to know who's in the city, if you understand my meaning.' The searcher points vaguely towards the city walls. 'It's *that* way, on Skinner's Row, hard by the castle. You can't miss it; it's got a clock on the tower.'

Looking down the quay, Nicholas can see a section of city wall that has been smashed in; and, behind it, the shell of a house with no roof.

'I thought the rebels lacked ordnance,' he says. 'Are they already close enough to bombard?'

The searcher laughs. 'Mercy, no. The rebels wouldn't know which end of the match to light. That was last year, that was. Some shallow-pate managed to set off the black powder they was unloading. One hundred and forty barrels of the stuff.' He puffs his cheeks and spreads his palms to indicate the magnitude of the explosion. 'Took away half of Fishamble Street, Cook Street and Bridge Street in one clap; and almost as many souls as barrels went with it. They'll get around to the rebuilding in time, but at the moment we've other woes to occupy our minds.'

'Can you tell us where we might find a bite to eat?' Bianca asks.

'I hope you don't have large appetites. Food is scarce.'

'Why? The city isn't under siege, is it?' Nicholas says.

'Not yet. But the rebels have burned most of the harvest and carried off half the cattle.' He gives a knowing smirk. 'That and the fact that Dublin has more billeted soldiers feasting on it than it has rats. And we have a *lot* of rats.'

'We'll need a bed,' Nicholas says.

'I should think so,' says the searcher, casting another sly glance at Bianca.

'Can you advise?'

'Well, given that you're official, I'd suggest the castle again. But don't expect comfort. Even if you've got a title, you'll likely have to sleep on straw.'

'Is there a tavern?' Bianca asks wearily.

The man looks at her in disbelief. 'A tavern? You're in Dublin, Mistress; what do *you* think? Try the Brazen Head.'

✠

The walk from Wood Quay into the city is a game of hazard played against carts laden with fodder for the cavalry horses, waggons piled with newly turned pikes, squealing pigs being driven to the shambles, and groups of young gallants in the gaudy doublet and trunk-hose costume of amateur officers, all careering through the streets with no more regard for the hurt they may do the civilian population than they hold for the enemy. And piled head-high on almost every vacant space, a steaming midden filling the air with the stench of decay. Dublin seems a poor prize. Nicholas wonders why the rebel Earl of Tyrone would want it.

'I'd expected somewhere larger,' Bianca says as they walk up a narrow street lined with equally narrow houses. 'This is no bigger than Bristol. Have we come to the right place?'

Small Dublin may be, but the port searcher was right: it contains more troops than any town Nicholas was ever in. Some of them look to him like veterans of the war in the Low Countries, serious fellows with unreadable faces, who sit quietly in doorways and against walls while they whet their blades, cut neat lengths of wick for their matchlock firing pieces or trim cock feathers for the fletches of their arrows. But the majority appear no more martial than the file he had seen mustering at the Southwark Fair – underfed and under-equipped, looking as though they would rather be anywhere but here.

As the port searcher promised, they find the Tholsel with ease. Bianca is the first to spot the clock-face on the tower above a clamorous mob of about fifty people. For the beating heart of civic government, the building looks surprisingly down at heel. The glass has been removed from the windows and some of the lead has been stripped off the roof, presumably to be melted down for musket shot. It reminds Nicholas of a wool-exchange long after the trade has moved to another town. Jostling their way inside, they find themselves in a gloomy hall full of wood-panelled cubicles and benches, where the clerks to the Lord Justices and the Lieutenant-General's staff toil under an avalanche of paperwork, doing their best to obey instructions that change almost as soon as they are given. The accents they can hear are from half the shires in England, the bureaucratic plainsong of the English administration. Here and there they can detect the softer, lilting speech of the Anglo-Irish, and even the mysterious music of native *Gaeilge*.

'I had hoped we might keep our presence here quiet,' Nicholas says as they attempt, by a process of elimination, to locate the clerk responsible for the strangers' roll. 'Now it's going to be on record.'

'Do we really *have* to register?'

He nods. 'They'll have people checking on any tavern that you and I would care to lie down in. New faces will raise questions. I wouldn't rate our chances highly if someone takes it into their heads that we're rebel spies.'

'Name?' says the register clerk, barely looking up.

'Dr Nicholas Shelby,' Nicholas says. He gives Bianca an apologetic glance. 'And Goodwife Shelby.' I've never called her that, he thinks. It sounds like someone I don't know.

'Would that be a doctor of medicine or a doctor of theology?'

'Medicine.'

The clerk makes an entry on his roll, drawing the nib of his quill in slow, scratchy perambulation over the parchment. He looks up, his eyes bloodshot from his labouring in the gloom, and scratches his nose with an ink-stained finger. 'You should make yourself known to the mayor's clerks. Physicians are as scarce as cardinals in Dublin.'

'I'm not here to practise physic. I'm here to carry out an official commission,' Nicholas says, handing the clerk the letter he'd shown the port searcher. 'You'll see from this that I'm from the Stationers' Company at St Paul's, in London. I've come to speak to Master Edmund Spenser. Do you know where I may find him?'

'That depends on which Master Spenser you want,' the clerk says obtusely.

'There's more than one?'

'Several.' The clerk anoints the air with the tip of his quill, counting out the options. 'There's Mr Spenser the muster-master, in which case I would refer you to the Lieutenant-General's office. There's Mr Spenser the secretary – you're best seeking out the Sheriff of Munster if you want to speak to him on council business. If it's Mr Spenser the landowner, you'd be best seeing his bailiff at Kilcolman. If it's the Mr Spenser they say will likely be the next Sheriff of Cork—'

'It's the poet I need to see. *The Faerie Queen* – that fellow.'

'Yes, I know,' says the clerk.

'You mean, they're all the same man?'

'A very prominent citizen is Master Spenser,' the clerk says proudly.

'It's so much easier on Bankside,' Bianca whispers into his ear. 'If you want to find a poet there, all you have to do is shout, "I'll stand the next quart of knock-down."'

Nicholas hushes her into silence.

Mercifully, before Nicholas can lean across and strangle the man, he hears a voice calling from the adjacent cubicle:

'I believe I may be of assistance to you—'

✠

His name is Piers Gardener. An honest fellow, loyal to Her Majesty Queen Elizabeth in all matters, including religion – from an Anglo-Irish family of modest but sound reputation. And any Gardener worth his salt, he assures them, knows his way around Ireland like a flea knows its way around a dog.

He has a young, guileless face, framed by gentle blond curls, and the trusting brown eyes of a milk-calf. Bianca would give him no more than twenty years. His beard is making its best effort to grow, though it's still a long way from a good harvest. In the gloom, she could swear there are patches of flour on his jerkin and hose.

'Fear not, Mistress,' he says, catching the question in her eyes. 'I'm not a ghost.' He pats his breast. A tiny, pale cloud falls away from his fingers. 'They call us the *grey merchants*. It's the dust we pick up from always being out on the road.' He smiles at her with endearing frankness. 'You should see me when it's hot and the sun is high. I look like a miller.'

'And the nature of your merchandise?' Bianca asks, wondering if this is merely the opening patter in what will prove to be nothing but a bald attempt to sell them something.

'Sheepskin and hides, mostly,' he tells her. 'Munster... Leinster... Ulster... there's few places in this isle where the name Piers Gardener is not known, nor his honesty held in high regard.'

'I'm sure that's true,' says Nicholas, trying to keep the doubt from his voice. 'But can you help us find Edmund Spenser?'

'But of course,' Gardener replies. 'He is at Kilcolman. I was there only last week. I can take you to him, if you would like.'

'For a price, I suppose?' Bianca suggests.

Gardener looks hurt. 'No more than the price of renting a horse to ride. I have to go that way on official business.'

'Official?' Nicholas says. 'You're a government man as well as a merchant?'

'I have the honour to be engaged as scrivener to the Surveyor of Victuals.'

Gardener explains that it is the duty of the Surveyor to record the fullness, or more usually the depletion, of the barrels of stockfish, oatmeal, butter, biscuit, cheese and sack to be found in the cellars of the many isolated garrisons of Her Majesty's soldiers currently scattered throughout Ireland. Naturally, one would no more expect the Surveyor to count the victuals himself than expect the Lord Treasurer to count the coins in the Treasury. The menial work he leaves to someone better suited to it: someone who travels widely on his own account. At present, Gardener tells them, his position is unofficial. It will cease to be unofficial just as soon as the Surveyor of Victuals prises the requisite funds out of the Treasurer-at-War.

Here it comes, thinks Bianca: the appeal for money. Gardener's patter is a slick as that of a Bankside street-trickster. 'But at the moment, of course, you have no income...' she suggests, inviting his pitch.

A look of horror clouds Piers Gardener's innocent face. 'Mercy, Mistress!' he protests. 'I am no swindler, if that is what you are thinking.'

For a moment the three of them are trapped in an uncomfortable silence. Bianca wonders if she's been too harsh on Master Piers Gardener. Then the register clerk waves them aside with his quill, beckoning the next newcomer to Dublin to step forward.

'We'll let you know,' Nicholas says. 'We've only arrived within the hour. We haven't eaten or rested, and decisions made in haste may not always be the wisest ones.'

'I understand, Master,' says Gardener in a carefree manner. 'But I would loathe to see the two of you gulled. Dublin is full of bad fellows who will cheat a stranger as soon as wish him good morrow.'

Nicholas asks, 'If we have need of you, Master Gardener, where may we find you?'

'Either here or on St Bride's Street at the sign of the Peacock,' Gardener says. He gives a rueful smile, as though Nicholas has just shown a losing hand at *primero*. 'But I do urge you to think carefully about my offer. Horses will be hard to find in the present circumstances, and you'll discover it very costly to have armed men about you.'

Bianca shoots Nicholas a look that says, *You didn't mention anything about us requiring armed protection.*

'I thought Munster was quiet at present,' he says, echoing her thoughts.

'You'll have been travelling; you may not have heard the news,' says Gardener. 'The rebels are at Limerick. They've burned some of the settler plantations roundabouts. But I know the safe roads and pathways, and I know the people. I can vouch for you, as well as guide you. If you're thinking of leaving today, I would advise you to take up my offer. Remember: the watch will shut the city gates at dusk.'

Gardener gives a courteous bow, reminds them where they might find him, and heads for the door.

The instant before he reaches it, it flies open, almost hitting him in the face. A man rushes in, shouting triumphantly, 'They're bringing rebels in! Three of the papist swine. Come and see!'

Swept up in the rush, before Nicholas and Bianca know it, they are standing outside the Tholsel amid a small crowd, their ears assaulted by a noise similar to the one the audience at the Rose makes when the villainous Turk or the Pope walks on-stage – a throaty mix of derision and loathing.

A low cart rumbles into the square, drawn by a tired and dejected-looking pony, its hocks caked in mud, its huge dark eyes placid and unconcerned. Leading the beast are two men in buff jerkins and knee-high boots, their mouths grinning with vicarious triumph.

'Well, at least we shall see what manner of fellows have thrown the Privy Council into such a terror,' Nicholas whispers.

Bianca looks at the passing cart, expecting to see a trio of bearded, painted warriors in plaid – huge mountain men with deep, glaring eyes and snarling mouths. Instead she sees nothing but sheaves of straw, piled up to the rim of the cart. Otherwise, the cart appears to be empty. It trundles slowly past, the axles grinding discordantly in their collars, a dancing crowd of jeering onlookers following in its wake. Perplexed, she lets her eyes follow.

As the cart moves away, Bianca gets a sight of its open tailboard – and three human heads, propped upright on the planks against the straw, staring at her with their sightless young eyes.

She turns to Nicholas, her hands flying to cover her open mouth, too shocked to ask the question: *What manner of hellish place have you let Robert Cecil bring us to?*

6

The Brazen Head, the port searcher had said. Prophetic advice, Bianca thinks. Staring down at her, from a board hanging out over the lane, is a garish, disembodied face, painted in brilliant red with yellow flames for hair.

Her hands are still trembling from the macabre sight she'd witnessed only a few minutes before. She wonders why it has so affected her. A whole coronet of severed heads sits atop the southern gatehouse of London Bridge. She cannot cross the top of Long Southwark, or go over the Thames into the city, without passing beneath them. But those are the heads of traitors, condemned by judicial process. What must have befallen the three boys whose heads she has just seen lying on the floor of the cart seems to her more like vengeful murder. Not one of them had been older than dear Timothy, her taproom lad at the Jackdaw. She had heard that Ireland was a barbarous place, but she had never expected *this*.

'A glass of sack might settle you,' Nicholas says as they enter. 'I think I need one, myself.'

'They looked so young,' Bianca says sadly, shaking her head to cast off the image that seems painted on the inside of her eyelids.

'They were rebels. Rebellion against the Crown is no trivial matter. The punishment cannot be trivial, either.'

'You condone *that*?' she asks, staring at her husband. 'You, a man who's made healing the sick his guidepost?'

'No, of course not,' Nicholas says defensively. 'But insurrection cannot be treated with a gentle hand, or else all semblance of order might be overthrown.'

'You sound like Robert Cecil.'

'I accept such punishment is harsh, but there is purpose to it.'

'Purpose?' she exclaims.

'If you burn your finger on a candle's flame, you are unlikely to thrust your hand into a fire. For your whole body, that burnt finger was a mercy.'

'I would never have taken you for a tyrant, Nicholas,' she says, surprised by his response.

'I didn't say I agreed with it. But those rebels raised their swords against the queen's lawful rule. Robert Cecil would say that's tantamount to raising them against God.'

'But *you've* rebelled against God, Nicholas,' Bianca says gently. 'You told me so yourself. When your first wife died carrying your child, you railed against Him. You denied Him.'

'Yes, I did.'

How easy it is now, he thinks, to revisit memories that had once almost driven him to the sin of self-destruction. Bianca has given him the strength to do that. And she has given him more: she has given him little Bruno.

'Then should *you* not be severely punished,' she asks, her voice softening further, 'for seeking to overthrow *His* order?'

He tilts his head back and stares at the sky, as though appealing for help from above.

'I *have* been punished,' he says. 'God has sent me a wife who is so clever she can take my thoughts and tangle them into a knot, which she can then magically unravel, and – *lo* – I discover they were not my thoughts at all, but belonged to some other fellow, and now I cannot fathom *what* I believe!'

She smiles at the way the Suffolk burr strengthens in his voice when his heart is at its most open. 'Would you prefer a wife who did nothing but sit at home, sewing and reading her psalter?'

'Do you mean at this *precise* moment—'

She jabs him with her elbow. 'You're right about one thing, though.'

'What's that?'

'That glass of sack. After today's shock, I might need more than one.'

✠

Their luck is in. Not only does the sack hit the mark, but there is also a room about to be vacated. They order their glasses refilled while the bedding is refreshed. A trencher of stringy mutton and a hunk of manchet bread is all the kitchen can provide. The meat has globules of yellow fat on it and the bread is stale. But the sack is sweet, and it washes away the awful images in Bianca's mind. While she drinks she casts a professional eye around the Brazen Head.

The first thing she notices is the number of soldiers. At least she assumes they're soldiers, by the swords and poniards they wear at their belts, and by the lusty songs they keep belting out about killing papists or rolling maidens in the hay. There is little consistency in the uniforms they wear, nothing as colourful or as disciplined as the troops she's seen in Padua or Venice.

'Are these the fellows the queen is relying upon to save Ireland?' she asks Nicholas.

'Apparently. No wonder the Earl of Tyrone's rebels have had the better of them. Let us pray Robert Cecil is wrong about the Spanish coming to their aid. If they do, Ireland will be theirs inside one month. Were that to happen, they could be in England within two.'

The wine and the thought of a comfortable bed that does not lurch to the movement of the waves, like a drunkard dancing a volta, makes Bianca tired. She promises herself to stay awake long enough to write a letter to Bruno that Rose can read to him. She has steeled herself not only to his absence, but to Nicholas's desire for him to enter Robert Cecil's household when he is older. Much as the thought pains her, she knows it will only be to Bruno's harm if she stands in the way.

'By the golden chariot of bright Phoebus! It *is* you. I knew it, the moment I set eyes upon you.'

The voice that breaks into her thoughts has a languid confidence about it, the voice of a man unaccustomed to rebuttal. A voice she remembers.

'Oliver! What on earth are you doing in Dublin?'

Looking up, she sees an elegantly dressed man perhaps a year or two younger than herself, clad in a bright-yellow brocade doublet and dark-blue kersey trunk-hose. The body is as nonchalant as the voice, one hand spread against his waist, the other balled under the smooth chin. His brown hair is cut close to the scalp. The finely wrought guard of a rapier lies against his hip like the head of a faithful hound. He is the very model of the English gentleman-dabbler in the military arts.

And then she remembers the man Vyves, and his invitation to Ned Monkton at the Southwark Fair: *We could use a doughty fellow like you in the ranks of Sir Oliver Henshawe's company...*

'It is *Sir* Oliver now, Mistress Bianca,' Henshawe says smoothly. 'Dubbed by the Earl of Essex himself, at Cádiz.'

'Cádiz? So you never got to Madrid?'

'Madrid?' He gives her a puzzled look. 'I don't recall mentioning—'

'You told me once that you were going to steal King Philip's wedding ring and put it on my finger.'

'Did I? All I recall is you laughing at my attempts at verse.'

'Laugh at *you*, Oliver? I'm sure I never did.'

'You left my poor heart as tattered as a Spanish battle flag,' Henshawe says, laying an elegant hand to his breast to emphasize the extent of his torment.

'I'm sure it's been patched since. English maids at your station are renowned for their needlework.'

Henshawe gives Nicholas an empty smile. 'And am I to believe that this dull fellow is your husband?'

Is this a clumsy attempt at manly badinage or just plain rudeness? wonders Nicholas. Henshawe's pretty face is too smooth, too unreadable.

'Yes, this is Nicholas,' Bianca says, laying a restraining hand on his arm. 'And he didn't have to offer me stolen jewellery in order to woo me.'

'Someone told me you were a farm labourer's son who became a physician,' Henshawe drawls. 'Is that so? Would that I might find such a clever alchemist. I'd be eating gold for breakfast and supper.'

Rudeness, plain and simple, Nicholas decides. He resists the urge to land a fist on Henshawe's jauntily tilted chin. A brawl here, in such company, would not go well for him.

'My father is a yeoman,' he says calmly. 'He has title to the land he farms. And I earned my doctorate in medicine. I didn't inherit it.'

The riposte slides off Henshawe's self-regard as if it were plate armour. 'No matter,' he says, turning his attention again to Bianca. 'We may consider it a fine example of how a man may make his way in Her Majesty's England – if he has a mind to it.'

'I see your gentlemanly manner is as polished as I remember it, Oliver,' Bianca says sweetly. 'I cannot possibly imagine why it failed to captivate me. For someone who can't recall promising me a wedding ring, you seem to have taken an inordinate interest in the man I *did* marry.'

'You forget that my family has an estate at Walworth. One cannot pass across London Bridge without first passing through Southwark. And one cannot linger in Southwark without hearing gossip. You, of all people, should know that,' Henshawe says. Then his untroubled smile disappears, as if cut off by the executioner's axe. 'But if you've decided to leave Bankside and settle land in Ireland, you have chosen a poor time to do it. The rebels have run off most of the settlers' cattle and burned their crops. We're here to stop them taking all Munster.'

'We've not come to settle,' Nicholas interjects, growing tired of Henshawe's supercilious performance. 'I am on official business for the Stationers' Office in London. I've come to speak with Master Spenser, the poet.'

'Spenser?' Henshawe says with a lift of his brow. 'He's out at Kilcolman, I believe. You'd best hurry. I came through there a week ago and I could smell insurrection on the air.'

'Do you think an attack is imminent?' Nicholas asks, chewing a morsel of mutton and trying to sound unperturbed.

'Our spies say a brace of rebel chieftains, O'Moore and Tyrrell, have some two thousand rogues under arms, ready to launch a sally from Limerick. If Tyrone lets them off the leash, you wouldn't want to be there when they come.'

'We plan to leave tomorrow. We have no cause to stay here,' Nicholas says, trying not to give Henshawe the satisfaction of thinking he's leaving in a hurry.

'I'd heartily advise taking an escort,' Henshawe says. He gives Bianca a smooth smile as he taps the hilt of his sword. 'Why don't I come with you? Bookish men are all very well in a cloister' – a glance at Nicholas – 'or a hospital. But here in Ireland it's better to have a fellow with a goodly length of steel in his scabbard by one's side. I'm sure the Earl of Ormonde – the Lieutenant-General – will grant me leave when he learns the value of the prize I'd be guarding.'

Nicholas turns his eyes to the soldiers in the taproom, wondering if Henshawe is trying to bait him for their entertainment or his own. But they are too engrossed in their drinking and dicing to have noticed. Personal then, he decides – Henshawe, the spurned lover, the rejected stag trying one last stamp of the hoof. Pathetic.

'We already have an escort, thank you,' he says.

'We have?' Bianca queries in surprise.

'Yes. It's all arranged,' Nicholas announces confidently. He waves the lump of mutton impaled on the end of his knife at Henshawe. 'Now, if we *might* be permitted to finish our meal...'

Henshawe looks at Bianca. She smiles with pretend regret. 'I'm sorry, Oliver. You're too late – as ever.'

A little grunt of defeat escapes from the back of Henshawe's throat. As he turns away, he mutters, 'Please yourselves. But I would allow no wife of mine to go wandering off into the wilderness in search of a poet. I'd make sure she knew her station.'

Before Nicholas can reply, Bianca gives Henshawe a brief but challenging smile. 'Perhaps, Oliver,' she says, 'that's why I decided not to wait for you to get back from Madrid.'

✠

'*What* escort?' Bianca asks impatiently when they're alone in their chamber. 'You told Oliver Henshawe that we have an escort. We don't.'

'Yes, we do,' Nicholas says, easing himself back against the bolster of the small tester bed. 'Master Piers Gardener.'

'The fellow at the Tholsel? The one with the dust?'

'What was it he called himself – a grey merchant?'

'But we barely know him. For all we know, he could be the worst trickster in Ireland.'

'He told us he knew the discreet roads, the people. Who better to put our trust in, given what your Sir Oliver Henshawe said in the taproom?'

'He's not *my* Oliver Henshawe, Nicholas.'

'I get the impression he rather wanted to be.'

'Nicholas,' she replies irritably, 'Oliver Henshawe has seen the inside of every stew on Bankside. He must have near-bankrupted his father with the money he spent on doxies and dice. It's a miracle he's not riddled with the French gout. If you want me to be blunt, he was never my lover. This is all about jealousy, isn't it? Anything rather than accept help from someone who once paid court to me.'

'It has nothing to do with jealousy,' Nicholas protests unconvincingly. 'I wasn't the uncivil one.' He adopts a gallant's drawl. '*Someone told me you were a farm labourer's son who became a physician... better to have a fellow with a goodly length of steel in his scabbard...* I could have punched him in his supercilious face.'

'That would have been a good stratagem – attacking an officer in a tavern full of his own soldiery.'

'I suspect they would have cheered me. The point is, if Henshawe is right about the threat, we'll need someone who knows the lie of the land. Someone who can guide us without attracting every rebel within riding distance.'

'Couldn't we just stay in Dublin and send Spenser a letter?'

'We could have stayed on Bankside and done that. I suspect it would have had much the same result.' He swings his legs over the bed and slips his feet into his shoes.

'Where are you going?' Bianca asks.

'Speaking of letters, you have one to write to Bruno. Send him his father's love. I'm off to St Bride's Street, to the sign of the Peacock, to speak to our grey merchant.'

✠

Piers Gardener is as good as his word. By the time the clock bell at the Tholsel rings ten the next morning he has procured three hobbies – tough little horses that look sound enough for the journey to Kilcolman Castle. Nicholas braces himself for the bill. He may be using Robert Cecil's coin to settle it, but a speedy means of escape from a city in fear of attack comes at a premium, and the keepers of the Cecil privy purse have a habit of rejecting anything they consider above the going rate – that usually being the rate pertaining during the reign of the third Edward.

In fact the price Gardener asks is a reasonable one. 'No one in Munster overcharges me,' he says, 'not if they want my recommendation to the Surveyor of Victuals.'

By noon – just twenty-four hours after they arrived in Dublin – Nicholas and Bianca pass through the stout city walls by St Nicholas's Gate, which Bianca proclaims a clear sign of good fortune to come. They follow a line of little thatched houses to a second, smaller archway beside St Patrick's Church, and so out onto the Cork road. The late-September air is cool, a hem of grey cloud brushing the tops of the mountains that Nicholas can see on the horizon. To his right he glimpses an encampment huddled amid the alder trees on the opposite bank of a rushing stream of dark water.

'Are these the Lieutenant-General's men?' he asks Gardener.

Gardener laughs. 'Mercy! Even the Earl of Ormonde's men aren't *that* ragged.'

And indeed, as they draw closer, Nicholas can see the tattered tents made of scraps of hide, the turf-clad shelters and the thin, dispirited faces of the camp's inhabitants as they tend their fires and cooking pots. Skinny cows and sheep graze disconsolately between the trees.

'Refugees,' Gardener explains, his golden hair dancing about his gentle face in the breeze, 'English settlers from Ulster and

Leinster, mostly. Tyrone and his fellows have burned them out of their plantations. There's no room for them in Dublin – not that one in a hundred could afford. The Pale around the city is the only land left to shelter on.'

As they ride on, Nicholas cannot help but notice the look of doubt that has entered Bianca's amber eyes. He does not press her. He knows what she's thinking: that he is a fool for agreeing to come here. He tries not to imagine the fountain of molten anger that will flow if, upon reaching Kilcolman, they discover that the great secret Edmund Spenser wishes to reveal to Robert Cecil turns out to be nothing more than the fevered excesses of a poet's imagination.

✠

Piers Gardener turns out to be the ideal guide. His travels across Ireland as scrivener to the Surveyor of Victuals – making meticulous note of the provisions needed by the isolated English garrisons – means he can find food, a hearth and a comfortable place to sleep even when the landscape seems devoid of all human habitation.

On the first night, as Bianca is beginning to think they have become utterly lost amid a range of wild hills whose crests are buried in the rapidly darkening clouds, a tiny hamlet emerges out of the mist. On the second, as night begins to overtake them on a narrow path through a great expanse of bog, convincing her that they are doomed to drown when the hobbies inevitably stumble off the track, a simple hut of grey stone suddenly appears, huddling against the bracken of the rising hillside ahead. They reach it just before the last of the light goes.

And this smooth-faced boy with the saint's halo of blond curls proves to have more skills than simply knowing where to find shelter. A scion of an ancient Anglo-Norman family from

Waterford, he has learned enough of the Irish language to speak to those they come across who are not English settlers, but folk whose roots go deep into the ancient heart of the land, back to a time before St Patrick first hoisted his crozier aloft to bring God's grace and mercy to the pagans. Some of them seem to Bianca like characters from tales of legend and myth where solitary women of great beauty cast spells in high towers, and men with unshakeable ideals embark on hopeless quests. Others look broken by toil or close to starving. Many of these people appear to have no fixed home, or choose not to have. Through Gardener, she learns that they come and go as the land and the mood take them, moving their small herds of cattle and sheep from pasture to pasture, or their labour from plantation to plantation. The timelessness of the landscape seeps into Bianca with the chill and the rain. It is a place as far away from the heat and colour of Padua as she can imagine: rolling hills of bracken turning to amber, gold and scarlet as autumn approaches; craggy grey outcrops of stone jutting like buried dragons' teeth. Occasionally, when the land rises, they glimpse a smudge of smoke against the grey sky where it touches the horizon – a burning farmhouse or a sacked manor, Gardener tells them, his child's face darkening. Signs, he says, that even though Tyrone's forces are mostly in Ulster well to the north, here in Munster he has friends amongst the local population.

At night, when they reach whatever place Gardener has assured them will offer shelter and food, the welcome proves to be ungrudging, though always muted. It seems the scrivener is well known – trusted even. Nicholas and Bianca dine simply on oatcakes and buttermilk, or fish taken from fast-flowing rivers. They warm themselves beside smoky hearths of peat and sleep on pelts and fleeces. No one asks who they are and, from what Bianca can gather, Gardener does not volunteer the information.

But she catches the frowns and worried glances when the subject moves to what she assumes is the rebellion.

On the third night they lodge on the fringe of a dense stand of fir trees that stretches as far as Bianca can see, in a single-storey cottage made of mud-brick and stone with a turf roof.

It has rained again during the afternoon. As she dismounts in front of the simple dwelling, she can hear the lachrymose singing of the wood as the uncountable droplets fall into the dense undergrowth. From somewhere deep inside the trees, the haunting cry of an owl carries on the damp air. By now she is ready to believe she has entered a world of sprites and spirits, or even the legendary *Longana*, the creature her Italian mother told her about when she was a child – a creature with the face of a beautiful woman and the hirsute limbs of a faun, who lives in the forests of the Veneto and can smell the future on the wind.

The owner of the cottage is an ancient woodcutter with lined grey skin like runnelled sand when the tide is out. He greets them without fuss, bestows an inexpressive hug upon Gardener and beckons them all to his hearth. His wife is a slight, silver-haired woman, dressed in plain broadcloth. Something about the couple makes Bianca believe they are more kin to the dark wood than the world beyond – if they even know there *is* a world beyond – for although Bianca cannot understand the words that pass between them and Gardener, there is none of the urgency that would suggest the exchanging of news. But they are welcoming to her and Nicholas in a quiet, reserved fashion.

They ease their hunger with vegetable pottage flavoured with wild garlic, ladled from a communal cauldron on the hearth. The woodsman offers them rich, dark ale from a clay jug. As they relax, Gardener explains that the woman is a *Seanchaí*, a keeper of ancient stories.

Bianca leans forward to learn more. She is already remembering how, in Padua, her mother enchanted her with tales. Mostly they had been about the Caporetti women of ancient times, and their mythical ability to turn almost anything that grows into a healing balm or a fatal poison. For her, the excitement in the stories was never just about the women's skills, but about who was the beneficiary or the victim. So now, if there is an intriguing tale to be told, Bianca is always ready to hear it – even if it does have to be translated for her by a young lad who seems barely old enough to have acquired stories of his own. As she settles back against the earthen wall of the cottage, her face thrown into sharp relief by the firelight, she leans into Nicholas so that they might share, as one, whatever is to come. She feels like a child again: eager, slightly apprehensive, ready to be transported into a magical realm.

And so, on their third night on the road, huddled together in a dark cottage on the edge of a weeping wood, with Piers Gardener translating, Bianca and Nicholas hear for the first time of the Merrow: the woman who walks out of the sea to capture the hearts of men.

✠

There are families in Munster that claim their descent from the Merrow, the *Seanchaí* explains in a soft, lyrical voice that belies her great age. These mythical women live in the ocean, she says. They converse with the sea and the air, and thus have knowledge of the future. They are beyond beautiful. No man, however resolute, can withstand their sweet song. They grow rich upon the treasure from drowned wrecks. Sometimes, when lust takes them, or the loneliness of the deep ocean becomes too much to bear, they swim ashore to seduce a land-bound mortal.

The *Seanchaí* relates a haunting tale of one such Merrow, and the man she came ashore to woo. It ends with the man, and his son, standing heartbroken on a beach, staring out at the empty ocean.

'So be warned,' the *Seanchaí* says, when the story has drawn to its close. 'A man can never keep a Merrow long. One day she will return to the sea, leaving her husband and their children bereft and consumed by an impossible longing.'

'I always wondered why you take such long walks beside the Thames,' Nicholas whispers. 'Are you planning to swim away?'

Bianca jabs him with her elbow. It is a good tale, she thinks. Retold well, it should boost the takings in the Jackdaw on a cold night in winter – especially if Timothy the taproom lad plays a haunting accompaniment on his lute.

Nicholas, who has grown up to the tales of strange creatures dwelling in the Suffolk marshes, says in his practical physician's voice, 'How is it that the Merrow do not die, as a fish dies when it is brought from the sea into the air?'

The *Seanchaí* gives him a sympathetic smile, as though he is a poor fellow cursed with the dullest of brains. 'The Merrow wears a magical hat,' she explains. 'She must take it off when she comes out of the sea.' She looks at Bianca and raises a gnarled, cautionary finger. 'Be careful, Mistress,' she says. 'If you find a Merrow's hat on the shore, watch out. She has probably come to steal your husband's heart.'

7

In the Jackdaw tavern on Bankside a company of players is arguing volubly about whether they can claim exemption if the city aldermen send their sheriffs into the playhouses to conscript men for the Irish war. Outside, it is raining. Inside, the fuggy air turns the windows the colour of dusty charcoal. The St Saviour's bell has just tolled nine. Only the hardened drinkers remain, and those – like the players – whose occupation does not require them rising with the dawn.

'I *cannot* go to the wars!' Ned Monkton hears one cry. 'I am engaged at the Curtain, to play the part of Shallow in Master Will's *The Merry Wives of Windsor*.'

'But you *must* go to the wars. You'll feel at home, dear lad,' comes the reply. 'Every part I've ever seen you take was a bloody battle.'

Ned knows that, of all the factions who drink in the Jackdaw, actors are the most prone to riotous behaviour. Too much knock-down and the outcome will likely be either weeping self-pity or drawn swords.

He is keeping a tally of the jugs and victuals they have ordered. Being a stranger to writing, he is using an invented notation of his own. He can write the numbers well enough, but for letters Ned has to use symbols that are comprehensible only to himself, Rose and Timothy. It works well enough. It's known in the Jackdaw as *Ned-hand*.

He still feels a surge of pride whenever he looks around the rebuilt Jackdaw. Sometimes he walks out into the lane to assess the tavern as though he were a thirsty traveller in search of rest and company. Then he thinks: Rose and I achieved *that*.

On these occasions he is careful not to boast. After all, it is really the bricklayers who are responsiblc for the almost-straight herringbone masonry stretching some forty feet between a tallow shop on one side and a private house on the other. The row of diamonds that decorate the base of the upper floor jutting out above his head – rendered fetchingly in alternating yellow and red, and each the size of a man's hand – is down to the artistry, and sobriety, of Bankside's painters. (Rose hadn't let them touch a drop of knock-down until they'd finished.)

When, from the lane, he stoops to peer inside, the distorted view through the lozenges of window glass into the taproom is by courtesy of the glaziers. The casks, counter, benches and booths, the low ceiling beams and the pillars that support them – all of which prevent him seeing as far as the stairs to the lodging rooms, even when the windows are clean – are the work of the joiners. Nor can he claim responsibility for the thatched roof, or the rebuilding of the two narrow wings at the back that enclose the yard and the brew house, and where, in the eaves of one of them, Master Nicholas had his attic lodgings – until he and Mistress Bianca at last accepted what the rest of Bankside had known for months.

But none of these would exist as they do today if Ned and Rose Monkton hadn't overseen the rebuilding in Nicholas and Bianca's absence. Quite an achievement, he thinks, for a fellow who can neither read nor write and who had previously overseen nothing but the binding of the dead at St Thomas's hospital.

The street door opening causes him to look up from his work. Two men enter. He recognizes the taller at once. It is Vyves, the lank-haired, one-eyed muster ensign he had seen at the Southwark Fair.

The other man is smaller, with a flushed, porcine face fixed in a frown of permanent disgruntlement. On his head is a tall, thimble-shaped felt hat, gleaming with rain.

'God give you good morrow, Master Ned,' says Vyves, shaking his cloak as he approaches the counter. He has exchanged make-shift military for a tattered open-necked jerkin of green frieze.

'And to you, too, Ensign Vyves,' Ned replies. ''Aven't seen you in 'ere before. It's late, but you're welcome, all the same.'

'We drinks usually in the Turk's Head,' Vyves says, looking around in admiration at the new – if not exactly pristine – interior of the tavern. 'But we thought we'd give the new Jackdaw a try. And very nice it is too, if I may make so bold. What say you, Master Strollot?'

'Very nice indeed,' agrees the other man, taking off his thimble-hat as though he was in church.

'Master Ned, meet my friend, Gideon Strollot,' Vyves says expansively.

Strollot gives Ned a treacly smile. 'Junior clerk to the alderman of Cornhill Ward.'

Ned's eyes are drawn to a belly straining at the seams of a grey broadcloth doublet. 'You're welcome, both,' he says, thinking Strollot a little old to be a junior anything. He must be at least forty. 'At the Jackdaw we asks only that if you *must* curse, you do so inventively; and call no man a liar unless you can prove it. 'Part from that, if your coin is 'onest, we'll take it.'

'I still say he would have made a very fine pikeman,' Vyves says to his companion as Ned pours a jug of stitch-back from the cask.

'He's big enough to fill in for ten,' Strollot says appreciatively.

From in front of the cask, Ned says over his shoulder, 'I've put my fightin' days behind me. I 'ave no quarrel with any man, let alone one in Ireland.'

'But they're rebels,' says Vyves. 'Wasn't *that* long ago they held the Pope himself to be their master. And besides, what if the Spanish make a landing, to assist them in their sedition?'

'Well, the Dons 'aven't managed it yet, 'ave they?' Ned points out. 'Your average Don is about as good at armada-rin' as Ned Monkton is at dancin' a galliard. Neither of us floats very well.'

He fetches two tankards from the shelf and sets them beside the jug of ale.

'We'll need three, if it's no trouble,' says Vyves. 'We's expecting company.'

Ned brings the extra tankard. 'One 'a'penny, if it pleases.'

Vyves hands over the coin. 'But aren't you outraged at the cruelties the rebels are inflicting upon our innocent settlers over there: infants dashed against walls, men's heads cut off an' used as footballs?'

'I look at it like this,' explains Ned, scratching his great auburn beard. 'Anyone who decides 'e'd rather make his 'ome in a wasps' nest, in pref'rence to the one he's already got, can't complain much if 'e gets stung, can 'e? Why go? There's land enough in England, isn't there?'

'They go in order to bring God's light to a heathen country,' suggests Strollot sternly. 'To civilize it, and bring it to an understanding of Christian law and good custom.'

'An' 'ow's that goin' at the moment, would you reckon?' Ned asks, leaning across the counter in a conversational manner.

Vyves lifts the jug of ale. His one eye gleams knowingly. 'If the queen sends the Earl of Essex at the head of a *proper* army, like they say she's going to, we won't hear another squeak out of the Irish from now until the crack of doom – Spaniards or no Spaniards. You mark my words.' And with that, he takes his tankard and heads for a nearby empty bench, Strollot trailing him like an inquisitive sow.

In the far corner the players are getting to their feet, their voices rising, their gestures becoming more theatrical. Ned goes over to calm them down. He calls Timothy to fetch them more knock-down. Then he goes back to his tallying until the street door opens again.

Laying aside his quill, he watches the newcomer stop just inside the door and look around, obviously searching for someone he knows. Lanky, not yet out of his teens, he looks strangely familiar. His eyes alight on Vyves and Strollot, sitting at their ale. At once he takes on a deferential shortening of the body – the way a servant might if he was about to make a guilty confession to an unpredictable master.

Now Ned recognizes him: he's the young fellow from the muster file at the Southwark Fair, the one who exchanged a few words with Master Nicholas. He can hear in his head the boy's answer to Nicholas's question:

To Ireland, if it please Your Honour – to kill the papist rebels...

His curiosity pricked, Ned watches the lad slide onto the bench in front of Ensign Vyves, who lifts the ale jug and fills the third tankard, then pushes it towards the newcomer. But the lad ignores it. His shoulders stoop, his back bends, his head twists sideways a little. The abasement seems limitless. He is saying something that, at this distance, and with the noise coming from the actors' table, Ned is unable to hear. But presumably it's a request for money. Because Strollot pulls a purse from his jerkin, rummages in it, then puts his fist into the lad's suddenly grasping palm. And with that, the fellow jumps up and leaves, without even lingering long enough to take a single sip from the tankard of stitch-back.

That alone is enough to rouse Ned Monkton's suspicions. He thinks: whoever heard of a soldier passing up a free drink in a tavern – especially a newly mustered green-pate facing the imminent prospect of losing his head to a rebel's knife?

But what is he doing still on Bankside? The muster marched away almost three weeks ago. He should be in Ireland by now. He has obviously not deserted, although Ned wouldn't blame him if he had. A deserter wouldn't go within a league of the man who mustered him, unless he wanted to end up with a length of stout rope for a scarf. There must be some other reason he's still in England.

Ned runs through the possibilities. The cod's-head must have dropped a heavy pike on his foot. Or he's inadvertently stabbed himself while sharpening a poleaxe. And now that he's recovered sufficiently, he's come back to collect his pay. That would explain the coin Strollot handed him. What does it matter anyway? Ned asks himself. What concern is it of mine?

He goes back to his Ned-hand.

But for some reason that he cannot explain there is an itch in his mind that demands scratching. His pen gets barely as far as making the mark that assigns a jug of cardinal's courage and a plate of brawn to the account of John Dromley, the wherryman, before another thought strikes him.

Why was it Strollot who paid him, and not Vyves?

Strollot is an alderman's clerk. He's not a military man. He has nothing to do with the muster. What business does *he* have paying a soldier?

In his memory, Ned tries to repaint the picture he's just seen. This time he gives Vyves the purse. Perhaps that's what actually happened, he thinks, making a pout that fails to move a single strand of his great red beard. Perhaps I remembered it wrong.

The actors are getting raucous again. Ned decides it's time to have another word.

And so he forgets all about what he's just seen. He puts it out of his mind. The itch subsides. Within a minute or two it has gone entirely, as if the gangly lad who should be in Ireland had never walked through the door.

8

Kilcolman Castle glowers over the fertile valley like a keep guarding a disputed border. It is a flinty grey tower house, dour and forbidding, set between the pine-clad slopes of the Ballyhoura Mountains and a wide, marshy lake. Now that the rain clouds have gone, the lake is a mirror glass in the afternoon sunshine.

According to Piers Gardener, Edmund Spenser has owned the estate for a decade. The valley itself looks well tended and profitable. Someone must have been keeping watch from the tower, because the owner of Kilcolman is waiting for them at the gate in the outer wall. In his middle forties, Spenser has the appearance of a scholar or a chaplain. Nicholas can picture him in the cloisters at Cambridge, discussing theology with his students. Yet while his hair is now receding at the temples, the neatly trimmed moustache flicked up at the ends and the small wedge of beard suggest he likes to keep abreast of fashion, even in remote Munster.

Before Nicholas can introduce himself, Gardener says, 'I have brought you visitors, Master Spenser. This gentleman is Dr Nicholas Shelby, a physician – from London.'

Nicholas is speechless. In Gardener's presence he has been careful to portray himself only as a messenger from the Worshipful Company of Stationers. As far as he can remember, he hasn't mentioned medicine once. So how does Gardener know? Then he recalls a snatch of his conversation with the clerk at the Tholsel in Dublin. *Would that be a doctor of medicine or a doctor of theology?* The scrivener must have overheard. And he's just made Nicholas's task even harder.

'You are welcome, Dr Shelby,' says Spenser, as though random visitors turning up in his valley is a regular occurrence. 'But I have no need of physic. As you can see, I am in good health.'

'I don't doubt it. But I'm not here in any medical capacity,' Nicholas says. 'I've been sent on behalf of the Worshipful Company of Stationers.'

'Is it about my pamphlet, *A View of the Present State of Ireland?*' Spenser asks, a gleam of anticipation in his soft, brown eyes. 'Is it going to allow me a printer at last?'

'That is something I am sure we can discuss, sir,' Nicholas says evasively.

It seems to satisfy. 'Then you had best come in and take your ease,' Spenser says. 'You, too, Master Gardener.' He looks at Bianca. 'And you also, Mistress—'

'Bianca. I'm Nicholas's wife.'

Is that a fleeting, suspicious lift of a delicate Spenser eyebrow that Nicholas notices? If it is, then he knows what his host is thinking: since when did the august gentlemen of the Stationers' Company indulge its representatives by financing the accompaniment of their spouses?

'Bianca was accompanying me to Dublin on another matter,' Nicholas says, seizing the first vague explanation that enters his head. 'I suggested she stay in the city, but she told me she would rather spend time in the company of England's greatest poet than amongst a garrison of soldiery.'

His self-regard burnished just enough to overcome suspicion, Spenser protests. 'Oh, I would hardly place myself in such a pantheon, Dr Shelby. You see before you naught but a humble poetaster.' And with a sweeping gesture, he invites them in.

As Nicholas enters the poet's gloomy fastness, he wonders how easy it is going to be to gain Spenser's trust, now that Gardener has spoken loosely. Evidently a core of distrust lies beneath the poet's outer pleasantry. And not only distrust about his new visitors. Because why else, Nicholas is thinking, would a man who chooses to settle in this pleasing valley hide himself away behind the walls of a fortress? Perhaps, like the Merrow in the tale the old woman told them last night, Spenser can see into the future. Perhaps he sensed on the wind that one day rebellion would come to this peaceful place. Maybe that is why he will deliver his secret only to a messenger who has Robert Cecil's complete trust.

Supper is a stilted affair, like a family reunion where no one dares raise the matter of the skeleton in the cupboard. For the most part the pressing issue – the rebellion – is studiously avoided. The Spenser family prefers to learn the latest London gossip. Has the Earl of Essex convinced the queen to make him her Lord Lieutenant in Ireland? Does anyone yet dare speak of the succession? How grand was old Burghley's funeral? Did anyone shout, 'Thank God the corrupt old puppeteer is dead'? While Nicholas and Bianca scatter what pearls they think might entertain, Spenser listens with the studied concentration of the scholar – a man weighing the fashions and frivolities of London life against its affairs of state, as if to judge the nation's true humour. His wife Elizabeth – half his age – follows each nod, each purse of the lips and '*no – really?*' with dutiful attention. Sylvanus and Katherine, a son and daughter from a previous marriage, listen with the sort of fascination to be expected of children approaching adulthood in a remote rural home far from the excitement of the city. An infant son, Peregrine, can be heard wailing somewhere deep within the house, like a prisoner incarcerated in a dungeon. Bianca feels a stab of guilt and calls herself a callous, uncaring Medea for abandoning little Bruno. And all the while, a small supporting cast of servants hovers around the table board like grey spectres at a burial.

Nicholas dances as nimbly as he can around Spenser's enquiries about the Stationers' Company and its deliberations over the poet's pamphlet. Whenever pressed, he falls back on the vague excuses that are all Cecil's people have provided him with.

'You know how it is these days – no one wants to be the fellow to lose his right hand to the axe because he's inadvertently published something Her Majesty disapproves of... The price of paper these days is making everyone very cautious...'

'But they've had the *View* for over a year, Dr Shelby.'

'And then there's the fact that the Company is run off its feet, rooting out all those barrels of proscribed papist books being smuggled in from the Spanish Netherlands...'

But every now and then the cupboard door is opened. The skeleton is revealed. Then Piers Gardener is the one who must provide the answers.

'What was the mood in Cork when last you were there?... Is it still quiet along the Blackwater?... When does the Lieutenant-General, the Earl of Ormonde, think Tyrone will venture into Munster in force?'

'Why do you not seek shelter within the Pale, at Dublin, Master Spenser?' Nicholas asks over a chunk of rosy salmon taken from the nearby Awbeg stream.

'I have faith in the power of the Crown, Dr Shelby. The Lord Justices are considering appointing me Sheriff of Cork. How would it look if I were to run away from my duties? Besides, I have some three thousand acres here at Kilcolman, and more elsewhere. My absence from the estate might embolden those in

Munster who harbour rebellion in their hearts. I would not see such profitable land defiled. Then there's my library, and all my manuscripts.'

Now Nicholas understands why Spenser was so reluctant to leave Ireland. 'Do you not fear the isolation?' he asks. 'You are very vulnerable here.'

Spenser's confidence is unshakeable. 'Kilcolman has stood for centuries. It was built when the Munster chieftains were warring amongst themselves. We have our own water supply, and enough provisions to hold out until Dublin sends us relief. What do we have to fear from a band of rebellious peasants?'

Nicholas thinks of the wooden gates in Kilcolman's outer wall, which they had passed through on their arrival. Stout enough – but light a few fardels of brushwood against them and it wouldn't matter how thick or how high the stone walls were.

With a rattle, Gardener lays his knife and spoon on his plate. 'Master Spenser, Mistress Spenser, your board has been as welcoming as ever. But I must beg to be excused. The hour is late, and I must be on the road early.'

'To Cork?' says Spenser.

'Aye, the sooner I am there, the less time the garrison will have to cover their tracks if they've been over-ordering their provisions and selling the surplus.'

'Thank you for bringing us here safely, Master Piers,' Nicholas says. 'Will you pass this way again on your return?'

'I had not planned it,' Gardener says. 'But I am at your service, should you have need of me.'

Spenser offers to provide two of his servants as guides for the return to Dublin.

'In that case,' says Gardener with a smile, 'I wish you both God's good peace. If I do not see you tomorrow, let us hope we shall meet again soon in a happier Ireland.'

Before Nicholas and Bianca retire to a small candlelit chamber with a narrow, arrow-slit window that opens onto a void blacker than any Nicholas has seen, Spenser takes them to his study. Opening a chest, he hands Nicholas a sheaf of pages tied with a ribbon. 'Take this,' he says. 'Something tells me you haven't read it. It's my pamphlet – *A View of the Present State of Ireland*.'

'I'm just the messenger,' Nicholas says.

Immediately he sees the question form in Spenser's cool eyes. *From the Stationers' Company? Or from Robert Cecil?*

'The messenger from London,' he adds hastily, and not entirely satisfactorily. 'From the Stationers' Company.'

'I always find it hard to sleep in a new bed. Perhaps this will help,' Spenser says with a self-deprecating smile. 'I don't expect you to read it all. You've had a long journey' – he places the pages into Nicholas's hands – 'whoever sent you.'

✠

'No wonder they won't license anyone to print this,' Nicholas says, waving a page of Spenser's manuscript. 'To call it incendiary doesn't do it justice.'

A pale band of morning light from the narrow window slices in two the opposite wall of the chamber. A candle gutters by the bed.

Beside him, Bianca shakes off the lingering cobwebs of an interrupted dream: little Bruno sitting on a riverbank, fidgeting with joy, while she – his Merrow of a mother – tries to walk out of the water to reach him, the distance between them never shrinking.

'You haven't been reading that all night, have you?' she says, yawning.

'No, but I've been awake awhile. I thought at least I'd better skim through it – pick up where I left off last night.'

'Is it as tedious as the *Faerie Queene*?'

'Only if you think starving a population to death by famine tedious.'

Bianca props herself up on one elbow, the better to look Nicholas in the eyes. Waves of dark hair spill over one shoulder of her linen night-smock. '*What?*'

'Our great poet is not the quiet man he appears. He has some deeply troubling thoughts on how best Ireland may be pacified.'

'What are you saying – he wants the people to starve?'

'For their own benefit, of course. Apparently they are a simple race who need only strong government to bring them to order.'

'And he thinks famine is the most efficient way to bring that about?'

'He thinks it's the speediest, and therefore least costly.'

'But how does he propose to do it?'

'Chop down the forests, destroy the crops, force the rebels and their cattle off the land – preferably so that they face a winter where they must eat the cattle or starve, thus robbing them of their only wealth. After that, they will be not only peaceable, but apparently grateful, too.'

'And who is going to bring about this monstrous event? The English settlers?'

'Reading between the lines, the Earl of Essex, with an army of ten thousand men and a thousand horse. That's what Spenser recommends in this.' Nicholas throws the manuscript onto the coverlet. 'He even spells out what bridges to build for the army to cross, where garrisons should be established, how many men in each...'

Bianca lies on her back and runs her fingers through her hair to tame its morning wildness. 'But at supper he seemed such a reasonable fellow. Surely the Privy Council wouldn't countenance such a monstrous thing. Even Robert Cecil isn't *that* callous.'

'I'm sure he'd argue against it. But he's only one man. The Council might have thought this *View* of Spenser's too rich to stomach last year, but things in Ireland have changed. Now there is open rebellion. If it spreads, they might decide Spenser is right and urge the queen to agree to his proposals.'

'And Essex would seize the chance with both hands, wouldn't he?'

'Indeed he would. He's already in the queen's presence chamber almost every other day, petitioning her to make him Lord Lieutenant. With an army at his back, he would descend upon this island like a great pestilence.'

Bianca looks at the manuscript as though it were an adder she'd just discovered sleeping under her pillow. 'Is *this* the great secret that Spenser will reveal only to someone Robert Cecil trusts? Is that thing why we're here?'

'That's what I don't understand,' Nicholas says. 'The Stationers' Register has already read it, which means so has the Privy Council. Cecil must already know exactly what it contains. Spenser must be aware of that.'

'So *that*' – a jab of her finger as if to keep the manuscript at bay – 'isn't why he wanted Sir Robert to send Spenser a trusted messenger?'

'Edmund Spenser isn't a fool. He must know that Mr Secretary Cecil has either read every word of this... this *insanity* or his secretaries have done so for him. So, you're right. This cannot be his secret.'

'Think of him as a patient who's reluctant to admit to his symptoms,' Bianca suggests. 'You'll get him to talk eventually.'

'I was hoping I might enlist you.'

'Me?'

'You're more subtle and persuasive than I am.'

Bianca mulls over the suggestion for a while. 'There will be a price,' she says.

'Name it.'

'You must promise never to make me sit through another night of verse at Greenwich – unless it's one of Master Shakespeare's new comedies. Men with grand schemes and deep secrets will be the ruin of this world.'

✠

How to persuade a monster to share his monstrous thoughts?

Should I just be bold and come straight out with it? Bianca asks herself as she prepares to corner the poet in his garden later that morning. *Tell me, please, Master Spenser, will you have us eat our children to reduce the number of infant beggars on the London streets? Should we burn our elderly for fuel when winter bites? Can you think of a crueller punishment for traitors than the scaffold? Have you forgotten all compassion in your cold, stone carapace in the wilds of Ireland?*

And yet Edmund Spenser looks to her such an unlikely ogre. She can see him now, stooping to better appreciate a clump of late-flowering heleniums – the most unlikely Horseman of the Apocalypse she can imagine. He places one palm on his hip to massage some inner ache or twinge. How, she wonders, can a man who dwells in a tranquil valley, who finds beauty in verse, possess a heart that can countenance the idea of starving a whole population in order to force their compliance? She shudders at the thought of being in his presence. Still, she's promised Nicholas to do her best. And Edmund Spenser won't be the first man she's charmed into being less discreet than he might otherwise have intended.

In the event, the cat turns out to be Spenser, and Bianca the mouse. Even as she's about to greet him with some trivial nonsense to put him at his ease, the poet straightens from his inspection and smiles.

'Mistress Shelby, I trust you slept well.'

'It's Bianca. All my friends call me Bianca. And yes, I slept well, thank you.'

'Good. And your husband – the man who says he's from the Stationers' Company, but knows as much about printing as I know about needlepoint?'

It is said without the slightest malice. He could be repeating a pleasing joke they had all shared over the supper board last evening.

'I don't know what you mean,' she says, feeling her cheeks redden.

'Come now, Mistress Bianca. I've had all night to think about this. The Stationers' Company doesn't indulge its messengers by allowing them to take their wives with them on their travels. And since when did it employ physicians to do its bidding? Dr Shelby has come a very long way to waste time on subterfuge.'

'I think you should speak to my husband,' Bianca says, hearing the sound of her own artifice shattering.

'Oh, I intend to, Mistress Bianca,' Spenser says, smiling as though he's uncovered a child's white lie. 'But I have a feeling I already know who sent him.'

✠

'Why didn't you simply tell me when you arrived?'

Spenser pours Nicholas a glass of malmsey from a polished pewter jug and gestures him towards a pair of high-backed chairs set beside the study hearth. He has ordered a fire lit, perhaps to make the act of confession more domestic. The rain beats against the windowpane in a conspiratorial whisper.

'Sir Robert thought a measure of discretion would be in order,' Nicholas says, conscious of the slight falter in his own voice.

'Mr Secretary Cecil doesn't trust me, does he?'

'I'm sure that's not the case.'

'No matter; the feeling is mutual. His father, Burghley, was a snake. I don't suppose the son is any different.'

'Perhaps it might be better if we were candid with one another,' Nicholas suggests.

Spenser gives a tight little laugh. 'Candid? It is not I who have attempted to deceive.'

'For which I am duty bound to apologize,' Nicholas says, trying to limit the damage. 'My deceit was only at Sir Robert's insistence.'

'Ah, but so many deceits are swirling in the winds of this rebellion, Dr Shelby. Sometimes the small ones can turn out to be more dangerous than the great. How am I to gauge the measure of yours?'

'Sir Robert understands the need for caution as well as do you. He wished only for me to form an opinion of you before I disclosed why I had come.'

'Oh, I already know Mr Secretary Cecil's opinion of me,' Spenser says. 'Some time ago I wrote some verses about Lord Burghley. They were... shall we say, *less* than flattering. I can understand his son's reluctance to trust me.'

Exasperated, Nicholas asks, 'How can there be trust if you will not tell me what it is you wish Sir Robert to know?'

For a moment he is sure the poet is going to end the conversation, turn his back, dismiss his guest and retreat into that inner remoteness that has its visible expression in the flinty walls of Kilcolman. Then Spenser emits a sharp little cough. He turns back to face Nicholas, the resolve clear in his eyes.

'Tell me, has news reached Robert Cecil yet of the wrecking of the Spanish ship?'

9

They hear the screeching of the gulls long before they hear the murmur of the sea. The wind moans through the wild grass, a monotone lament that Bianca can believe has not paused for breath in centuries. Between the riders and the distant headland, the ground slopes away towards a low grassy saddle-back, the central spine between two bays. Beyond it, a steeper incline rises towards the cliff top. Nicholas wonders how Spenser has managed to bring them to this inlet amongst all the others along his fractured coast. It strikes him that he must have been here before.

It has taken three days to reach the coast. At night, they have rested in the houses of Spenser's settler friends. More than once they have noticed fear in the eyes of their hosts.

'Refuse to go,' Bianca had said, when Nicholas had told her of Spenser's proposal. 'Tell him you've had enough of his secrecy.'

'Robert Cecil will want to know of this,' he'd replied. 'He doesn't employ me just to treat his children when they catch an ague.'

And Nicholas had known in his heart that he was right. Even though Cecil would likely already have received word of a Spanish wreck from other sources, he would want to know the details: what size of vessel, how many troops it might have accommodated, whether there are still pennants hanging from the wreckage, whose design might reveal what grand admiral she sailed under. A single wreck can tell you a lot about Spanish intentions. Most of all, Cecil would want to know if any ciphers had been recovered. Nicholas already knows there were no survivors. Spenser had told him that a company of English cavalry had been in the area when the ship was driven onto the rocks. They had killed all who managed to struggle ashore.

'*There*, do you see it now?' shouts Spenser, bringing his horse to a stop and thrusting out an arm towards the cove to their right.

Nicholas narrows his eyes as he searches. The bay sweeps away from him in a wide arc, the bluffs beyond the narrow beach lifting until they run against another rugged promontory some quarter of a league away. He can see no wreck lying in the sheltered water. Wherever the vessel has come ashore, it has not been run aground on the beach in an attempt to save the crew.

'Fix your eye on the cliffs at the far edge of the bay, where it meets the open sea,' Spenser commands. 'Then come inland a way, following the water line – about an arrow's shot. Look for the breaking waves.'

And then Nicholas sees it: a darker smudge between the sea and the cliff. Not a whole ship. Not even a dismasted hull, but part of a high stern-castle, the regular lines of planking the only indication of something man-made lying smashed against the irregular rock face.

'The waves have had their sport since it went aground,' Spenser says. 'Another month and there'll be nothing left but driftwood.' He looks at Bianca, a concerned frown on his studious face. 'There were dead men here, Mistress,' he says. 'They may not have been removed. Are you sure you wish to continue?'

'I have a strong stomach, Master Edmund,' Bianca says. 'You need not fear. I will not wilt.'

She considers changing her mind almost as soon as they have ridden off the grassy saddleback and down into the cove.

Nicholas is the first to pull a face at the smell of death. The stench – that sweetly cloying assault on the senses that can defeat all but the strongest, or most callous, resolve – is only too familiar to him from his time with the Protestant army in the Low Countries. 'I think you should wait back there,' he suggests.

'I'm not a timorous child, Nicholas,' Bianca says, remembering the three severed heads she'd seen in Dublin and mustering a courage she does not feel. 'I have as strong a stomach as any man.'

'I know,' he says gently. 'But this will not be a pretty show. They have lain here awhile.'

In grim silence they ride down through the bluffs towards the beach.

The first corpse they come across wears a pair of tattered sailor's slops and nothing else – no shirt, no shoes. He must have been the one who evaded the cavalry the longest, Nicholas thinks. He lies on his back, half-hidden in a clump of gorse, his eyes pecked out by the gulls. Nicholas cannot place his age, because decay has swollen the body, distorting the features, stretching back the grey lips to reveal an uneven snarl of teeth. Like a fashionably slashed doublet studded with pearls, the mottled torso gapes black wounds where maggots crawl.

Bianca feels the gorge rise in her throat. Even more than the sight, it is what it suggests that sickens her. This man must have thought himself blessed by God's mercy for having survived the wreck. Then he had seen the soldiers waiting for him on the beach.

'I think, perhaps, you were right, Husband,' she says. 'I shall wait, back there – where we turned down into the bay. I can shout if anyone approaches.'

Nicholas smiles at her determination not to let distress make a purposeless bystander of her. 'That is a wise idea,' he says, though they haven't seen another soul for hours, and by the time he and Spenser reach the wreck, they'll be too distant to hear her call above the wind and the crash of the waves. Taking one hand from the reins, he reaches out and lays his gloved fingers against her cheek. 'I'm sorry that you had to see this. I shouldn't have let you come.'

She smiles back at him, brushing aside a tangle of dark hair that the wind has blown across her face. 'You couldn't have stopped me, Nicholas. You should know by now that Caporetti women by tradition take unkindly to constraint.' As she turns her horse away, she calls back, 'Though you might have expected the daughter of a line of famous poisoners to have developed a stronger stomach.'

✠

Where is the honour in slaughter? What glory does it bring to kneel astride a man already half-drowned, pull back his head by the sodden hair and cut his throat? There is only one word that Nicholas can find for what the bay reveals to him: murder.

He counts at least twenty bodies before he and Spenser reach the wreck. He can imagine how these poor, floundering fellows must have thought God had bestowed His mercy upon them, saving their bones from whitening on the ocean floor. He can picture them now, exhausted, crying out in relief, *Thank Jesu! We're saved* – even as the shadows of their killers fell across their outstretched arms.

Some seem to have been hunted down for sport. Their remains are scattered amongst the scrub. None has shoes, or a jerkin. Several are naked. Nicholas assumes that somewhere in a nearby garrison, or in Waterford or Dublin, Wexford or Cork, there are young men from England, or mustered from Irish counties, who are sporting a newly acquired item of clothing. He wonders if they've managed to wash the bloodstains out, or whether – when they sit together at a tavern bench – they display them like trophies.

Nicholas remembers the file of unlikely recruits at the Southwark Fair muster. How long, he wonders, does it take boys like those to become monsters? What had they seen, what had they been told, to turn them from laughing plough-hands and farm labourers into implacable killers? He remembers, too, the three heads propped on the back of the cart that he saw in Dublin. A sudden wave of disgust sweeps over him. Is bestiality to be the means by which Robert Cecil and the others in the Privy Council maintain the queen's laws, the queen's realm, the queen's religion, here in Ireland?

I am not some unworldly innocent, he tells himself. I know full well what men can do. I've seen the same savagery in the Low Countries, perpetrated by both sides – Catholic and Protestant. I know that neither holds the monopoly on sanctimony or cruelty. But if *this* is the mercy we show to a score of Spaniards whom even the sea has declined to take, what right do we have claiming God's authority over our enemy?

Ahead of him, Edmund Spenser is peering down from his saddle. Nicholas rides over to join him.

Spenser is staring down at a corpse. It is that of a man of some substance, judging by the quality of his hose and the barbered ringlets of black hair that lie around his shoulders. He lies with both arms outstretched, as if crucified. The fingers of each hand are missing: hacked off for the rings they wore. Close by lies a travelling chest, resting forlornly on the sand. It looks too expensive to belong to a sailor, even a ship's master. It is finely carved, with brass guards on the corners, each embossed with a lion's head. Prised from its hinges, the discarded lid lies tossed into a nearby clump of grass. The chest is empty.

'Have you found something?'

'No, nothing,' Spenser says.

Is that a note of anxious disappointment in the poet's voice that Nicholas can hear? He recalls his earlier impression that Spenser may have been here before.

Riding on along the beach, they reach the remains of the wreck.

Driven ashore by the wind and the sea, it is a sizeable part of the ship's stern-castle. Around twenty feet high and a little more in length, it has come to rest tilted against the cliff, the forward, shattered end jammed into a fold in the cliff's face. The lower, rounded part of the hull has been smashed in as the sea dragged it across the rocks, so that what survives reminds Nicholas of the upper half of an egg dropped onto a floor. Now that the tide is out, barely a foot of water gurgles in and out through jagged fractures draped with kelp. Pounded for weeks by the tide, she makes a sorry sight, a ghost of the fine face she once presented.

'The forward part of her must lie out beyond the headland,' Spenser says. He points to the promontory and the jagged rocks that surround its base. 'I would hazard those are what broke her in twain.'

'And that's where the rest of her crew will be,' Nicholas says solemnly.

'Aye, they may have been papists, but they were men for all that, and far from home.'

'The question is: why?'

'She must have been dismasted in that terrible storm we had.'

'I meant, why was she so far from home?' Nicholas says quietly.

Spenser offers no opinion. So Nicholas says softly to the cold, dead timbers of the wreck, 'What mischief were you up to in these waters, I wonder?'

He contemplates the ruined stern-castle for a while. Then, to Spenser, 'How did you know it was a Spanish ship?'

'Because Sir Oliver Henshawe told me so. If you had stayed in Dublin longer, no doubt you would have heard the story.'

Taken aback, Nicholas sees in his mind the grinning, aristocratic features of the man he met in the Brazen Head in Dublin, the man who had once paid court to Bianca.

'Henshawe? Was it his troops who did *that*?' he asks, glancing back at the beach. 'I can't say I like the man, but I hadn't taken him to be a butcher.'

'You know Sir Oliver then?' Spenser says warily.

'Not really, but Bianca does. He once paid suit to her, in London. He said he wanted to marry her,' Nicholas says with a laugh. 'I don't think he had the slightest notion—'

'You know that Sir Oliver is one of the Lieutenant-General's officers, here in Ireland?'

'Yes, we met him in Dublin. As I say, I found him objectionable.'

Spenser looks visibly troubled. 'Did you mention you were coming to visit me?'

'Yes. He offered to provide an escort. Why, do you have some manner of quarrel with Henshawe?'

'No, nothing,' says Spenser, a little too hurriedly to be convincing.

'Of course he was just plain Oliver Henshawe when Bianca knew him. He said he'd been knighted at Cádiz by the Earl of Essex. I would have thought that might put him in your favour.'

'Why would you think that?'

'Because I worked out from your pamphlet that you consider the earl to be the best man to bring Ireland to order.'

'His Grace has been a firm friend to me. Admiring him does not mean I have to admire *all* of his officers.'

Dismounting, Nicholas tethers the reins of his horse to the

limb of a stunted gorse bush and walks out across the wet sand and into the water. Spenser watches him from the shore.

First he wades around to look at the wreck end-on. The rudder has been torn away from the stern-post, leaving only one large empty iron ring twisted out of shape by the force of the sea. About two feet above his head is a narrow gallery protruding from the ship's hull, where the master or an admiral might have found himself a little privacy. Above that, the stern narrows, framing a weathered painting of a haloed saint holding a shepherd's crook. At the very peak is a lantern on an iron post, the translucent horn smashed in.

Nicholas then turns his attention to the side of the ship. The gallery wraps around the corner of the stern and the quarterdeck to run along the hull for about twelve feet, canted down at an angle. There is an open doorway set into the hull wall halfway along, barely large enough for a man to squeeze through. The door itself has been torn off. Inside, Nicholas can see only blackness. From a carved frieze running below the gallery, the weathered wooden faces of Castilian lions peer out forlornly at a world they can no longer menace.

Reaching the point where the captain's gallery ends, no more than the length of a hand above his head, Nicholas notices a circular hole cut into the planks. He guesses its purpose at once: a private jakes, where the master might relieve himself without having to go forward to the grating beneath the bowsprit used by the rest of the crew. Rejecting the idea of using the lip of the hole for purchase, he jumps up, grips the outer rail of the gallery and folds his knees under his body, swinging for a moment as he gauges whether the rail will hold his weight.

'What are you about, Dr Shelby?' Spenser calls out. 'Surely you're not planning to go inside.'

Nicholas drops back into the shallow water. 'Of course I'm going inside. She's a Spaniard. And judging by that body back there, she was carrying someone of note. There could be papers, or ciphers, that Henshawe's men may have missed.'

'You've lost your reason, Dr Shelby,' Spenser protests. 'This wreck has been battered by the elements since it came ashore. For all you know, those timbers may have no more strength in them than kindling. You would have to be bereft of reason to go up there and poke about inside.'

'Bereft of reason, or in the service of Robert Cecil,' Nicholas laughs. 'They're one and the same really.'

He jumps up again, seizing the rim of the gallery, swinging his body sideways to get a foothold on the hull. A wave slides in, breaking over his dangling feet.

It takes Nicholas three attempts to get enough purchase to pull himself up. But on the third, he finds himself standing on the slanting gallery, legs astride the jakes hole, breathless, wet, his arms aching, but triumphant.

Moving up the incline towards the stern, he reaches the open doorway leading into the master's cabin.

'Is all well?' Spenser calls out.

'Well enough.'

'Take care, Dr Shelby. We are a long way from help.'

The door is barely large enough for a grown man to pass through. Nicholas has to stoop to enter.

Inside, shafts of mournful daylight pierce the salty grime on the small stern windows. The reflection of light off the water makes swirling patterns on the deckhead inches above his skull. There is an almost overpowering stench of salt water and rotting kelp.

He is standing on a tilted deck that slopes away some ten feet to the other side of the hull. The cabin wall there is all but smashed to pieces against the rock face. To his right is a narrow void about five feet wide, where the shattered beams that support the floor of the cabin are jammed fast against the fold in the cliff. The noise of the sea is somehow amplified in this little space, the hull acting as a soundbox. With every surge of water on the rocks below his feet, a roar echoes around the small chamber. He feels as though he's trapped at the back of a cave, facing an incoming tide.

Looking about, the first thing that strikes Nicholas is that the cabin is a simple one for a man of importance, if that's what the corpse with no fingers was. There are no signs of comfort, other than a wooden cot attached to the side with the door in it, and the remains of a second on the far side. A row of cupboards runs beneath the stern windows, gaping like ransacked tombs, their doors flung open or torn from their hinges. A bank of sand, kelp and shattered glass and timber has fetched up against the demolished cabin wall where it lies against the cliff. A single pewter jug lies spout downwards, half-embedded in the mess.

Looking at the gaping cupboards, Nicholas wonders if Henshawe's men have been here before him, searching for the same haul he himself had hoped to find. If they have, so be it. Even if it ends up in the hands of Robert Devereux, Cecil is bound to hear of it when Essex lays it before the Privy Council. Still, thinks Nicholas, it would have been nice to have been the man who found the key to the Dons' ciphers.

Nicholas is mulling this thought in his mind when a wave, larger than the others, rolls in out of the ocean. It breaks against the cliff barely twenty feet away. The din inside the cabin is deafening. A blast of spray bursts up through the gap by the fold in the cliff face, making him fear for an instant that the wreck has broken loose. Losing his balance, he staggers.

The blow takes him utterly off-guard. The breath leaves his lungs in an agonized grunt as he topples. Too stunned to stop himself, or even register the secondary pain of hitting the deck, he slides sideways towards the gap between the shattered cabin floor and the cliff.

And then he is falling. Falling into blackness. Falling into a bottomless ocean. Falling towards the crabs feasting on the bones of those who never made it as far as the beach.

10

The wind has picked up a little, dragging tendrils of grey cloud over the headland. Bianca pulls her riding cloak tighter about her shoulders. From her place on the grassy saddleback, she looks again towards the far side of the right-hand bay. She can just make out the two horses where the bluffs meet the beach. But she can see no sign of Nicholas or Edmund Spenser. It would be exactly like Nicholas, she thinks, to go climbing over the wreck like a schoolboy in an apple orchard. She curses herself for being weak. Dead men don't frighten her. She should have stayed with her husband.

The bay to her left is the smaller of the two, but its beach is more substantial. With the tide out, the damp sand stretches out almost halfway to the narrow mouth of the cove. She thinks, with a pang of longing, how pleasing it would be to play with little Bruno on these empty sands. Far better for him this wild freedom than the close, stultifying confines of Cecil House with all its formality. Better for company the sea, the wheeling gulls and the wide sky than boys who looked down upon him and tutors who spoke only Latin.

A band of shallow water cuts the bay neatly in half, running diagonally from one side to the other. Perhaps one hundred paces before this runnel reaches the far cliffs it turns sharply into a wider channel that leads to deeper water and the open sea beyond. Unlike its grim neighbour, this cove looks a peaceful place. It has a timelessness that makes her think she might be the first person ever to ride a horse over that pristine sand. She remembers with sudden delight a moment from her girlhood in the Veneto: she and her friend, Lorenza Montegalda, galloping through the marshes beside the lagoon on horses borrowed from Lorenza's father. They had told Signor Montegalda that they wanted to pick flowers. In truth they had desired only to watch the bronzed, muscular young fishermen at work, to call tantalizingly to them like sirens and then ride off at high speed.

Bianca turns her back on the bay with its stench of death, and urges her horse down off the grassy saddleback, across the bluffs and onto the beach. Reaching the sand, she puts her heels to her horse's flank.

The salty wind purges her spirit, fans her hair into a dark halo, brings her joys remembered from childhood. The faster Bianca drives the galloping horse, the more cleansing it becomes. All she can hear is the rushing of the air, the thundering of her mount's hooves and the joyous exclamation of her own breathing. Even though the tide is out, they move together in a mist of spray like a single creature of the air and the sea, scorning the land and its tediously solid sobriety. She is fourteen again, astride Signor Montegalda's horse, hearing the fading catcalls from the fishermen, all the world hers for the taking.

She brings the horse to a halt beside the runnel of water. Even though the wind scythes the surface into little dancing wavelets, she can see now that it is shallow. She could wade through it without getting her knees wet. A brief shaft of sunlight escaping the scudding grey clouds makes it gleam invitingly at her. The horse catches her thoughts and starts to fidget. There is not a stretch of water anywhere, she thinks, that demands to be galloped through more than this.

It takes only a few moments, but every one of them is a joy, like running through a waterfall on a hot day to see if you can escape getting wet. Horse and rider arrive on the other side of the runnel panting with exhilaration.

Being this far out into the bay gives Bianca a sense of floating between the sea and the land. It is an extraordinary feeling of freedom. Reluctant to turn the horse around and head back to the bluffs, she lets her eyes wander over the rocks, watching how they lift into the high headland. From the edge of the cliff, a single seabird dives like a gleaming white arrow towards the water.

Bianca follows its plunge. Behind it, the rock face is little more than a blur to her. Yet something out of place, some anomaly in the background, registers in the back of her mind. She watches as the bird lances into the water, raising hardly a splash. A moment later it breaks the surface, a fish fatally trapped in its bill. The head goes back, the fish vanishes. Caught in the instant, it is a short while before Bianca lets her eye return to the cliff face, searching for what had caught her attention.

There – on a shelf of rock about four feet above the water. It looks almost as if someone's arm is beckoning to her, a lazy wave, the sort of greeting an old friend might make. Taking up the slack in the reins, Bianca urges the horse forward into a slow walk towards the cliff.

✠

'Dr Shelby... Dr Shelby...' Each word is a dagger thrust into Nicholas's skull.

With consciousness comes pain, and a confusion that makes his head spin. For a moment his senses cannot find the slightest familiar thing upon which to anchor themselves. He is not in the sea, though his legs are soaking wet. He is not on the land, though he lies on stone. He is not in the air, though he seems to be flying. It is daylight, though he is in darkness. He feels someone cautiously gripping his outflung hand.

'Dr Shelby… It's Edmund Spenser. Can you hear me? Are you alright?'

And then a wash of pale daylight as Spenser steps back from the narrow space between the wreck and the fold in the cliff into which Nicholas has fallen. Looking around, he sees that he is spreadeagled on the rocks, the shattered floor of the master's cabin some four feet above his head.

'Can you move your limbs, Dr Shelby?'

The prospect of lying badly injured in a rocky Irish cove, leagues from help, while the tide come in sends a wave of fear through Nicholas's body. He flexes his limbs. They ache, but they work. He eases himself off the sloping rock and rolls towards the light. Spenser reaches in to help him. Another wave funnels a cascade of water over his legs, icy cold but shocking him into full consciousness.

'God's mercy was with you, Dr Shelby. You could have drowned,' Spenser says, as he helps Nicholas wade through the water towards the beach.

'I must have walked into something, up there in the cabin.'

'I heard you cry out. You're lucky you didn't break your neck, Dr Shelby.'

'How long was I senseless?'

'Only a moment or two. My greatest fear was that if another wave came in again, you might drown. Are you in pain?'

'Just aches, mostly.'

Spenser smiles in self-reproach. 'Mistress Bianca will take greatly against me for letting you climb up there in the first place.'

Nicholas places one palm behind his head. It comes away wet, but with salt water, not blood. 'I've had a lucky escape, it seems.'

'You found nothing up there, I take it?'

'No, nothing. If there were any papers, Henshawe has recovered them. Or the sea swept them away. Nevertheless, Sir Robert is bound to ask me if I took steps to see for myself.'

Spenser helps Nicholas away from the wreck. As he climbs into the saddle of his horse, the effort makes him wince. Bianca is going to be incandescent when she sees the bruises.

'You still haven't explained to me why you wanted to bring me here,' he says to Spenser.

'Here to the wreck? Or here to Ireland?' Spenser answers, swinging into the saddle.

'Both – while we're about it.'

Spenser thinks about this for a while in silence. His hands, clasped about the reins, churn, causing his horse to fidget. He seems to be struggling between the merits of confession and secrecy. Eventually secrecy wins.

'I must speak to Cecil face-to-face,' he says, determination hardening his scholarly features. 'Only to Cecil.'

'Has something occurred since you wrote to him?' Nicholas asks. 'Has something changed?'

'I can say no more, Dr Shelby,' Spenser replies, his eyes almost pleading. 'It must be to Cecil, Dr Shelby. *Only* to Sir Robert Cecil.'

Nicholas persists. 'But you told Sir Robert to send you someone he trusts. He trusts *me*. That is why I came to Ireland. That's why I'm *here*, now.'

But Spenser has retreated into that inner, unbreachable bastion that Nicholas detected on his arrival at Kilcolman.

As they begin to ride out of the bay, Nicholas glances at Spenser's breeches. They are stained and wet, just like his own. Did they get that way when the poet climbed into that space between the wreck and the rocks to see if I was alive? wonders Nicholas. Or did the poet follow me into the master's cabin? Did I walk into a beam by accident? Or did the only other living person in this cove attempt to kill me, losing his nerve when he realized he'd failed?

He glances again at Edmund Spenser. Refusing to trust, he thinks, can work both ways.

✠

Long before Nicholas reaches the grassy saddleback between the bays he can see that Bianca isn't there waiting for him. The knoll is empty. A sudden wrench of alarm makes him drive his horse onwards. Has Spenser lied to him about how long he was senseless? Were there supposed to be two more bodies left to the gulls on this beach? The poet doesn't strike him as a practised murderer. But where is Bianca?

And then, as he tops the rise, he sees her – far out in the next bay, across a band of water, sitting on her horse close to the cliff. Relief is followed swiftly by shame for having condemned Spenser so quickly. Perhaps, he thinks, there is something in the air of this island that lets distrust grow like spiders' webs.

Riding down the bluff, he can now see in the churned-up sand the visible evidence of his wife's irrepressible spirit. The hoof-prints run parallel to the land and then turn sharply out towards the stretch of shallow water that cuts the sandy bottom of the bay in two. He wonders what has led her so far out. Exhilaration or something more?

Dismounting, he sits down at the boundary between the bluff and the beach, his knees up under his chin. His body is beginning to ache from the fall. He is cold. His legs are soaked, his back damp from lying on the rocks. He begins to shiver. He shouts to attract Bianca's attention. But the onshore wind and the sound of the sea beyond the bay throw his voice back at him. He whistles. She turns towards the beach and, after a few moments searching, lifts one hand in recognition.

'What in Jesu's name have you been doing?' Bianca asks when she is close enough to see the state of his clothes. 'You look as though you've been for a swim, fully dressed. And you, too, Master Spenser.'

'I slipped. Fell amongst some rocks,' Nicholas says, telling himself it doesn't really count as a lie. 'Master Spenser fished me out. We both got a little wet.'

She rolls her eyes. 'You can't ride far in wet breeches. You'll catch a chill. Worse, you'll get sores in your privy places. And where am I to find liverwort around here to make into a balm?'

'A fire will dry us off in no time. I've flint and tinder in my pack,' Nicholas says. 'What were you doing, all the way out there by the cliff?'

'Something caught my eye. It turned out to be a big pile of rope washed up against the rocks. It must have come from the wreck. A length of it was flapping about in the breeze.' She opens her hand to reveal a soggy, dark ball of fabric. 'But I did find *this* caught up in it.'

Nicholas takes the material, shakes it out and holds it up for inspection. He can see now that it's a length of black lace, large enough to cover a woman's face. 'It's very fine. Expensive, I would have thought. Might be Flemish.'

'It looks as though it's a woman's veil,' Bianca says, 'the sort of veil I was made to wear in Padua when we attended Mass – a mantilla. Or a bridal veil, perhaps.'

'I saw no women amongst the dead,' Nicholas says, nodding at the other cove.

'Perhaps it was cargo.' Bianca sighs at the picture that has just entered her mind, a picture of a doomed young maid calling to her distant lover as the waters close over her. 'Perhaps the ship was carrying a girl to her wedding. Poor soul. She might be lying out there at the bottom of the sea. And somewhere is a young man waiting for a love that will never come to him. I'm going to keep it – as a memento mori.' Bianca folds the material with great care, placing it in the pocket of her riding cloak. She looks out at the empty ocean. 'After all,' she says wistfully, 'the poor souls who perished here will have nothing else to be remembered by.'

✠

The bluffs prove a rich source of driftwood. Nicholas finds a hollow that gives shelter from the wind. Using the flint from his pack, he soon has a fire going. He and Spenser sit as close as they can to the flames, feeling the heat warm their legs and waiting for their breeches to dry. Rubbing the back of his head to ease the ache in his skull, Nicholas casts a glance at his companion. He doesn't look like a man inclined towards opportunistic murder. For a moment Spenser holds his gaze, then looks away. A sign of guilt? Nicholas wonders.

When Bianca moves away to fetch more fuel, Spenser says bluntly, 'You think it was me, don't you?'

'What do you mean?' Nicholas replies, faintly embarrassed.

'At the wreck – you think I climbed up after you. Struck you from behind. I could see it in your face just now.'

Nicholas shifts uncomfortably. 'No, of course not.'

'If you think I could easily climb up into that cabin without you noticing, you're deluding yourself. You hit your head. You slipped. I warned you not to attempt it.'

'I'll ask you again, Master Spenser,' Nicholas says as the two men don their still-damp clothes. 'Why did you bring us here?'

'Trust cannot be bought on a promise, Dr Shelby,' Spenser says evasively, rubbing his hands along his thighs as if to speed up the drying. 'Sometimes you need to see the coins placed on the table. And sometimes the transaction needs a witness.'

'Your versifying is too clever for my ears, Master Spenser,' Nicholas says with a shake of his head. 'I'd rather we spoke plainly. Somehow I have the feeling you know what that ship was carrying. I think you've been here before.'

Spenser gives him a look as unbreachable as the walls of his Kilcolman bolthole. But a Suffolk yeoman's son is nothing if not stubborn. Nicholas jabs a finger in the direction of the other beach. 'Were you at the slaughter? Were you with Henshawe when he did *that*?'

'Before God, I swear I was not,' Spenser protests.

Bianca's voice at his shoulder makes Nicholas turn his head. He hadn't heard her return.

'Oliver? Oliver Henshawe?' she says.

'According to Master Spenser, it was Henshawe and his men who were responsible for the deaths of those poor fellows across the way. It appears your old suitor is not a gentleman at all, but a merciless butcher.'

'Is that true?' Bianca asks Spenser.

Hurt, denial – even fear – sweep across the poet's face like scudding clouds heralding rain. 'I was not a witness to what happened on that beach,' he says, casting a worried glance towards the wreck, as though he expects to see the dead propped up on their elbows, hands cupped to their ears, their corrupted bodies straining to catch his words. 'But it would be best if Oliver Henshawe didn't know you were here with me today.'

'Why not?' Nicholas asks.

'You should know that whatever happens on this island, the Earl of Essex hears of it first from Henshawe before all others,' Spenser says. 'Be very cautious in what you say when that man is present.'

'But the Earl of Essex didn't send me here, Master Spenser,' Nicholas says. 'Mr Secretary Cecil did. Besides, what do *you* have to fear from the Earl of Essex? You told me he was your friend.'

'We should be on our way,' he says. 'When we stand together before Mr Secretary Cecil, then you shall have your answers. In the meantime let what you have seen here be enough.'

And with that, Spenser again retreats behind that invisible wall of his, leaving Nicholas to wonder how many secrets one man can hold within his head.

✠

They sleep that night in the home of yet another English settler and his family. An air of impending disaster pervades the house. The husband is outwardly calm, but the eyes of his wife and children are quick with fear. They have heard rumours that supporters of Tyrone are burning farms barely a day's ride to the north. Their Irish estate workers no longer give them the deference they once did. They have taken it as a sign they could be next.

'Why haven't they fled to the safety of Dublin, or Cork?' Bianca asks later, as they lie together in a guest chamber.

'This is all they have. If they leave the land, there will be nothing for them but the relief of alms and charity. Then there's the faith.'

'Religion? Is that why they stay?'

'They haven't come here simply to farm. They've come to settle the land for Luther and Calvin. If they abandon it now, England will be set about on either side by enemies who owe their loyalty to the Pope. The Dons will land in force, unopposed – welcomed even. England could not possibly defend herself from Spanish armies in the Low Countries *and* Ireland.'

'You told me at Kilcolman that Spenser's pamphlet implies he believes the Earl of Essex is the perfect general to subdue the rebels,' Bianca says.

'Yes. But that's hardly surprising. Devereux has been Spenser's patron for years. Spenser couldn't have achieved what he has without the earl's help. They're practically friends, in so far as an earl may befriend a mere poet. Essex, Southampton – those sorts of fellows keep poets like lapdogs.'

'So why did Spenser tell us to be wary about what we say in Oliver Henshawe's presence? What was it he said – something about Oliver being Devereux's ears in Ireland? Surely he'd *want* Essex to hear what we said, if he thought it important? Yet I could see the fear in his eyes when you and he spoke of Oliver and the awful things done at the wreck.'

'Now we know what he's capable of, being afraid of Oliver Henshawe seems reasonable enough to me,' Nicholas says. 'Did he let slip his killing side when he was wooing you with verse?'

'If you mean did he kick stray dogs or pull the wings off butterflies, then the answer is no.'

Nicholas wonders how much to tell her about the deep feeling of distrust he had for Spenser during their time alone at the wreck. He decides against it. What would be the point in alarming her? In the end, all he says is, 'I formed the impression that Spenser had been to that bay before. After all, how did he lead us there so easily?'

'Do you think he took part in the slaughter, with Oliver?'

'I don't know. For all the hard words in that pamphlet of his, he's a poet, not a butcher.'

'But he could have been a witness to the massacre.'

'He swore before God that he wasn't.'

'Do you believe him?'

'I don't know what to believe.'

Bianca thinks for a moment. 'Even if Spenser wasn't actually present, he must have visited the site before today. That would answer your suspicion that he found it too easily.'

'That's reasonable enough.' Nicholas yawns and lays his head back on the bolster, wincing as his scalp touches the straw-stuffed linen. He rubs the spot to ease the dull ache. 'Spenser isn't just a private citizen,' he continues reflectively. 'He's held civic office. Perhaps he went there to compile a report for the Earl of Ormonde in Dublin.'

'There could be another reason,' Bianca says slyly.

'And what might that be?'

'What was a Spanish ship doing in Irish waters in the first place, Nicholas? Passing by? Or landing?'

Nicholas's jaw drops. Then he rolls his eyes. 'Oh, my devious wife! That must be the Caporetti coming out in you.'

Bianca slaps his arm. 'Don't laugh at me,' she says primly. 'If Spenser *had* been there before, what if it wasn't a wreck he had expected to find? What if he'd thought to find an intact ship, at anchor. Live people instead of dead ones.'

'What would England's foremost poet – the man who writes endless verse in praise of Gloriana – be doing making a rendezvous with a Spanish ship? Do you think he's a spy, for the Spanish?'

'No, but perhaps he knows who is.'

'But why go to the length of taking us there?'

'To cover himself?' Bianca suggests. 'To gain Robert Cecil's protection, before Essex can put him to the rack to find out what he knows? Just because they're friends, that wouldn't stop Essex putting Spenser to the hard press if he thought he might be a traitor.'

'So instead he turns himself over to Robert Cecil? Why would he do that?'

Bianca waves her hands, clutching for invisible straws. 'Nicholas, I don't *know*.'

'Take heart, sweet,' Nicholas advises. 'If Edmund Spenser is set upon speaking only to Robert Cecil, that means you and I can return to England on the first available ship.'

Bianca's eyes gleam with joy at the prospect of seeing Bruno again. Then her wide grin turns into an elfish smile. 'It means I can return,' she says.

'Am I not to come with you?' Nicholas asks, sensing her playfulness.

'You'll be too busy staring out to sea with a mooncalf look on your face.'

'And why will I be doing that?'

Bianca slides out of the bed. She goes to her travelling cape, hanging from a peg on the door. Coming back, she slips in beside Nicholas and holds up the rectangle of black lace that she found in the bay.

'A mantilla is a form of headwear, right?'

'Yes.'

'So, it's really a sort of hat, isn't it?'

'I suppose it could be said so.'

'A hat that I found lying on the shore.'

'Ah, now I see,' he says with a grin, remembering the tale told by the *Seanchaí*. 'A Merrow's magic hat.'

'My clever husband has it at last! They cannot live out of the water without it. Perhaps, somewhere not so very far away, a woman of the sea is calling to a mortal man so that she can steal his soul. I should be on my guard, if I were you, Husband.' She holds the scrap of veil before her face, only partially hiding her coquettish smile.

'Never fear, Wife,' he says. 'I shall be aboard that postal pinnace with you and Master Edmund. Your Merrow will be wasting her time. No matter how sweet she may sing, she can never outcharm a Caporetti.'

✠

Barnabas Vyves has made the Jackdaw his regular haunt, or so it seems. Ned Monkton has watched the muster ensign with the missing eye play his trick four nights in a row. It's a simple form of gulling, he's noticed: tell a stirring tale about the hard fighting at Cádiz, fix the victim with a brave glare of your one remaining eye and wait for the sympathy to flow. *A jug of ale for this brave hero, and on my coin...*

Ned knows the story is nonsense. Master Nicholas had proved it so at the Southwark Fair. But if Ned were to ban every teller of a tall story from the Jackdaw, Mistress Bianca would see no return on her investment. And anyway Vyves is canny enough not to try it on the regulars.

For the first three nights Vyves performed alone, picking his spot and waiting for a likely target to pass. But tonight the man called Strollot has joined him. Ned cannot help thinking they look like the worst kind of Southwark purse-divers, huddled together as though conspiring against the entire world. He tries hard to put the notion aside. Master Nicholas and Mistress Bianca, and most of all Rose, have taught him to think better of his fellow man – however disreputable they might look – than once he did.

Tonight, as Ned turns his attention elsewhere, he remembers the lanky recruit with the agitated manner who had taken coin from Strollot some days ago, and how it had occurred to him then to question why the alderman's clerk had paid him off, and not the man who had called him to the muster. But tonight the Jackdaw is busier than usual. The players are back and twice as voluble. Ned has other things on his mind than Barnabas Vyves and his trickery. His consideration of what passed between the ensign, Strollot and the gangly recruit must wait for a quieter moment.

11

They reach the outer gate of Kilcolman with barely an hour of daylight to spare. The stone tower gleams like a stubby beacon in the setting sun. It looks as welcoming as a fortified house can appear. But to Nicholas it is like a shout heard in an empty landscape: impossible to ignore, an invitation to any marauding rebel force.

The stout wooden gates open only when they approach close enough to be identified. In the courtyard Nicholas dismounts and helps Bianca down from the saddle. Since his first arrival, he has had his doubts about Spenser's Irish bolthole. It is nowhere near as impregnable as its owner thinks. What he hears as they sit down to eat in the main hall doesn't allay his concerns.

'I am informed by my steward that the rebels have sacked Mallow,' says Spenser. His voice sounds brittle. 'That's barely three leagues away. They've descended on the Buttevant estate like pharaoh's locusts – stripped it bare of sheep, cattle and horses. All the corn has been burned and more hamlets fired than can be counted.'

'Are we next, Father?' Spenser's teenage son Sylvanus asks.

Nicholas feels his appetite for the venison pottage wilting, despite its aroma.

'I am informed that the Earl of Ormonde has led a force out of Dublin,' Spenser says. 'He's on his way with pike and horse to chase them off.'

'More heads on the backs of donkey-carts then,' Bianca mutters under her breath.

'What's that you say, Mistress?' Spenser asks, leaning forward to catch her words.

'Nothing of consequence, Master Spenser. It merely strikes me that this isle is too beauteous a place to abide bloodshed. Perhaps it would be better for all if there were no men in it.'

'You should tell that to the rebels, Mistress,' Spenser says, giving her a scornful look. 'Buttevant's losses alone will likely run into thousands: enough to keep an earl in luxury for a year. And those rebels – who appear to have your sympathies – they kill while they pillage. They're not above dashing out the brains of infants. And I may tell you plainly, *they* were the ones who taught us about lopping the heads off prisoners.'

Katherine Spenser emits a tight little gasp of revulsion.

'I didn't say I sympathized with them,' Bianca says, trying to sound civil. 'I wouldn't wish *anyone* to lose their heads, or their brains.'

Spenser takes a spoonful of pottage. He draws the juices in with a sucking noise. 'The rebels must be brought to common civility and obedience,' he says, running the tip of his tongue around his lips. 'And *soon*. Otherwise this realm will know nothing but strife until it sinks beneath the waves at the Last Judgement. Blood spilt now will prevent more blood spilt later.'

'And Oliver Henshawe and the Earl of Essex are the men you would have spill it?' Bianca says.

Nicholas tries not to smile at the startled look on Spenser's face. Clearly he is unaccustomed to womenfolk voicing opinions at his table.

'The hero of Cádiz? Of course,' Spenser says, dismissing the servants with a wave of his hand. 'We need a competent general here to restore the island to peace.'

'And what if the Earl of Tyrone has no need of Robert Devereux's peace? What if he just wants the English settlers to go away?'

'What in the name of Jesu are you suggesting, Mistress – that we should abandon this land? There are English families here who can trace their line back to the Conqueror.'

'But who invited them?' Bianca asks, holding Spenser's gaze.

Under the board, Nicholas lays a cautionary hand on Bianca's thigh. There will be time enough, he thinks, to make an enemy of Edmund Spenser.

But Spenser seems not to have heard. Or if he has, he's not inclined to address the question. 'Ireland is England's western rampart against foreign enemies,' he says in a schoolmaster's tone.

'You mean the Spanish?' says Bianca.

'Of course. If they were free to assemble a great host here, they could almost step across into England. Would you see our monarch overthrown and our people forced into the papist heresy again, as they were in the reign of the bloody Mary?'

'Are you inciting me to treason, Master Spenser?' Bianca asks sweetly, wondering what Spenser would say if he knew she was a Catholic. 'A most ungallant manoeuvre at the supper board, if I may say so.'

Nicholas notices Elizabeth and Katherine Spenser staring at Bianca with a mixture of horror and admiration.

Spenser says, 'Your wife is very – *forthright*, Dr Shelby. Is that the new fashion in London?'

'Don't ask me. I hail from Suffolk,' Nicholas says, making a play of savouring his venison. 'We have small concern for fashion there.'

'Apparently, I'm a *shrew*,' Bianca says.

'According to Mr Secretary Cecil,' Nicholas adds hastily. 'I've said nothing of the sort.'

Bianca gives a dismissive toss of her head. 'I have it on the Master Shakespeare's own authority that I inspired him to write his *Taming of the Shrew*. He drinks in the Jackdaw more than occasionally. The saucy rogue didn't dare name the shrew after me, of course. He called *her* Kate. He made Bianca the more biddable daughter. Lost his nerve, I suspect.'

Nicholas clears his throat. 'Thank you for a very fine supper, Master Spenser,' he says, trying to sound as conciliatory as he can. 'With your indulgence, we shall take our ease outside, in the fresh air. When do you propose we return to Dublin?'

'Tomorrow, after I've ensured my manuscripts are safely hidden away. There's a tunnel below the house that runs out into an old quarry. I'll have the servants store them there, along with my valuables.'

'This tunnel – do you trust your servants not to betray its existence?'

'If you mean my steward and the immediate household, then without question. I picked them myself. They are good Englishmen. As for my estate workers and tenants – well, the tunnel is strongly gated and locked. It will be secure enough until order is restored.'

'But you said Kilcolman could hold out against an army, and now you're leaving,' Bianca pipes up.

For the first time Nicholas can see real uncertainty in the poet's eyes. He toys with the handle of his spoon. 'Only because I *must* see Sir Robert Cecil. I would not leave Kilcolman otherwise.'

For a moment, Nicholas thinks Spenser is about to make free with his thoughts, to open the gates of his inner fortress and reveal the truth behind his appeal to Mr Secretary Cecil to send him a trustworthy man. The poet opens his mouth to speak. But then the eyes lower. Spenser lays aside the spoon as though it has become loathsome to him. The cold stone walls close in again.

✠

Outside, the air is crisp and cold. The windows in the grim tower are shuttered. A torch burns in a sconce set into the courtyard wall. The dancing pool of light it casts could be the only sign of life in the entire valley. Kilcolman is surrounded by an immense and oppressive silence.

'There's little profit to be had in antagonizing him,' Nicholas says.

'Has Robert Cecil demanded that I should like him?'

'Of course not.'

'I find him abhorrent. How can a man who writes verses about damsels and knights, about love and chivalry, believe what he does?'

'I wasn't sent here to ask,' says Nicholas.

'Do you not care?'

'Of course I do. I would no more see that old *Seanchaí* and her husband made skeletal by famine than you would. But that is not why we are here. My task now, given that Spenser won't speak freely to me, is to see him safely to Cecil House. That will be easier if you don't bait him.'

Bianca puts her hands together demurely, like a maid at prayer. 'Yes, Husband. I shall be obedient to you in all things.'

Nicholas laughs, his voice oddly loud in the darkness. 'That will be a novelty.' He takes her arm in his. 'But I do have to confess there's a lot about Edmund Spenser that troubles me.'

'Apart from him wanting to subdue the population of Ireland by famine?'

Nicholas dodges her thrust. 'He's publicly insulted the Cecils in print, yet he's determined that he has a message only Sir Robert must hear. He wouldn't leave Ireland to speak with him face-to-face, but now he wants to go into England as quickly as may be arranged – even though he believes Kilcolman can hold out against a rebel attack. He takes us to a shipwreck, but he won't tell us why. He favours Essex as the hammer to beat the rebels into submission, but holds a secret he's frightened Essex might discover – at least that's the impression I got, after his comments about Oliver Henshawe. He's a puzzle, I'll say that for him.'

When they re-enter the tower house, Spenser is already issuing orders. Nicholas and Bianca stand at the foot of the winding stone staircase that leads to the poet's study. Servants hurry past with sheets of bed linen to wrap the manuscripts in, and a selection of baskets and wooden boxes to transport the product of the great man's genius to a place of safety where uneducated peasants can't use it for lighting fires.

'So much for his unbreachable valley hideaway,' Bianca observes. 'It looks as though he expects an attack at any moment.'

Spenser's steward hurries past, clutching a sheaf of parchment bound with legal ribbon.

'May we be of assistance?' Nicholas asks pleasantly.

The man twists on the first step and looks back over his shoulder. His cheeks are puffed, his brow damp with sweat. He is a man who believes that exertion is a visible measure of a task's importance. 'All is well, Dr Shelby,' he says confidently. 'Master Spenser is a demon when he has a purpose.' He wipes a bead of perspiration from the tip of his nose. 'I almost forgot: he bade me tell you we leave for Dublin immediately after breakfast. I shall ensure there are horses saddled for you.'

As they squeeze past the hurrying servants on the stairs to their chamber, Bianca begins to laugh.

'What amuses you, sweet?' Nicholas asks, his hand sliding against her backside as they climb.

'I was just reflecting – at Greenwich I almost fell asleep during *The Faerie Queene*. You'd think a poet who can set such a commotion as this in play would at least write verse that kept you awake. You were right, Husband. Edmund Spenser is a puzzle.'

✠

Nicholas wakes to a twinge of pain in his back. He rubs at what he supposes is a bruised muscle, sustained during his fall in the wreck. Or perhaps his body has begun to complain at these long days spent in the saddle. He remembers how fit and strong he had been as a boy, working on his father's farm. Despite the trials he has endured during his service to Robert Cecil, a physician's life is not nearly so demanding. I'm getting flabby, he thinks. Exertion is required when I return to Bankside. A series of lessons at the Guild of Fencing Masters might be in order, a punishing schedule under someone who knows what they're teaching: Joseph Swetnam or George Silver. Bianca will tease him unmercifully, of course. But a queen's physician is a gentleman, and gentlemen wear swords. If he has aspirations to join their number, it might pay him to know how to use one.

He eases himself onto one elbow. The candle flame has died. He can see almost nothing in the chamber. Yet there is a definite line of light edging the side of the narrow window. He peers at it for a while. It can't be dawn already; he hasn't slept long enough.

Then the light goes away.

Nicholas lowers himself back onto the pillow. Beside him, Bianca mutters something incoherent in her sleep.

He is about to close his eyes once more when the entire window lights up, flares briefly, then dies to a dull glow. Nicholas throws back the coverlet and goes to the window slit. Outside, in a night that his senses tell him should be as dark as Purgatory's cellar, he can see flames dancing along the top of Kilcolman's outer wall.

12

Spenser leads them up a twisting flight of steps and out onto the flat roof of Kilcolman Castle. A servant bearing a burning brand follows behind. After the warmth of the chamber, the night air is cold. Bianca pulls her riding cloak tight about her shoulders. Nicholas puts an arm around her. She cannot see where the land and the sky meet. The valley is lost in the darkness. But below her there is light aplenty. A fire is raging on the far side of the main gate, and a swarm of what appear to be fireflies mills in the blackness beyond. At first she thinks they are sparks from the fire. But they move with a definite purpose. She realizes they are lighted torches.

Down in the courtyard the servants have set up a human chain to bring water from the Kilcolman well. Nicholas can hear the sound of it being dashed against the inside of the wooden gates. Rising tendrils of steam tell him the fire that the rebels have set outside has gained a foothold.

'Thank Jesu my tenants have stayed loyal,' Spenser says, his voice sharp and pettish. 'Otherwise these rogues would have come in through the tunnel from the quarry and caught us all in our beds.'

'We're not saved yet, Master Spenser,' Nicholas says brutally. 'That fire has taken hold. If those gates burn faster than your people can douse them with water, you'll have more need of that tunnel than for the storage of manuscripts.'

'Then we'll stay here. The entrance to the tower itself has a stout enough bar.'

'And give the rebels another door to burn?'

Spenser's son, Sylvanus, joins them on the roof. 'Do you think we should flee, Dr Shelby?' he asks.

'We'll hold out, boy,' Spenser says harshly, cutting him off. 'The Earl of Ormonde's forces are on their way.'

'You could be waiting for days,' Nicholas says.

'We have food and water. We can hold. I know we can.'

Nicholas looks down over the parapet again. The fire at the gate is spreading. 'You have no choice, Master Spenser,' he says. 'You cannot long defend Kilcolman against armed rebels, not with only a handful of servants, however stout these walls are. You don't even have a proper armoury. We must go now, before it's too late.'

Still Spenser hesitates. 'But all my documents, my manuscripts—'

'What about your family?' Nicholas says, trying to stop himself from shouting. 'What about your servants? Do you care less for their lives than you do for your verse?'

Spenser stares at him. In the light from the servant's torch, Nicholas thinks he can see tears in the poet's eyes.

A cheer goes up from beyond the wall. A tongue of flame, larger than the others, shoots up into the night. The rebels have added fuel to their fire. Nicholas takes Bianca by the hand and turns back towards the stairwell. To Spenser he says, 'We don't have much time. If we remain here, and they break through that gate, this tower will not save us. We'll be trapped here. And if there's only one amongst those rebels who can read, and he finds your pamphlet, I wouldn't be expecting any inclination towards mercy, if I were you.'

As the torchlight flickers on Spenser's face, Nicholas watches the fight go out of him.

'You said the tunnel leads to a quarry,' he says.

Spenser nods. 'It's about three hundred paces beyond the outer wall.'

'Will it hide us from sight?'

'In this darkness, yes.'

'We'll need horses if we're to stand a chance of getting clear. Stumbling about on foot in this blackness, we could end up anywhere.'

Spenser turns away from the parapet. He points across the tower roof. 'There's a small, gated sally-port in the outer wall, over there. The tower and the flames should hide it from those traitors at the gate. We can lead the horses through that.'

He orders Sylvanus to take some of the male servants to the stables to saddle as many mounts as they can. Then he calls to his steward to fetch the key to the sally-port and a dagger. When they arrive, he hands them to Sylvanus. He has one last instruction for his son.

'If any of the servants attempt to steal this key, or prevent you relocking the gate once the horses are through, use the dagger on him. Meet us in the quarry. And for Jesu's sake, make no noise.'

Sylvanus stares at the dagger in disbelief, but takes it anyway. Then he turns and heads for the stairs.

Back inside the tower house, order is breaking down. Some of the female servants are close to panic. Spenser's wife, Elizabeth, has forgotten her earlier jealousy. Now she all but clings to Bianca, like a child woken from a nightmare. Little Peregrine wails in a maid's arms. Servants rush here and there like chickens surprised by a fox. In Spenser's study, Nicholas watches as the poet stuffs pages of his *View* into a leather bag. Nicholas would prefer to see the pamphlet burned and the hateful propositions in it buried in the rubble of Kilcolman's inevitable sacking. But now is not the time to antagonize. He confines himself to a terse,

'If you're determined to save something, I'd suggest you choose something more practical than that.'

'The Earl of Essex will need this – if he is to rescue this island for Her Majesty,' Spenser says defensively. He threads the fastening of the bag through its buckle and pulls it tight. 'Besides, up on the roof you implied that were it to be discovered here, it would prick the rebels to even greater fury.'

'Then let us hope we don't fall into their hands. If they find it on your person—'

'I'll take that risk.'

'Where is the nearest English garrison?' Nicholas asks.

'A day's ride to the south, at Cork. We can be sure of sanctuary there – I've been recommended by the Privy Council for sheriff of that town. They're hardly likely to close the gates to me.'

'Cork it shall be then,' says Nicholas.

Spenser shakes his head. 'It's closest, but between us lies Mallow. You heard at supper that the rebels are around the town in force. Do you propose we try to fight our way through? Or shall we have our horses *fly* over them, Dr Shelby?'

Nicholas ignores Spenser's petty jibe. 'Where else then? Hurry! Every moment we wait here is a gift to those people at the gate.'

'There's a garrison at Waterford, to the east. But it's over twice the distance.'

Nicholas steadies his breathing, forcing a viable plan on his racing thoughts. A wrong decision now could mean death later.

'We go east then,' he says decisively. 'We keep the Ballyhoura Mountains to our left, and our faces towards the dawn. That way, we won't run the risk of getting lost and stumbling into the rebels.'

'And if the rebels guess we're heading for Waterford?' Spenser says. 'What then?'

'If we're careful, they won't know we've gone until they've broken through the outer wall, then burned their way through the tower gate. By the time they discover the house is empty, we should be well away. Let's hope they spend a good while ransacking this place before they think about coming after us.'

'That is easy for you to say, Dr Shelby,' Spenser says harshly. 'The loss of Kilcolman and three thousand acres of good land will not come out of *your* purse.'

Not a thought for your wife, your sons or your household, thinks Nicholas. Not a word about how we shall herd your servants together in the darkness, or what might befall them if they lag behind.

'But you will still have your life, Master Spenser,' he says, trying to keep his voice civil. He jabs a finger at the bag slung over Spenser's shoulder. 'And *that* – for what it's worth.'

Spenser lays one hand on the bag, as though to defend its contents from Nicholas's contempt. 'Have you not considered the fact that Waterford will give the rebels twice the time in which to catch up with us?'

'They won't catch up with us because we won't go to Waterford.'

'But... but you said—'

'Once we're clear of Kilcolman we'll swing south, then turn and approach Cork from a different direction. If we're lucky, we may even run into the Earl of Ormonde's force.'

Spenser considers this for a brief moment. 'That *is* feasible, Dr Shelby. We can cross the Blackwater at Fermoy. For a physician, you seem to have an unusually military mind.'

'I served a season on campaign with the forces of the House of Orange, in the Low Countries. If you think a mob of rebels is a peril, trying evading a troop of Spanish lancers.'

Spenser gives him a look of new-found admiration. 'When we have the leisure, you must tell me how you managed it. I might make it the subject of a poem.'

As they hurry down towards the cellar and the entrance to the tunnel, Bianca says, 'Nicholas, you've never told me about hiding from Spanish lancers.'

'Why would I? It would only have caused you alarm.'

'How did you evade them?'

'Simple,' Nicholas says, giving her a sly grin. 'I hid. In a midden.'

Bianca wrinkles her hose. 'You hid in a *dung-heap*?'

'Don't look so revolted. It had unexpected benefits. You'd be surprised how many sickly pistoleers suddenly discover they're miraculously cured when their company's physician smells of horse-shit and rotten vegetables.'

13

In the liquid grey light before sunrise, Nicholas reins in his horse. He looks back over his shoulder into the departing night. Beyond Spenser's party he can see a dozen stragglers on foot, standing out against the misty fields like the grey stones the giants of antiquity seeded in this strange land so long ago that everyone has forgotten their purpose. The tower at Kilcolman has disappeared from sight behind the trees and the soft rise of the ground. Not even the glow of the fire is visible. In the darkness it has taken them hours to make barely two miles.

'Now that we can see our hands in front of our faces, we must make better speed,' he says to no one in particular. He is impatient to continue. Now that daylight is approaching, they are more vulnerable than ever.

Close beside him, Bianca gives a smile of encouragement, her face pale and drawn in the twilight. She has said little since they escaped from Kilcolman. Not a word of complaint. Not one hint that she blames him for casting her into this chaos. It occurs to Nicholas that he would rather have her riding beside him than a company of horse armed with loaded wheel-lock pistols.

'I know where we are,' Spenser says, as though heading east had been his idea all along. 'We're less than two leagues from the Nagle plantation at Ballynamona. I know the Nagles well; an old Anglo-Irish family. We can be there within a couple of hours.'

'Then let's pray the rebels haven't attacked there, too,' Nicholas says, putting voice to a fear that's been nagging him since they left – that the assault on Kilcolman is only part of a general uprising within Munster.

Ballynamona turns out to be a brand-new tower house, but built much in the style of Kilcolman. By the time it comes into view, sunrise has filled the valley with autumnal light, turning the trees from black to gold. Cattle graze peaceably in the surrounding fields. A thin column of smoke rises, unperturbed, from the chimney. For Nicholas, it is the first indication that his decision to take Spenser and his party eastwards was sound. Nevertheless, their arrival brings an abrupt end to Ballynamona's innocent tranquillity.

The lord of the Nagle household is a man of about Spenser's age, with the reticent wariness of the border settler. He listens without comment as his neighbour tells of the attack on Kilcolman. When Spenser has finished talking, Nagle shrugs as though the prospect of imminent attack is a minor tribulation during a day's toil in the fields.

'Sounds to me like Tyrone has grown tired of waiting for the Council of Munster to treat with him,' he says. 'With those fools in command at Dublin, I'm surprised he's stayed his hand this long. Have you lost everything, Master Edmund?'

'I fear I have lost my dearest offspring, Master David.'

David Nagle casts a quizzical glance at Sylvanus, who stares at his boots in discomfort; then at Katherine, who looks at the ceiling in resignation; and finally at little Peregrine, clinging to his mother's coat and sniffling fractiously with tiredness.

'I speak of my manuscripts,' Spenser says without a trace of cognizance. 'I had to leave behind the original *Faerie Queen*. I fear the rebels are using it to wipe their traitorous arses at this very moment, the savages.'

Feigning weariness, Bianca leans against Nicholas. 'They say everything under heaven has a purpose,' she whispers.

Nicholas covers his mouth with his palm and stares at the ceiling.

David Nagle gets slowly to his feet, gathers his family and his servants together in the main hall and announces that they will join Master Spenser and his band on the ride to Cork. Safety in numbers, he declares. The cattle will come, too. 'Damned if I'll let Tyrone and his barbarians have them,' he says, calling for his riding boots.

And so the party grows, joined by the Nagles themselves, a clutch of Nagle daughters including a babe in swaddling clothes, their retainers, servants and farmhands and, following on behind, enough cattle to keep them all in milk and beef for several years. The cattle alone, Nicholas thinks, are bait enough for any marauding rebels. But he has little say in the matter.

Fording the Blackwater near Killavullen, they pick up even more stragglers. From a warren of caves on the south bank of the river emerge tired and frightened villagers, farm workers, shepherds and herdsmen. The rebels are in Mallow – burning, pillaging and murdering, they say as they emerge cautiously from their hiding places. Fermoy is taken, and all hanged who would not swear allegiance to the Pope. God has punished the English for daring to set one single foot on Ireland's soil.

Nicholas takes these claims with a pinch of salt. He remembers how, in the Low Countries, rumour was as much an enemy as the Spanish, and able to move a good deal faster. He is relieved, therefore, when – in the early afternoon – they encounter a solitary rider, waiting for them at the top of a heather-banked defile.

'I'm guessing the Earl of Tyrone's fellows have chased you out of Kilcolman, Dr Shelby,' says Piers Gardener, a wry smile playing on his smooth young face. 'And you, Master Spenser – I hope they have not used you too roughly.'

'All my manuscripts, the original *Faerie Queen* – probably destroyed,' Spenser says, his eyes tight with weariness.

'It pains me to hear you say so,' Gardener says. 'I'm sure that had Tyrone himself been with them, he would have saved your achievements from the flames. They say he is a cultured man.'

'He's a papist traitor, that's what he is,' snarls Spenser.

'I have heard it said that he wishes only for the queen to acknowledge his right to govern his own people, the O'Neills; for them to be subject to their own Irish law; and for them to practise the Catholic religion.'

'And welcome the Spanish in, while he's at it,' grunts David Nagle.

'Is the way clear into Cork?' Nicholas asks.

'It's clear, Dr Shelby. The Earl of Ormonde's force is barely a league beyond the walls. You'll be safe there.'

'Will you ride with us?'

Gardener looks back down the defile and out across the open countryside to where the Nagle cattle are making their slow progress. 'I don't suppose they were speaking of cows when they said there is safety in numbers, Dr Shelby. But yes, I will ride with you.'

He smiles and gives Bianca a gracious tilt of his head in recognition.

'I'm glad you did not fall into the rebels' hands on your journey, Master Gardener,' she replies courteously. But inside she is wondering if perhaps a little of the old *Seanchaí*'s ability to see things other people cannot has rubbed off on Piers Gardener. Or maybe he was just guessing that Edmund Spenser's fine tower house at Kilcolman had been burned, rather than merely ransacked, when he spoke of saving the poet's achievements from the flames.

✠

That night, while Nicholas and Bianca lay their cloaks down on bracken and wait for sleep to ease the aches of the ride, in the Jackdaw tavern on Bankside, Rose Monkton is preparing the taproom for the next morning. The last of the serious drinkers has departed, the empty jugs are washed and cleared away, the soiled rushes on the floor gathered up and the flagstones swept. Ned Monkton sits in a corner checking his Ned-hand, before adding it to Rose's tally of the day's takings. Timothy the taproom lad is squaring away the benches and boards before tamping down the fire for the night. Upstairs, in the Monktons' chamber, little Bruno Shelby is fast asleep on the truckle beside the bed.

When the street door opens and Constable Osborne of the Bankside watch puts his head around the jamb, Rose's first assumption is that he's after something warming to sustain him on his tramp through the lanes. It can be a wearisome burden, keeping the queen's peace and ensuring the bellmen call the hours – as their duty requires – instead of falling asleep beside the brazier up by the bridge gatehouse.

'Sorry to disturb, Mistress Monkton, but there's been disorder on Mutton Lane. We need somewhere to lay him out.'

Before Rose can enquire what manner of disorder, or who requires laying out, Osborne holds the door open while four of his watchmen manhandle a heavy bundle into the tavern. They gently deposit their burden on the floor by the hearth. It is the body of a young man, his shirt soaked in blood, his alabaster face lolling against the watchman's gaberdine they have wrapped him in.

From her place beside the fire, Buffle, the Jackdaw's dog, rouses herself, stretches studiously, pads over and sniffs at the bloodstained gaberdine, then at the nearest flesh, a curled hand. Rose hurries over and scoops her up.

'Take Buffle to the top of the stairs,' she tells Timothy, offering him the animal. 'If Bruno wakes, keep him occupied. I don't want 'im climbing off the truckle and seeing this.' Turning to Constable Osborne, she says, 'God's mercy, what 'as 'appened to this poor boy?'

'Cut-purses, I should warrant,' says Osborne sadly. 'Probably from beyond the parish. Our local thieves tend to draw the line at killing.'

'Where did you find 'im?' Rose asks, kneeling to lay a motherly hand against the cold cheek.

'Outside the Mutton Lane shambles. We thought at first that he'd drowned himself in ale and fallen asleep. When we tried to rouse him, then we sees the blood. He's taken a thrust to the side, like he was caught unawares.' Constable Osborne scratches his head. 'I don't know what's become of this city, Mistress Rose, I truly don't. They could have just taken his purse and sent him on his way. There was no need for this.'

'Do you know who 'e is?' asks Rose.

'No, never seen him before,' says Osborne.

And then Ned steps forward, rubbing his great auburn beard as though to dislodge the correct memory.

'It's the lad from the muster at the Southwark Fair,' he says. ''E was in 'ere a few days ago.'

'Does he have a name, perchance, Master Ned?' Osborne asks.

'Not known to me, if he 'as,' Ned replies. 'Nor any luck, neither – to get slain on Bankside when 'e was s'pposed to be fightin' in Ireland.'

'Luck?' echoes Osborne with a snort of derision for the whims of fortune. 'Well, he's beyond luck now, poor sod.'

14

Piers Gardener raises his hand to signal a halt. Ahead of him the fields slope away towards the shore of Loch Machan. 'At least another dozen, since I was last here,' he says in grudging admiration. 'The Privy Council must have anticipated Tyrone's move into Munster.'

Anchored out on the water are more ships than Nicholas can count.

'Pity they didn't anticipate it sooner,' mutters Edmund Spenser from a little way back.

Even at this distance Nicholas can see the bright banners signifying the different companies. Small pinnaces shuttle between the ships and the shore, landing men and supplies. The whinnying of horses drifts across the loch as they are lowered onto wooden barges to bring them ashore. It will take hours, if not days, to land the reinforcements aboard these ships, Nicholas reckons. By then Tyrone could be arraying his forces beneath the walls of Cork, if he's half the general that rumour would have him be. He lets his eye wander over the scene.

On the far headland, where the River Lee gives onto the loch, a newly built fort stands watch, with a circular tower clad in wooden scaffolding.

'Blackrock Castle,' Spenser tells him, seeing the direction of Nicholas's gaze. 'Another enterprise that was too long in the making. Pity those fools on the Privy Council didn't understand that the queen's rebellious Irish subjects were as much a danger to the peace of her realm as any enemy that might come at her by sea.'

'How far now to Cork, Master Piers?' Nicholas asks.

'Within the hour,' Gardener replies.

The group is smaller now than when they left Kilcolman: only Nicholas and Bianca, Spenser, his son Sylvanus, and Gardener. The others – including Spenser's wife, Elizabeth, daughter Katherine and young Peregrine – are with David Nagle and his household and the rest of the people from Kilcolman. The third group, the herdsmen and the cattle, are far, far behind. For Nicholas, the decision to allow each person to attach themselves to a group best fitting their own pace had been a hard but necessary one. The sooner the lead element reached Cork, the quicker help – in the shape of an armed escort – could be dispatched to the aid of the stragglers.

Resuming its journey, the party follows the north bank of the Lee towards the town, keeping company with a line of pinnaces carrying colourfully arrayed pikemen, halberdiers, musketeers and harquebusiers, all loudly confident after their voyages from Holyhead, Chester or Bristol.

'At least they're eager to be ashore,' Nicholas says.

'I pray they've brought their own victuals,' Gardener replies. 'Feeding this lot will take more than just Master Nagle's herd. And where to put them all? There's barely a patch of land around Cork that isn't a temporary refuge for a settler and his family. If you want my view, it would be best if soldiers and settlers alike sailed back to England.'

'All will change when the Earl of Essex comes,' Spenser calls out. 'He'll know how to pacify this land.'

'First he must convince the queen to appoint him to command,' Gardener says. 'His father almost bankrupted himself financing settlements in Ireland. If Her Majesty is wise, she'll not let Robert Devereux anywhere near this island. It's seen off one Essex already. It can chase away another.'

'You're a defeatist,' calls Spenser.

'No, sir. I merely state what I know.'

They ride onwards along the riverbank. A cold, salty wind begins to blow in off the loch. But within the hour, just as Gardener had forecast, they look out over the marshes to the high, turreted walls of Cork.

Riding across a wooden bridge and into the town through the North Gate, they enter what is – when left to its own devices – a prosperous community of some four thousand souls, mostly merchants, their families, the folk who labour for their comfort, and the men who load and unload the ships that carry their wares in and out of the Watergate. But today Cork is bursting at the seams. Nicholas takes in the packed alleyways, the graveyards with their bands of refugees from the countryside huddled between the headstones, the houses packed with people who've sought shelter from the dangers of the countryside with friends and relatives. Here and there, he sees bands of soldiers in groups of ten or twenty. They look up as he passes by, their eyes deep and wary, because even with reinforcements on the way, they know there aren't enough of them to mount a proper defence of the walls. The sleety air is heavy with the stink of human and animal waste. To Nicholas, it looks like a town waiting for the arrival of pestilence.

The men who matter in Cork are to be found on Tuckey's Quay, down by the Watergate, housed in one of the two stone towers that guard the entrance to the town's mercantile centre. Here, Spenser presents Nicholas and Bianca to the mayor and members of the Council of Munster.

'God be praised you're safe, Master Edmund,' says the mayor, John Skiddy, a pudding of civic rectitude tied at the neck with a starched ruff. 'We had feared the verminous traitors had strung you up from a tree.'

'Has the Council appointed me sheriff yet?' Spenser asks in reply.

'I fear we've been a little busy,' the mayor says with a wince of regret.

Nicholas listens while Skiddy reveals the extent of the misfortune that has engulfed Munster. The list of villages and settlements sacked by the rebels seems endless. The number of cattle, sheep and horses taken runs into the thousands. Too many fields despoiled to even count. Kilcolman, it appears, is but one of many tower houses ransacked or burned. There are reports of settlers hacked down trying to defend their lands, or having their noses and their ears cut off and sent away to instil terror in their neighbours.

The rebels' successes have taken everyone by surprise. Even the imminent arrival of the Earl of Ormonde and his troops from Dublin cannot, it seems, raise a smile on the frightened faces of the councillors.

'If Essex were here,' says Spenser, 'all would be different.'

But Robert Devereux is not here. And even if he were, from what Nicholas can judge by listening to Skiddy and the councillors, he'd need a much greater force than is currently disembarking in Loch Machan. It occurs to him that Elizabeth, by the Grace of God, Queen of England, Ireland and France, is in imminent danger of having her regal title unceremoniously trimmed a little.

✠

The port cuts into Cork from the east, like a thumb thrust into a ball of dough. Protected on the side facing the marshes and the loch by the town walls and the barrier that gives Watergate its name, the channel is flanked by extensive wharves and warehouses.

An atmosphere of anxious uncertainty hangs over the docks like a sea fog. Ships of every size cram the inlet, from small pinnaces to barques of two hundred tons or more. But there is no one to unload them. Every stevedore or waterman in Cork is helping the army to disembark. Piles of deer pelts, barrels of tallow, sacks of grain and flax, baskets of salted fish lie unattended on the quayside. In the customs house and the surrounding taverns the merchants sit gloomily at their ale or their dice, muttering amongst themselves about how much they'll lose if the rebels take the town before Ormonde comes to their rescue.

'Bristol?' queries the harbourmaster when Nicholas has made his request. 'You want passage for three people, to Bristol?'

'Or Holyhead. Chester or Minehead would be equally suitable. Any English harbour, really.'

'For what purpose?'

'Privy Council purpose,' says Nicholas.

The harbourmaster slaps the flanks of his jerkin with his hands and laughs. 'Good try. You'll have to be more specific.'

'I am the queen's physician. I need to return to England.'

'The queen's physician, eh? Ill, is she? No quacks in London to look after her?'

'That's not the point. I must have passage to England.'

'But you won't tell me why?'

'Am I required to?'

The harbourmaster gives him a mocking smile. 'In the present circumstances, yes, I fear you are. You might not have noticed, but there's rather a lot of people who would prefer to be anywhere in the queen's realm at the moment than Munster. And I've heard every excuse you can imagine; though before today I hadn't heard the one about being the queen's physician.'

'I'm telling you the truth,' Nicholas insists.

'Of course you are. But while this present emergency prevails, I have orders not to allow anyone on a vessel who does not have a written passport from the mayor and the Council. And *they* won't write one until the Earl of Ormonde arrives to tell them they can.'

✠

The next day, when word reaches Cork that Ormonde is only hours away, the mood in the town lifts like morning mist in summer. The citizens become animated. Their former fatalistic lethargy vanishes. Even the church bells ring out each hour with vigour instead of slow despondency.

Even so, the force that Ormonde brings in is, to Nicholas's eyes as he and Bianca watch the earl ride in through the North Gate, woefully understrength. If all they have heard of Tyrone's abilities is even half-true, the mix of undernourished Irish levies and mustered English – barely five hundred strong – will need more than the reinforcements disembarking on Loch Machan to win back Munster.

But the early signs are good. The earl brims with urgent efficiency. Even before his men have cleared a space to set up their tents and cooking cauldrons on a patch of open ground in the lee of St Peter's churchyard, he dispatches messengers to summon the mayor, the corporation, leading citizens and eminent settlers – Edmund Spenser amongst them – to the church's nave to hear his assessment of the present parlous state of affairs.

Standing beside Spenser outside the church, Nicholas and Bianca watch Ormonde stride in, accompanied by his senior officers – amongst them, Nicholas notes to his dismay, Sir Oliver Henshawe. 'How gallant,' says Bianca teasingly. 'He's had himself attached to the earl's staff so that he can ensure I'm safe.'

'I'm surprised he could steal the time away from all that slaughtering he so enjoys,' Nicholas replies testily.

Bianca keeps silent. She still finds it difficult to match the young man who paid court to her – earnestly chivalrous on the outside, but with his inner awkwardness obvious to any woman who had the eyes to see it – with the murderer of helpless survivors of a shipwreck. Instead, she keeps her eyes fixed on the person everyone hopes will be the saviour of the city.

Ormonde is a small man, well into his sixties, his white hair cropped close to the scalp. Clad in mud-splattered field armour, with a burgonet helmet held under one arm, he clatters as he strides into the church. Climbing into the pulpit, he proceeds to deflate the newly buoyant mood as effectively as if he'd stabbed a blown-up pig's bladder with the fine Lombardy rapier that he left with a page by the door, in deference to the Almighty.

'The rebels are as unsoldierly as a band of Morris men,' he tells the gathered worthies. 'But they are fierce fighters. And wicked with it. They do not give battle like honest fellows. They will not stand against pike, musket or horse like Christian soldiers. Instead, they resort to deception and ambuscade. When we come close to them, they let loose a volley or two, then slip away into the forests. When we have passed, they fall upon our tail like hungry rats. They attack at night, slitting the throats of our sentries. They raid our baggage trains and foraging parties. Our wounded are butchered where they fall. We cannot be everywhere, and so they burn and plunder at will—'

Nicholas hears Spenser mutter, 'Don't I know it?'

'But you need not fear,' Ormonde assures them, his voice ringing as though he were delivering a fiery sermon. 'Cork is safe. Cork has walls and a garrison. And now it has Thomas Butler, Lieutenant-General of Ireland and Earl of Ormonde, to watch over it.'

Cheers from the assembled worthies.

'Thinks highly of himself, doesn't he?' Bianca whispers in Nicholas's ear.

Ormonde rises – either on his toes or on his own hyperbole – the better to lean over the rim of the pulpit. His gaze is as tenacious as the bite of a mastiff at a bull-baiting.

'As you can see with the eyes that God gave you,' he continues, 'reinforcements from England are arriving by the day. And not just into Cork, but into Youghal, Wexford, Waterford and Dublin. Her Majesty the Queen has given me all authority to crush this traitorous uprising and bring her peace to Ireland. That is what I intend to do. And Cork will be the wellspring from which victory flows.'

St Peter's rings to more animated hosannahs. But Nicholas is not convinced. He can recall any number of stirring speeches he'd heard from commanders in the Low Countries. And the Low Countries are still at war. He imagines this island may not be as easy to subdue as Ormonde – or the queen – might suppose. But his immediate concern is how to get Ormonde to allow him to take Spenser to England.

✠

'I need your help, sweet,' Nicholas tells Bianca later in their cramped lodgings under the eaves of Spenser's house. Bianca's mouth purses in mock resignation. 'I *know*, Husband. I've grown accustomed.'

'I mean, I need your help to get us out of Cork.'

Sitting up in the narrow bed, Bianca leans forward to avoid the rafters, so that her heavy waves of dark hair hide her face from him. 'What would you ask of me?' she says, her voice turning from teasing to serious.

'Your former suitor, Oliver Henshawe, the butcher of shipwreck survivors – I need you to seek a favour from him.'

'I didn't care much for Henshawe when he was paying suit to me. I care for him even less after what we saw on that beach. Do I have to?'

Nicholas sighs. 'He's the surest way I can think of to get an audience with the Earl of Ormonde. And we need Ormonde's passport to leave Cork. Petitioning him could take weeks.'

'What is it I must do?'

'Seek him out and talk him into asking Ormonde for a meeting. Tell him I'm the queen's physician; that should help. It might put his nose out of joint, too – which would be pleasing.'

'What if Henshawe doesn't believe me?'

'You can describe the banqueting hall at Greenwich in detail, can't you? I don't recall you falling asleep.'

'You'll owe me dearly, Husband. You know that, don't you?' Bianca says, placing one hand on his thigh in a manner that is far from cautionary.

'I know, Wife,' he says, placing his hand over hers. 'I've grown accustomed.'

✠

It doesn't take Bianca long to locate Henshawe. Sir Oliver has commandeered himself a pleasant lodging near the Red Abbey Tower, ejecting its previous occupants and making himself and his servant at home. When Bianca is shown into his chamber she finds him bent over a table, cleaning a fine Flemish wheel-lock pistol. Holding up the weapon to the light from the window, he inspects the polished horn inlay of the stock and nods in satisfaction.

'Took this off the body of a Spanish gentleman who'd had the gall to come sailing by,' he says proudly. 'Had to clean it up a little, but it's as fine a firing piece as you'll find in any armoury. Ironic really – the Don brings it here to do England harm, and it ends up in my hands doing execution on traitorous Irish rebels. They do say God works in mysterious ways.'

'When you were paying court to me, I never took you to

have a stony heart, Oliver,' Bianca says, her voice laden with disappointment.

'You think me cruel?'

'At the shipwreck – that was nothing but murder.'

For an instant she thinks he's going to lose his temper. But then his face takes on a sad, almost hurt expression.

'Let me tell you something, Mistress Bianca,' he says calmly. 'My grandfather, whom I loved deeply, went to the flames as one of Mary Tudor's victims. My father only escaped a bonfire by fleeing abroad. Would you see those monstrous times returned to England, to Ireland? Those Spaniards you concern yourself with would have everyone in these isles in thrall to the Antichrist. What I and my men did on that beach – what we do in Ireland – is protect the immortal souls of every man, woman and child of the one true faith. If that requires the occasional cruelty, then I will answer to it before God. And I know how He will judge me.' He lays the weapon aside and leans back in his chair, swinging his elegantly hosed legs over the corner of the table. 'Now, what have I done to deserve the presence of so much beauty in such an ugly place?'

'You were once so courtly, Oliver,' she says, alarmed to find herself slightly chastened. 'This fight for my immortal soul seems to have coarsened you somewhat. Am I to remain standing in your presence?'

To her surprise, he blushes. 'Forgive me,' he says. He gets up and pulls another chair over to the table. Then, expectantly, he resumes his former languid pose.

To lift the mood, she says with a girlish laugh, 'I've come to accept your proposal of marriage. I've tired of my lumpen oaf of a husband – the one who drew himself up from a humble farmer's son to become the queen's physician. I thought I'd be better off with an empty vessel prettily painted.'

'So, you've come here only to tease?'

'You were always easy to tease, Oliver. You took yourself so seriously.'

'A third son doesn't have the expectations of the first,' he tells her, as though it's a secret he has never imparted to anyone before her. 'He has to work hard. He has to take risks, like tying his banner to that of the Earl of Essex and nearly getting his head carried away by a cannonball at Cádiz. Your husband is not the only one to have had to make his own way in the world.' He studies her, his eyes glinting with unasked questions, and no little regret for what he imagines might have been. 'You didn't tell me until now that he was the queen's physician.'

'You didn't ask, Oliver.'

'So he's not a quack or a charlatan, like most of the others? Like the ones who let my lads die because they believe a spell can heal a sword thrust?'

'Quite the opposite, Oliver. Nicholas has served as an army physician in the Low Countries. He doesn't believe in spells and drawing up a horoscope to make a diagnosis. But he does know how to mend broken bodies, if they can be saved. I assume there are plenty of *those* in this isle. He can be of some goodly use to the Earl of Ormonde.'

'How do I know you're telling the truth?'

'Ask him yourself.'

'He doesn't *look* like a queen's physician.'

'Have you ever been to Greenwich Palace, Oliver?'

'Once or twice, in the company of the Earl of Essex.'

'Nicholas and I attended a performance of *The Faerie Queen* there only a few weeks ago. I can describe it to you, if you'd like: the Flemish hangings... the design on the doors... anything you care to ask – on the assumption, that is, that you really *have* been inside.'

Henshawe regards her with new-found respect. He smiles at

Bianca as winningly as he ever did. Then he takes his feet off the table.

'Tell me, how may I be of assistance?'

✠

The Lieutenant-General has his temporary headquarters in the chapel of a friary, thrown down by the queen's father and turned over to a storehouse. The faded paintings of the saints still adorn the walls, though the air smells not of incense but of salted herring awaiting export to Chester.

'Do you see how deep the papist heresy runs on this island, Dr Shelby?' Ormonde asks abstractedly, when a halberdier in full plate escorts Nicholas into his presence. He is pointing to the upper torso of the Virgin Mary and the head of the infant Jesus peering out from behind a row of barrels. 'We prised this land out of the Pope's clutches years ago, and still no one has bothered to whitewash over its idolatry.'

Nicholas throws together a few consolatory words, forgotten the moment they have left his mouth.

'Sir Oliver tells me you are a physician much in favour with Her Grace, the queen,' Ormonde continues.

'Sir Oliver exaggerates, my lord. I have had the honour of being summoned by her on a few occasions. Mostly I am physician to Sir Robert Cecil.'

'Really? Are you one of those physicians who quotes Latin over his patient while the poor fellow's malady carries him off?' Ormonde asks in a blunt, soldiery manner. 'Or perhaps an expert in the various shades of piss and pus?'

Nicholas smiles. 'You paint the College of Physicians as accurately as Master Hilliard paints his portraits, sir.'

Ormonde looks him up and down as though making a military assessment of an enemy's dispositions.

'I had expected a queen's physician to be a grey-haired old sorcerer with a tome full of enchantments and a fat purse,' he says. 'Yet that is not what I see before me.'

'I learned practical physic on campaign in the Low Countries, with Sir Joshua Wylde's company of pistoleers. It was a while ago now, but very instructional.'

'Are you a follower of the Frenchman, Paré?'

'Very much so. We had Protestant Italian and Swiss physicians in the army who used his techniques. I learned much from them. And I've studied anatomy under Professor Fabricius, in Padua.'

'And are you a hot-iron man or a silk weaver?'

Nicholas smiles, knowing he's being tested. 'A silk weaver, my lord. Silken thread will tie off a severed blood vessel with far better results than brutal cauterizing with hot iron.'

Ormonde seems impressed. He nods in approval. 'And now here you are, in the midst of a rebellion. If you've come to Ireland to settle a plantation, Dr Shelby, you've picked a choice time in which to do it.'

'No, I am here on private business. It is that which brings me to you.'

'How may I be of assistance?'

Nicholas tells him of the brick wall he'd come up against at the Watergate.

Ormonde asks, 'And the reason you desire this passport?'

'I wish to escort Master Edmund Spenser to England.'

Ormonde laughs, like an order barked out on a parade ground. 'Spenser? The poet fellow?'

'Yes, my lord.'

Ormonde looks puzzled. 'Why does Spenser want to go to England?'

It would be so easy, thinks Nicholas, to tell Ormonde that he has been sent by Mr Secretary Cecil to learn what Spenser is so eager to reveal, and that Spenser now demands to speak to Cecil face-to-face. But in his mind he can hear Cecil's words as clearly as if Sir Robert were standing here in this old friary. *There are certain people I would prefer didn't learn that I have a new man in Ireland...*

'Her Majesty the Queen has expressed a desire to hear more of Master Spenser's art,' he says. 'She thinks very highly of him.'

Ormonde seems unconvinced. 'Highly enough to send her physician to fetch him?'

Nicholas has prepared for just such a question. He adopts the air of the hard-done-by. 'Her Majesty's whims often come without warning, my lord. She does not always instruct the most appropriate person, only the nearest. She decides, and then she commands.'

The Lieutenant-General's response is not what he expects. Ormonde slaps his hands on his breeches, throws back his head and laughs. 'Well, I pity you, Dr Shelby. Christ's nails! Have you ever sat through a rendering of Spenser's verse? It's the most rambling bilge I've ever heard.'

Nicholas struggles to keep the mirth out of his voice. 'Her Grace has a higher appreciation of the artistic form than I do, my lord.'

And then the mastiff's bite of a gaze bares its teeth again in Ormonde's eyes. 'Well, I fear Her Majesty's pleasure will have to be denied for a while. The answer is "no".'

'My lord?' Nicholas says, taken aback.

'I fear that I cannot write a passport for you, Dr Shelby. Or for Master Spenser. Certainly not at this moment. For a start, Spenser is a prominent citizen who has held several important positions on this island. How will it look to the populace if they hear he has scuttled away to safety in England?'

'But, my lord – you surely cannot intend to stand in the way of Her Grace's wish.'

However, Ormonde is unmoved. 'In the matter of verse, I most surely do,' he says gruffly. 'It may have escaped your notice, but part of our sovereign majesty's realm is threatened by traitorous rebels. There are poor fellows amongst my army that have suffered grievous hurts from them. There will undoubtedly be more to come, when I close with Tyrone and defeat him. My men need a competent physician almost as much as I need another muster of pike and horse.' He gives Nicholas a challenging stare. 'Unless, that is, you'd prefer your fellow countrymen to ail and die for lack of a surgeon, while you sit comfy in the queen's company, listening to poetry?'

'Of course not, my lord,' Nicholas says quietly, feeling his control over Robert Cecil's commission vanish like a handful of ice thrown onto a fire.

'Consider yourself assigned to Sir Oliver Henshawe,' Ormonde says, bringing the short audience to a close. 'He will direct you as he sees fit. Once the situation here in Munster is resolved, Her Majesty may listen to Spenser's horse-dung until her ears bleed. In the meantime, Dr Shelby, I fear *you* are a prisoner of your own undoubted abilities.'

15

The coroner's inquisition into the murder of Lemuel Godwinson, a seventeen-year-old shepherd's apprentice from the manor of Camberwell in the county of Surrey, and recently slain on Bankside, opens on a chill October morning beneath a grey, indifferent sky. The jurors themselves are no more charitable than the weather. It doesn't take them long to reach a verdict.

'On the matter of the coroner's inquisition post-mortem upon the body of Lemuel Godwinson, previously viewed lying dead at St Thomas's Hospital by Thieves Lane,' the jury foreman intones laboriously as he brings the hearing to a conclusion, 'I believe we are all in accord.'

He looks at his fellow jurists for dissent. Finding none, he continues.

'I propose to inform the Surrey justices of the peace that Master Godwinson was assaulted by persons unknown, and died during the melee while attempting to prevent his purse being cut away. Which anyone – short of a Don, a Frenchie or a Turk – ought to know is not a wise thing to do on Bankside. Particularly at night, with no witnesses. May the good Lord have mercy on the poor lad's soul.'

Ned Monkton adds his own amen to all the others.

Throughout the hearing Ned has sought to remain unobtrusive, no easy feat for a fearsome-looking fellow such as himself.

He is not comfortable around juries of any stamp. The branded M on his thumb has made him so. But he has come out of a sense of curiosity, and also out of respect for the young recruit whose body began its official passage to the hereafter on the floor of the Jackdaw's taproom.

The verdict comes as no surprise to Ned. What does is the fact that Gideon Strollot and Barnabas Vyves have somehow managed to inveigle themselves onto the jury.

Their presence disturbs Ned considerably. Vyves's appearance – being the man who called poor Lemuel to arms – he can just about explain. But Strollot? Yes, he's an alderman's clerk, a man of some small dignity and therefore as likely to serve on a jury as any other; but on that day when Vyves brought him to the Jackdaw, didn't he say he was from Cornhill Ward? What is a fellow from Cornhill doing on a Southwark jury?

And there is something else troubling Ned today. Why is it that no one has asked why young Lemuel Godwinson was on Bankside the night he died, and not fighting the papist rebels in Ireland, where at least his demise would have incurred the grateful thanks of his sovereign lady, Queen Elizabeth?

He steps forward from the small knot of the bored and the curious who have gathered to watch the proceedings. ''Scuse the liberty, Master Foreman,' he says. 'But I 'as a small question to ask.'

The foreman recognizes him at once. Ned's appearance anywhere tends to be notable, and few are inclined to deny him his right to be heard, especially when he's asking nicely.

'Ask away, Master Monkton,' the foreman invites.

Ned takes off his cap and says, as respectfully as he can, 'I was merely wonderin' what poor Lemuel was doin' in Southwark, when 'is company is away fightin' in Ireland. I mean, a fellow doesn't get mustered to spend 'is time playin' dice or visitin' the play'ouse, does he?'

'I fear I cannot help you, Master Monkton,' says the foreman. 'The question might be more properly addressed to Ensign Vyves, I think.' He turns to Vyves, inviting him to bring light to the general darkness.

Vyves leans back in his chair. The lank hair swings around his neck like a grey veil. He adopts a look of admiration.

'A cleverness to match your size, Master Ned,' he says. 'I can see as how nothing slips by *you*. Wasted, that's what you are. You should hold some position of authority in this realm – like Lord Chancellor or Master of the Rolls – instead of running a tavern.'

'I'm only askin',' says Ned. 'Besides, it's my Rose what runs the Jackdaw – for Mistress Merton.'

'Well, you're an observant fellow, regardless,' says Vyves. 'But I can set your mind at rest. Young Godwinson was kept behind due to the fact I needed someone to assist me in the procuring of pike and powder. We can't send our fine young fellows off to fight the papist traitors with naught but the courage in their hearts, now can we?'

'I should think not,' says the foreman in agreement.

Vyves gives Ned a condescending smile. 'After all, lead don't turn itself into ball, black powder don't mix itself, an' pikes don't grow on trees, do they?'

'Well, they does, actually,' Ned points out respectfully. 'Pikes is made of wood. You 'as to lop a strong, straight branch an'—'

The foreman cuts in, 'I think Master Vyves has answered the question, Master Monkton, if it pleases.'

And Ned is forced to conclude that Vyves's answer is plausible enough. He is about to step back when a thought strikes him. Craving the foreman's indulgence a little further, he turns to Gideon Strollot.

'I was just wonderin', Master Strollot, 'ow come you're sittin' 'ere on this 'ere jury? Seein' as 'ow you're from Corn'ill, that is.'

Strollot's porcine face beams happily. 'I happened to be with Master Vyves when he was invited. I thought it right to offer myself. A man's civic duty may call at any time, and at any place. When it does, he should not refuse the summons.'

The foreman nods approvingly. 'I trust that answers your enquiry, Master Monkton?' he says. 'Now, we are a *little* pressed for time—'

What makes Ned ask his follow-up question will remain a matter of conjecture for him for a long while to come. He will later put it down variously to an innate stubbornness, a mistrust of the law, a general feeling of suspicion about Gideon Strollot and Barnabas Vyves or just plain genius. But he will always look back to this moment and say he felt a guiding hand on his shoulder.

'So, am I right in thinkin' that if you're from Corn'ill, and poor Lemuel Godwinson was from Camberwell, that would imply you've 'ad no preevus knowledge of the deceased?'

Strollot gives a smile of amusement for a common man's clumsy attempt at legal formality. 'Quite right, Master Monkton. Never saw him before in my life.'

'Before you saw 'is body laid out in the crypt at St Tom's, that is?'

'Exactly.'

Not wanting to risk a quarrel with the bearded giant before him, the foreman asks cautiously, 'Might I ask precisely *where* this line of enquiry is bound, Master Monkton?'

But before Ned – who is not sure himself – can answer, Barnabas Vyves interrupts.

'I fear, Master Strollot, that it must have escaped your memory,' he says helpfully – a little *too* helpfully, in Ned's opinion.

'You *have* met young Godwinson before. The deceased came into the Jackdaw's taproom while you and I were discussing the next muster demand from the Privy Council, *if* you remember.'

Strollot spreads his arms, to show that even the most blameless of men can sometimes fall prey to an honest mistake.

'Then I confess my error, gladly,' he says generously. 'One meets so many people when one is engaged upon one's civic responsibilities.'

Civic responsibilities? thinks Ned, watching a line of sweat-beads break out on Strollot's pink brow. He's an alderman's clerk, not the Lord Mayor. And he's just been dug out of a hole by his accomplice; though accomplice in quite *what*, Ned would be hard pressed at this precise moment to say.

'I think that must be the last of your questions, Master Monkton,' the foreman says, wondering how he's going to silence Ned if he chooses otherwise.

But Ned, wisely, admits that it is. He admits it all the way back to the Jackdaw – even while he tries unsuccessfully to convince himself that he must have been mistaken that day in the taproom. And that it wasn't Gideon Strollot he saw pay Lemuel Godwinson for an errand run, but Barnabas Vyves. And that there is a plausible explanation why an alderman's clerk from Cornhill should stir himself to sit on a coroner's jury in Southwark – on the other side of the river.

16

Cork has not fallen. Cork is not even under siege, though from the conditions within the walls it would be easy to think it was. While Ormonde is out chasing the rebels through Munster, a steady trickle of sick and wounded men flows through the North Gate. Food is scarce. Hunger bites. The rain seems to have forgotten how to stop. Nicholas really fears an outbreak of pestilence. He has seen it happen before. He knows how quickly a town may become one great bone-yard, with the only difference between the living and the dead being the waiting.

Bianca raises the possibility of hiding aboard a ship bound for England. But like all good commanders, Ormonde has already made his preparations for the possibility of such an ambush.

'He has imposed martial law,' Nicholas reminds her when she suggests the idea. 'We'd be deserting. That's a hanging offence.'

Bianca's only consolation is that Nicholas's position as Ormonde's advisor in matters of physic gives him access to the mail pinnace that plies between Cork and Bristol. While Nicholas pens a letter to Cecil, encoded with the cipher they use for privy correspondence, telling Mr Secretary Cecil that he will bring Spenser to London when Ormonde allows it, Bianca writes a letter to Rose at the Jackdaw. She accompanies it with her own versions of the stories the old *Seanchaí* told her and Nicholas that night on the ride to Kilcolman. They are to be read to little Bruno before bed. She takes care to give the story of the Merrow a happy ending – a marriage. In her mind, it is a way to remember the owner of the lace mantilla she had found at the cove, and whose body she assumes is lying at the bottom of the ocean.

With no hospital worth the name in Cork – the old friary's medicinal garden has long since been turned over to vegetables – the wounded from Ormonde's march from Dublin through Munster are housed in a warehouse at the Watergate. They lie on dirty straw, cared for by only a few camp-followers. Using the earl's authority, Nicholas gets to work. He presses into service the town's barber-surgeons and a number of women skilled in using the healing plants to be found in the surrounding countryside. He musters some of the refugees to help remove the filthy straw, scrub the dirt and the dried blood from the flagstones and lay fresh reeds cut from the marshes. He calls upon Cork's licensed apothecaries and entreats them to assist Bianca. They bridle. *A woman?* To be set over us? He tells them she is licensed in London by the Grocers' Company, the guild that controls the apothecary's art. Still they resist. The Grocers might think it right, but God surely does not. Whoever heard of such a thing? What next: women physicians? When they witness the level of her skill, most of them change their opinion. Those who don't are too afraid of her to complain further.

With the help of the barber-surgeons, Nicholas assembles a serviceable collection of knives, tweezers and lancets. Anticipating amputations, he sharpens saws and stores them in pairs, so that if one breaks halfway through, another is immediately to hand. From the local shambles he purloins a wickedly curved boning knife, so that when he cuts through flesh and muscle, it will automatically pull back from the bone, leaving a clear space for him to apply the saw. From the same place he gathers a stock of pigs' bladders for stretching over the freshly stitched stumps.

In the chamber above the warehouse, Bianca sets a cauldron in the hearth for boiling brank-ursine, which she makes into poultices for setting broken bones. She gathers a collection of stone jars to hold the ingredients for plaisters: St John's wort, pimpernel and comfrey; meadow rue for killing lice; juice of syanus, which the farmers call hurt-sickle, to close the lips of wounds. When not at Nicholas's side, she goes out into the marshes beyond the walls to gather up marsh-mallows, using the roots to make a decoction to restore those who have bled too freely. She also boils the roots in wine, making a draught to ease the suffering of soldiers and refugees alike who are afflicted by the bloody flux, brought on by bad water and the damp climate.

Keep busy, she tells herself. Work is the answer to all those troubling questions that keep sleep at bay. Questions like: *What manner of mother leaves her infant son behind to go swanning off to Ireland?* And: *What manner of wife would contemplate leaving her husband to face these trials alone?*

With the makeshift hospital open for trade, they go to work. For his part, Nicholas finds the demands made on his skills invigorating, if exhausting. It is good, once again, to be practising a physic that he knows to be purely practical. No need to cast a horoscope before he deals with a wound or a fracture. A man in agony from a sword slash doesn't care a damn if his doctor can recite the *Aphorisms* of Hippocrates in Greek or Latin. The owner of a torn spleen doesn't give a fig for the argument currently dividing the College of Physicians – does the organ purge the body of black bile, as Galen claims; or produce blood, as Aristotle would have it do?

Surprisingly, Oliver Henshawe turns out to be the least of Nicholas's worries. After what he had seen at the sight of the wreck, he had expected to find Henshawe utterly unmoved by the plight of his own wounded. Yet he seems genuinely concerned for his men.

'You have an unusual faculty for this business,' Henshawe tells him on one occasion, and not patronizingly, but with genuine admiration.

'Thank you,' Nicholas replies. But he can't help adding, 'It's a pity you didn't bring back some of those Spaniards who survived the wrecking of their ship. I might have been able to keep them alive. They might have told us what they were about.'

'Oh, I know what they were about,' Henshawe laughs. 'They were intending to parley with the rebels, to contrive a landing in support of Tyrone. They made an attempt last year. Only the weather saved us.' He gives Nicholas a sickly smile of assumed brotherhood. 'I know you have sworn an oath to do no harm, but God never meant that to apply to the Spanish.'

Nicholas has noticed Edmund Spenser growing increasingly agitated, particularly when he's around Oliver Henshawe. Mayor Skiddy has instigated regular conferences to order the regulation of the town: allocate rations, organize watch patrols, address weaknesses in the walls. Throughout – when he's not restating his opinion that only the Earl of Essex can set things right in Ireland – Spenser sits in the corner of Skiddy's apartments in the King's Tower on Tuckey's Quay, looking like a man awaiting the verdict of a jury in a capital trial. This discomfort is most visible whenever Henshawe is around.

Why is Spenser so afraid of him? Nicholas wonders again. After what he witnessed at the shipwreck, especially if he was there while the killing was taking place, it makes every sense that Spenser should fear such innate brutality. But hadn't Spenser told him that Henshawe was Robert Devereux's man in Ireland? He can recall the poet's words exactly: *Whatever happens on this island, the Earl of Essex hears of it first from Henshawe... Be very cautious in what you say when that man is present...*

So if Spenser believes Essex is the best man to defeat the rebellion – and if Essex is Spenser's patron and friend – why does he fear Henshawe so?

✠

A week later Henshawe returns from chasing off a band of rebels attempting to sack a plantation at Ballinahina, to the north. He brings with him a soldier whose thigh has been badly gashed by a lucky strike from a poleaxe. Nicholas follows the man's comrades as they carry the casualty to the temporary hospital down by the Watergate. He is a rake-thin lad of barely sixteen, with a pitted grey face and darting, frightened eyes. His pain has pitched him into delirium. He cries out in anguish, a jumbled, plaintive wail of misery: he is damned for all eternity... he has defied God's will by taking innocent lives... he has profaned, and now he faces judgement... the Virgin Mary has come down from heaven to punish him. The poor boy only falls silent when Bianca takes his hand and walks with him beside the litter.

The hospital is dark and quiet when they carry the lad in. Someone calls in a hoarse, pain-racked voice, 'Whose company? Is he from Sir Henry Norris's regiment? My brother is with Sir Henry.'

The only answer he gets is a muttered, 'No one gives a shit for your brother, Tib Kelly. Pipe down and let us sleep.'

'Lay him down here, by the door,' says Nicholas, indicating a clear space on the bed of fresh reeds.

The light spilling in from the entrance is pale and sickly. Nicholas calls for a horn lantern to work by – he will allow no candles in the warehouse, a blazing hospital being somewhat prejudicial to the chances of a patient's recovery. When he cuts away the bloody, mud-stained woollen leggings, Nicholas sees the Devil's purple lips smiling back at him. Surrounded by dried blood, they leer in corrupt invitation. He leans closer, expecting to catch the stink of putrefaction. But all he can smell is blood and the cold scent of damp wool and sweat from the boy's dirty hose.

Nicholas knows he will have to work quickly. If the wound is neat and he can prevent it becoming diseased, the boy has a chance. But if there is extensive damage to the surrounding flesh, tendons and muscle, perhaps even to the bone, he will have consider amputating the limb. That, he thinks, is almost as likely to kill the patient as the infection.

Nicholas has always considered himself competent with a saw. His success rate – around six out of every ten amputations resulting in the survival of the patient – is acceptable by any measure that the College of Physicians cares to impose. But it's been a while since he performed the procedure. He calls for a jug of potcheen and a jar of honey. The spirit will help cleanse the wound and the honey will soothe and delay any infection. The potcheen will have the added benefit of dulling the lad's senses if Nicholas needs to amputate. In the Low Countries he could take off a limb inside the first three verses of 'We Be Soldiers Three'. As he cleans the wound, he sings it to himself, to get the speed of the saw fixed against the rhythm of the song, should he need to:

We be soldiers three,
Pardonnez-moi je vous en prie,
Lately come forth from the Low Countries
With never a penny of money...

Now that the wound is cleansed, Nicholas can see that the boy has been luckier than he knows. The blade must have been well honed. It has carried deep into the muscle, but brought with it only a few strands of woollen hose, and it has missed the femoral artery by less than a finger's width. Remembering the boy's ravings, he says, 'You were wrong, my lad. The Virgin Mary was on your side, not the rebels'.'

He stitches the wound with animal gut and anoints it with the honey. Then he wraps it tightly in a warm poultice that Bianca has prepared. Now the boy's fate is up to God or, more likely, luck – because Nicholas has observed that when it comes to healing, God's attention too often seems occupied elsewhere.

Over the following days he is relieved to see the lad recover. Within the week his patient is able to hobble on his good leg. His appetite is restored, though no one in the town can rely upon the prospect of a full belly. On the eighth day after he was brought in, Nicholas sits beside the lad and tells him how lucky he is. There is every chance he will make a full recovery. Only one thing has not healed: the lad's certainty that he is damned.

'War makes men behave like beasts,' he laments to Nicholas. 'I had not thought to see such things. I had not thought to *do* such things.'

Nicholas wonders if the lad was with Henshawe at the wreck site. But when he asks, he receives only blank incomprehension.

'No, this was no shipwreck – this was at Ballinahina. We hanged a whole rebel family,' he says sadly. 'Children an' all. We should not have done that. The husband went silently to his maker, with naught but hatred in his heart for us. But the woman cried out that the Virgin Mary had risen out of the sea to protect Ireland from our cruelty, and that our work that day was blasphemous and against God. She cursed us to hell.' He lays his hand on his bandages. 'Very next day, I caught *this*.'

Nicholas knows from his experience in the Low Countries that a man's worst wounds are not always the visible ones. When the boy has talked himself into silence, he says,

'If you want me to, I'll tell Sir Oliver that your wound has made you unfit for further service. You'll be back in Surrey before you know it, the bold hero – setting all the village maids' hearts a-flutter.'

The lad gives him a bewildered look. 'Surrey, sir? Where in Ireland is Surrey?'

'*Surrey*, in England.'

'They'll not send me to England, will they?' the lad asks, a plaintive look clouding his young, thin face.

'Don't you want to go home?'

'Aye, sir – but not to England. My home is in Leinster. My father came over to work land at Rathcoffey, before I was born.'

'I must have misunderstood,' Nicholas says, confused. 'I thought you were with Sir Oliver Henshawe's regiment.'

'Oh, I am, sir. And as proud as Hector to be so – or I *was*, until I saw what manner of fellows he keeps.'

'But I thought Sir Oliver's regiment recruited in Surrey. I've seen their muster ensign at work at the Southwark Fair – a thin fellow with one eye. I can't recall his name at present – Voles, or Vibes, something like that.'

'Don't know no Voles, Master. All the fellows I served with were mustered in Leinster.'

'Is there *no one* from England in your company?' Nicholas asks, confused.

'Save for the officers, not to my knowledge, sir.'

As Nicholas goes about his business attending to the other patients, he puzzles over what the young lad has told him. The memory of that day at the Southwark Fair sharpens. He can hear the muster ensign clearly as he tried to recruit Ned Monkton:

We could use a doughty fellow like you in the ranks of Sir Oliver Henshawe's company... Sixpence a day all found. Glory by the cartload...

Now he can even remember the man's name: Vyves. So where, he wonders, are Oliver Henshawe's English recruits?

Solely out of curiosity, he mentions it in passing to Henshawe himself.

'You know how disorganized the Privy Council is,' Sir Oliver says with a dismissive smile. 'We should thank God they've sent us a single reinforcement. My brave fellows are still languishing at Chester, for want of a ship. I'll be lucky to get them before Christmas.'

'So you have to raise amongst the local Irish?'

'Aye. And poor fellows they are too, by and large. Most of them slink off to join the rebels the moment their officers look the other way.' He looks up at the wintry sky and curses. 'You can't trust anything in this island. You can't trust the sky not to rain, the land not to swallow you, and the people not to stab you from behind the moment you turn your back. By the way, have you heard the news?'

'What news?' Nicholas says.

'Philip of Spain is dead. That's one more bastard on his way to the eternal fires of damnation. Now we have his son to play the match against. They don't give up, these Dons. Cut down one, and another springs up to take his place – like sown dragon's teeth. Unless we kill them all, I'm beginning to think we'll never be free of their papist scheming.'

With the arrival of November's gales, Munster seems to be slowly sinking into the sea. Black water wells out of the ground like bad blood, filling each new footstep as the Earl of Ormonde's forces struggle across the county. While his tenacity and vigour have prevented immediate catastrophe, the earl cannot win a decisive victory. Tyrone stays safe in the wilds of Ulster, sending small parties of rebels out to lure the English forces into the marshes and the bogs, the dark forests and the narrow passes between the mountains. But Ormonde is too old and too canny to fall for such tricks. As a consequence, the flow of wounded returning to Cork dwindles to a trickle.

The reinforcement of Ormonde's locally mustered companies is gathering pace. More ships than ever are braving the winter seas, making their landfall at harbours along Ireland's eastern coast – Dublin, Waterford, Youghal, Cork. They come from further afield, too: from Padstow, Plymouth and even Southampton and the Solent. Their decks are crammed with Englishmen newly mustered by the queen's Privy Council: two thousand raised in the west from farms, towns and hamlets throughout Cornwall, Devon, Somerset and Gloucestershire; another thousand from Worcestershire and Warwickshire. Not all of them are as disciplined as Her Majesty might wish: the band of four hundred that so bravely marches out of London mutinies on the road to Chester, making off with the regimental funds.

But no matter, because although these bands gathering to the colours like flowers blooming in a meadow in summer are mostly masterless vagrants, callow farmhands or released indentured labourers, a letter has been sent to Sir Francis Vere, commander of the English forces in the Low Countries. He is ordered to dispatch two thousand of his own battle-hardened troops to Ireland. And the rumours are growing apace that the army will indeed have a new marshal: none other than Robert Devereux, Earl of Essex.

✠

With Ormonde's campaign stalled, most of the patients in Nicholas's makeshift hospital down by the Watergate are civilians, suffering the effects of the weather and malnourishment. Ormonde sends word he is lifting his prohibition on men of importance leaving Cork. The Council of Munster appoints

Edmund Spenser – still awaiting his confirmation as sheriff of Cork – to carry official dispatches to the Privy Council in London. The poet welcomes the news like a man reprieved from the block.

On the ninth day of December 1598, with a harassing wind driving tangles of black cloud over Loch Machan, Nicholas, Bianca and Edmund Spenser are rowed out to the *Calliope*, a compact little barque bound for Holyhead.

Nicholas watches the *Calliope*'s mainsail begin to unfurl the moment their oarsman comes within hailing distance. He is glad his commission for Robert Cecil will soon be over.

For her part, Bianca is hard pressed to stop herself grinning insanely at the prospect of holding little Bruno in her arms again. Calliope, she reminds herself, was the Greek muse of poetry. A fitting vessel, then, to carry England's greatest poet. A good omen – surely?

17

Under a cold mid-December sky three riders – two men and a woman – cross the open fields to the west of Charing Cross. It is late afternoon, the sun little more than the fading light in a dying eye. The ride from last night's resting place – a Windsor tavern that Bianca said had no right to call itself by the name – has been a trial of chilled extremities and stiff limbs. But they have made the journey from Cork in just under eight days. Bianca fights back the tears. They are tears not of discomfort – though she would have cause enough – but of joy at the prospect of seeing her son again.

Turning down King's Street towards the Court Gate at Whitehall, they leave their mounts at the official post stables, signing their hire – and the cost of a postboy to return them to Bristol – to the account of Mr Secretary Cecil.

As Spenser prepares to leave for the Privy Council offices at Whitehall, where he will deliver the dispatches he has carried from Ireland, he says something that rocks Nicholas on his heels.

'I cannot go to Cecil House. It is out of the question.'

Nicholas stares at him blankly. 'But you said you would speak to no one but Sir Robert,' he protests, struggling to master his growing anger.

'And so I must. But not at Cecil House. It is too public.'

'What are you so afraid of?'

'I cannot risk His Grace the Earl of Essex knowing that I have held a privy meeting with Mr Secretary Cecil.'

'Have you *any* idea how hard it is to get an audience with him?' Nicholas asks petulantly. 'It's easier to find an honest bawd in a Bankside stew.'

But Spenser is adamant. 'It *must* be somewhere discreet.'

Nicholas promises to do what he can. 'Where are you going to stay?' he asks.

Bianca glances at him, fearful her husband is going to offer Spenser a room in their lodgings at the Paris Garden.

'When I am in London, His Grace the earl allows me to lodge in a property he owns on King's Street,' Spenser says. 'Once I have delivered the dispatches, I shall go directly to Essex House to seek the keys.'

Nicholas recalls something Cecil had told him before his departure: *You could thatch Essex House with all the poets the noble earl likes to keep there. Essex promotes them, encourages them, indulges them... He could be planning to entrap me into some enterprise he can use to my disadvantage with Her Majesty, using Spenser as bait...*

Watching Spenser walk away, Nicholas struggles to fathom his sudden change of heart. But he can find no answer. Whether he is bait or not, one thing is clear. Whatever secret he is carrying, Edmund Spenser is scared stiff of his supposed benefactor, the Earl of Essex, catching even a scent of it.

His thoughts are interrupted by Bianca throwing her arms around him.

'We're almost home, sweet,' she says happily.

Nicholas wonders how he's going to break the news to her that the only suitably privy place for a meeting between Spenser and Cecil that he can think of is their lodgings at the Paris Garden.

'Yes, home,' he says distractedly. 'And let us stay here until our feet grow roots.'

✠

A light dusting of snow whitens the downstairs windowsills of the neat little timbered house that lies on the north side of Southwark's Paris Garden, close by the river Thames. Beyond the glass, flakes the size of moths flutter gently to earth against an alabaster sky. Looking out on the cold, ghostly world through the windows of the modest chamber that passes for the great hall, Nicholas can imagine an army of Norsemen encamped along the riverbank, warming itself around its fires and cooking cauldrons.

It is five days now since he, Bianca and Edmund Spenser arrived in London. Five days during which Bianca has barely allowed little Bruno out of her sight. Retrieving him from the Jackdaw, she had feared he might have no recollection of her whatsoever. But her concerns have proved groundless. He is a precocious lad, quick to learn, eager to hear her tales – mostly invented – of the strange and distant land from which she has returned. At this moment Bruno is in the parlour, disjointedly recounting them to three surprisingly indulgent Cecil bodyguards, while their master – the queen's principal Secretary of State – warms himself in front of the fire in the main hall.

Cecil is wearing the scholar's plain black knee-length gown he brought back from his studies at the Sorbonne fifteen years ago, Nicholas notes. It still fits. The Parisian tailor who made it cut the cloth to flatter the wearer's crooked back. He looks like a well-to-do lawyer who's dropped by for a chat and a glass of sack. He casts his gaze around as though marvelling at how a couple with an infant son could tolerate living in a space that, at Cecil House, might serve as a storeroom for the pewter.

'You should find yourself somewhere more fitting for a queen's physician,' he says. 'Build yourself a decent place at St Giles. I can arrange a good mortgage for you with a banker, if you wish.'

'And can you also arrange for the sick on Bankside to cure themselves?' Bianca asks waspishly. 'Let St Giles find its own physicians.'

As if he hadn't heard her, Cecil asks, 'Where *is* Master Spenser, by the way?'

'I'm sure he will be here shortly, Sir Robert,' Nicholas says. 'With Christmas approaching, the traffic on London Bridge can often be impassable. And, with respect, you didn't give us much of a warning.'

'You can do that if you arrive by private barge,' Bianca says. She does not find it easy to make polite small-talk with the man who once threatened her husband that he would hang her for a witch if he didn't agree to spy for him, and who thinks turning her son into the model of an English courtier is somehow appealing to her. Nevertheless she fetches a bottle of good malmsey and marchpane comfits from the kitchen and does her best to make the Secretary of State feel welcome. She still hasn't fully forgiven Nicholas for offering their home as the place for Cecil and Spenser's privy meeting.

The rapping of a fist against the street door puts an end to her embarrassment.

'God give you good morrow, Mr Secretary,' Spenser says, making a laborious bend of the knee to Robert Cecil. The light dusting of snow on the shoulders of his gaberdine cape drips onto the floor. He takes it off and hands it to Nicholas, as if to a servant. Nicholas drops the cloak onto a chair, not really caring if the melting snow dribbles down the insides.

Cecil gives Spenser a lingering look of reproach. 'Good of you to join us, sirrah,' he says. Then, bluntly, 'Tell me, Master Spenser, in Ireland do they consider me a saint?'

Spenser stares at Cecil, not knowing what to say. 'Why, no, Sir Robert,' he manages. 'That would be blasphemy.'

Cecil gives a slow exhalation that could signify weariness. Or the savouring of long-delayed revenge. 'Yet a saint's forbearance appears to be exactly what you expect of me.'

'I do not follow you, Sir Robert.'

'I seem to recall a pamphlet that was widely circulated some years ago...'

'A pamphlet, Sir Robert?'

'A vile satire on the probity of Her Majesty's courtiers. It was entitled "Mother Hubberd's Tale". Do you recall it, by any chance?'

Spenser swallows hard. 'I believe I might, sir.' He studies the buckles on his shoes, muddy from the walk from King's Street.

'I can't quite hear you, sirrah,' says Cecil, twisting the knife a little. 'Would you kindly repeat that?'

'Sir Robert. I confess it – I was the author of the said pamphlet.'

Cecil's little body seems almost unable to constrain his indignation. 'You were clever, I'll give you that – a fable about an ape that usurps the throne of the animal kingdom, aided by a cunning fox,' – a stern wag of Mr Secretary's right index finger – 'but the fox was meant to be my late father, Lord Burghley, Her Majesty's most faithful and devoted servant. And *you* traduced him as a manipulative schemer.'

'The character was an amalgam, Sir Robert,' Spenser says wretchedly. 'Lord Burghley was never named.'

'Funny, then, how all London came to the conclusion it was him. I have no doubt that in Mistress Merton's tavern the most common sort of fellow was all but prostrate with mirth.'

Bianca glances at Cecil with a look that says, *Leave me out of this.*

'If you desire an apology, Sir Robert, I offer it freely,' Spenser says. 'I was a much younger man then. Young men tend to be intemperate.'

'Well, you have a bold face, sirrah, and no mistake. What I find hard to understand is why you sent me a privy letter about some matter of great import that you believe should be brought to my attention. Why should I care to hear a single word you have to say about anything?'

Spenser weighs his words before speaking. 'Because, Sir Robert, like your lord father, you care for Her Majesty's continued preservation.'

But Cecil is that rare man, a courtier who scorns flattery. His face hardens and the dagger point of beard pricks forward in Spenser's direction as he looks up at the taller man.

'If you've made all this fuss simply to have me read your writings on the present state of Ireland, you've wasted your time. I read it when you presented it to the Stationers' Register. I have no intention of advising Her Majesty that we starve the population of Ireland in order to make them biddable to her rule.'

'This has naught to do with my *View*, Sir Robert. It concerns another matter entirely.'

'Then you had best explain yourself, Master Spenser, before my limited tolerance for your scurrilous versifying is spent.'

'It has to do with the Spanish, Sir Robert. And it is of such importance to the safety of this realm that I *had* to be sure news of it reached no other member of the Privy Council.'

Knowing that Robert Cecil does not expect mute passivity from his intelligencers, Nicholas says, 'I believe Master Spenser means the Earl of Essex, Sir Robert.'

Spenser glances at him. '*Particularly* the Earl of Essex.'

A gleam of curiosity blooms in Robert Cecil's eyes.

'Go on.'

'I am right, am I not, when I say that the Cecils and the Devereuxs have what one might call "opposing views" on the present struggle with Spain?' Spenser says.

Cecil allows himself a grudging smile. 'Indeed. One might.'

'We all know,' says Spenser, gaining confidence, 'that the Earl of

Essex would fight the Dons through the gates of hell if he thought it would burnish his name. Whereas the Cecils – your late father, Lord Burghley, most prominently – are more...' He searches for the right words, ones that will not deplete the small credit he thinks he's managed to prise from Cecil, now that the matter of former insults has been laid aside. 'Shall I say, *practically* minded?'

Cecil considers this for a moment, his clever little face giving away nothing.

'My father's view – *my* view – is common knowledge at court, Master Spenser,' Cecil says at length. 'This continual war is a burden the realm can ill afford: armies to field in the Low Countries *and* in Ireland; a navy to build and sustain, lest the Dons send yet another armada against us... A fellow doesn't have to be the Lord Treasurer to see that after four bad harvests in a row, the conflict lays a heavy hand on England's prosperity. It would be best if it were ended.'

Spenser lets out a slow breath, like a man who's had a lucky escape. Then he says, 'What if, Sir Robert... it *could* be? What if a peace between the two realms were possible?'

Cecil's eyes narrow. 'That's nonsense. Only last year a second armada was attempted against us. Now that King Philip is dead, his son will seek to win the glory his father was denied.'

'Not if he could be persuaded otherwise.'

It is said with such confidence that Cecil is, for once, taken aback.

'What are you saying, Master Spenser? What does a poet know that the queen's Secretary of State does not?'

Again Spenser chooses his words with care.

'What if I were to tell you I have had secret correspondence from a certain faction in Madrid?'

Cecil eyes him with curiosity. 'Then I would call you a traitor,' he says slowly. 'And you know full well what England does with traitors.'

'But what if that faction feels – as do *you* – that this war has grown too burdensome to continue? What if the correspondence includes the proffering of an olive branch: what then?'

'*Does* it?'

'It will, Sir Robert – *if* it is delivered into the hands of the right person.'

Robert Cecil's eyes fasten onto Spenser like a falcon's talons on a particularly plump pigeon.

'You've come a long way, Master Spenser. Perhaps it would be only courteous to hear what you have to say.'

✠

It begins, Edmund Spenser says, with a man named Father Robert Persons. A man exiled from his homeland – a quarter-century past – because of his faith.

'We met as young men,' Spenser explains. 'He was at Oxford, I at Cambridge. We were not contemporaries; I was seven years the younger. But I admired Persons, even though his religion was abhorrent to me. When he was forced out of Oxford for being a Catholic, he fled abroad. He wrote to me on several occasions, but he never sought to proselytize. Eventually he sought refuge in Spain. There, he won permission from King Philip to establish a seminary – at Valladolid. But I suspect you probably know that.'

Mr Secretary Cecil would consider it a grave dereliction of his duty if he didn't, Nicholas thinks as he watches the interest shine in Cecil's eyes.

'We know the location of most of these Jesuit vipers' nests, Master Spenser,' Cecil confirms. 'Robert Persons is, indeed, a name known to us.' He gives Spenser a grim smile. 'It will be even more familiar, should he dare to return. An appearance on the scaffold tends to give a man a measure of public notability.'

'Father Persons has no intention of returning, Sir Robert.'

A note of contemptuous anger enters Cecil's voice. 'No, he just sends others. He leaves it to *them* to come here and attempt to corrupt the queen's subjects away from her religion.'

But that is not where Robert Persons's present energies are focused, Spenser explains quickly. While he would rather his chosen faith was the lawful religion of England, Father Persons has no desire to see his homeland devastated by a Spanish invasion.

'How noble of him,' Cecil interjects sourly.

More important than Robert Persons, Spenser explains, are the priest's close friends amongst the supporters and patrons of the seminary at Valladolid.

'A number of them can rightly claim to be Spain's most influential courtiers. And by no means are they *all* thirsty for English blood,' Spenser says. 'Some of them believe it would be better for both realms if a peace treaty could be achieved.'

'A peace treaty?' Cecil says. To Nicholas, it is the first time Cecil has appeared wrong-footed.

These courtiers, Spenser explains, are prepared to use their influence to convince the new king, Philip III, that he would gain more glory in God's eyes by bringing peace to a troubled world than by emptying the Spanish treasury in a futile conflict against the stubborn English – a conflict neither can win outright.

'Spain, too, has suffered poor harvests,' Spenser says, 'and English depredations upon the silver fleets coming home from the New World means that treasury will not be easily refilled. In plain words, Sir Robert, Spain is in the same hole as we are.'

For a while Robert Cecil remains silent. To Nicholas's eyes, his slight frame seems to contract as though gathering up the competing passions swirling within. Eventually Cecil asks, 'Tell me, Master Spenser – how does a peddler of verse come to know such things?'

For the answer to that, Spenser says, we must imagine ourselves back in Cork. Not the Cork of the present, a town beset by the travails of rebellion, but the Cork of some two years ago. Spenser is in the town to sign the lease for his property there. He has not heard from his friend in Spain for several years. Indeed, he has all but forgotten Father Robert Persons.

'The first letter to arrive was delivered by the master of a Portuguese carrack from Oporto, unloading sugar and spices at the Watergate.'

Spenser invites his little audience to imagine his surprise upon discovering the letter is from his former acquaintance. The subject is general: reminiscences of old times, old friends, a vague lament at the present state of the world.

And an invitation:

> *Reply, and tell me how things are with you, dear friend. Do not tarry. The bearer of this will stay in port not above seven days...*

And, indeed, Spenser does not tarry. Far from it. The letter intrigues him. But being a patriot, he is careful not to reveal in his reply anything that could be construed as aiding an enemy of the realm. If the letter were to be intercepted and read by the wrong people, a man could lose his head, his limbs and his vitals through such carelessness. Thus, when a second letter arrives two months later, he is wholly receptive to Father Persons's provision of a convenient cipher with which to encode all further communications.

Over the next several months the leisurely correspondence continues. Sometimes it is the Portuguese carrack that brings it. Sometimes it arrives on another of the many foreign vessels that ply their trade in Irish waters: an argosy from Genoa, carrying almonds, aniseed and brimstone; a barque from Flanders, its hold crammed with pewter, cabbages and capers; even one from

Scotland, carrying woven bed coverlets and fancy cushions for the comfort of the more successful Irish plantation owner and his lady.

The connection is clear to Spenser: every one of them could, at some recent time, have dropped anchor in a Spanish port.

It doesn't take long for Father Persons to move from mere reminiscence to more political matters:

> *How sad and displeasing to God that Spain and England are such determined enemies... Would not our Lord be pleased if men of peace might prevail?*

The most recent letters, reveals Spenser, have been more forthright. Father Persons – or whoever is standing in the shadows behind him – is certain that, with King Philip close to death and Queen Elizabeth halfway through her seventh decade, now is the time for men of character and godliness to look to the future:

> *And God be praised! Here in Spain, my dear and beloved friend, Edmund, there is one such fellow. I commend him to you most heartily. He is but one amongst several, a pious man of faith who wishes only that the bloodshed may cease, and that God's peace may again comfort the peoples of Spain and England, whatever their religious differences.*

His name: Don Rodriquez Calva de Sagrada.

✠

In the cold world beyond the window the snow is falling heavily now. Inside, the air has become heavy with the heat from the fire and the implications of Spenser's tale. Save for the crackling of the logs in the hearth and the poet's voice, all is silent. Even Robert Cecil has lost the compulsion to interject.

'Don Rodriquez was only one amongst several,' Spenser says. 'There are at least a dozen highly placed courtiers in the Escorial in Madrid who share his inspiration. They believe that as the crown of Spain passes from father to son, now is a propitious time to sound out the peace faction in England, to see if there is courage enough to bring this conflict to a close.'

Without waiting for Cecil's approval, Nicholas says, 'You speak of "was"— "Don Rodriquez *was* only one amongst several".'

'Yes.'

'Are we to understand that Don Rodriquez was aboard that wrecked vessel?' Cecil asks.

'He was escorting his daughter Constanza to her marriage in the Spanish Netherlands. It was the perfect opportunity to deliver the names of those nobles prepared to extend to England the hand of peace.'

'In person – to you?' Cecil suggests.

'Yes. Constanza was to act as translator. She would answer any questions I might have for Don Rodriquez. Apparently she speaks good English; Robert Persons was her tutor.'

'And then what?'

'Once the list was in my hands, I was to carry it, along with an assurance of good intent, to England.'

Robert Cecil asks, 'Where was this meeting to happen, Master Spenser?'

'At Kilcolman. Dr Shelby and Mistress Bianca have seen how remote it is. It was the perfect place.'

Nicholas says, 'No wonder you were so cautious when we arrived.'

Spenser turns to him, his face twisted with self-justification. 'I needed to assure myself that you really were Sir Robert's intermediary, and not in the pay of someone else.'

'By "someone else" I assume you mean the Earl of Essex.'

'Exactly. If His Grace had learned I was in communication with the Spanish, I could have given up any expectation of his continuing patronage. He would probably have considered me a traitor.' Spenser allows himself a grim smile. 'Indeed, it is likely my four quarters would now be nailed up and rotting on the city gates of Dublin, Cork, Wexford and Drogheda.'

'But there is someone you fear even more than Robert Devereux, isn't there?' Nicholas suggests.

Spenser lowers his eyes, the acknowledgement of a man who knows that courage is easier to find in verse than in real life. 'Yes,' he admits. 'I was beginning to think I could confide in you – until, on that beach, I heard of Mistress Bianca's former attachment to Sir Oliver Henshawe.'

'There was no *attachment*,' Bianca says indignantly.

'I was not to know that, Mistress,' Spenser replies, almost blushing.

Nicholas can hear in his head the words Spenser had spoken that day at the cove: *You should know that whatever happens on this island, the Earl of Essex hears of it first from Henshawe before all others... Be very cautious in what you say when that man is present...* He says to Spenser, 'Your sudden change of mood, when we were drying ourselves before the fire – I understand it now.'

Spenser gives him a slow, sad nod. 'You've witnessed for yourself what that man is capable of. How could I possibly have risked him learning why you had come to visit me at Kilcolman.'

Spenser is right, Nicholas thinks; Oliver Henshawe would rather burn in hell than see peace between Catholic Spain and Protestant England. 'Then why did you take us to the wreck?' he asks.

'If you were who you claimed to be – Sir Robert's man – you would at least be able to confirm that part of my story to him. I needed you to be a witness.'

'Instead you've had me wondering if it was you who struck me from behind – up in that cabin.'

Spenser gives a grim laugh. 'That was purely the result of your own temerity, Dr Shelby. I have not the robustness to climb up there as you did.'

Bianca scowls at Spenser with a venom that takes everyone by surprise. 'All this talk of a Spanish peace faction: you only want peace because you're afraid a Spanish invasion of Ireland would likely lay waste to your estates! That's the real reason, isn't it? It's nothing to do with the safety of the realm. It's all to do with your purse.'

For a moment Spenser just stares at her. Then he turns for succour to Robert Cecil.

'Sir Robert, this is intolerable. I will not be spoken to in such a manner by a *woman*.'

For the first time in his life, Nicholas observes Sir Robert Cecil attempt to stifle a spontaneous outbreak of laughter. As sternly as he can manage, Cecil says, 'Master Spenser, I have to tell you that if the queen's principal Secretary of State can get used to it, so you can you.'

'That body lying in the bluffs,' Nicholas says. 'The one with the ringlets and the severed fingers that you were looking at. Was *that* Don Rodriquez?'

'In all probability, yes. Robert Persons had described him to me.'

'I remember you looking at a casket lying beside the body. Did you think it might have contained the list? Because it was empty. Is it possible Henshawe has it?'

Spenser shakes his head. 'There was to be no physical list – at least not until Don Rodriquez was in my company. He's thought it too dangerous to commit the names to paper. They were in his head. I was looking into the chest for rings. I was to know him by a sapphire and two rubies. That would be his proof of identity. It was a forlorn hope, but I had to look.'

'You told us a moment ago that Constanza spoke good English, so that she could translate,' Nicholas says. 'Perhaps then she also knew the names.'

'That is possible. I was assured Don Rodriquez was a cautious man.'

'But we saw no female corpses on the beach, or in the bluffs.'

In the instant that Nicholas and Bianca's eyes meet in mutual understanding, Spenser says, 'I suppose she must have drowned. Poor child.'

And then Bianca speaks, quietly but to devastating effect.

'But what if she didn't drown?'

Cecil and Spenser stare at her as though she has just uttered some Delphic prophecy.

'The mantilla,' Nicholas says softly.

Then he remembers the injured boy he had treated in Cork, and his tale of how the woman whom Henshawe's men hanged had cursed them, warning them that the Virgin Mary had walked out of the sea to bring deliverance to Ireland. A wild fantasy born of fear and hatred or a piece of distorted gossip based on a kernel of truth?

'I found a black lace mantilla caught amongst some wreckage in the cove adjacent to the one in which the vessel was cast ashore,' Bianca continues carefully, as if a single wrong word might make the airy spirit she has conjured in her mind vanish before it can take on a more substantial form. 'We assumed it must have been part of a wedding trousseau – cargo perhaps.' She looks to her husband, a hint of triumph on her lips. 'But it could mean that Constanza survived the wreck. What if she walked out of the ocean – exactly like the Merrow? What if she's *alive*?'

PART 2

✠

Our English Caesar

18

There are parts of the shipwreck of which Cachorra has no memory. Those that do remain are seared into her mind. They play out in her dreams. Never in plainsong, always with an accompaniment: shrieking wind, waves slamming against rocks with the roar of a battery of cannon firing simultaneously. A cacophony of terror.

Sometimes when she wakes she can taste salt water in her throat. Then, if she clenches her fingers, she can feel the icy slide of rough wet rope as she struggles to free Constanza from the Devil's fishing net that had ensnared her. And above that din she can hear the voice of Don Rodriquez, the fear for his daughter turning his usually elegant Castilian into an animalistic howl of desperation. But as for the moment when the wave dragged the wreckage over the side – taking her and Constanza with it – that is an empty hole in her recollection, as deep and as dark as the ocean itself.

That she fought like a lioness to live, of that there is no doubt. And she has an impression – it must have been when she surfaced briefly – of being... *thrilled*?

Looking back, she understands that the imminent danger of dying triggered a much earlier memory: a memory of herself as a child, running out across the hot Hispaniola sand and into the breaking surf to help her fisherman father land his catch. That memory belongs to a child who was not then called Cachorra. That name had been taken from her when the Conquistadores came.

To her surprise, the heavy mat of rope and broken timber that carried them both overboard had proved their saviour. Buoyant, spread out on the water, it had become their life raft, carrying them on the surging current away from the *San Juan de Berrocal*.

When, at last, she had managed to drag Constanza and herself above the surface of the water, using every ounce of her strength to get them both at least partly onto the mat, she had time only to register the distant anguished face of Don Rodriquez staring at them from the quarterdeck of the wallowing, dismasted wreck before a new danger loomed: the prospect of being dashed to pieces against the knife-edged cliff that jutted out into the sea between two coves.

Again, the mat had saved them. It had acted in the manner of a sea anchor, slowing their progress, letting the heavy swell break through the lattice of debris as it charged towards the rocks, but also catching the return surge and keeping them from being dashed to pulp.

And then, somehow, Cachorra had known they were going to live.

If anyone had asked her in the strange days since then, she would have been unable to say exactly when she had felt a change in the motion of the sea. It could have been a few minutes or a few hours after they went over the side. But at some point she had become conscious that its power was no longer coming up from the depths, implacable and vast. It had slowed, become more languorous. It reminded her of one of the great fishes her father had struggled to land, his hands bleeding from his unshakeable grip on the line. It was as though the fight had gone out of it, and it wanted nothing more than to close its fishy eyes and sleep.

Eventually the mat had drifted onto a steep, shelving bank of rock that looked to her like a jumble of giant pewter plates. By that time the *San Juan* was lost from her sight. Mercifully, the thunder of the waves had drowned out its wrecking, along with the cries of those who had so temporarily survived. But it would be many days before Cachorra learned of their fate.

Letting go of the hemp, she had dragged Constanza onto the rim of the first level of rock, about an arm's length above the water. It had not been easy. Her shins and arms still bear the scars. But she had done it. She had saved them both.

It had taken her an age to calm Constanza's hysterical sobbing, but she had managed it. She had soothed her, sung lullabies to her, reminded her of the times they had giggled together at the more preposterous courtiers they had seen at the Escorial, like the old Duque de Navalpino, who had a wine-soaked nose the shape of a *berenjena*, and Conde Alejandro de Mandresa, whose leather hose squeaked when he strutted, making everyone think he was passing wind. Eventually Constanza's plump cheeks, gleaming with brine, had sagged into an expression that seemed to suggest acceptance, though Cachorra had judged it far too early to raise the matter of her father's likely survival. For a moment she had thought that a grateful Constanza was about to embrace her, to thank her for saving them both. But she had been wrong.

'Where is my mantilla?' Constanza had demanded petulantly. 'A lady of my quality cannot possibly go to the altar unveiled! My husband will consider me little better than a whore. How could you have let me lose it, you foolish girl?'

Exhaustion had made impossible the idea of wading to the safety of the beach. The water here was too deep, the rocks on either side still a danger until the tide dropped. Besides, the beach itself was some considerable way off, little more than a narrow strand of sand at the foot of a gorse-covered bluff rising steeply into a narrow defile. Cachorra had seen, halfway between their perch and the beach, a place where the floor of the inlet shelved up towards the surface, a line of white foam marking the spot. But beyond it the water was darker, deeper. She could remember enough of her childhood in Hispaniola to know the foolishness of second-guessing shifting sands, or underestimating riptides in shallow water.

She had looked upwards, hoping there might be a way to climb to the top of the headland. But her stomach had rebelled at the vertiginous rock face and the gulls wheeling in the sky high above. The salt water she had swallowed spewed itself over her already soaked needle-lace smock that Don Rodriquez had fetched from Venice for a price that would have bought an entire village in the Carib.

In the end she had decided there was no option other than to stay where she was. She would have to endure Constanza's blubbering and her own misery until the tide went out and she could safely wade ashore.

And that is what Cachorra had done. Shivering, dozing sporadically when the fatigue overwhelmed her, she had sought relief from Constanza's utterly pointless objections to their plight by listening to the crashing of the waves and trying to catch a distant echo of the breakers rolling onto a beach in the Hispaniola of her childhood.

It had been during one of these wide-awake dreams that she had seen, quite clearly, her older brother standing on the distant bluff, a horse grazing peacefully beside him. He had been staring out at her, as though he wasn't sure it was her, which was understandable – because Cachorra had been only six when she'd last seen him. She had wondered how he had managed to find his way to Ireland, and on a horse too. Cachorra had never seen a horse until the Spanish had come to her village, but she was sure they could not swim across an entire ocean. It had been that impossibility that had convinced her that what she was seeing was an illusion. It must have been conjured out of her mind by exhaustion, or some mischievous demon.

Only after shaking her head and wiping her soaked sleeve across her eyes – a foolish mistake on her part because the salt water made them sting even more – did she realize that he was still there, and that by all reason, and not least the paleness of his face, he wasn't her brother.

Still Constanza had refused to leave the rocks. Eventually Cachorra had grabbed her mistress by the edge of the stupid mantilla that Constanza had put on aboard the *San Juan*, determined to die a bride, if only in her dull little head. Then she had dragged Constanza bodily off the rocks. Even without wearing a waterlogged bridal grown, Constanza was not exactly the lightest jewel in the Escorial court.

When, at last, they waded ashore, the boy on the bluffs had stared at them as if they were magical sea creatures. He had turned out to be a rebel, keeping watch on the movements of a troop of English horse. And he had had enough wits about him to hurry them away to a safe hiding place. For that alone, Cachorra knows she will be for ever in his debt – if only because he had stopped her stumbling away towards the adjacent cove and seeing for herself the horrors that have festered in her darkest thoughts ever since.

✠

The door to the mean little byre opens, and Cachorra's memories flow out into the grey light outside like the retreating surf of her childhood.

'Are you rested, Mistresses?' the lad-who-is-not-her-brother says in lilting English. 'We are going to move you again. We cannot risk an English foraging party stumbling across this hiding place. The sooner we are on our way, the sooner we can deliver you into the safekeeping of the Earl of Tyrone.'

Cachorra nods to show her understanding. In the time since they waded ashore, she has had frequent cause to be glad that she, at least, had the curiosity to pay attention while her mistress received her English lessons from Father Persons. Indeed she had proved so adept at learning that Don Rodriquez arranged for Father Persons to give her additional tuition. 'Extra studies in religious devotion,' he had pretended to his daughter, lest she take offence at her maid being favoured. For his part, Father Persons had seen it as his mission to bring Christian learning to a benighted savage. Cachorra had had to beg Don Rodriquez to prevent the Jesuit from parading her before his companions at the seminary like a performing dog. But the effort is paying off now, because Constanza has so far resolutely refused to address anyone she considers of inferior position in anything but Spanish.

True to form, Constanza pipes an irritating whine:

'When are we going to Antwerp? My husband-to-be will be pulling his hair out. We must go to Antwerp. Where is my father?'

At least, thinks Cachorra, she's not complaining about the food again. She seems never to notice the look of shamed regret on the faces of those who bring them small bowls of oatmeal and hunks of bread. She seems wholly unaware that these people are sharing with them their own meagre provisions. Cachorra wonders how hospitable they would be if they were to learn the true reason why Don Rodriquez had come to Ireland. But that is something Cachorra is determined they must not learn. In the meantime, she can do nothing but wait for God – or her own cunning – to contrive a way of meeting the man her master has brought her and Constanza to this cold and dismal isle to meet.

And so once again, as she has done often since the wreck of the *St Juan de Berrocal*, Cachorra reverts to her role of servant – a role she has played since Don Rodriquez plucked her from the warm sand of a Hispaniola beach – and does her best to get the plump and resisting backside of Constanza Isabella Maria Calva de Sagrada off her bed and out into the rain.

19

To be alive but so unreachable – to Bianca it seems little more than just another form of death. To survive the ocean, only to drown in one's own invisibility. She holds the lace mantilla against her face, trying to catch a hint of perfume. All she can smell is dried salt water.

It is late evening. They have eaten pigeon pie at the Jackdaw, gossiped casually with friends as though the meeting with Cecil and Spenser had never happened, and returned home across the frosty Paris Garden to find their house now haunted by the imagined ghost of a young Spanish woman.

'Would you go back?' Bianca asks Nicholas speculatively as they sit together beside the fire. 'Would you try to find her?'

He thinks about this for a moment, elbow on knee, chin in hand. 'Even if I wanted to, how could I? If she's alive, the rebels probably have her. Even if they don't, Ireland is a big place.'

Slowly Bianca shakes her head, surprised by the hurt she feels for a woman she has never met and who at present exists only in her imagination. 'How frightened she must be,' she says, 'to have survived such a trial as a shipwreck... to fall amongst strangers in a land at war – to be so... so *lost*. I wonder if her husband-to-be has the slightest notion of what has befallen her?'

'Well, one thing is certain: judging by the way Constanza's presence has become known in at least *some* rebel circles, she hasn't told them Don Rodriquez came to Ireland to offer the chance of peace to the English.'

'What if she did?'

'They might throw her back into sea.'

'Nicholas! That's uncharitable.'

'The rebels need Spain's help to prevail against us. Even more so, now that Essex is appointed Lord Lieutenant. It looks very much as though, in Ireland at least, Spenser will get what he wants.'

'But you *would* try to find her – I know you too well.'

Her assumption brings a small, sad laugh to his lips. 'It will never happen. Hundreds will have perished in this rebellion already. There will likely be thousands more when Essex takes his army to Ireland. To save one lost woman amidst so much confusion' – a nod towards the window and the night beyond – 'why, it would be easier to save one of those snowflakes falling out there.'

'Robert Cecil could try, if he really wanted to,' Bianca suggests.

'How? He may have a few informers in the larger towns, places like Dublin, Waterford and Cork, but Ireland is a large and wild land. Much of it is now inaccessible to English forces. If Cecil attempts any kind of search, he'll give away his hand to Essex; and Essex is not partial to olive branches, certainly not Spanish ones. Besides, no one's going to risk sticking their heads into the wasps' nest in search of one Spanish maid.'

'Constanza could still stumble into English hands,' Bianca says plaintively. 'Then at least she might be ransomed.'

Nicholas dismisses the idea with a grunt. 'It happens, yes. But more likely is that she will simply disappear, swallowed up in the chaos. If she lives, she'll probably become someone's maid, or wife, or possession. Remember the European captives I told you about when I went to the Barbary shore? A few will still be hoping against hope that, one day, someone will ransom them. But the majority will have given up all hope of ever seeing home again.' He watches the snowflakes dashing themselves to destruction against the window, leaving only a glistening memory of their brief existence. 'No. The thought of it is just a fancy. Even Robert Cecil must admit that the chance Don Rodriquez was offering has been lost – along with him *and* his daughter.'

✠

'You've missed the excitement,' Ned Monkton tells Nicholas the next day as they sit together in the Jackdaw's taproom, watching Bianca and Rose fuss over little Bruno. 'There was a slayin' while you were away.'

'On Bankside? That's not exactly uncommon, Ned. Who was it?'

'Do you recall that young fellow you spoke to at the Southwark Fair?'

Nicholas searches his memory without success. 'I must have spoken to several people that day.'

'The one like a beanpole,' Ned prompts. 'The lad who'd answered the muster.'

The vague recollection of an awkward young lad with a schoolboy's glow on his cheeks hoists itself into Nicholas's consciousness. 'Oh, *him*. Yes, vaguely.'

'Well, he's dead.'

'Even less uncommon, given that he went to Ireland.'

'No,' says Ned, wondering how a man clever enough to be a physician can sometimes be so block-headed. ''E died *'ere*, on Bankside. They says it was a purse-cutting gone wrong. But I 'ad me doubts. Still 'ave, to be 'onest.'

'Are you sure we're talking about the same fellow? The one I'm thinking of should be in Ireland, with Sir Oliver Henshawe's company.'

Ned nods towards the hearth. 'Constable Osborne and the watch brought 'im one night a while back. Laid 'im down right there.'

At once Nicholas is back in Cork, kneeling beside Henshawe's boy with the wounded leg. He remembers the confusion in his eyes when he told him he would soon be home in Surrey.

My home is in Leinster... All the fellows I served with were mustered in Leinster.

And he remembers Oliver Henshawe's response when he'd asked him about the band mustered at Southwark:

You know how disorganized the Privy Council is... My brave fellows are still languishing at Chester, for want of a ship.

'So what was the lad doing in Southwark, when he should have been in Ireland?' he asks Ned, his interest suddenly pricked.

'That's what I wondered.'

'Did you ask anyone?'

'I asked that one-eyed muster ensign, Vyves.'

'And what was his reply?'

'That Godwinson – that were the poor fellow's name – was kept back to 'elp gather in the plate and powder needed for the company.'

'That's plausible enough, I suppose. Perhaps it *was* just a robbery that went awry.'

Ned rubs his chin, tangles of auburn beard spilling through his fingers. 'There was somethin' else that struck me as odd.'

'Go on.'

'Well, this Vyves 'as taken to drinkin' at the Jackdaw. An' a while before 'e died, young Godwinson came in. He looked real discomforted. Vyves 'ad this friend with him – Strollot by name, an alderman's clerk from Cornhill; looks like a sow what's chewed on a lemon. They all 'ad a little parley together. Then piggy-Strollot hands Godwinson some coin and 'e leaves. Few days later 'e gets brought in 'ere, cold as yesterday's brawn.'

'Do you believe these two men were somehow connected with the boy's death?'

'I 'ave no reason to think it, Master Nicholas, but my mind keeps wranglin' on it.'

'There could have been any number of reasons why they met together.'

'Aye, but what I can't get my 'ead around is that it was Strollot what paid 'im – not Vyves. That puzzled me. I mean, it was Vyves what was 'is master.'

'Perhaps he ran some errand, performed some service for Strollot. Maybe that's why it was Strollot who paid him.'

Ned gives Nicholas a look of pained uncertainty, a simple man doubting the value of his own thoughts.

'Out of curiosity, I went to the coroner's inquisition. I was right foxed to see Vyves an' Piggy 'ad got themselves appointed on the jury. I asked Strollot about knowin' young Lemuel – Godwinson, that is, or rather that *was* – but Strollot denied havin' met 'im. Vyves 'ad to correct 'im.'

'Maybe he simply made a mistake.'

Ned accepts the proposition equitably. He places his great palms flat on the table. 'Maybe 'e did. But I'd be more inclined to believe it if I didn't 'ave the impression neither of those two 'ad told anything but a lie since the moment they was spawned. It's just a feelin' I 'ave, a feelin' what won't go away.'

'Have you thought about speaking to a magistrate?'

Ned lifts his right hand and presents Nicholas with the underside of his thumb. The scarred *M* of the branding stands out like a signal. 'I don't care much for being near magistrates,' he says in a low rumble.

Nicholas colours. 'I sorry, I didn't mean to...' His voice trails off into silence. Ned's official punishment for his efforts to disprove the false case made against Nicholas – that he had been involved with the queen's late physician, Dr Lopez, in a plot to poison her – is a constant reminder to Nicholas of the price his friend has paid for loyalty.

'I'll speak to Constable Osborne,' Nicholas says. 'We'll see what Vyves and Strollot were up to on the night Godwinson was murdered.'

'Oh, they'll 'ave an alibi,' Ned says. 'Folks like them always do.'

✠

Robert Cecil has appointed the little house in the Paris Garden to be the place in which to drain Edmund Spenser of the last drops of intelligence in the matter of Don Rodriquez Calva de Sagrada. Cecil himself stays away, sending a procession of grey, legal-looking men to do the work for him. Bianca tolerates the intrusion, knowing there is little she can do to deny the principal Secretary of State. Besides, their presence seems to make Constanza's existence more corporeal. She imagines a waif-like beauty with wide eyes, lost, frightened and wandering in a vast, dripping forest like the one where the *Seanchaí* lived.

Nicholas, being a trusted Cecil intelligencer and the nearest thing to a witness, is allowed to attend these sessions. Sometimes he is even the subject. They are held either in the main hall or – if the weather is not too wintry – in the small orchard garden beside the house.

Describe the captain of the Portuguese carrack who brought the first approach from Robert Persons... Were the letters all in the same hand?... What position did Don Rodriquez hold at the Escorial?... Have you ever, even inadvertently, let slip anything in the presence of Robert Devereux or anyone connected to him that might hint – however tenuously – at your correspondence with the Royal College of St Alban, the Jesuit seminary set up by the traitor Robert Persons at Valladolid?

Spenser grows visibly irritated by the questioning, but Cecil's men are skilled. The more the poet protests, the more indulgently reasonable they become. Nicholas sometimes wonders who Cecil might send if Spenser ever decides not to cooperate. Then he has a clear image in his mind: the bulky, ungentle body of the servant, Latham, peering down on the palsied rebel prisoner in the cellar beneath Cecil House.

When not acting as a go-between, Nicholas returns to his physician's practice on Bankside. It does not pay, other than in chickens, fruit or labour. For income, he has Cecil's stipend. With the Jackdaw and her apothecary shop on Dice Lane, Bianca is the real money-earner. What Nicholas makes from the few richer patients he permits to visit him from across the river, he sends to his father at Barnthorpe.

As Christmas approaches the sessions with Spenser become less frequent. The poet has given up everything he knows that might be of use. The grey men from Cecil House find other subjects for their quiet persistence. For Bianca, this decline reminds her of mourners drifting away from a graveside. A grave in foreign soil, in which a young woman – still very much alive – stares up at the cold December sky, whispering softly and with fading strength for someone to come and pull her out.

There is ice on the Thames. Not thick enough for a Frost Fair, but rather a floating patchwork of giant white water-lilies. After three drunken visitors to Bankside attempt to walk back across the river, rather than take the bridge, and pay the price, the treacherous, shifting surface is left to the slithering gulls, ducks and swans. The clear water in the arches of London Bridge where the water-wheels turn, and along the outer curve of the river at Whitehall where the current flows fastest, is as dark as a demon's soul. The wherrymen steer their boats cautiously along the jagged channels between the floes, and charge the passengers huddled beneath their heavy winter cloaks an extra ha'penny each way for the trouble.

At Whitehall the mood is a strange mix of Christmas merriment seasoned with venom. On the surface, the courtiers go to chapel, dine, dance and disport themselves with customary polished elegance. But behind the façade, the Cecil and the Devereux factions spit their silent enmity at one another with every mannered exchange.

This is supposed to be a Christmas to remember, a celebration before the Earl of Essex leads an army of some sixteen thousand foot and a thousand horse to subdue the queen's rebellious subjects across the Irish Sea. The subsidy rolls have been consulted to raise the money to pay for it, the muster expanded to almost every county, and young men of quality with an eye to making a reputation by the sword – and more than a few older ones who have been languishing without gainful employment since the expedition to Cádiz – are flocking to Essex House to plead their case for inclusion.

On Christmas Eve one of Cecil's gowned ghosts arrives at the house in Paris Garden. He brings a summons to court. The Lord Chamberlain's Men are to perform Master Shakespeare's *The First Part of King Henry the Fourth*, and Dr and Goodwife Shelby are invited. Nicholas accepts graciously, though he knows that – just as they had when they'd attended *The Faerie Queene* – they will be standing behind several hundred far more important guests, all arranged according to their luminosity in the courtiers' cosmos, with only the brightest being allowed anywhere near the royal sun.

On the twenty-sixth day of December, as the bells of St Saviour's Bankside ring ten in the morning, under a sky as dull as the eyes of dead fish, Nicholas and Bianca take a boat upriver to the Whitehall public river stairs, leaving young Bruno in the care of Rose and Ned at the Jackdaw.

'Whitehall, Dr Shelby?' asks the wherryman, one of the tavern's regulars, with a conspiratorial laugh. 'Has the queen raised another boil on her royal arse that needs drawing?'

'If she has, she won't be allowing me anywhere near it, Jed Tubley.'

'We're going to see a play, by Master Shakespeare,' says Bianca as the oars send fragments of thin ice spinning on the water like shattered sugarloaf.

'Will the Earl of Essex be there?' says the wherryman, as though proximity to glory – even at this distance – might bring a little of it his way.

'I would guarantee it,' Nicholas replies.

'It must be a rare fine thing to be so close to England's new Caesar that you might reach out an' shake his hand,' Jed Tubley says in wonder.

'We'll be allowed no closer to the Earl of Essex than we will to the royal backside,' Nicholas assures him.

'Aye, well, even so, you've come up in the world, Dr Shelby – an' you, too, Mistress Merton.'

As Tubley puts his back into the rowing, Nicholas lets his hand trail in the water. The icy shock rushes up his arm, making him gasp.

You've come up in the world, Dr Shelby.

He looks back at the receding grey shape of the Mutton Lane water-stairs. In his memory, he sees himself as he was on a cold night eight years ago, walking those wet planks resolutely towards the edge, ready to let the river have him, driven to self-destruction by his failure to save his first wife, Eleanor, and the child she was carrying.

And the river would have had him, too, if the temperature hadn't been warmer than today, and his body strong... and if Bianca Merton hadn't made the decision to come to England and purchase a tavern on Bankside... and if her taproom boy hadn't gone down to the riverbank that morning to dispose of a pail of slops... *Ifs*. Nothing but *ifs*. What is life, he wonders, if not a careless cavalcade of happenstance?

Tubley delivers them to the Whitehall privy water-stairs – no public jetty for a passenger who is very nearly a queen's physician. Nicholas and Bianca present their invitations to one of the Lord Chamberlain's liveried ushers. Passing through the Shield Gallery, its walls hung with pasteboard escutcheons bearing mottos and aphorisms in praise of the woman whose majesty is the heart of this sprawling, labyrinthine place, they pass along narrow corridors, across courtyards like roofless dungeons, up winding stone staircases and into a world of priceless hangings, magnificently moulded plaster ceilings and floorboards so polished that they reflect the light from uncountable candles, like a still lake beneath a clear night sky.

In Whitehall's great hall rows of benches have been set out, cushioned for the rumps of the quality at the front, bare wood for the lesser mortals at the back. An excitable chirruping rises to the high ceiling set with gilded stars. But Nicholas's eyes are not drawn to the setting, or the fine dress of the men and women gathered here. His gaze is for Bianca alone. Her dark hair, tamed – for once – beneath a French hood, her boyish form flattered by the cut of a satin de Bruges orange gown that will require a significant outbreak of ill health amongst his wealthier patients to pay off, her complexion still blessed by the Italian sun, she is – for him – a treasure greater than he could find if he walked the halls and chambers of Whitehall Palace from now until the Thames itself turned to sand. Not even the imminent arrival of Gloriana herself can make him think otherwise.

The heavy floor-to-ceiling doors of the watching chamber swing open. The chattering dies, cut off as though an axe has fallen.

First comes a band of cherubic young choristers, trilling a sugary paean to majesty. Then the Bishop of London, Richard Bancroft, strides in, his white cassock and black stole at odds with a face that looks as though it has come straight from a drunken night in a Bankside dice-house. He is accompanied by a dean and four acolytes. Then a row of trumpeters, whose deafening fanfare makes Bianca wince.

When the queen herself walks in, behind a hedge of pearl-studded, silver-threaded silk, the hall falls silent, the echoing trumpet notes fading away in the far reaches of the plaster cornices. Then there is a great sighing, like a sudden wind through a forest, as three hundred sets of clothes rustle over three hundred genuflecting bodies. As she passes, Nicholas notices her eyes dart momentarily towards him. Their cold appraisal takes no more than an instant. Then the thin, painted lips crack the plaster-white face in the briefest of tiny smiles. Staring at her back, Nicholas is unsure whether it was a smile of approval or a marking for later censure. But Bianca has seen it too. Her arm slides around his, pulling it against her body in a congratulatory hug.

In Elizabeth's wake glide her privy councillors and senior courtiers. Mr Secretary Cecil bustles in with his uneven gait, like a man about to put his shoulder to a stuck door. He nods to Nicholas, who makes a second formal knee. Bianca gives him a grudging little dip that looks more like a passing spasm of cholic than a curtsey. Whispering, Nicholas identifies the two men with Cecil. The first is Henry Brooke, the eleventh Baron Cobham, son of the former Lord Chamberlain who gave his patronage to the troupe of players performing this afternoon. Cobham is a dull-looking man about Cecil's age. He towers over the diminutive Principal Secretary like a particularly placid bear over his bearward; all that's missing is the chain. The second man is about decade older than the other two. He has a thin, contemplative face, though he looks untroubled for a fellow who's just lost his Irish plantations; but then the world knows that nothing short of the Second Coming could discomfort Sir Walter Raleigh.

And in hot pursuit of the Cecil faction come Robert Devereux's snapping leash-hounds. Essex himself strides in like a young Charlemagne, his hose gartered, his cloth-of-gold half-cape swishing fetchingly despite there being not so much as a breath of a breeze because all the windows are shuttered. With him are his stepfather, Sir Christopher Blount, whom Essex has been trying, without success, to have appointed to the queen's Council for Ireland, and the young Earl of Southampton, his preferred choice for General of Horse in the coming campaign. Bianca is intrigued when Nicholas points Southampton out to her. Who can fail to be spellbound by such a fair fellow? Especially when all London knows that the gentle face with its resplendent curtain of flowing locks is a disguise for a brawler who's tupped one of the queen's ladies-in-waiting, put an egg in the henhouse and – worst of all in the eyes of his monarch – married the girl.

Behind Southampton comes a clutch of poets and versifiers favoured by Essex House, amongst them Edmund Spenser. He walks by without so much as a nod. Bad manners or self-preservation? Nicholas wonders.

The queen sits. Everyone else sits. Onto the stage comes dear old Will Kemp, the most popular player the Lord Chamberlain's Men possess. He's a big fellow, almost as large as Ned Monkton, but without the fearsome mask. He bows deeply to the queen, makes a clever opening address and the play begins.

Nicholas finds himself as entertained as any other in the watching hall, no matter their status – right to the moment when Will Kemp, playing the role of the fat knight Falstaff, makes his speech about thc quality of the men he has mustered to the service not of Elizabeth, but of the fourth King Henry, in preparation for the battle of Shrewsbury:

'Slaves as ragged as Lazarus... No eye hath seen such scarecrows... I'll not march through Coventry with them, that's flat...'

Mindful of the derision he's heard in the Jackdaw for the quality of the present muster for Ireland, Nicholas looks around to see if the audience is going to laugh. But in the presence of the queen and the Privy Council – nothing. Just the occasional knowing turn of a head to a partner or a companion. He wonders if Master Shakespeare is going to get his knuckles rapped later by the Lord Chamberlain and the Master of the Revels.

But in his own mind, Nicholas is seeing again the fellows he tended in the makeshift hospital in Cork, and the lad who should have been with them – the lanky, unmartial Lemuel Godwinson, murdered by persons unknown on Bankside. And while he does so, something makes the hairs on the back of his neck stand up. A sense of being watched.

He looks around at the attentive audience, their faces all fixed on the performance. Except one.

On the last row of benches, where the latecomers have sneaked in unobserved, he catches a movement. A head turning away from him. Evading his gaze. A familiar head. As handsome as Southampton, but far more murderous by comparison. A death's head, Nicholas cannot help thinking, as Sir Oliver Henshawe returns his attention towards the stage.

20

When the performance is over the men from the Office of the Revels strike down the few pieces of painted scenery and carry away the benches. The hall is readied for the part Nicholas dreads most: the dancing. He tries his best. With Bianca resolutely holding back her laughter, he murders a galliard and does serious injury to a pavane. With the best grace he can muster, he accedes to the requests of other men to dance with his wife. For the two Williams, Shakespeare and Kemp, he is happy to withdraw. He knows them from their regular visits to the Rose theatre, and their accompanying diversions to the Jackdaw. Kemp has that unexpected grace that is sometimes the secret of large men. He leads Bianca through an athletic volta, to the acclaim of the other dancers. Even the queen applauds. Nicholas catches with his eyes, if not his ears, her brief aside to Robert Cecil. From the direction of her gaze and the softening of her mouth he can tell she is asking after the beauty in the orange satin de Bruges. It makes his heart swell.

Even Robert Cecil requests a *fedelta d'amore*. Half the size of Kemp but with no less grace on the dance floor despite his ill-made body, at the end he wins Bianca's unstinting applause. As for the others who request his wife's favour – Walter Raleigh, George Carey, the Lord Chamberlain, a lecherous old satyr old enough to be her father, and Southampton, who seems in his own mind to be the only one dancing – these Nicholas stomachs as charitably as he can. Until the Earl of Essex sweeps over.

Making a laborious bow to Bianca, Devereux asks Nicholas for his permission to dance a measure with the most gracious and comely lady in the chamber – saving the queen's presence. '*If* it meets with your indulgence, Dr Shelby.' His voice manages to be both oily and arrogant at the same time.

Bianca throws Nicholas a questioning glance. It's obvious she's not sure what to do. But what husband can deny England's new Caesar?

Nicholas reassures her with a brief nod. Then he says something in acquiescence to Essex that jumbles in his mind the moment the words are out, and which he then spends some time trying to recall, in case what he actually said made him sound like a cuckold. Giving up, he looks around the hall for Edmund Spenser. He spots him talking to an official from the Office of the Revels. Mindful of the poet's reluctance to be seen by the Essex faction conversing with anyone connected with Robert Cecil, Nicholas hails a passing liveried servant to deliver a discreet message. Then he leaves the hall by a narrow stone arch that gives onto one of the small quadrangles that he noticed on his journey from the Whitehall water-stairs.

Outside, the air is cold and misty, the daylight barely penetrating between high brick walls dotted with clumps of moss. Nicholas thinks he could be standing at the bottom of a deep cistern from which the contents have slowly leaked away. The place smells of sour, watery decay. He suspects the servants use it as a latrine.

'You didn't tell me Henshawe was back in London,' Nicholas says when Spenser joins him a few moments later.

'I didn't know myself, until this morning,' Spenser tells him. 'He arrived yesterday, carrying privy dispatches for His Grace the earl.'

'I caught him watching me. Do you think he has any suspicion that you've had an audience with Mr Secretary Cecil?'

'If he had, I dare say I would not be here. I'd either be under interrogation at Cecil House or in the Tower.'

'I seem to recall Sir Robert telling me that you were once in charge of the muster in Munster. Is that true?'

'"In charge" is too grand a description, Dr Shelby. I was appointed one of the commissioners for the muster in that country. Why do you ask?'

'Merely a passing interest – it was just a scene in the play, the one in which Falstaff decries the quality of the troops levied for the king's army.'

Spenser laughs. 'Yes, nothing changes, Dr Shelby, does it?'

'No, I suppose not. I was wondering if you knew where Sir Oliver Henshawe raised his company.'

'I fear I cannot help you. I've taken no part in the recent musters. Why do you ask?'

'No matter. Merely a passing interest.'

'If it's their quality that concerns you, I wouldn't worry. My lord Essex will soon have affairs properly in hand.'

'I'm sure he will,' Nicholas says, hearing a diplomat's practised insincerity in his own voice and wondering where it came from.

'By the way, Dr Shelby, has Sir Robert decided what to do about Constanza Calva de Sagrada?' Spenser asks, dropping his voice to a whisper.

'I don't think there's much he *can* do,' Nicholas says. 'Perhaps he will ask you to send a message to Robert Persons in Valladolid, asking the peace faction to send another emissary. Mr Secretary Cecil doesn't confide such matters to me, I'm afraid.'

'If there's nothing else you require of me, Dr Shelby, I'd best return to the revels,' Spenser says. 'I'd rather not be discovered holding secretive privy meetings with Mr Secretary's physician – if it's all the same to you.'

After Spenser has gone, Nicholas waits a few minutes before re-entering the hall. He soon spots Bianca fending off a group of ladies-in-waiting, all suddenly eager to make the acquaintance of the unknown woman who had danced with the Earl of Essex and caught the queen's eye. They remind him of a gaggle of geese after the corn has been scattered.

'You look flushed, Husband. Have you been engaging in an assignation outside while I was dancing with His Grace?' Bianca says, touching his cold cheek with her fingers.

'More to the point, did the noble earl sweep you off your feet?' Nicholas asks as he draws her away.

'What a strange man,' she replies. 'It was like conversing with a locked wardrobe: a polished front, sharp edges, and you come away wondering what's hidden inside.'

'I mean, was he a good dancer?' Nicholas lies.

'You wouldn't expect otherwise, would you?'

'When he asked to dance with you, he called me by my name. That's a worry. It means he remembers me.'

'Yes, in a manner of speaking. He asked me if you weren't the physician who was accused with poor old Dr Lopez of trying to poison the queen.'

'God's nails! What did you tell him?'

'I told him he *should* remember you. I reminded him that four years ago you spent several uncomfortable hours locked in a room at Essex House waiting to be arraigned for attempted regicide – before I persuaded Robert Cecil to get you out.'

'And what was his reply?'

'He said he wasn't responsible for miscarriages of justice. He said, if you wanted an apology you should seek it from the Attorney-General.'

'It's just that I had hoped he might have forgotten.'

Bianca leans against him, her breath warm on his cheek. 'Well, fret not, Husband. In truth, I think he's rather impressed with you.'

'Impressed? How? Other than the Lopez affair, Essex doesn't know me.'

'Apparently Oliver Henshawe has been singing your praises.'

'Henshawe? *Really?*'

'About what a fine physician you are.'

'Oh.'

'I thought you'd be pleased. I've been afraid you'd end up getting into a quarrel with Oliver – punching his pretty face. Or, worse, challenging him to a duel.'

'I'm Nicholas,' he says, laughing, 'not the Earl of Southampton. Brawling and duelling are *his* diversions.'

'And *Nicholas* can lay aside any jealousy he might feel for Oliver Henshawe, can't he?'

'He can, sweet,' he says, kissing her briefly and caring not a jot about decorum. 'Because now he has the Earl of Essex to snarl at.'

Bianca leans further into her husband, feeling the reassuring warmth of him, the sturdiness of a yeoman's son still in him. 'Look on the bright side,' she says closely into his ear. 'You might not be as fine a dancer as Robert Devereux, Husband, but nor do you have a reputation to lose in Ireland.'

✠

Twelfth Night, and a sharp, sleety rain falls on Bankside. It advances and retreats along the narrow lanes in bitter little skirmishes, battering against the Jackdaw's foggy windows like fingernails drumming on the stretched skin of a tambour. Inside, a goodly fire is raging in the hearth, keeping hot a great cauldron of steaming wassail. Timothy, the taproom lad, is tuning his lute for the evening's festivities. Bianca is helping Rose to prepare mince pies in the kitchen. In the taproom Ned Monkton is polishing a pewter tankard on the sleeve of his jerkin. He holds it up to check his distorted monster's reflection in the metal.

'Wonder if 'e'll be in tonight,' he says out of nowhere.

'Who?' enquires Nicholas, laying aside his personal copy of Professor Fabrizio's *Pentateuchos chirurgicum*, given to him by the author to mark his departure from the Palazzo Bo medical faculty at Padua.

'That one-eyed muster ensign with the stringy grey 'air – Ensign Vyves,' says Ned, giving Nicholas an alarming squint. ''E's not been in since you an' Mistress Bianca returned. I don't often take against people on a whim, but there's somethin' about that rogue what troubles me. I'd be int'rested to know what you make of 'im.'

'Come now, Ned,' Nicholas says, laughing. 'You must have heard about the great hero raising a grand army to win glory in Ireland? Essex can't do all that by himself. Master Vyves will have been too busy combing the hamlets and villages for men to muster for Henshawe's company.'

'Well, wherever 'e is, the Devil's luck to 'im,' says Ned, setting the tankard on the shelf with all the others. 'I'd sooner be hanged in London for stealing a chicken than slain in Ireland 'cause my belly was empty on account of the bad 'arvest.'

'Be patient. If he's going to come, it will be tonight.'

'An' 'ow does you fathom that, Master Nicholas? 'Ave you've drawn 'is stars – one of them 'oroscopes what physicians draw up when they make a 'nosis?'

Nicholas gives him a frown that might be considered censorious, were it not accompanied by the hint of a smile. 'You know I don't hold with that, Ned. I'm banking on the fact that the Jackdaw will be full tonight – plenty of customers who haven't heard his line about losing an eye at Cádiz.'

'You could be right,' Ned says approvingly. 'I don't s'pose 'e's got many other places to be on Twelfth Night. 'E don't strike me as the sort to be spendin' it in the bosom of a doting family.'

And with that, he picks up another pewter tankard to buff, leaving Nicholas to his book.

✠

As darkness falls, the Jackdaw begins to fill. For the celebration of Epiphany, Bianca has splashed out on half a sugarloaf, grating it into hot ale with ginger, cloves and butter to tease customers away from the Good Husband and the Turk's Head. It seems to be working. Children from the nearby lanes are playing Hoodman Blind, cannoning around the tables and getting under the adults' feet, earning themselves cuffed ears and kicked shins for Twelfth Night presents.

When Barnabas Vyves walks in, shaking the rain from his lockram cloak, Ned glances across to where Nicholas and Bianca are sitting in conversation with the wherryman Jed Tubley and his family. Nicholas, too, has spotted him.

The muster ensign takes off his cloak, draping it over one arm. He's wearing a quilted red military sleeveless jerkin, patched and stitched, over his civilian shirt, and a belt with a leather powder flask and a metal bullet-mould hanging from the strap. He could scarcely have advertised himself better if he had walked in wearing a full suit of plate armour.

Nicholas is in no hurry. He lets Vyves settle himself into a window seat, noticing how the man scans the faces in the tavern. Nicholas can tell he's not assessing their suitability for the muster; his eyes linger on too many men well past fighting age.

It doesn't take long for someone to notice Vyves's empty eye socket. Nicholas watches as the ensign opens the flap of his powder flask, then upends it over one waiting palm to reveal not a cascade of black powder, but a single farthing – half what he requires to purchase a jug of ale. He points to his empty orbit and adopts a expression of stoic but noble suffering. Though Nicholas cannot hear the words above the general hubbub, he identifies a mouthed 'Cádiz' and an 'Essex'.

The stranger orders a tankard from the counter and joins Vyves at his bench. While they drink, Nicholas contrives to take surreptitious glances at the pair without Bianca or the Tubleys noticing. The two men could be players acting their parts, he thinks: Vyves the wounded old campaigner with hair-raising tales to tell, the other the wide-eyed neophyte basking in reflected glory, nodding now and then in sympathy or admiration.

When the listener has finished his ale, and presumably heard enough to satisfy his curiosity, he returns to his companions. Nicholas excuses himself with a throwaway line about needing to speak to a patient and walks over to Vyves's table.

'You must be wishing you could make the Dons pay for such a grievous hurt,' he says, opening the conversation.

Vyves looks up, a venal gleam in his single eye at the arrival of such an easy prospect.

'Oh, fear not, good sir. Barnabas Vyves gave as good as he got.' Then he adds, as an afterthought, 'Do I *know* you? You look familiar.'

Nicholas gives a casual laugh of good-fellowship. 'Spend any time on Bankside and soon everyone looks familiar. Can I stand you an ale? It's the least I can do for a veteran of Her Majesty's wars.'

'I'll drink with any man what hates the Dons.'

Nicholas waves at one of the taproom servants and makes a sign for two jugs of knock-down. 'Where was it – the Low Countries?' he asks Vyves, looking uncompromisingly at the empty eye socket.

'Nay, at Cádiz, with the Earl of Essex.'

'The very man to settle the queen's quarrel with the Earl of Tyrone – our English Caesar.'

'There's none better she could send,' agrees Vyves enthusiastically.

The ale arrives. Nicholas raises his tankard in a salute.

'You're a patriot and a grand fellow,' says Vyves, returning the compliment. The single eye peers over the rim of his pot. 'Are you *sure* we haven't met before?'

Nicholas heads him off with a question of his own. 'I expect you're looking forward to standing in the ranks behind His Grace.'

Vyves lets out a throaty laugh. 'I've served my time in the breach, thanks all the same. Besides, I have work to do here in England. Important work. I'm in charge of the muster for Sir Oliver Henshawe's company.'

Nicholas does his best to look suitably impressed. 'That's still dangerous work, Master Vyves. I heard one of his men was murdered here, before Christmas.'

'Aye, young Godwinson. A terrible thing, an' no mistake.'

'A brawl, perhaps?'

'A purse-cutting. Silly sod tried to resist.'

'You were there?' Nicholas asks, as casually as he can manage.

'Gracious, no! That night I was drinking in the Turk's Head, with Gideon Strollot. He can vouch for me – he's an alderman's clerk.'

'Vouch?' repeats Nicholas. 'Marry, Master Vyves! I wasn't asking you to defend yourself.'

Vyves leans across the table, a thin cyclops with a dirty grey mane. 'I've seen you before, I *knows* I have.'

Nicholas ignores the statement. 'Whose company did you say you were mustering for?'

'Sir Oliver Henshawe's. A great warrior and a fine gentleman.'

'Is he in Ireland at present?'

'No, he's here in London – advising the Earl of Essex. What do you want to know for?'

'And his company, is *that* in Ireland?'

'Bringing the queen's mercy to the rebels,' Vyves assures Nicholas. Then, with a deep, cruel laugh, '*If* you gets my meaning.'

Nicholas says in a mild, observational tone, 'I've encountered some of Sir Oliver's fellows – in Ireland.'

'You've been in Ireland?' Vyves asks, a note of suspicion in his voice.

'They were all locally mustered Irish, or English settlers. Not a recruit from Surrey amongst them, or not that I could tell.'

Vyves shakes his head. The lank grey locks swirl around his thin shoulders like the rain falling outside. 'You must have been mistaken,' he says. 'I'm told the mists of that isle can sometimes rob a man of his faculties.'

'Perhaps you're right. Perhaps it was another captain's company I was thinking of,' says Nicholas, feigning a look of embarrassed confusion.

And in response Vyves's face lights up with what Nicholas could swear is relief. 'When was it you spoke to these fellows?' he asks.

Nicholas pretends to search his memory. 'I think it would have been sometime in November. Why?'

'Well, that explains it,' Vyves announces, as though he's solved a puzzle that would have defeated Archimedes. 'The muster we sent to Ireland got held up in Bristol, for lack of ships to carry it.'

'I'm sure that was it,' says Nicholas pleasantly, even as he hears Henshawe's answer when he'd asked the same question in Cork: *You know how disorganized the Privy Council is... My brave fellows are still languishing at Chester, for want of a ship...*

Disorganized the Privy Council may well be, thinks Nicholas. But not so disorganized as to send one part of the same muster to Bristol, an eight days' march west, and the other to Chester, at least thirteen days from Southwark and in a quite different direction.

Nicholas is about to call Vyves out on the error when Ned Monkton walks past carrying a jug of stitch-back to an adjacent table. The muster ensign looks up at him. And then at Nicholas.

'That's *it!*' he says, almost shouting. 'You're the one who was with Master Monkton at the Southwark Fair' – a jab of one dirty thumb into the empty eye socket – 'the saucy rogue who tried to gainsay my Cádiz medal.'

Cursing his ill luck, Nicholas tries to forestall disaster. 'I'm sure you mistook my words for insult, Master Vyves. I meant no—'

But it's too late. Looking around the taproom as though fearing an ambush, Vyves has now spotted Bianca.

'An' *that*'s the comely maid you were with that day! I'd remember *her* if I recalled naught else.' His single eye glares malevolently at Nicholas. 'You're baiting me, whoever you are. You're playing a match with a poor fellow wounded in Her Majesty's service. I'll have none of it!'

Kicking back his stool, Vyves waves his folded lockram cloak at Nicholas as though trying to ward off some great evil. He is on his feet and halfway to the door almost before Nicholas has left the table.

As Vyves barges out, he collides with someone attempting to enter. For a moment they meet in an unseemly and confused embrace. Then Vyves disappears into the night, leaving Nicholas to stare at the young man trying to compose himself after being unceremoniously pushed against the jamb. A young man in possession of a set of fine golden locks, if the Christmas rain hadn't plastered them to the pale cheeks of his gentle face.

'Dr Shelby,' says Piers Gardener with evident relief. 'I've been half-drowned trying to find this tavern. I asked for you all around St Paul's. I even went to the Stationers' Hall. They hadn't heard of you. I'm beginning to think you weren't telling me the truth about your visit to Edmund Spenser.'

21

Whether it is said in jest or in deadly earnest, it leaves Nicholas speechless.

'Aren't you going to make me welcome?' Gardener asks, whatever doubts he may just have expressed seemingly forgotten. He gives Nicholas the broad smile of the utterly innocent.

'Of course, forgive me,' Nicholas says hurriedly. 'God give you good eventide, Master Gardener. I must confess you are the last person I expected to walk into the Jackdaw on Twelfth Night.'

To his relief, Bianca appears at his shoulder.

'Master Piers, what a happy surprise! Whatever are you doing in London?'

'There has been a change of Surveyor of the Victuals, now that the Earl of Essex is to take the field,' Gardener says. 'Sir George Beverly has been appointed in Ireland. I have come with his letters to the earl. It is the first time I have been in London; nay, in all of England. It is such a *large* city. I have never seen such a place. I can walk from one side of Dublin to the other in the time it takes the Christchurch bell to ring an hour's quarter. Here I feel I might walk all day and not traverse it. How do you not all get lost in such a place?'

'We find a tavern and ask for directions, Master Gardener,' Nicholas explains with a smile.

Bianca readies a table and orders hot wassail to take the chill out of Gardener's cheeks. 'When we were with you last in Ireland I recall you were hoping your position might be made permanent,' she says. 'I take, from your presence here, that your wish has been granted.'

'Seven pounds per annum,' says Gardener proudly.

'You mentioned you'd come from St Paul's, asking after me amongst the Stationers' Company,' Nicholas reminds him.

'Aye, they seemed not to know of you,' says Gardener. 'I'm sure that when we met in Dublin you said you were visiting Master Spenser on the guild's behalf. Was I mistaken?'

Nicholas feels himself colour. He prays that, in the low light from the hearth and the candles, Gardener hasn't noticed. 'It was a privy matter,' he says, trying not to hurry his words, 'regarding Master Spenser's rather controversial pamphlet on the present situation in Ireland. Only the president of the guild and a few of his closest officers knew about my journey.'

'Ah, that explains it,' says Gardener, beaming as though a heavy burden has been lifted from his conscience.

Bianca enquires where he's lodging. A storeroom floor somewhere deep in Whitehall, he tells her – a place he can never find by the same route twice in a row. She insists he at least spends tonight at the Jackdaw; there is still one straw mattress free in the communal lodging room on the top floor beneath the attic, and enough venison pottage left to nourish a slight but hungry frame. He asks the price. Bianca assures him there isn't one, not for the man who saved their lives in Ireland.

While Gardener warms himself before the fire, they press him for news. The hospital in Cork is still functioning, they learn, though mercifully the winter weather has kept it mostly free of men wounded in battle with the rebels. The word in Dublin is that the Earl of Tyrone is holed up in Ulster, awaiting the onslaught of Essex and his army in the spring.

'Have you seen Spenser yet?' Nicholas asks. 'He's very much the pride of the Essex faction at present.'

A fleeting shadow passes across Gardener's face, a sudden hardening of the smooth features, a momentary dying of his former goodwill. And then, in an instant, placidity is restored. He smiles. 'I have not yet had the pleasure. Perhaps when the festivities are over.'

Bianca turns the conversation to the trivial, letting Gardener find his ease in his new surroundings. Only when he has emptied his bowl of pottage and drunk his wassail does she asks casually, 'Tell us, Master Piers, before you left were you still often on the road?'

'Endlessly, Mistress,' Gardener replies, adopting the look of a man asked to attempt the impossible. 'But in Ireland, as you will have discovered when you were there, the term "road" is a tricky one to pin down.'

She allows him a sympathetic smile. 'And did you still rest at night in those extraordinary places? I'm thinking of the *Seanchaí*.'

'Aye, I prefer them to the settlers. They are good folk, Mistress. Their kind were in Ireland centuries before even the Conqueror's people went there. The land would have no soul without them.'

Nicholas thinks he knows where Bianca's questions are leading. He casts her a cautionary glance.

'I recall that night we heard the *Seanchaí* tell us the tale of the Merrow, the woman who walked out of the sea to entrance menfolk,' she continues. 'It was a fine tale. I fear all we can offer you here is Timothy and his lute.' A thought strikes her. 'The Morris men will dance, tomorrow. That's always... engaging.'

'I shall be grateful merely to be in your company, Mistress,' Gardener says gallantly.

'I don't suppose, Master Piers, that the tale of the Merrow has surfaced again, has it? – in those places you visit on your lonely travels.'

'The Merrow?' he replies, raising an eyebrow.

'Any claims of a beautiful woman walking out of the sea to enchant all those silly men? You haven't heard any rumours like that during your peripatetic wanderings?'

And for a moment, before Gardener answers that no such tales have reached his ears, Nicholas could swear he sees the fleeting return of suspicion to their guest's innocent gaze.

✠

The following day Piers Gardener returns to Whitehall. Nicholas bids him farewell with mixed emotions. He cannot lay aside the feeling that Gardener's visit to the Jackdaw was not made solely out of friendship. True, in the time it had taken to ride from Dublin to Kilcolman, he and Bianca had struck up an easy companionship with their guide, but it had not been the sort of friendship that might entice a man to walk from Whitehall to Bankside in the pouring rain on a cold Twelfth Night. Just how speculative, he wonders, were Gardeners' enquiries around St Paul's and at the Stationers' Company? Even as he catches a glimpse of Gardener in the lane beyond the window, striking out in the direction of the southern gatehouse of London Bridge, he can hear again the words that had caught him so off his guard:

They hadn't heard of you... I'm beginning to think you weren't telling me the truth...

Had Gardener really been joking?

The memory jolts Nicholas back to the previous night, and his conversation with Barnabas Vyves. He goes in search of Ned Monkton, finding him in the brew house behind the tavern yard.

'You're right, Ned,' he says, 'Vyves is lying through his teeth – but what *about* I can't begin to fathom.'

He recounts how Vyves had claimed that if Sir Oliver Henshawe's company wasn't in Ireland, then it was held up at Bristol, and how Henshawe had told him the recruits were waiting for transport at Chester.

'Something is going on, Ned, but I'm damned if I know what.'

'You think Vyves was involved in poor Godwinson's murder?' Ned asks, effortlessly rolling a barrel across the flagstones as though it were made of pigskin and full of air.

'If he was, he has an alibi – in his friend Strollot. And I would guess if we were to ask Strollot, he'd say Vyves can vouch for him. Are you sure there were no witnesses to the boy's killing?'

'Nay, Master Nicholas. Constable Osborne and 'is night-watch found the poor lad on the corner of the Mutton Lane shambles and Black Bull Alley. He was dead when they found 'im. Not 'nother soul in sight, or so they said.'

'Well, Ned,' Nicholas says reluctantly, 'perhaps we'll just have to accept that it was what they claim: a purse-cutting that went awry.'

Ned dusts off his huge forearms. 'Aye, well, the fact remains that Barnabas Vyves and Gideon Strollot are kings – kings amongst arseworms. An' naught can make me think otherwise.'

And with that, he goes back to his labours.

✠

It is Plough Monday – the first Monday after Twelfth Night – when the ploughs are blessed and prayers given for the summer to come. Bianca always ensures the Jackdaw is part of the accompanying festivities; in the taproom, shepherds, farm labourers, cowherds and drovers are as common as wherrymen or players from the Rose theatre. If she opens the bedroom window of the Paris Garden lodgings and leans out of the jutting first floor she can just about see the millpond beside the Pudding watermill. In spring she can hear cattle lowing in the fields below the pike pools. The southern edge of Bankside is where the city ends and countryside begins.

Save for a few outbreaks of raucous intemperance, the day passes without incident. Until the following morning, two hours before dawn. when the bucolic tranquillity of the Paris Garden is shattered.

The hammering at the street door brings Bianca instantly out of a repetition of the dream she had at Kilcolman in which little Bruno waits fretfully for his Merrow mother to wade out of the sea to comfort him – a task that is beyond her because her feet keep being sucked down into the ooze of the seabed. She shakes the dream out of her head. The noise, she thinks, must be loud enough to wake the Archbishop of Canterbury from his slumber in Lambeth Palace, two miles upriver past the Lambeth marshes. She lets out a stream of invective, involuntarily delivered in Italian.

It does nothing to stem the din. Believing that someone must be in desperate need of Nicholas's physic, she delivers herself a stern rebuke and makes her way cautiously downstairs, conscious of Nicholas's grumbled protestations as he dresses. Taking the heavy key from its hook beside the street door, she turns the lock – and finds herself blinded by the flames of a torch held by a man whose black garb makes him all but indistinguishable from the night outside.

'Where is Dr Shelby?' a voice demands to know.

'I'm here,' says Nicholas. 'What's the matter?'

'Come with us, please, Dr Shelby. Sir Robert has need of you.'

In the torchlight, Nicholas can now make out one of the men from Cecil House, a member of the team of inquisitors who'd been here at the Paris Garden lodgings before Christmas. He's accompanied by two others, also vaguely familiar. His sleepy mind takes a moment to realize they must have come by private wherry, landing at the Falcon stairs.

'Is Sir Robert ill?' he asks. 'Is it his children?'

'Sir Robert is in good health,' the man replies. 'So are his children. It's the poet he wants you to visit – Master Spenser.'

'Spenser? Where?'

'King's Street. We're to take you there directly.'

'What ails him,' Nicholas asks, 'that he has need of my attention at this hour?'

'He has little need of attention, sir,' the man says. 'He's dead.'

22

Nicholas sits huddled in the stern of the private wherry, bleary-eyed and freezing cold. There will come a time, he assures himself, when he becomes accustomed to these sinistrous night-journeys on the river, summoned from his sleep by Robert Cecil. But not tonight. Tonight he is hurrying over a river that he is beginning to think is not the Thames but the Styx, the watery boundary between the living and the dead. Looking around in the pre-dawn darkness at the oily black heave of the water and the infrequent pinpricks of lantern light on the north bank, he half-expects to see the ferryman Charon poling his skiff out of the night to guide him down into Hades. I will have a fine welcome there, he thinks. He peers over the edge of the wherry and imagines the ghosts in the dark water beneath him. There's little Ralph Cullen, whose murder started him on his fall when Eleanor, his first wife, died. Ned Monkton's younger brother Isaac, whose eviscerated corpse helped him find Ralph's killer. The crazed Swiss physician who planned to turn the world upside-down. And Mistress Warren, who thought she could use a perverted physic to bring back her dead lover... They are all there, staring up at the river's surface with their dead eyes, watching him pass by. It is a relief, he thinks, to be summoned to a death on dry land.

But what manner of death? Robert Cecil surely hasn't called him out in the small hours of the night because Edmund Spenser has died of natural causes.

They glide in silence to a halt alongside the Court water-stairs. A member of the Whitehall night-guard in breastplate and morion helmet escorts Nicholas through the warren of buildings and out into King's Street, over the narrow Long Ditch bridge – their footsteps sounding unnaturally loud in the stillness – before delivering him, without having answered even one of Nicholas's attempts at casual conversation, to a narrow timber-framed house set in a row of similar frontages close by the path to Canon Row. A brief parting of the clouds washes the street for a moment in grey, funereal moonlight. The street door is open. Head down – somehow secrecy seems expected of him – Nicholas enters. A narrow flight of steps awaits him. He climbs quickly. The boards creak loudly, making a mockery of his subterfuge.

Lantern-light flickers on the upper landing where Cecil is waiting for him, a little black raven in its night-roost.

'The night-watch found him a little after the second hour,' he says, showing Nicholas into the small sleeping chamber. 'The street door was ajar. The watch has a dislike of unlocked doors around Whitehall at night. They're worried someone might find a way through the yards or over the roofs and into the privy areas. A little difficult from the top of King's Street, I'll grant you, but better diligent than lax.'

Nicholas is standing in a low-ceilinged room dimly lit by the lantern carried by one of Cecil's two attendants. Both, he notices, are armed with rapiers and wheel-lock pistols. They stand back a little from the bed on which Spenser lies, their faces slack with tiredness. Cecil, however, looks as though he's just had a good breakfast after a night of uninterrupted sleep.

Spenser is lying on the coverlet, his legs straight, the top part of his body turned so that his sightless face is set towards the door. One arm is bent across his chest, as though he's hugging himself in his sleep. He is wearing a plain linen night-shift, rucked up over his hairless legs.

'Is this how they found him?'

'Exactly as you see before you,' Cecil says. 'They went in with the intention of reminding him to be more cautious. They found him as you see him now.'

'How did they know who it was?'

'Not because the watch are aficionados of poetry, that's for certain,' Cecil answers with a cruel laugh. 'The captain of the watch came to see Spenser when he moved in before Christmas. They like to know when a new face appears so close to court. Fortunately he's one of my fellows.'

'A sudden death within the royal verge is a task for the queen's coroner,' Nicholas reminds him – as if Cecil didn't know. 'Why call upon me?'

'Because before anyone else lays a hand on Edmund Spenser, I want you to tell me if he was murdered.'

'Do you think that's likely?'

'After our meeting with him at your lodgings on Bankside, what do *you* think?'

'Murdered by who?'

Cecil adopts a speculative air, as though he were a philosopher debating some arcane argument. 'Let us imagine for a moment that Spenser's fears had been realized: that the Earl of Essex had learned of his communications with Spain...'

'Then he would have had Spenser arrested.'

'Perhaps the perpetrator was from beyond these shores – one of the rebellious Tyrone's assassins.' Cecil's smile is one of superiority, not mirth. His little mouth purses with a wry sharpness. 'As you well know, Nicholas, Master Spenser had certain... shall we say "harsh" views on how the rebellion in Ireland should be put down.'

'You think he was murdered because of his pamphlet?'

'Men have lost their lives for writing words far less contentious,' Cecil says, indicating the body on the bed as though it were an exhibit in a cabinet of curiosities.

'They could have killed Spenser in Ireland. It would have been easier.'

'But there are *some* in England, Nicholas, who would have happily done it for them.'

'You mean Catholics?'

'You should know, Nicholas. You married one.'

'Yes, I did,' says Nicholas, as though he's only just remembered. 'That must be it: Bianca laid a charm upon Master Spenser and he died of induced melancholy. There is an alternative.'

'Is there?'

'Perhaps it was someone from court. Perhaps they'd had to sit through his *Faerie Queen* or his *Shepheardes Calendar* once too often.'

'This is not the time for flippancy, Nicholas.'

Nicholas moves closer to the bed, beckoning the holder of the lamp to do the same.

'Does Essex know?' he asks.

Cecil shakes his head. 'Not yet. The noble earl will likely be abed, in the arms of Bacchus. Or more likely one of his poets – a living one.'

First Nicholas makes a general study of the place of death, a narrow tester bed unfurnished with any hangings. He sees no sign of a struggle. The bolster bears only a single indentation, a little to the left of centre, presumably made ante-mortem by Spenser's head. The body itself lies at a slight angle on the rumpled coverlet. Spenser's yellow-soled upturned feet hang over the end of the frame.

Enlisting the aid of one of Cecil's men, Nicholas drags the nightshirt over the dead man's shoulders and discards it. Then he arranges the corpse so that it is lying on its back, the empty eyes fixed on the sagging ceiling beams. The slight resistance in the cold limbs tells him Spenser hasn't been dead more than a couple of hours.

Now Nicholas inspects the neck. He finds no bruises below the neatly trimmed beard, no weals or scratches made by fingers tightening about the windpipe. A single goose feather has lodged beneath the lobe of the right ear. He pulls it from the chilled skin and holds it up to the lantern. It appears undamaged. Observing the absence of a pillow, Nicholas examines the bolster for signs of feathers working their way out through the fabric. He finds none.

He places the feather gently on the coverlet and peers into the gape of the mouth, searching for evidence of smothering: other feathers caught between the teeth or on the tongue. There is not enough light for him to be sure, so he is forced to explore the inside of the dead man's mouth with his fingers. He finds none.

Next, he carries out a careful inspection of the eyes and the face. He searches for broken blood vessels and blotches, signs that might suggest suffocation. It is no easy task in the lantern light, but he thinks he sees a partial reddening of the right eye, and a few purple marks under the skin.

Although there are no bloodstains visible, Nicholas inspects the torso for punctures, on the remote possibility that Spenser was run through elsewhere, cleaned up and brought here to be so arranged as to suggest that he died in his sleep. A close inspection tells him that Edmund Spenser's body bears nothing more sinister than the blemishes any man might accumulate over almost five decades of life.

'He could have been poisoned, I suppose,' Nicholas says, returning his attention to Spenser's dead face. 'There's a little dried spume at the corner of the mouth. It might mean something. There again, it might be merely the residue of the death-rattle.' He sniffs the area around the nostrils and the sagging jaws. 'Some venomous substances leave a noxious scent after being ingested,' he explains. Then, glancing at Cecil, 'In the case of sulphur, for instance, residue can be expelled from the nose.'

He moves to inspect first one side of the head and then the other. 'There's no discharge from the ears, so we might discount poisoning by arsenic.'

'It's extraordinary what you physicians have to learn,' Cecil says.

Nicholas thinks it best not to tell him that he's gained most of his understanding of the art of poisoning from Bianca. Her mother was a Caporetti, and in the Veneto the Caporetti line is said to have begun with the woman who mixed the poison that Agrippina used to dispatch her husband, the Emperor Claudius. There again, he thinks, it would be a sure-fire way of avoiding any further summons to court.

Stepping back, he says, 'Some venoms inflame or discolour the internal organs. We could have the body moved to the barber-surgeons' hall on Monkswell Street. I'm not a member of that guild, but I'm sure they'd accede to an order from you and let me open it up, just to be sure.'

'Christ's sweet wounds!' gasps Robert Cecil in an expiration of horror. 'You're speaking of England's foremost poet. We can't cut him up like a mutton carcass at the shambles.'

Satisfied that he has done his best in trying circumstances, Nicholas thanks the keeper of the lantern for his assistance and says to Cecil, 'There *are* a few signs this might not be a natural death. But I fear that, at present, I cannot in all honesty tell you Edmund Spenser was murdered.' A reflective pause. 'But knowing as I do his history, neither can I say for sure that he was not.'

Cecil nods gravely, as though he is about to read Spenser's eulogy right here in this humble little chamber. 'Well, we can be sure that the queen's coroner will say he died of natural causes.'

'How can you be certain of that?'

'Because I have every expectation that he will wish to *remain* the royal coroner.'

'So what will happen now?' Nicholas asks.

Cecil gives him a courtier's practised smile. 'You and I shall depart. When it is light, a clerk from the Office of the Revels – a very *junior* clerk, I imagine – will attempt to visit Master Spenser on some matter of business about his dreadful versifying. He will have instructions to insist, should Master Spenser be asleep. He will notice the door is unlocked—'

'And you and I shall never have been here?'

Cecil's smile has a chilling confidence about it. 'No more so than fleeting wraiths in a graveyard.'

As they descend the stairs, he calls back over his shoulder, 'No doubt there will be a great wailing and a general gnashing of teeth. You know how esteemed these poet fellows are. We shall all be invited to mourn the loss of another Virgil, another Ovid. My money's on Westminster Abbey.'

'You told me that it was the night-watch who found the street door ajar,' Nicholas says to the bustling, uneven shoulders below him.

'Yes, a little after the bellman passed on his rounds. A stern word or two is in store for *that* fellow, I'll warrant. He failed to notice.'

'Then if Spenser *was* murdered, he must have known his killer,' Nicholas observes.

'There may be duplicate keys.'

'Spenser told me a while ago that the Earl of Essex was paying for these lodgings while he was here in London.'

The restlessness Nicholas senses in Cecil, as he considers this, seems to need a larger stage than the narrow confines of the little house. Cecil waits until they are out in the street before replying. The clouds have torn a little. A low moon drips fleeting puddles of grey light over the silent gatehouse that guards the way into Whitehall.

'I keep asking myself if it might be conceivable that Devereux had him killed,' he says softly. 'He may have learned of Spenser's communications with the Spanish peace faction – decided to cut it off at the first branch, rather than risk the delay of arraignment and trial. Perhaps he was concerned that if the approach by Don Rodriquez were to become known, others on the Privy Council – perhaps even the queen herself – might consider it favourably. Without Spain to hate, Devereux would be a much smaller man.'

'I would be lying to you, Sir Robert, if I were to tell you with conviction that Edmund Spenser had been murdered. I cannot say so without cutting him open,' Nicholas restates plainly, wondering if Cecil needs even his air laden with conspiracy before he can breathe it. 'I'm sorry if that is not what you want to hear, but you didn't bring me here for anything other than my professional opinion.'

Cecil leads him towards one of a pair of pedestrian gateways flanking the main arch of the King's Street gatehouse. With barely a sound, the tall wooden doors swing open. Nicholas assumes Mr Secretary's approach has been expected, observed through some spyhole. But it would be easy, he thinks, to believe that they have sprung wide solely at the command of this crooked little man's immense will.

'You're mistaken,' Cecil says, his voice echoing in the archway as they pass through.

'About Spenser?' Nicholas asks, as he senses rather than sees the guards step aside to allow them entry to the inner courtyard.

Ahead he can just make out the façade of King Henry's great hall against the deeper darkness.

'No,' says Cecil, with the finality of a lawyer about to demolish an alibi. 'About your professional opinion being the *only* reason you're here.'

23

They have spent a full fortnight in the cellar owned by a family that Cachorra now knows to be Anglo-Irish, a concept that at first took a little explaining to her. She had previously assumed there were only two types of folk in Ireland: Irish or English.

They have allowed her and Constanza to join them for Mass. This takes place in their modest single-storey house of stone, capped by a turf roof. It is always a packed affair, attended not just by the family, but also by others from around the little valley. The celebration is given by a priest who, when not clad in his threadbare vestments, looks like a mountain shepherd, all beard and sinews. Constanza insists on sitting at the front and receiving the Eucharist before anyone else. In the fourteen days she has been here she has not addressed anyone in English. When it is over and the spirit of God has again suffused their souls, the shepherd-priest hides his regalia in an old wooden box, which he reburies behind the cow byre. It is an inconvenient resurrection, but necessary. Cachorra has been told that if soldiers from Dublin or Cork were to find it, or to stumble across the house while the Mass was in progress, they might well hang everyone in the valley. To avoid this, the children are sent to the high places around the house to keep watch. The health of their immortal souls can wait for later.

Last night, for the first time in a long while, Cachorra was able to make confession of her sins. She asked the priest if it was a sin to wish to be desired by a man.

Not if he is your husband, the priest had told her.

'But what if it was my master?' she had replied.

'Then it is lust, and indeed a sin,' was the answer. A double sin, in fact, if the man desires in return.

But despite what the priest told her, Cachorra is unconvinced that the dead *can* sin. Because in the weeks and months since the shipwreck she has accepted reality: that Don Rodriquez is dead and is in heaven.

Today she and Constanza are to be moved again; another step in the laborious journey into Ulster and – if God wills it – to the court of Hugh O'Neill, the Earl of Tyrone. In anticipation, Cachorra has woken early, before cockcrow. It is pitch dark in the cellar. Beside her, Constanza is dreaming whatever vapid dreams Cachorra supposes flit through her mind like shadows in an empty room.

Cachorra does not hear the petulant wheeze of Constanza's snoring. She is in a place far removed both in time and distance from the pile of musky sheepskin on which she lies, her eyes closed even though it is pitch black in the cellar. She is lost in memories of a time before Constanza, and what she can hear is the crashing of white surf against a golden shore, and the screeching of the cuca birds in the palm trees. She is six years old – and sitting hunched in a bamboo cage like a turkey waiting for the pot. The cage is but one in a line. The others are full of everything that was worth looting from her village. There are no other humans in the cages, and for all Cachorra knows, none left alive in all of Hispaniola, because the men standing in conversation nearby are Ciguayo raiders and their knives are still crimson from the slaughter.

However much it pains Cachorra to admit it, the Ciguayo must have deserved their victory. Because otherwise why else would they be standing on the beach in conversation with the gods?

Cachorra has no doubt at all that these other creatures are gods, though they look similar to all the other mortal men she has encountered in her six years. Though their colour and their faces are different from any Carib, they possess human heads, arms and legs. But they are indeed gods; no question about it. Because no mortal would possess detachable iron skin, or arrive in a great longhouse that floats upon the water and belches fire and thunder from its windows.

Cachorra watches, wild-eyed, as one of the gods points at her crate. He is as magnificent as she would expect a god to be, though not nearly so old. He has a sharp, angular face and a mane of gleaming black ringlets. She hears him utter the word *caníbal*.

Or at least she imagines *now* that she hears him utter it. Because at the time she could not possibly have understood the meaning of that Spanish word. At the time she had yet to hear the word *Hispaniola*. It was not a place known to her. Even her own name, *Cachorra*, was knowledge she had yet to acquire. All this would come later, when she had learned the language of the man who rescued her from the Ciguayo for the price of a single, gleaming gold coin. But at the time she had understood the meaning behind the word *caníbal* at once, because one of the raiders had made play of munching on his own wrist, which the gods seemed to find hugely amusing.

For Cachorra, this had been an insult too far. Her people were not *caníbales*, they were honest fisherfolk. True, the important men of the village might carry around with them a desiccated relic of a revered forebear – a wizened black hand or a foot perhaps – but these were freighted with solemn sanctity. She would no sooner eat a person than she would a toadfish. So when this god with the iron skin and the black ringlets had cut through the cords keeping the lid of the crate shut and reached in to pull her out, the jewelled rings on his ringers blazing like stars fallen to earth, she responded with the outraged fury of a wildcat, even though – inside – she was terrified halfway to death.

'I named you on the spot,' Don Rodriquez had told her later – much later – when she could speak his language and had put out of her mind every memory of her life prior to that day on the beach. '*Cachorra de Leopardo*. Leopard cub.'

And in all the years since Cachorra had entered his household to serve as companion, and then maid, to his daughter, Don Rodriquez had never once behaved towards her in any way other than as a man of honour. When his wife had died, five years ago, he had not – as far as she could tell – considered for a moment taking her to his bed in consolation, as some men would happily have done. If he had, she thinks ruefully now, she would have agreed in an instant. A strong friendship had grown between them, as far as there could be between master and servant. He was relatively young, barely forty, still striking, and the age difference between them would not have made even a formal union unusual. Every widower in his circle had married a younger woman. After all, a man must produce heirs or else have his name erased from history.

Eventually, on the eve of their departure aboard the *San Juan de Berrocal*, in one of the companionable private moments they shared when Constanza was at her *vihuela* practice or at chapel, she had found the courage to ask him why he had resisted a longing that she knew he harboured. In reply, Don Rodriquez had taken her hands in his and smiled. 'What has always stood between us,' he explained sadly, 'what has always made marriage impossible, is knowing that there is a part of your soul that still dwells somewhere in the steaming jungles of Hispaniola. I would only ever have half of you. Besides, I know what the wives of my fellow courtiers would say behind your back: Look at the Carib servant – the *naboría* – who bedded a grieving fool for his gold. And I would never have you suffer *that* insult.'

How she wishes now that she had persuaded Don Rodriquez Calva de Sagrada otherwise. How she wishes she had stayed with him in that black, spinning terror of the storm, and that the sea had taken them both together. For Cachorra is sure now that he is dead. She has asked more than once if any but she and Constanza survived the wreck. The only answer she has been given is a silent one, framed in sad, regretful smiles.

But fate has decreed that she is to live, just as it decreed that – in Hispaniola twenty years ago – Don Rodriquez would happen upon that beach, on that day, at that moment.

And Cachorra thinks she understands why she has been spared. It is to finish what he began. To repay him for saving her that day on the beach.

That is why, she realizes now, Don Rodriquez insisted she should be in attendance when he was battling to hammer into his daughter's recalcitrant brain a list of names. Twelve names, in fact. And each one as grand a name as was ever committed to memory – for fear of what might befall its owner if it were ever to be written down.

24

Dawn is still an hour away. In the Green Yard of Whitehall, Nicholas is walking through a graveyard where the risen ghosts all wear clerks' robes and black bonnets. He catches glimpses of them in the puddles of meagre light cast by the torches on the precinct wall, emerging from their tombs in the side of the great hall, bent from sleep not yet fully cast off, scurrying away through the sharp morning air to labour behind the few dimly lit windows that seem to float like watching eyes in the darkness.

'You are to return to Ireland,' Cecil told him barely a minute ago, though from the heavy silence while he waits for a reply, in Nicholas's mind it could well have been an hour.

Cecil had spoken so casually that at first Nicholas was sure he had misheard him. But now, after he has had time to digest the curt instruction, he senses that – from the moment the hammering on the door of the Paris Garden lodgings woke him – he has always known it would come.

Cecil's prompting breaks the silence. 'Well? Have you nothing to say to me?'

'If you're prepared to wager on me finding Constanza Calva de Sagrada, then I highly recommend you never go anywhere near Bankside, Sir Robert. You'd be destitute inside a week. Other than the mantilla that Bianca found, and a wild rumour about the Virgin Mary that seems to have been confused with folk law, there's no real evidence she survived the wreck.'

They walk on along the path that runs back beside the ancient, flinty walls of the great hall to the wing occupied by the officers of the Exchequer. No one challenges them; Mr Secretary Cecil's silhouette is immediately identifiable in the torchlight.

'That is not the sole purpose of your return, Nicholas,' he says without looking up. 'But I confess it would be a welcome benefit.'

'Then why do you want me to go back?'

'The order does not come from me. It comes from the queen.'

'The queen?' Nicholas repeats, astonished. 'Why does Her Majesty desire me to go back to Ireland?'

'She is concerned for the proper care of the army that the Earl of Essex will command. You have been a military surgeon. You're not one of the old charlatans who customarily advise her on matters of physic. It makes perfect sense. Of course, from *my* perspective, it would be a great boon if, while you were there, you were also able to discover the whereabouts of the daughter of Don Rodriquez.'

'Is this commission a request or a command?'

'Whatever Her Grace requests is a command, Nicholas,' Cecil says, looking up at him with an empty smile. 'You will receive formal note of it, under her seal, before you leave.'

'Does she know she's written it?' Nicholas asks caustically, remembering the letter from the president of the Stationers' Company that Cecil had provided him with when he left for Dublin.

'I was there when she made her wishes known,' Cecil assures him. 'You should be honoured.'

'Do I have any choice in the matter?'

'None of us have a choice in whether or not to serve our gracious sovereign lady, Nicholas. You may as well ask if you have the choice of obeying the Almighty or not.'

Nicholas is about to say, 'I have, *often*', but decides it's wiser to let the words die on his tongue.

'When am I ordered to depart?'

'Not for a while. Probably not until the spring. It will take some time for Ireland's new Lord Lieutenant to assemble his great army. But I suspect you will be summoned by Devereux at some point. I understand he has heard great things of you.'

Henshawe, thinks Nicholas. I've been recommended to the Earl of Essex by a murderer. He wonders if Henshawe's arrival in the city has anything to do with Spenser's death. He dismisses the thought. Essex would have had better ways of dealing with Spenser's contact with the Spanish peace faction than sending a clumsy butcher like Henshawe.

'Bianca will throw a bate worse than a falcon that's had its prey snatched away,' he says, as if that might change the queen's mind.

'I've already considered that. She can go as your apothecary. After all, a woman could be of use, if you were to find this Constanza.'

'You've thought this through, haven't you?'

There is a modesty in the smile Cecil gives him that is quite out of character. 'I am Her Majesty's humble principal secretary. It's my *job* to think things through.'

Only when Nicholas is sitting in the stern of the wherry taking him back to Bankside does the truth hit him: Cecil has convinced the queen to send him to Ireland to spy on Robert Devereux.

In the swaying light from the boat's lantern, he reads again the brief letter with its heavy seal dangling on a length of fine ribbon:

> *To our trusty and beloved servant Master Nicholas Shelby, greetings… It is our desire that you should go into Ireland with the forces of our Earl of Essex, our true and valorous friend and Lieutenant… there to make service in physic unto our troops hurt in the suppression of the rebellious Tyrone…*

Elizabeth R

Nicholas stares ahead at the sickly pallor of the coming dawn, his stomach chilled by the ease with which Robert Cecil has played him. And he can hear Bianca's voice over the wind and the splashing of the oars:

Must you forever dance to Robert Cecil's tune?... It was a pact with the Devil. I should never have let you make it.

She's right, he thinks. A pact with the Devil. And his soul exchanged in payment.

✠

Bianca kneels on the hard earth and hacks at the cold finger of sanicle root. She imagines that it runs from her hand down through the earth, out of her little riverside physic garden set between Black Bull Alley and the Mutton Lane shambles, and all the way to Cecil House, thickening as it rises through the foundations, through the gaps in the floorboards, into Mr Secretary's study, where it seamlessly melds into his lower limbs. It is Cecil himself that she is striking at with her knife. Cecil, whose malign roots seem to spread everywhere.

The Devil take Robert Cecil and all his works.

Bianca has come to her secret place with the intention of fetching the fragment of sanicle to pound into mulch and boil in wine, to make a healing decoction for the bawd at the Arbour of Venus on Kent Street. One of the bawd's poor, undernourished girls is showing symptoms of the French gout. The bawd is an unforgiving woman. If the girl cannot be cured, she will likely be turned out, joining the growing ranks of those made destitute by the bad harvests and the quarrel with Spain. Nicholas has gone to the stew to do what he can for her.

In a way, Bianca is glad he has been called away barely an hour after returning from King's Street. His news, she thinks, is best considered in solitude, and with a task at hand to stop her thoughts spinning out of control.

The Devil take Robert Cecil and all his works.

Spenser – dead. That's shock enough. But to return to Ireland because the Crab wants a spy in Robert Devereux's camp: that is a poison sharper than even a Caporetti could mix.

As she hacks at the sanicle root, in her mind Bianca tries to lay a solid foundation upon which to construct the edifice of her response.

First, Nicholas is *not* to blame. Even though instinct had made her want to hammer at his chest with her fists and call him weak, to tell him to defy Cecil and spit on his shadow, she knows that would have been unfair, untrue and unwise. Nicholas is in the Crab's service only because of her. If she were not a Catholic, Cecil would have no hold over him. Second, she must accept Nicholas's assurance – because her husband is an honest man – that what drives Mr Secretary is not simply a scheming and devious disposition, but an unbreakable loyalty to the realm and its monarch. Whatever ill methods he might employ, he acts only for the queen's protection and, by extension, her subjects. He does what he thinks is right, and the Devil can worry about the method.

Haven't I done exactly the same thing?

Bianca remembers a cold, starlit night on London Bridge, and the sound of two bodies striking the water below, the bodies of men who had intended Nicholas mortal harm.

Have I not sinned in protecting those I hold dear? she asks herself. Did I not sanction – nay, *contrive* – the deaths of those men solely to save Nicholas's life? What right do I have, then, to condemn Sir Robert Cecil?

And then there is Constanza Calva de Sagrada. She, too, has cast her own enchantment. Bianca cannot deny it. And she knows Nicholas feels the same. She wonders if, perhaps, they have both fallen under the Merrow's spell.

Finally, there is the inescapable matter of the queen's command.

Bianca has read the words for herself, stared in awe at the imperious signature. Nicholas can no more deny his queen than fly to the moon. It matters not if Cecil has whispered in the queen's ear, directing a growing approval of her new – and undeniably striking – physician. She could mix no balm, distil no concoction, cast no enchantment that could overturn the written order of a monarch.

No, Nicholas must go again to Ireland.

And *therefore*, she whispers as the sanicle root finally yields to the knife's blade, I must go with him. I must keep watch on the precious talisman that came to me out of the river that cold October dawn eight years ago.

We shall go as one. Because when I saved Nicholas from himself, and he saved *me* from Cecil, we forged the links that bind us. We forged them willingly. They bind us still, even more so now that we have Bruno. But the fact remains: Nicholas and I are two comets that have wandered by mistake into the wrong sky. For as long as we blaze, we blaze together, but otherwise alone.

25

It is a lavish funeral for a man who claimed he was barely more solvent than a beggar. But then Robert Devereux is paying. Whence does the earl's generosity stem? Nicholas wonders. From an appreciation of Spenser's verse? Or from the poet's approval – his validation?

A sharp frost crackles underfoot as the cortège approaches the great North Door of Westminster Abbey. Ahead the dean awaits to receive the coffin, his hands together in reverence for a man he doesn't know, and whose views on the subjugation of the Irish rebels might, Nicholas dares to hope, appal his Christian sensibilities. Behind the cortège a trail of poor folk, paid to attend, do their best to adopt a grieving look. Count yourself fortunate, Nicholas thinks, as he glances back at their pallid faces from his place in the procession, that you don't know how the great poet would have wanted you brought to order, if you were rebellious enough to dare protest your lot.

Inside, the Abbey is dark and cold, the steps of the pall-bearers as they traverse the flagstones echoing like a slow, rhythmical lament.

They've all come, Nicholas notices. There's young Ben Johnson, a smaller version of Ned Monkton, but who shares the same fierce scowl; Will Shakespeare, whose eyes when they look into yours, Nicholas has often noticed, seem to be fixed on a part of yourself you haven't met yet; Walter Raleigh, who considers himself no mean versifier; Southampton, patron of poets… and all those clever fellows favoured by Essex House, who throw copies of their own verse into the open grave dug close to Chaucer's tomb in the South Transept and weep. Listening to the eulogy, Nicholas finds his thoughts not with Spenser, but with his wife Elizabeth, and Katherine, Sylvanus and Peregrine, mourning without the comfort of ceremony, or even a body, in beleaguered Cork. Nicholas has written a letter of commiseration and sent it with the Cecil House post. A natural death, he has assured them, brought on by the calamity of losing Kilcolman. What good would it do, he thinks, to tell them otherwise – if there ever really was an 'otherwise'?

✠

It is no small task to equip England's Caesar with a host befitting his new estate. Sixteen thousand foot and one thousand horse cannot be supplied out of thin air. Nor can they be assembled swiftly. The general muster gathers pace, sweeping up unemployed veterans and farmhands with little or no knowledge of where on the surface of the globe Ireland may be found. Meanwhile, men with an eye for profit line up at Whitehall, at Cecil House, at Essex House – anywhere a contract is on offer. Because an army cannot bake its bread without ovens, so the humble brick suddenly attracts a premium; fish cannot be salted and dried if there are not nets to catch them. To feed a company of a hundred men requires more cooking pans than may be found in a small village. They cannot march without an adequate supply of water butts, or take their ease afterwards without ale or sack to drink. And they cannot be armed without such a forging and hammering of plate as might deafen all the angels in heaven.

In early February, with London swathed in icy fog, Nicholas is summoned to Essex House. He wonders what sort of reception he will receive.

He is shown into a smart, panelled audience chamber with high windows giving onto the opaque void that hides the world outside. Essex lounges on an elaborately carved oak settle, his feet on a stool, a leather-bound volume of Virgil's *Aeneid* beside him. He is dressed in a doublet of cream satin set with pearls the size of buboes. Ranged on the floor around him is a cluster of young gallants, would-be stars in orbit around a would-be sun. To Nicholas, the scene smacks uncomfortably of a court-in-waiting. Perhaps the queen is right, he thinks, not to trust this ambitious man too far.

With disdainful faces, like scent-hounds lying at their master's feet, the gallants regard Nicholas – dressed in a simple broadcloth coat – as if he were a servant who's had the temerity not to use the back stairs. Amongst them, he notes, is Sir Oliver Henshawe.

'Dr Shelby, I see you've arrived safely,' Essex says, looking up. 'How these watermen find their way on a day like today, only the Almighty knows.'

'I came across London Bridge, my lord,' Nicholas says.

'You walked? I should have thought to send a carriage. How uncivil of me.' Essex gestures him to the empty settle on the other side of the hearth. 'How's that comely wife of yours – the Italian one. We danced, at Whitehall, I recall.'

'She's well, my lord. But sadly, only half Italian.'

'I'll warrant that will be the *lower* half,' Essex says, holding Nicholas's gaze provocatively.

For a moment Nicholas is lost for a reply. Hearing Henshawe's guffaw, he begins to colour. Is Devereux trying to provoke him with a coarse joke?

'Her *feet*, Dr Shelby. Her feet,' Essex says with a smirk. 'She must have learned her measures in Italy. She dances better than any English maid I've met – excepting Her Majesty, of course.'

'Of course,' Nicholas says, as though he was in on the joke from the start. But the old memories of his first year at Cambridge – and the frequent brawls with gentlemen students who thought baiting a Suffolk yeoman's son such good sport – still smoulder and are easily rekindled. He looks Essex square in the face and says, 'She remembers it well, my lord.'

'I trust so,' says Essex.

'She described it as being like dancing with a locked wardrobe: it doesn't seem to feel anything, and you come away wondering what's hidden inside.'

The scent-hounds stir, but no command to bite follows. Their heads turn towards their master, looking to him for guidance. For a while Devereux's face shows no emotion. It is a picture of studied languor, the eyebrows neatly plucked, the curls caressing the brow, the hazel eyes observant but expressionless.

And then Essex begins to smile. 'Well, my friends, let us hope our new physician's skill is as sharp as his wit.' He looks directly into Nicholas's eyes. 'Tell me, what do you think was it that convinced Her Majesty to choose *you*, of all physicians, to send to Ireland with me?'

The implication could not be clearer, thinks Nicholas. Essex knows. Whatever he may be, he's no fool. It must be blindingly obvious that my attachment to the Irish enterprise is down solely to Robert Cecil's persuasive tongue.

'Her Majesty, I am told, has some small regard for me,' he replies, understanding now that, in Devereux's eyes, he is a marked man. 'I have served as physician to Sir Joshua Wylde's company in the Low Countries. I have studied anatomy under Professor Fabricius in Padua. And I'm young enough, and in good enough health, to bear the climate of Ireland. Would you rather she had commanded old Baronsdale from the College of Physicians to attend you, my lord? I hear the greatest battle he has faced recently is the walk from his lodgings to the College guildhall on Knightrider Street.'

Essex considers this awhile. Then he gives a little laugh, as if to himself. 'I am sure you will acquit yourself admirably, Dr Shelby. Sir Oliver, here, was most impressed with your work in Cork, weren't you, Oliver?'

Henshawe, sprawling on one elbow, purses his lips in grudging approval. 'Better than any quack I've ever encountered.'

'And old Ormonde thinks you could raise Lazarus from the dead if you put your mind to it,' Essex adds. 'So we must be thankful for your company, Nicholas Shelby.' A glance at his coterie, and a grin. 'Well, my brave fellows, with our new physician to watch over us, I dare say we shall all return from Ireland in better health than when we left.'

The gallants find this hugely amusing. Nicholas does his best to take their laughter in good spirit. There can be no future, he thinks, in deliberately making himself an outcast amongst Essex's companions. He offers up a silent prayer of thanks that Bianca is coming with him. Serving these men alone, without her at his side to confide in, would be worse, he thinks, than a year's confinement in the Tower.

'So, Dr Shelby. Let us get down to practical matters,' he hears Essex say. 'Marsh fever will be a major ill we shall have to contend with. My father learned *that* when he campaigned in Ireland. I fear fever more than I fear Tyrone. What are your recommendations?'

Practical matters. That's the answer, thinks Nicholas, as he outlines a regime for keeping the men's feet and clothes dry and their tents warm but well ventilated. Concentrate on the practical matters. Forget that Essex knows he has a Cecil spy in his headquarters. Forget the impossibility of ever finding Constanza Calva de Sagrada. Do what you did in the Low Countries: spend as much time amongst the soldiers as you can;

avoid the nobles, the would-be glory-seekers, the pretend philosophers who write their verses even as the blood dries on their swords; eschew the butchers with pretty faces like Henshawe, and hope for a swift victory.

But Nicholas cannot help thinking of Ormonde's assessment of the rebels he secretly admired. *Unsoldierly as a band of Morris men... But they are fierce fighters... They do not give battle like honest fellows... They will not stand against pike, musket and horse like Christian soldiers... they fall upon our tail like hungry rats.*

Looking at these primped gallants who have flattered their way into Devereux's regard, Nicholas wonders if any of them – regardless of what knowledge they may have had of making war against the Spanish – understand quite what it is they're letting themselves in for. He has a suspicion that fever is going to be the least of Robert Devereux's worries.

✠

On Bankside there is work to be done. Bianca's apothecary shop on Dice Lane could furnish scarcely a fraction of what is needed. So contracts must be concluded with the spice merchants and grocers on Petty Wales on the north bank of the river, close by the Tower: anise, pepper and parsley for making decoctions to treat lungs troubled by the damp air rising from Irish bogs; hyssop and pine nuts to boil into an *aqua mulsa* to treat peri-pneumonia; wormwood and mint to make syrups for treating the flux brought on by rations left too long in the casks. All these ingredients, and more, must be sourced and barrelled, space for their transport aboard the fleet negotiated with the navy's victualling clerks. Gratefully, Nicholas leaves the bulk of this work to Bianca. The merchants already know her well. Thus the deals Bianca strikes must surely be the only ones in all England where the final customer – the Royal Exchequer – is not robbed blind.

For his part, Nicholas visits as many of Essex's commanders and captains as he can reach. The earl has put out the word that his new physician has experience on the field of battle, that he is no dusty academic. They treat him courteously, but seem to think he won't be needed much – save for those who've served previously under Ormonde and know the score.

He receives a letter from the College of Physicians, reminding him that it is a physician's duty to diagnose and prescribe, not to physically *treat*. Taking off limbs, setting bones or stitching wounds is best left to members of the Worshipful Company of Barber-Surgeons, the letter points out. 'They'll probably be glad when I've gone,' he tells Bianca as he tears it up and uses the scraps to light that evening's fire. 'First they couldn't abide me because I question the medical canon, now they can't abide me because the queen invites me to her presence chamber.'

At Cecil House, Sir Robert is dismissive when Nicholas reveals that Essex has deduced why Nicholas has been appointed. 'I wouldn't have expected otherwise. I'd have thought the same,' he says, as though it's all simply part of the courtier's game.

But if Cecil is to be apprised of his rival's progress, the means by which he receives the news must still be secure. Nicholas is instructed to employ the cipher he and Cecil have always used for privy correspondence. But who can be trusted to carry it? asks Nicholas. The new Lord Lieutenant of Ireland will control the post. He will have clever secretaries who can open and reseal a letter, making it look to the receiver quite untouched. And some of those secretaries may be so clever that they might even be able to unlock the code. What then?

You won't send them through the official post, Cecil informs him airily. And so Nicholas must commit to memory the names of the masters of the ships who are in the principal secretary's pay: Graham of the *Arrow*; Acliffe of the *Sweet Reward*; Boyce of the *Goshawk*... 'Wherever possible, route your dispatches through Chester,' Cecil says. 'The captains know which post-riders are in my service.'

Nicholas has not forgotten the rigours of his time in the Low Countries. But he was more than a decade younger then. In preparation, he improves his fitness. Every other day he spends an hour in the company of Master George Silver from the Guild of Fencing Masters. His only previous experience of swordplay was at Cambridge, during a short-lived and futile attempt to fit in with the gentlemen students. Now he sweats and aches in a frantic effort to master the *stop-hit*, the *riversa*, the *mandritta* and the *stoccata*.

'You're not a dancer, are you?' says Silver – a grizzled fifty-year-old with three times the stamina of his younger pupil, as Nicholas tumbles clumsily to the floorboards in his Blackfriars studio.

'Not really,' Nicholas replies, climbing to his feet for some more humiliation. 'I'm a farmer's son. A carrot tends to give itself up without much of a fight.'

'I suggest a backsword, rather than a rapier,' Silver says. 'With only one edge to the blade, you're likely to do less harm – to yourself.'

And all the while, the muster gathers pace.

✠

Barnabas Vyves has not returned to the Jackdaw since the day Nicholas caught him out in his lie about the whereabouts of Oliver Henshawe's recruits. Bristol or Chester? A mistake, or a deceit?

There is every reason to believe he is busy scouring the towns and villages of Surrey, raising men for the earl's army, a task that leaves him no time for taking his ease – and other men's misguided charity. Or at least there would be, if he hadn't made such a hasty exit when he'd realized who he was speaking to.

When Ned Monkton hears from Talbot Appletree, the plumber's apprentice – who has stopped by for a jug of knock-down after repairing the public cistern behind Winchester House – that *he* has heard from Will Baldock, the warden of the old Bermondsey Abbey, that on the morrow a parade is to occur there in which a troop bound for Ireland will drill with their pikes, he decides to attend as a spectator.

The day brings a spiteful east wind that sets the banners on the flagpoles at the Rose theatre crackling like pistol fire. A convoy of wagons bringing hay up Long Southwark gives Bankside a shower of dry rain when the straps come loose and the dust escapes on the breeze. Low clouds as grey as old linen fly westwards as though they can't escape the city fast enough.

On the open ground beside the ruined abbey a troop of about sixty men stand in three ragged lines, their faces pinched and deathly white. Ned wonders idly if they've decided to do their dying before marching off to war, to get it out of the way. Like the muster at the Southwark Fair, they are a picture of improvisation, their plate, padded tunics and morion helmets consistent only in their dissimilarity. The recruits do their best to look suitably bold, while – to Vyves's shouted commands, delivered in a quite unmartial falsetto – they practise their advances, their shouldering, their porting and their trailing. They finish with a flourish, presenting their pikes to face an imaginary cavalry charge: anchoring them under the right foot, the shaft thrust upwards at an angle and braced against a bent left knee, the right hand swinging over it and across the semi-crouching body to draw the sword and point it along the pike as a secondary defence. This they manage with only a few stumbles from the less robust and coordinated amongst them. The small crowd shows its approval with a rousing cheer. Tyrone's papist rebels are assumed to be already vanquished.

As the recruits take their ease, their frosty breath torn away like cannon smoke, Vyves catches sight of Ned. For a moment he seems uncertain what to do. His high, domed forehead gleams like alabaster in the pale light. The long, lank hair and the single eye give him the appearance of a disreputable faun escaped from an enchanted glade. Then he walks over, puffing out his chest, as if he believes it might actually intimidate.

'What are you doing here?'

'Thought I'd come to see what the Earl of Essex keeps in the way of grey'ounds,' Ned replies amiably. 'This lot look like they couldn't catch a cold, let alone a coney.'

'Don't you worry, Master Ned,' says Vyves. 'A week or two under Sir Oliver's captains an' these lads will soon have the rebels running back to their bogs.' He nods towards one of the recruits, a pimply, whey-faced lad hanging onto a pike with all the assuredness of a man who's been handed a chain at the end of which is a wild beast. From the tip, a banner showing a boar's head against a red chevron ripples angrily on the wind.

'I'll take your word for it, Ensign Vyves,' Ned says. 'Any likelihood of *you* goin' with them?'

By the look Vyves gives him in reply, Ned might think that he's just suggested selling the Crown Jewels to the French.

'Without sound fellows in England to make the arrangements, an army is naught but a band of wandering vagabonds,' Vyves announces confidently.

'I 'aven't seen you in the Jackdaw of late, Ensign Vyves,' Ned observes. 'Run out of folks to gull, 'ave you?'

Vyves attempts to peer around Ned's bulk to see if Nicholas is lurking somewhere in the crowd. Satisfied he is not, the ensign confides, 'I came to the conclusion that particular part of Bankside is unwelcoming.'

'Unwelcoming? It most surely was so for poor Lemuel Godwinson,' Ned says.

Vyves's gaze flickers over Ned's impassive face. 'What you implying?'

'I 'eard from Dr Selby you 'ave an alibi for that night.'

'I do. I was with Master Strollot. And he was with me.'

'A right pair of turtle doves.' Ned looks up at the fleeting clouds as though they might vouchsafe an answer. 'An' who can prove otherwise?'

Vyves's manner hardens. 'Just 'cause you're a big bugger doesn't mean you can accuse an honest fellow of committing a felony and expect no consequences.' He glances at Ned's balled fist. 'Don't think I haven't noticed that brand on your thumb, Master Monkton. If I or Master Strollot were to tell a magistrate it was *you* who murdered young Godwinson, and swore an affidavit to that effect, you'd *hang*. There's no pleading the Holy Book a second time.'

To Ned's eternal credit, he keeps himself in check. And when he tells her of the incident, Rose will kiss him and say how proud she is. The Ned Monkton of old would have laid Barnabas Vyves out cold, regardless of how crucial he is to the conduct of Her Majesty's war in Ireland.

✠

In the courtyard of the Jackdaw, Ned and little Bruno are fighting to the death. In fact Ned has died twice already, his great body lying motionless on the flagstones until Bruno resurrects him by clambering onto his chest, tugging at Ned's beard with one hand and waving his wooden sword over him to cast a life-restoring spell with the other. Nicholas offers helpful advice on their swordplay.

'I've been meanin' to say – I saw Vyves again,' Ned says as he gets to his feet for a third bout. 'He was musterin', or whatever he does. ''Course he's not goin' to Ireland with 'em. 'As to stay 'ere in England, to run the war for the queen.'

Nicholas laughs. 'Then we're defeated before Essex reaches Chester.'

'I still know that little arseworm is up to somethin',' Ned says, dusting himself down and picking up his wooden sword. In his huge hands it looks like a poor man's crucifix. ''E threatened me.'

'That takes a brave man,' Nicholas says. 'I hope you didn't—'

'Nah,' says Ned with a shake of his great fiery head. 'I's a different fellow now, you know that.'

'All the same, Ned, tread carefully. I don't want you getting into trouble while I'm away.'

'It's that poor lad, Lemuel Godwinson, what I can't get out of me 'ead. Looked so pitiful when Constable Osborne brought 'im into the Jackdaw that night. Someone should pay for that. An' I 'ave a conviction that Vyves knows more 'bout it than 'e's lettin' on.'

'All the same, if there's no evidence to prove Vyves and Strollot were involved, there's little to be done, Ned. And I remember what happened last time you tried to take the law into your own hands. You almost ended up on the gallows. Think of Rose.'

'Aye, you're right of course,' says Ned as he adopts his guard in preparation for a joyous lunge from Bruno. 'It's naught to do with me. I must learn to keep me nose out of other people's business.'

✠

Upstairs, in the Monktons' privy chamber, Rose and Bianca are weeping on each other's shoulder.

'I'm the worst mother in all Christendom,' Bianca sobs. 'Worse even than Medea – the one who murdered all her children.'

'Medea was a pagan,' Rose wails in reply.

'Then I'm the worst mother in all creation!'

'Bruno was fine last time – 'e'll be fine again this time,' Rose assures her, honking through her tears like an over-excitable goose. 'There will be no cause for you to fret. Ned and I will take good care of 'im; you know we will.'

'Promise me one thing,' Bianca says, releasing Rose from her grip but leaving her hands on her friend's shoulders as though to bind them both in an unbreakable blood-pact.

'Anything,' Rose assures her, observing her former mistress through the watery screen of her tears. 'Anything.'

'Don't let him dress Buffle up as a knight's charger. They both contrived to ruin my best Flemish kerchief.'

In fact Nicholas and Bianca are not due to leave until the day after tomorrow, with the baggage train and the great trail of camp-followers: hammermen to repair damaged plate armour; farriers to shoe the horses; bakers and millers to produce the bread; powder-makers to mix gunpowder for the falconets, muskets and pistols, and to sieve the correct size of grain for each; and women to cook, tend, comfort and – though no one is inclined to consider the possibility at present – bury the dead. Tomorrow, the twenty-seventh day of March, London will turn out to bid farewell to Robert Devereux as he leaves to join his army at Chester; hence the city's general mood: the pain of parting. Neither Bianca nor Nicholas is immune to it. But at least taking your farewells early means there is time for one more tearful embrace between friends, one more chance for a little boy to slay a red-bearded giant and win his father's applause.

26

It is the first building of any real substance that Cachorra has seen. It stands in a small, easily guarded valley beside a winding river cloaked with alder trees, its stern grey walls softened by moss and weathered by centuries. A great herd of cattle ranges over the grassy slopes. Rain washes the valley, the cattle and the house, drifting on the wind in a procession of misty veils. Drawn up before the small portcullis is a band of some twenty men. She knows they are warriors by the swords that hang from their belts – swords so large it must take both hands to swing them. Some carry spears and axes. All are bearded, their hair long and unkempt. They look like beggars. Yet they bear themselves like kings, proud and ferocious. And their dress! Cachorra has never seen the like. Cloaks and tunics, like the ancients might wear; tartan hose with the pattern cut on the bias; cloaks that wouldn't look out of place – or so she imagines, for she has only ever heard of such things from Father Persons whenever one of his English lessons ended up in a discussion of the Latin classics that always put Constanza to sleep – on an enemy chieftain about to do battle with the Romans. Some wear nothing on their legs at all, but go about with their lower limbs quite uncovered, their privy regions barely covered by the hems of their tunics. Accustomed, if only at a distance, to the general magnificence of a Spanish gentlemen in his war plumage, Cachorra doesn't know whether to be scandalized or admire them for their fortitude. How, she wonders, do they not catch their death of cold?

'If there isn't a proper bed with proper pillows, and hot water to wash with, I shall damn this island as the most barbarous place on God's earth,' mutters Constanza in her sharp Castilian as their guide leads them towards the entrance. 'And if I hear any more of their dreadful pipe music – all that wailing and groaning, like a bull being slaughtered – may my ears be for ever shut up.'

I wish *you*'d shut up, sighs Constanza to herself.

The fighters part to let the two women pass. The portcullis rises with a heavy rumble into the roof of the gatehouse.

'Why do they stare so?' Constanza asks. 'Haven't they seen women before? Why do they look at you, rather than me? Why do they not show me the proper courtesies? Why can they not speak to me in Spanish – are they uneducated? Not that I would ever dream of replying if they did. Not for a moment. The meanest of our servants at Valladolid wouldn't have dared to attend my father dressed like *that*. Look at the ones without britches! Is this a bordello they have brought us to?'

One slice from the blade of one of those great swords, thinks Cachorra, trying to restrain herself. *One slice*. That's all it would take.

'My mistress wishes to know what they are saying?' she asks wearily, turning to their guide, the lad who led them to safety after the wreck, who has been their constant protector.

'They say that only now will they believe the myth of the Merrow,' he says with a grin. Then, seeing the look of perplexity on Cachorra's face, he adds, 'The Merrow is a woman of the sea, who comes onto the land to steal away the hearts of men. They also want to know if all the other women who live at the bottom of the ocean have skins the colour of a chestnut.'

'Then tell them this,' says Cachorra with a bright laugh. 'I *am* this woman they speak of. And I am dark because I come from stronger rootstock than their pale oaks.'

In the courtyard beyond the gatehouse four men stand in conversation. As Cachorra approaches, one of them turns and steps forward, not so much in greeting as with curiosity. He is a tall, imposing man in a quilted jerkin hung with studded plates of armour, each no larger than a playing card. The metal moves with the action of his body, like the skin of the armadillo that Cachorra had so wanted to become when the Ciguayo took her. In age, she would place him close to fifty. He has a thoughtful face, proud and well bearded, but with an underlying sadness to it. His dark hair is receding, leaving a deep widow's peak down the centre of his brow, as though his skull has been cleaved in two. For a man who has come close to wresting Ireland from the English, he looks like as though he has tasted only bitter regret.

Their guide kneels, beckoning Cachorra to do the same. Of the three, only Constanza remains upright as he announces in his bravest voice: 'His Grace the O'Neill, Earl of Tyrone!'

✠

It is a fair day on which to bid England's fairest earl God speed. London wakes at cockcrow to a bright, clear sky. At St Paul's Cross and in churches throughout the city prayers are offered for Robert Devereux's protection and the success of his great enterprise in Ireland. By the time the bells ring out the second hour of the afternoon, a great throng of Londoners has gathered in the Strand beyond Temple Bar. The street vendors are making a killing, selling oysters, baked apples and hot pies. The scent of battle is already in the air: the sizzling fat of roasted mutton in mortal combat with the sour reek of fresh horse-dung. Whenever someone comes out of Essex House – even a humble messenger or a servant – a great cheer rises from the crowd. No one appears troubled by the grey clouds that are beginning to drift across the sky.

On Bankside, Ned and Rose have chosen not to attend the earl's departure. Overt displays of wealth and assumed glory do not sit comfortably with Ned. But a parade is a parade. Rose convinces him to join her by the southern gatehouse of London Bridge, to watch Sir Oliver Henshawe's company march up Long Southwark and across the bridge to join up with the earl's column on the Strand. Henshawe himself appears martial enough, riding beneath his banner – the boar's head against a red chevron rippling from his lance – though he's too pretty for Ned's liking. Barnabas Vyves struts a few paces behind Henshawe's horse, his one eye glaring fiercely, his lank grey hair blowing about his shoulders. Ned wonders how far he'll go before he leaves the column. He's sure Vyves has no intention of exposing himself to any real danger.

Henshawe's company is less impressive than its captain: the same ill-fed, awkward farm boys, discharged apprentices, rescued vagabonds and paroled jailbirds that Ned has observed before, though they have just about managed to learn the complexities of marching in step. But the people who have come out of their houses to watch them pass seem contented by the sight.

On the Strand young Bruno squeals with excitement, jabbing his stubby little fingers at the gatehouse of the imposing mansion that he can see from his vantage point atop Nicholas's shoulders.

As the church bells fall silent, four trumpeters in bright orange tunics announce that the moment has come. A troop of pikemen in voluminous trunk-hose and steel breastplates march out and wheel into the Strand, their pikes waving like the masts of a little fishing fleet trying to keep their station in a heavy swell.

And here he comes!

A great roar goes up, sending the birds bursting out of the trees. Astride a charger that seems intent on taking flight with them, its head bucking, the spume splashing as it mouths the bit, sits Robert Devereux, the Lord Lieutenant himself, the Earl Marshal of England, the queen's champion – even if her favour *has* palled a little of late in the face of his constant pleas for advancement.

Clad in his finest armour of polished black plate, etched and gilded with intricate patterns that seem to swirl with a life of their own in the fading sunlight, Essex looks as though he is off to a joust. On his head is a handsome burgonet, the visor raised to allow the common folk to gaze upon his features in suitable admiration. From its crest a plume of white swan feathers dances in the freshening breeze. He is younger than Nicholas by a few years, yet he looks like a man who has had long enough on earth to conquer almost every part of it. Now he is off to claim the remainder.

Beside him – and almost as grandly mounted and attired – are his closest aides: the Earl of Southampton and Sir Christopher Blount, his stepfather. They make a show to stir the heart of every man, woman and child in the crowd.

Except for Bianca, who has never understood why men so enjoy the prospect of war. And Nicholas, who knows its true cost.

As he watches the spectacle, and the first drops of rain begin to fall, he can't prevent his memory taking him back to his time at grammar school, and in particular a Latin lesson. For weeks afterwards he had been unable to walk through the woods near Barnthorpe without experiencing a fit of the terrors. Because the lesson had involved translating a passage from Tacitus: the historian's account of the fate that befell the Roman general Publius Quinctilius Varus, who marched his army into the Teutoburg Forest to subdue the rebellious Germanic tribes, just as England's new Caesar intends to do in Ireland.

Varus had marched in with three full legions, Nicholas remembers reading. An invincible force, or so Varus had believed. But he had been wrong. Because sixteen centuries later their bones are still there, mouldering beneath the dripping foliage.

PART 3

✠

... Greate dammadge to her Majestie...

A View of the Present State of Ireland

EDMUND SPENSER

27

It is the first day of June, and it has been raining solidly for a week. The rain seems to know in advance where to find the eyeholes in a gaberdine cloak, or the way through the points of a quilted jerkin. It rusts the studs, hinges and swivel-hooks of plate armour, soaks the leather liners so that Bianca and her women can scarcely gather enough melilot and ground moss – bruised and boiled in water – to treat the chafing. Caesar's army no longer marches. It stumbles, slips and staggers. Nothing dries. Cord matches will not stay lit, so that when the rebels launch an ambush – a skill in which they seem to have been tutored by the Devil himself – they cannot be driven off with shot from the matchlocks and calivers. Instead they must be held at bay with the longbow, or else fought at close hand with sword, pike and poleaxe. The air itself seems drowned. It is becoming a torment without mercy: heartless, implacable and unconcerned whether you are an earl or a common horse-boy. It has no regard whether you are made of wool, leather, wood, steel or flesh. It will rot, rust and reduce you, and keep on raining. It is the second Flood. And this time no one has a place on the Ark.

In his tent, Nicholas studies the parchment roll on which he records the daily scything of sickness through the English army. To the accompaniment of the relentless liquid hammering against the canvas, he wonders if the Lord Lieutenant's once-grand enterprise will simply dissolve away before the skies clear. He aches with tiredness. He has caught only fragments of sleep for days. The sick-roll blurs before his sore eyes and he falls momentarily into a trance.

First had come the grand ceremony: Essex accepting his sword of office in the cathedral at Dublin. It was followed by wise counsel from men like Ormonde: *wait*. Wait until the rivers have given up at least some of the winter deluge. Wait until the tracks and bogs are a little easier to navigate. Wait for the pastures to ripen, so that enough cattle may be fattened to feed the army. Because Tyrone is canny. Tyrone is waiting in the north, in his Ulster fastness. It will take all that and more to reach him, let alone defeat him.

But England's Caesar is hungry for the glory he thinks is his due. The father was ruined by Ireland. The son will not wait for revenge. Essex orders a pointless meandering to the west and to the south, through Leinster and Munster. A few castles held by tiny, unsupported rebel garrisons surrender to him. Undefended towns throw open their gates and welcome him with loud but shallow protestations of loyalty. He takes it as a *form* of conquering, and it goes to his head. He thinks he is invincible.

And all the while, for every slight advance there are setbacks. The ambushes become ever more audacious and bloodier. He garrisons the towns he passes through not with fit men but with convalescents. The rest tire and sicken. The more experienced amongst them – those who have been taken from the army in the Low Countries – are beginning to give voice to the unthinkable: that whatever else Robert Devereux may be, when it comes to Caesars, he is more a Claudius than a Julius.

And still it rains. Dear loving Jesu, how it rains.

'Nicholas? *Nicholas!*'

Bianca's voice, breaking into his thoughts, makes him think for a moment that he is back on Bankside. Then the drumming of the rain on the canvas takes him again, like a nagging toothache that will not ease. Rubbing his aching eyes, he looks up from the campaign chest that he uses as a table.

Bianca ducks through the entrance of the tent they share, pitched amongst the baggage train and camp-followers. They are lucky. Those without such a luxury are forced to shelter under the trees, or in the lee of the wagons beneath whatever cover they can find or steal.

She has been out treating three men who – being previously farmhands from Warwickshire and thus uneducated in the science of combustion – thought that lighting a fire might be made easier by stealing a bag of black powder from the armourers. They had thrown it on the meagre flames that their flints had managed to strike out of the damp kindling.

'Are they improved?' Nicholas asks.

'The two with burnt hands bear their hurts well enough,' she replies. 'As to the third, there is no sign yet of his sight returning.' She wipes her brow with the rim of her hood before pulling it back over her shoulders. 'This place is thick with alder. I can make a decoction that might soothe. What are you doing?'

'The sick-roll – again.'

'Some of the women were saying we move tomorrow.'

'For Limerick, to receive supplies,' Nicholas tells her. 'Oliver Henshawe told me, while you were away.'

'What was *he* doing, skulking around the baggage train?'

'He said the constant rain was giving him a headache. I told him he had plenty of company.' Nicholas glances at the stack of pots and jars in the corner of the tent. 'Have you any oil of camomile and spikenard left? I told him you might be able to spare him a little.'

'Do you think Essex will take this rain as a sign from God that he should admit defeat and go home?' she asks.

'He hasn't yet,' Nicholas replies. 'I had hoped this would all be over quickly. Now I fear it could go on till the winter. I think you should go home. Be with Bruno.'

'Do you think I don't consider it every day?'

'I could arrange it. There's bound to be a ship at Waterford. And that order from the queen says nothing about a wife.'

Bianca places her palm against his cheek. The rain has chilled her flesh, but the touch feels warm to him. She says, 'How could I abide such a thing? How could I leave you here?'

'Are you frightened the Merrow will come and enchant me?' he asks, trying to lighten her mood.

Bianca looks again at the misty landscape beyond the tent. She laughs. 'When the *Seanchaí* spoke of the Merrow coming out of the sea, she said nothing at all about her bringing the ocean along for company.'

Nicholas is about to kiss her, to escape the immediate world if only for a few moments, when a shadow falls across the canvas and a figure fills the entrance.

'Dr Shelby, you are commanded to attend His Grace – at once.'

Nicholas recognizes Sir Henry Norris, one of Devereux's senior commanders.

'Is he sick?' Nicholas asks.

'Whatever else ails him, his anger seems healthy enough,' Norris says, pulling the face of the long-suffering subordinate. He is an old soldier, well into his fifties, a twinkling eye softening his flinty exterior. He glances at Bianca. 'I wouldn't tarry if I were you, Physician – however pleasing the cause might be.'

Nicholas throws his gaberdine cloak over his shoulders and follows Norris outside into the rain.

The army is encamped around Cahir Castle, given up by the rebels after a desultory bombardment. The oxen for hauling the artillery graze peacefully in the water meadows beside the River

Suir. A few have wandered into the tented lines of the baggage and powder trains. Nicholas and Henry Norris must shoo a pair out of their way with shouts and wild gestures as they hurry across the furrowed mud towards the grey walls of the castle, their boots spraying ochre torrents from the puddles. Nicholas asks again why he's being summoned.

'A reverse,' is all that Norris will tell him.

'Is the earl wounded?' Nicholas asks, chiding himself for a momentary wish that Essex has achieved a martyr's end in battle and they can all go home.

'Only in the heart,' Norris tells him, rolling his eyes at the cascading clouds.

✠

Essex is in the great hall of the castle. Surrounded by his senior commanders, he is reading a dispatch. His hair, at court so generously curled and primped, now hangs about his face like the torn remnants of an old sack. His skin has an unhealthy pallor. There is sweat on his brow. On the surface, he looks to Nicholas like a man in the late stages of quatrain fever. However, his body is shaking not with sickness, but with rage. When he notices Nicholas and Norris enter, he calls out, 'Dr Shelby, do you have a cure, perhaps, for cowardice, mutiny and sheer bloody incompetence?'

'Your Grace?'

Essex thrusts the dispatch at the messenger who brought it, as though he would make him eat it. 'Kill or cure?' he demands to know of Nicholas. 'As of this moment, my preference would be to kill.'

Nicholas looks to Norris for help.

'Tell him, Norris,' Essex barks.

With a diplomatic cough, Norris says, 'We have suffered a reverse – to Sir Henry Harington's force, at Arklow—'

Essex breaks in angrily, '*Reverse?* Two hundred or more dead! Men I can ill afford to lose. And all because the old fool Harington allowed the O'Byrnes to catch him unprepared. Those the rebels didn't kill broke and fled, almost to the walls of Wicklow. Captains deserted their men. English pike – *English*, mind, not Irish levies – broke and ran like frightened women. I tell you this, Harington is for prison. If he wasn't a privy councillor, I'd hang the bastard myself.'

'Your Grace, these are words spoken in haste,' says Norris. 'Reflection will put this setback in a better light.'

But Essex is not to be calmed.

'If Harington's men – those few who didn't desert – think they were flying to safety when they quit the field, I have news for them: I'm going to hang every damn one of them!'

Nicholas observes all this with growing alarm. He wonders if Norris has summoned him because he fears Essex is about to drop dead of apoplexy.

'Your Grace, surely you don't mean that,' says Norris soothingly.

'Watch me, Norris,' Essex snaps. 'I'll knot the ropes myself.'

'Sir, I urge you to be calm,' Norris says. He turns to Nicholas for support. 'Tell him, Dr Shelby: such extremity of the choleric humour is not good for him.'

Nicholas thinks it wiser to let the storm blow itself out.

But it seems the thunder has only just started to roll. Essex jabs a gloved finger at him. 'What manner of physician are you, sirrah? I've more of my army lying in a sickbed than standing in the ranks. Explain to me how so many men can sicken so quickly.'

Perhaps the earl lives in such rarefied air, thinks Nicholas, that he hasn't realized it's been raining for ever, and that the cold, the deep bogs, the mud, the bad water and the poor food have taken their inevitable toll on men less extraordinary than himself. He opens his mouth to say as much, but Essex cuts him off.

'It's not sickness, Doctor. I'll tell you what it is. It's *cowardice*. A mean wickedness of the spirit, bordering on treachery. They'd rather feign illness than face the enemy.'

A menacing jab of a gloved finger in Nicholas's direction.

'And *you* excuse it.'

Nicholas feels the heat rise in his cheeks. 'That is unjust and untrue, Your Grace. The men are sickening because of the conditions, their lack of proper equipment and victuals. I treat as many as I can, with what I have. If there is fault in this army, it does not lie on *my* shoulders.'

For a moment the officers surrounding Essex just stare at him. To his surprise, Nicholas finds himself standing his ground.

'If Your Grace is displeased with my service here in Ireland, it is within your power to send me back to England. I'm sure the queen will understand.'

Norris puts his palm against his forehead and closes his eyes. One or two of the earl's officers glance at their master to observe the anticipated eruption of anger. But Devereux keeps himself in check. He waves them all away, ordering only Nicholas to remain. When they are alone, he says,

'I will tell you plainly, Dr Shelby, I am in a troubled humour.'

'Your responsibilities would weigh heavily on any man, my lord,' Nicholas tells him, surprised by the earl's candour.

'It's naught to do with responsibilities. I am accustomed to responsibilities. This is a deeper melancholy.'

'If I am to assist, Your Grace, I must first know the symptoms.'

Essex turns his back upon Nicholas, as though leaving it to someone else to speak on his behalf, even though everyone else has retreated into the shadows of the great hall.

'I have moments of great weariness that come upon me. I have no appetite. My body is sometimes afflicted with sharp pains. Do you think, perhaps, it is the first sign of marsh fever?'

'May I be permitted to make an examination, Your Grace?'

Reluctantly Essex faces him. He sits in a chair while Nicholas looks into his eyes – and notices the broken blood vessels around the irises, marks the greyness of the skin, searches for open lesions that don't appear to be healing.

'Do you have any chancres about your body?' he asks.

'Only where my armour chafes against wet flesh. They'll go when it stops raining. If it ever does.'

Nicholas gives a slow, sympathetic nod. 'I'll have my wife prepare a balm of moneywort and honey. That should ease them. As for the internal pains, it could be that you are afflicted by a kidney stone. I'll ask her to grind a medlar kernel and some parsley root into a powder to add to your wine. That may help.'

'Do so,' says Essex gruffly. Then, as though it is the hardest symptom of all to confront, he says, 'I do have a temper, I will admit that. But recently it comes unbidden and with a fury that startles even me. I see enemies everywhere. And I don't mean the rebels. Can your wife mix me a powder for *that*?'

For a while Nicholas considers the challenge in silence. Then he says, 'A man would have to be made of rock not to find this campaign debilitating, Your Grace. It is a testimony to your constitution that you're not in the hospital alongside all those other fellows, whose ability to bear these trials you so despise.'

'You mean, you don't know what's wrong with me?' Essex says bluntly. 'Were Ormonde and Henshawe wrong when they sang your praises?'

Nicholas laughs. 'I *could* study a flask of your urine, or bleed you, but I don't think that would help. Besides, if you know anything of me – and after Her Majesty appointed me, I *assume* you made enquiries – you will have heard me spoken of as being something of a heretic when it comes to physic. I hold a great deal of what is written by the ancients to be false. I believe our present understanding of medicine to be flawed. Therefore I resist making diagnoses unless I can be sure. And I don't offer cures beyond what I know will work. My instinct tells me that you demand too much of yourself. If a man sets himself an impossible task, melancholy is to be expected when he fails to achieve it.'

Essex studies him for a moment in silence. For Nicholas, it is an uncomfortable inspection. Then the earl says, 'You're not seriously suggesting that I relinquish command of the army, are you? My enemies at court would fall upon me like jackals. Her Highness would discover an enmity in her heart for me as would never again be extinguished.'

'If you are truly in search of the cause of your melancholy, Your Grace,' Nicholas says, remembering how Ireland had destroyed the earl's father, 'then I believe you should seek the explanation not from me, but from within yourself.'

Essex almost springs out of the chair, throwing it backwards. As it crashes onto the flagstones, he shoos Nicholas away as though he were no better than an impertinent chambermaid. 'Enough! Be gone,' he shouts. His once-handsome face scowls with malevolent fury. There is spittle in the corner of his mouth. 'Ormonde and Henshawe were wrong. You're just a quack, like all the others. And a quack in the pay of Robert Cecil, more's the like. In this army, it seems, you don't have to flee the enemy to be a traitor. Get out of my sight, Shelby, or by God I'll hang you from the gibbet alongside Harington's men. Maybe then the queen will send me a physician who knows his business.'

✠

'The pox? The Earl of Essex has syphilis?'

In their tent, Bianca stares at Nicholas in astonishment. He shakes his head to throw off the rain.

'How can you tell, after such a brief examination?'

Nicholas lays aside his gaberdine cloak. 'Oh, I'm not *that* clever. Old Dr Lopez, the queen's physician, once told me there was a rumour the earl was infected.'

'And look what happened to *him*,' Bianca says in alarm.

'He does show some symptoms of the dormant stage of the disease: the sudden wild swings of mood, the pains, the broken blood vessels in his eyes, the chancres. But I could hardly ask him to let me inspect his privy member, could I?'

'Please God, say you didn't tell him.'

'Of course not. I may be wet through from this accursed rain, but my brains haven't dissolved quite yet.'

'Do you think he knows?'

'I can't say. I wouldn't imagine his own physicians in England have dared to tell him.'

Bianca shakes her head in disbelief. 'That's all we need. We're trapped with an army well on the way to being defeated, in a place that seems to be sinking into the sea, in the hands of a pox-ridden adventurer beset by a chronic mania, who might decide to hang us if the mood takes him.'

'You forgot to include this: he knows I'm here to spy on him for Robert Cecil.'

'*Well*, that just puts the marchpane on the pastry, doesn't it?'

Nicholas sinks onto their pallet and puts his head in his hands. 'Do you think the Earl of Tyrone might have use for a physician?'

'We could try to slip aboard a ship at Waterford,' Bianca says.

'That would make us deserters. Then he'd have a real excuse to hang us.'

Bianca joins Nicholas on the pallet. She throws her arms around him, holding him close.

'I'm sorry,' he says. 'I should never have brought you back from Padua. We should have stayed.'

'If I had wanted to stay, Nicholas, I would have stayed. There was nothing for us there, not after Cousin Bruno died. Padua holds too many bad memories.'

'It's where our son was born.'

'And we brought his goodness with us to Bankside.'

'I know you miss him more than you admit.'

'I'm his *mother*.'

'When we finally escape from here, when we're back on Bankside, I'll renounce all ambition. I'll give up medicine and become a humble barber-surgeon: mend broken bones and stitch wounds. I'll do what I know works. The queen won't call me to Whitehall to hear about *that*. She'll soon forget who I am. And as for Robert Cecil – well, Bankside is as good a place as any for our Bruno to grow strong and true. He might not end up quoting Virgil and marrying a rich nobleman's daughter, but at least he'll know the difference between dissembling and straight talking.'

'You'll do what you know to be right,' Bianca tells him gently. 'You always do. Your decency is the most infuriating thing about you. But I've learned to admire it.'

They stay entwined for a while, each giving and drawing strength and comfort. Then Bianca looks up at the canvas about her head. It has stopped trembling.

'Nicholas, look,' she says. 'I think the rain is easing.'

28

Cachorra lays a hand against Constanza's clammy brow. Her mistress groans, turns her head away, dampening the pillow with her sweat and the little bubbles that froth at the corners of her plump lips.

What shall I do if she dies? Cachorra asks herself. What will be my purpose then? Where shall I go? Not back to Valladolid – there is nothing there for me now.

It is the awful weather that has laid her mistress low, Cachorra is sure of it. A few days in the heat of Castile and she would soon recover. But here, in this wet, cold, wild place, Cachorra fears her mistress will succumb to the sickness that came upon her only days after reaching what they had both assumed was a kind of safety.

The Earl of Tyrone has sent his physicians every day, old men as grey as the weather. They have bled Constanza regularly, holding up the glass beakers to study the colour of the blood against a candle flame. They have bathed her in icy water from the nearby river, given her purgatives that stink even worse than the resulting eliminations. They have made her drink water with barley stewed in it, with crushed violets, with marjoram and with agrimony. They have laid kerchiefs soaked in hot oil over her breasts. They have fed her a sludge of hares' brains to absorb whatever is causing her to tremble so. One even brought her a dead toad, bandaging it against her belly to draw out the dampness in her. In

Cachorra's mind, the only improvement in Constanza's condition is that her exhaustion has shut off her continual complaining.

The Earl of Tyrone has proved a gentle and courteous host. He is an imposing man, sturdy and bearded. Before she fell ill, Constanza had even deigned to speak to him in English. He has dispatched a messenger to Scotland, there to take ship for Antwerp. The fellow is carrying a letter to Constanza's intended husband in the Spanish Netherlands, telling him of the shipwreck and asking him to send men to bring her to him. What will they find when they come, Cachorra wonders – that he has been a widower for months without knowing it?

The letter, Cachorra reasons, will have an unintended – and undesirable – consequence. News of the shipwreck will eventually find its way from Antwerp to Madrid. Questions will be asked. Questions like: what was the *San Juan de Berrocal* doing off the coast of Ireland in the first place? If anyone asks her, she has already decided to play the innocent. What could a servant possibly know of her master's secret intentions?

Cachorra remembers the care her dear Don Rodriquez had taken to ensure that she understood the importance of his mission. The implication was clear, though never actually voiced. *If something were to befall me, I don't trust Constanza not to make a hash of things in my absence. I must therefore trust in you, my brave leopard cub.*

No, if they ask her, she will plead the ignorance of the lowly.

There is another fear troubling Cachorra as she wipes Constanza's brow, the kerchief cold and damp, as though the malady has seeped into it, infecting the linen. What if Constanza – in her delirium – cries out in English the true reason Don Rodriquez brought them to Ireland? It would be just like her contrary, mutton-headed mistress to blurt out things that are best kept silent. Now that she has spoken English in Tyrone's presence, she might even spill the truth: that Don Rodriquez had not come to Ireland to offer him Spain's support in his rebellion against the heretic English. How welcome would they be then?

Cachorra has long wondered if there might be some way, some stratagem, to find the Englishman, Spenser. But where in this damp, misty island *is* he? Has he heard of the shipwreck? Does he know there are survivors? Is he, at this very moment, leading men in search of them?

A terrible weight of responsibility bears down upon her. She feels her eyes begin to prickle as the tears well. The loneliness and the rain she can tolerate. She even allows herself a moment's resigned pleasure at the thought of her mistress being restored to her former cantankerous self. But failing Don Rodriquez Calva de Sagrada – *that* is too great a shame for her to bear.

✠

Ned Monkton dips a rag into a pail and scrubs vigorously at the little lozenges of glass set into the window-leads of the Jackdaw tavern. Rivulets of dissolved dirt stream down the brickwork below the sill. He rubs harder. Although Mistress Bianca is not here to show her disapproval of the amount of mud and horse-dung that gets thrown up by the traffic in the lane, Ned cannot escape the feeling that somehow she is able to see even the slightest lapse in housekeeping. Besides, she has Rose to ensure that standards are maintained. 'What if the queen were to happen by?' Rose had asked him barely an hour ago, as though Her Majesty was in the habit of popping over to Bankside for a jug of knock-down and a plate of oysters whenever the burden of monarchy became too great to bear.

Wringing the water from his cleaning rag, Ned is about to plunge it back into his pail when he feels something brush against his legs. He turns and sees a black-muzzled sheep studying him with narrow, uncomprehending eyes.

The lane is full of them. And standing on the perimeter of this woolly throng is a wiry, weather-beaten man of some sixty years or more. He too is staring at Ned, but with a great deal more acuity.

'I *know* you, I'm sure I do,' the man says in the slow drawl of someone for whom cities are strange and alien places. 'But you're not from Camberwell, I know that much.'

'Ned Monkton,' replies Ned helpfully. 'Most on Bankside knows me. But I ain't been to Camberwell, never.'

The shepherd's face lights up with a sad recognition. 'It's come to me! You're the fellow who was at the coroner's inquest into the death of my son, Lemuel. You stood up to them jurors like you was their equal.'

Ned lets his rag drop into the pail. '*You*'re Lemuel Godwinson's father?'

'Aye, up from Camberwell, with this flock. I's taking them to the Mutton Lane shambles. City prices are always better than country ones.'

'Stop by, when you've handed them off,' Ned says, smiling broadly because he knows his size and appearance can often alarm. 'I'll stand you a jug; set you up proper for the walk back.'

'I'd like that,' says the shepherd.

The smile he gives in return makes Ned think the man has been a stranger to mirth for some considerable time.

✠

'I never wanted Lemuel to volunteer for the muster,' Aaron Godwinson says later, as he sits with Ned in the taproom, looking out on the lane through the now-gleaming glass. 'An' his mother was set against it with all her heart. Ireland is no place for a Camberwell man. I blame myself for letting him make his mark on the roll.'

'Some thinks there's glory to be 'ad in takin' up arms. More fool them, I say,' Ned replies gravely. 'These days the 'edgerows 'ave more maimed veterans of the wars sleepin' under 'em than they 'ave 'edge'ogs.'

'But that's it, you see, Ned. Lemuel told his mother an' me that he didn't 'ave to go.'

'To Ireland?'

'Aye. But he'd still get paid a bounty for mustering.' Godwinson shakes his head at the lack of application in the young. 'I told him, "A fellow don't get money from the queen just 'cause she's feeling generous." Well, not unless it's alms on Maundy Thursday. But to tell the truth, we needed the money to help us through till spring. Times is hard in Camberwell at present.'

'Let me get this straight,' Ned says, laying down his tankard and leaning across the table. 'Your Lemuel thought he could join a company mustered for Ireland, but not 'ave to actually go there to do the fightin'?'

'Aye. Half a month's pay, up front – ten shillings. That's twice what he earned as my apprentice.'

'For doing nothin'?'

'Apart from spending a day learning his pike, and then marching around at the Southwark Fair for a bit, yes. Nothing but taking his ease. Lemuel said he'd be back in a week. He was. With the money.' Aaron Godwinson looks down at the table board as though he cannot bear to remember what happened next. When he looks up again, there are tears welling in his eyes. 'If only he'd stayed in Camberwell with me and his mother, he'd have been fine.'

Ned sees in his mind once again the tall, angular Lemuel huddled in the corner of the taproom with Vyves and Strollot... the coin changing hands.

'Who told 'im all this?' Ned asks gently.

'The muster ensign,' says Aaron, brushing the tears away with the back of a gnarled hand. 'That fellow with the one eye who was on the coroner's jury. Had a funny name. Stuck in my mind, when Lemuel told me. Vyves, I think Lemuel said. That's it: Barnabas Vyves.'

✠

That evening Ned seeks out a regular customer at the Jackdaw, a pouch-maker from Long Lane who has served in the Low Countries. He asks him how the muster is organized, to get clear in his mind the picture that is beginning to form there.

'The queen says to the Privy Council: sirrahs, fetch me one thousand fine men to fight the papist rebels, right?' the pouch-maker tells him.

'Right,' agrees Ned. 'What then?'

'The Privy Council bow and scrape and scuttle away to draw up the plans for the muster. So many men from Surrey... so many men of Kent... so many lads from Sussex... and so on. With me so far, Master Ned?'

Ned says he is.

'When the levies have been raised, each company parades before a magistrate or an alderman. The muster roll is signed by the captain or one of his officers, to confirm the troop has been properly assembled and equipped. Then the magistrate, or the alderman, or some other high person, hands over the money for pay and supply, enough to maintain the mustered men until they can be resupplied. That's several months, usually. Our captain paid for his drink and his whores out of our funds, I recall,' the pouch-maker says, pulling a sour face. 'We never did get our promised pay in full.'

'But you *did* go to the Low Countries?'

The man looks at Ned as if he's the dullest-brained fellow on earth. 'Of course we went to the Low Countries. We'd have been hanged, otherwise.' Seeing Ned's brow furrow in thought, he shakes his head and laughs. 'What? You think Her Majesty would pay good minted coin just to have her soldiery taking their ease at home in the taverns? Now that *would* be a muster worth signing on for.'

✠

Ireland is devouring Robert Devereux as efficiently as it devoured his father. In the process, it is turning him into a monster. True to his word, on the army's return to Dublin he imprisons the hapless Sir Henry Harington, cashiers his officers and, despite pleas from Ormonde, Henry Norris, Oliver Henshawe and even Nicholas himself, hangs one in every ten of Sir Henry's surviving soldiers.

Nicholas observes his wild swings of mood with alarm. They career from euphoric optimism to petulant despair. One moment he is all for taking his forces north into Ulster and defeating Tyrone in open battle... the next, he must run back to England and prostrate himself before his queen, because the court – by which he means Robert Cecil – has turned Elizabeth against him.

'There must be *something* you can prescribe for His Grace, to bring him out of this ill humour,' Henry Norris says to Nicholas the following day, while the corpses still swing gently in the wind, a reminder to all of the price cowardice carries.

Physic has not yet come up with a cure for hubris, Nicholas considers telling him. But he keeps his counsel. Is it Ireland? Or is the cause of the earl's distemper the malady no one dares mention? He considers offering the Lord Lieutenant mercury. But that would involve revealing his suspicions. *Your Grace – try taking* this, *it might soothe your temper, and it's considered most efficacious for those suffering from the pox.*

As an alternative, he prescribes a draught of sow-fennel and euphorbium boiled in vinegar, in an attempt to bring the earl's lethargy and frenzy into more of a balance. 'Perhaps this might ease your present discomfort a little and help you sleep,' he says, offering the cup.

Essex drinks the decoction grudgingly. 'If this an attempt to poison me, the way you conspired with old Lopez to poison the queen,' he tells Nicholas in a voice that chills him to the marrow, 'you'll be rotting in a noose alongside Harington's cowards.'

Nicholas reminds Devereux that the charge was bogus. That he was exonerated. But that night the earl complains of stomach pains, and it is Nicholas who cannot sleep for worry. The following morning he bumps into Henry Norris again, who reveals the true cause of the earl's discomfort. The post-pinnace from England has brought letters of stern rebuke from Her Majesty. She is not at all pleased with the army's progress. In her opinion, the small triumphs Essex has so far achieved are mere trifles – unworthy prizes that any half-competent general might achieve, even if he had stayed abed. The earl himself is forbidden in no uncertain terms from returning to England until he has accomplished what Her Majesty sent him to Ireland to do. Nicholas's relief is tempered by Norris's revelation that the letter contained a footnote bearing the signature of Robert Cecil, adding his own prohibition as principal Secretary of State against the earl's return. Another reason, Nicholas thinks, for Robert Devereux to take offence at my presence.

In the taverns of Dublin the earl's supporters are drinking themselves into a morose fury. The enemy now is not only Tyrone and his rebels, but those back in London who have whispered their poisoned words into the queen's ear. A few rash individuals, who think themselves protected by their distance from London, speak openly of begging Essex to take what is left of his army back to England, to purge the court of those they consider traitors. They believe they could compel the queen to honour their commander as they believe he should be honoured.

Nicholas duly notes all this in a cipher to Cecil and hands it to one of Mr Secretary's trusted captains when he goes down to Wood Quay to collect a consignment of iron pestles for Bianca's women to mix herbs in. He takes care to describe only a general mood of frustration, and he leaves out the names. His conscience is troubled enough, without having the deaths of a few weary, dispirited drunks weighing on it, and he'll be damned if he'll sink to the level of a common informer.

✠

Essex is not the man to let such barbs from his sovereign stand. Whatever else Ireland has done to him, it hasn't diminished his pride. In late July, with the crops standing unharvested in the fields, he rides out of Dublin at the head of a much-reduced force. His declared intention is to bring the clans of O'Connor and O'Moore, allies of Tyrone, into proper obedience to her sovereign majesty, before turning north into Ulster to finally lop off the gorgon's head. Norris and Henshawe go with him.

This time Nicholas is commanded to ride with the earl's headquarters. Whether this is because Essex thinks his constitution might be in need of physic, or because he doesn't trust his physician far from his immediate grasp, Nicholas is uncertain. Devereux's opinion of him appears to swing with the state of his health. When he's well, Nicholas is a Cecil spy and the worst man on earth. When he sickens, it's *Call for Physician Shelby. He's the only man on this isle, save me, who knows his business...*

'Stay in Dublin,' Nicholas begs Bianca before they leave. 'I have a bad feeling about this.'

'Then I would have Bruno *and* you to worry about.' She lays her hand against his cheek. 'I'm coming with you,' she says firmly.

He folds his arms behind his head, closing his eyes and bowing as if in deference to old memories. 'When my first wife, Eleanor, died carrying our child,' he says, 'I realized that I couldn't trust the physic I'd learned at Cambridge. I threw away my doctor's gown into the Thames in disgust.' He looks into her eyes again. 'Tell me: what shall I throw away now, if I were to lose *you*? The stars in all their multitude would not be nearly enough.'

'You won't *lose* me, Nicholas,' she laughs, kissing him on the forehead.

But in her mind – for a reason she cannot at that moment explain – Bianca is seeing Nicholas as the Merrow might see him: standing on the shore gazing out to sea in search of the love he cannot summon back. The image fills her with a deep sense of foreboding.

29

Nicholas reins in his horse on the edge of a great wood, much like the one where he and Bianca had encountered the *Seanchaí*. He pats the hot, slick hair of her neck in praise, smelling her sweat on the warm air. It is late afternoon, and for once it's not raining. On the grassy slope below the treeline, several hundred men are sitting or lying in the sunshine, resting from the march. Some are sharpening or cleaning their weapons. Others have snatched the chance of sleep. They lie like men already dead. Bianca is half a mile back, along with the baggage train.

Sir Henry Norris walks over to greet him. His breastplate is unlaced and he carries his burgonet helmet under his arm. He, too, is sweating in the unusual heat. 'When they arrive, you may set up your things over there, Dr Shelby. By that line of oaks,' he says. 'Though God willing, you won't be much employed today.'

'I thought His Grace intended to provoke the rebels into battle. Isn't that why we're here?'

'They won't dare sally out of Conna Castle, and that's a day's march further on, towards Lismore,' Norris says, grinning. 'They'll shout at us from behind their walls, and we'll march proudly by and thumb our noses at them. They're not so foolish as to pick a fight with us in the open.'

Nicholas spots Oliver Henshawe's banner flapping sullenly in the breeze. A thought occurs to him, and Norris seems just the man to answer it. 'I've heard His Grace air the opinion that he thinks but little of the men recruited from the local population,' he says casually, knowing he should tread carefully.

Norris gives a contemptuous laugh. 'Where were you born, Dr Shelby?'

'Suffolk, Sir Henry. Why?'

'Well, imagine trying to raise a troop of Suffolk men to fight their neighbours in Norfolk, and then give them old weapons, little money and even less food. Call them cowards when they waver. Hang them when they break. It's hardly a surprise if they then melt away into the forests and meres the moment your back is turned. We need more fellows who've served in the Low Countries and know the score. Better still, rogues who kill for money. We should have hired the Swiss.'

'Sir Oliver Henshawe recruits from his lands in Surrey, does he not?'

'Probably. Haven't asked him.'

'I only mention it because his company seems to be made up mostly of Irish conscripts.'

'We take what we can get, Dr Shelby. If the muster masters in England send us weak boys with no fighting spirit, we must make the best of what we have here in Ireland.'

'But Sir Oliver told me, before Christmas, that his men from England were stuck in Chester, awaiting transport. Where are they? Have they been somehow spirited away?'

'What are you suggesting, Dr Shelby?'

'I don't know. But where *are* they? Surely Sir Oliver would want every man he can muster to be here, with the earl's forces – especially given the rate of sickness amongst those who *are*.'

'Knowing how efficient the Privy Council can be, they're probably still in Chester,' Norris replies with a gruff, self-satisfied laugh. 'I wouldn't fret, Dr Shelby. They've most likely been used to stiffen some of the outlying garrison. Or they've succumbed to bog fever. I wouldn't concern yourself with such matters. Sir Oliver is twice the captain old Harington was. If anyone can put backbone into Irish levies, it will be him.' He points to the line of oak trees he'd indicated earlier. 'There, in the shade, should do nicely. But I think you'll not have much in the way of trade today. Maybe a few blistered feet, but nothing that's been valorously earned. Take the time to rest. I would – if I were you.'

✠

The sound of the army breaking camp brings Nicholas and Bianca awake. Looking out of their tent, they see the forest has disappeared, swallowed by the fog that has settled overnight like a shroud. In the twilight before dawn, it coalesces into half-human shapes that flit and writhe before vanishing again, to be replaced by new creatures that seem to spring out of the ground, live for a moment or two in strange animation before sinking back into the soil. It is as though all the ghosts of this conflict have gathered together in one spot to dance a pavane to the living. Voices seem flattened. The snorting and whinnying of the horses sound like the fading echoes left behind after a parade has passed by.

The baggage train is to remain where it is camped. It will move once the main force has cleared the track along the forest's edge and secured the land around Conna Castle. Go back to sleep, Nicholas tells Bianca. Sleep is almost as important as food or water. Like them, it must be seized when the opportunity presents.

He wakes again and thinks the rain has returned – a scattering of hail, perhaps, striking the canvas of the tent. Then he hears a shout from close by.

'Physician! Where is the physician? He is needed forward.'

Another scattering of hail, longer but more ragged.

Not hail, Nicholas realizes with a start that brings him fully to his senses, but the flat *crack... crack...* of caliver, petronel and matchlock being discharged.

Nicholas is all but dressed; no one has had the luxury of a nightshirt for days. He throws on his doublet, laces his boots and steps out of the tent into the chill morning air.

'I am Dr Shelby – over here. Who calls?'

A drummer boy, barely into his teens and clad in a muddy tunic too big for him, emerges from the fog, breathless and frightened. 'The rebels have launched an ambuscade, sir. They've caught our vanguard in the trees. You're to come at once.'

'How many hurt?'

'I know not, sir – only that you must come.'

Bianca appears at Nicholas's shoulder. He tells her to muster her women and have her balms and washes ready. Then he gathers three barber-surgeons from their sleeping place beneath a wagon loaded with cooking cauldrons and follows the lad back into the fog.

✠

Within moments Nicholas is sure they are lost. A tree looms out of the fog, like the mast of a sinking ship. Then another. He fears they are wandering into the forest. And if the rebels have launched an ambush, they are as likely to be there as anywhere. He tries not to dwell on the thought that – to some amongst the enemy – a severed head is as much a trophy as a living one still attached to a neck worth ransoming.

It is all he can do to keep the diminutive drummer boy in sight. The lad has a habit of fading alarmingly, forcing Nicholas to quicken his pace over the uneven ground. He hears the crash of bodies and horses moving through undergrowth off to his left, where he thinks the trees thicken. Are they rebels about to attack? Or are they our own men breaking in panic? Disjointed cries carry on the flat air. English or Irish? Victor or vanquished? From far off comes a chorus of unearthly high-pitched screams, suddenly cut off. Men? Women? Animals? Ghosts? He cannot tell.

And then figures emerge out of the smoky fog, like escapees from a house on fire. They are clad in dirty padded jerkins, their faces streaked with mud and sweat; large men, fiercely bearded, murder in their eyes – English pikemen. One of them, larger than the others, carries something slung across his back. He could be a poacher bringing home a deer, Nicholas thinks. Then he notices the dangling legs and knows the man is carrying a wounded comrade. His companions walk beside him, carrying the fallen man's armour: the greaves to protect the legs, the unlaced pauldrons from the shoulders, the plumed burgonet helmet, all muddied, bloodied and battered, trophies of someone else's victory.

The man carrying him stoops as he moves, weighed down by his burden. His face is impassive, the jaw set tight. In his eyes Nicholas can see a grim determination: to carry his charge for as long as it takes to find him aid – to the farthest reaches of hell, if necessary.

'Over here!' shouts the drummer boy. 'Here is the physician!'

One of the figures calls in reply, 'Thank Jesu! We have a good man here, most grievously hurt.'

The words seem to give the soldier carrying the body a final burst of strength. His legs look on the point of buckling, yet he breaks into the semblance of a run, an ungainly, desperate gait, as though he were the one with the wound. Reaching Nicholas, he sags to his knees and releases his burden. His companions drop the armour they are carrying into the mud. One of them throws down a bloodstained cloak. Then, with surprising gentleness for such fierce-looking fellows, they lift their charge from the kneeling man's shoulders and lay him on it. Nicholas looks down into the deathly-white face of Sir Henry Norris.

Despite the sickly alabaster light, Nicholas can see at once that Norris has lost a lot of blood. Beneath the streaks of dirt, his face is the same colour as the fog. He hangs on to consciousness by a thread, his eyes half-shut, his slack expression like that of a man robbed of his senses by a sudden terrible palsy.

Cutting away the cloth around Norris's shattered left leg, Nicholas tries to assess the extent of his injuries. It doesn't take him long to see that they are grievous. The whole knee joint has been destroyed, the ball of the tibia smashed to pieces, the patella staved in and the tendons and muscles shredded like a coney torn to pieces by a hound. Norris does little as Nicholas probes, other than groan softly as though troubled by heavy dreams.

'I must amputate at once, tie off the main blood vessel, or he'll die before we get him back to the shelter of the baggage train,' Nicholas says to the man who carried Norris out of the forest.

The man gives him a murderous look. 'I'll have no quack dishonour Sir Henry,' he says, placing one hand on the hilt of his sword. 'You butcher him, you die.'

'It's alright, he's the earl's physician,' says a voice. 'If Dr Shelby says the leg must go, then it must go. He's the best surgeon we have.'

Glancing up, Nicholas sees Oliver Henshawe emerge from the fog.

'Thank you, Sir Oliver,' he says. 'I'll do the very best I can, I promise. Is it safe to work here? I don't want to move Sir Henry any further than necessary.'

'Aye, it's as safe as anywhere on this damnable island,' says Henshawe. 'We chased the papist rogues off eventually.'

'Do you know if it was shot or pike?' Nicholas asks Norris's men. 'I need to know what might be in the wound.'

'Pike, sir,' one of them says. 'When he came out of the saddle, his horse stamped on him for good measure.'

Nicholas orders Norris held down lest he struggle. Two of his men kneel on either side, like pall-bearers. Norris does not resist. Indeed, he seems almost insensible. Nicholas pushes the knight's helmet under the ruined knee, to support the limb while he works. One of the barber-surgeons places Nicholas's physic chest close by.

'No point in wasting time,' Nicholas says, taking a determined breath.

First he employs a leather strap as a tourniquet. Then, on the inside of the physic chest's lid, he lays out the silk twine for tying off blood vessels. He pulls out two small saws and puts them beside the twine. With his head turned away, he reaches back several times until he knows he can grasp a replacement saw without having to think where it is, should the first blade break. Finally he pours the contents of a flask of arak spirit over the wound to wash away as much of the dirt and blood as he can.

Now there is only the action – and for that he does not need to prepare. It is lodged by practice in his memory. Taking up a long-bladed knife, which he knows to be sharp because he hones it as the last task of his working day, he kneels, placing one knee on Norris's left shin, close to the ankle. The knife slides into the flesh as if by itself, down to the bone in one fast orbit, angled so as to leave a flap of skin to cover the stump. Dropping the knife – no time for tidiness, he can clean it later – Nicholas's right hand moves back and finds the handle of one saw. He begins to murmur a familiar song:

We be soldiers three...

He sets the saw's teeth against the bloody bone.

Pardonnez-moi je vous en prie...

Swift, hard movements, the elbow locked to counter the resistance.

Lately come forth from the Low Countries
With never a penny of money...

It is not the fastest job he's ever done, but speedy enough. By the end of the third verse the limb is lying in the bloodied grass, like the cast-offs after a butchery session at the Mutton Lane shambles. Norris's men seem unwilling to approach it, as though it's an evil talisman. Nicholas picks it up by the ankle and throws it away into the fog. 'Well, he won't need it now, will he?' he says with a grim laugh in answer to their stares. 'We're not at Whitehall. There'll be no dancing the volta for a while for any of us.'

His words bring him up with a start. He realizes how easily he has fallen back into the black humour that had been the lingua franca of his days in the Low Countries – the soldier's antidote to the pain of cruel experience.

'I suppose he won't be needing both of *these* now,' says the man who carried Norris, holding up one of the bloodied leg greaves, before letting it drop back onto the grass with a clatter.

'That was a fine piece of carvery, Doctor,' says another in admiration.

They've accepted me, thinks Nicholas. At least now they won't seek revenge if Norris dies. I've seen *that* happen before.

'Will you stay with him, sir?' another asks.

'I take it that Sir Henry is not the only man hurt today. There must be others for me to attend.'

'We'll go together,' says Henshawe. 'But we'll need this damnable fog to lift if we're to recover those who cannot walk back.

If any are lying out there, I fear the rebels will not have shown them much mercy.'

A blood-red sun has lifted above the fog, thinning it into misty tendrils by the time Nicholas and his barber-surgeons have accounted for the wounded – some dozen men. None is as badly hurt as Norris, though almost all of them stare in terror at the indistinct figures approaching until the English voices reassure them. They have good reason. Several of the dead Nicholas encounters look as though their throats have been slit whilst lying immobilized from their wounds. Walking beside Oliver Henshawe, he cannot help but remember the bodies he had seen at the wreck site. What is it about this island, he wonders, that makes men forget the principle of mercy? Does hatred grow with the roots of the grass, the bracken, the heather, the trees themselves?

He is still wondering when he hears the cry go up, 'The baggage train! They've fallen upon the baggage train!'

✠

Nicholas stands in the shadows and stares in disbelief at the devastation. Now he understands the source of the noises he had heard in the forest on his way to treat Sir Henry Norris. A fleeing band of rebels have stumbled upon the encampment of the supply column. Too few – and too pressed for time to commit wholesale massacre – they have launched a spiteful little attack. Several tents have been pulled down and trampled. The cooking cauldrons have been overturned and their contents spilled. Grain sacks have been slashed open, a few of the smaller wagons looted. The oxen for the artillery have been set loose and chased off. And five camp-followers – all women – lie dead in the mud.

The tent Nicholas shared with Bianca is still standing. But she is nowhere to be seen. With mounting dread, he goes from body to body.

Later, he will confess to himself his shame for the surge of relief when each one turned out not to be her. But at this moment he is faced with one last place to search for her. He almost dares not look inside the tent, for fear of what he might find there.

The air inside the tent is sultry, heated by the morning sun. It feels like a physical barrier, resisting him as he enters, preventing the breath from leaving his lungs. A vision of blood and white skin reels before his eyes – and then is gone.

All the balms, pastes and medicines have vanished, as valuable as food to a fleeing rebel who lives off the land and has no recourse to an apothecary, a physician or a hospital. A few other useful items have been taken. Everything else is left untouched.

And of Bianca there is no trace.

30

How can the leader of a rebellion have time to spare for a cantankerous young woman of the Spanish nobility, even an ailing one? Hugh O'Neill, Earl of Tyrone, might be forgiven for having more pressing claims on his attention. Yet he has come to sit by her bedside more times than Cachorra can count. She knows the answer to her own question well enough. He thinks Constanza Calva de Sagrada is the daughter of an emissary sent by Spain to aid him in his battle against the heretic English queen.

'My physicians have done their best,' Tyrone says sadly as he takes his leave after his latest visit. 'I wish they could do more. Let me know if your mistress sickens further. I will call a priest to perform the Viaticum.'

'In Spain we have wise women skilled in ancient cures,' she tells him. 'Do you not have such people in Ireland?'

Tyrone laughs, his craggy face showing a benevolence that surprises her. 'Aye, we have as many wise women as we have poets and storytellers. Sadly, their arts are just as ephemeral. Some people will swear they can raise Lazarus from the dead, if you promise them enough gold half-crowns.' He pauses at the chamber door. 'Then there is the lack of roads, and the marauding English to consider.'

Constanza burbles in the deep fathoms of her unconsciousness, her skin shiny and wet to the touch. To Cachorra, she has become a child to be pitied rather than a trial to be borne, a tyrant to be despised. The change has as much to do with Cachorra's understanding of what it is to be defenceless as with the silent vow she made to Don Rodriquez to serve and protect his daughter. 'There must be something you can do,' she says, almost pleadingly.

'I have caused the word to be spread amongst the chieftains: that the O'Neill has urgent need of a skilful healer. Let us pray – for the sakes of both your mistress *and* my cause – that they find one before it's too late.'

✠

Today, having no tasks that cannot be delayed for a few hours, Ned Monkton walks the three miles to Camberwell. The summer sunshine lifts his spirits better than a bottle of *aqua vitae*. The meadows beside the lane hum their approval into the languorous air. The larks trill at him, urging him forward, congratulating him. He grins with pleasure, not just at the brightness of the day, but for the man he has become.

Ned has always thought himself as being a little dull in the wits. He cannot read or write. His younger years gave him little learning in anything beyond brawling and drinking. But then Rose, and Master Nicholas and Mistress Bianca, showed him a better road. And today – *this* day – he thinks himself almost as clever as any of them. Because today Ned is almost certain that he's fathomed the deceit being practised by Barnabas Vyves and Gideon Strollot.

'I don't want to cause you more 'urt than you've already suffered, Master Aaron,' he tells the shepherd when he tracks him down to a shelter made of interwoven willow branches, set in a lush meadow beside a stream, 'but I've 'ad my suspicions for a while now that your son wasn't the victim of cut-purses.'

Aaron Godwinson has his hand on the top of his shepherd's crook, the tip on the ground by his right foot. He tilts the crook forward in a little jab of command and fixes Ned with his rheumy eyes. 'Then I'd ask you to speak plainly to me and not dissemble.'

Ned so promises. 'It concerns what I believe to be a gullin'. A cheatin' of Her Majesty in fact,' he says.

'You'd best explain what you mean, Master Ned.'

Ned adopts a contemplative tone. 'Let us say, just as a proposition, that your master who owns those sheep out there is a kindly soul who cares for the comfort of 'is shepherd.'

'Fat chance of that, Master Ned,' Godwinson says with a loud snort.

'Maybe so. But let us say that 'e is. Let us say also 'e's *so* kindly that 'e commands me to give every shepherd in Surrey a jug of ale.'

'Why would he do that?'

'Bear with me, Master Aaron.' Ned opens one palm and spreads his huge fingers. He proceeds to count them off with the index finger of his other hand as he makes his case. 'This master of yours comes to me an' says, "Master Ned, I need one 'undred pots of knock-down for my fine fellows. 'Ow much will that cost me?" An' I tell 'im that a jug of my ale will cost him 'a'pence.'

'And fine ale it was, too, Master Ned. I thank you for it. You were generous.'

Ned dismisses the shepherd's appreciation with a brief shake of his auburn-bearded chin. '*Now* your master says, "That will do me nicely. Order me one 'undred, so that my 'undred shepherds may slake their thirst."'

'I can't imagine him doing that,' says Aaron Godwinson sadly. 'Not this side of the Last Judgement.'

'That's not the point, Master Aaron,' Ned says. He taps another finger. 'Now, I gives 'im the pots, an' in return 'e gives me…' Ned does the calculation in his head, 'over four shillings.'

'That's a lot of money to spend on making a shepherd happy,' Aaron observes. 'I'd have to work a fortnight to earn that much.'

'We even line up a few jugs on the counter, so 'e can see what 'e's gettin' for 'is money.'

'We do?' queries Aaron Godwinson.

Ned's right index finger lands firmly in the centre of his left palm. '*Then* we goes down to Camberwell and we buys us one 'undred jugs of cheap ale from another tavern what sells sheep-piss for only a farthin' a jug.'

'Why do we do that, Master Ned?'

Ned's fiery face lights up like a victory beacon, a blaze of triumph. 'Because *they*'re the ones we give to 'is 'undred shepherds. An' they costs *us* only two shillings!'

'And we keep the difference?' says Godwinson, catching on.

'You 'ave it,' Ned announces. 'Your master don't know 'e's being gulled. Your shepherds don't know they's being gulled – they's just glad for the ale. And *we* make two shillings! How much did your Lemuel sign up for?'

'Sixpence a day, that's what Vyves was offering.'

Ned frowns while he does the calculation in his head. In the little willow shelter, the air is heavy with the sound of the meadow, the gentle persistent humming of summer.

'If we was to muster a company of one 'undred men and take sixpence a day per man from the Exchequer to pay them, over an 'ole campaign season – say, six months – that's four 'undred and fifty pounds. 'Course we'd lose a bit of that in paying off the recruits we *did* muster, with 'alf a month's pay, but I ain't included what the Exchequer would pay us for food, transport, armour... You could probably make a thousand pounds. You could live like a lord.'

'But what happens to the recruits?'

'They go 'ome, just as your Lemuel did,' Ned says. 'I reckon if we spent the summer walking through Surrey, we'd come across any number of young lads who've signed up with Sir Oliver 'Enshawe, taken the money an' gone back to their farms and their smithies.'

A shadow of disbelief flickers over Aaron Godwinson's artless face. 'But won't the Earl of Essex notice that he's getting no soldiers, Master Ned?'

'But 'e *is* getting soldiers. That's the beauty of it. 'Ow much do you think it might cost to raise a levy of Irishmen?'

'I don't know. I only knows the price of sheep.'

'Well, I'd guess it's a lot less than sixpence a day per man.' Ned shakes his head in disbelief at the cunning ways some men find to cheat their fellows. 'I've lived on Bankside all my life, Master Aaron. I reckoned I've seen just about every gull goin'. But this one is a peach. That little arseworm Vyves is musterin' fellows 'ere in England, but 'e don't actually *send* them to Ireland. He pays them off an' keeps the queen's coin, making up the muster with cheap fellows across the water. That means 'is captain – that 'Enshawe fellow – is in on the gullin' too. An' that Strollot. They'd need *'im* to cover for them with the aldermen an' the magistrates.'

There is anguish in Aaron Godwinson's eyes as he says, 'Is that why my Lemuel was slain, do you think? They murdered him to keep their grubby secret?'

'P'raps your son's conscience troubled 'im,' Ned replies. 'They must 'ave got wind that 'e was thinkin' of tellin'.'

'I would like to think it so,' the shepherd says, gazing sadly out at the meadow and his flock. 'He was a good lad, at heart. Honest.' He falls to silence while he thinks of his son. Then he says, 'What are we to do, Master Ned? How can we do what Lemuel intended – bring these rogues to justice?'

'There's a problem,' Ned says, wincing. He raises his right thumb to show the scar of the branding. 'You may 'ave noticed *this*, Master Aaron,' he says uncomfortably. 'I killed a man. I ain't proud of it. It were in self-defence, but they sentenced me to 'ang. My Rose saved me from the gibbet. But they branded me anyhow.'

'One offence shouldn't damn a man's character for ever, Master Ned. I'll stand for you, if anyone should doubt your testimony.'

'It's not that easy,' Ned tells him regretfully. 'You see, I 'ad words with Vyves a while back, being as 'ow I 'ad my s'picions of 'im.'

The colour drains out of Godwinson's face. He grips his shepherd's crook as though he means to strangle it. 'You've broached this with him?'

'I 'adn't fathomed what he was up to then. But I knew somethin' wasn't right.'

'What did he say?'

'The rogue told me that if I didn't mind my own business, 'e and Strollot would sign an affidavit before a magistrate sayin' that it was me what killed Lemuel. If they were to do such a thing, Master Aaron, this time I'd 'ang for sure.'

Godwinson lets out his breath in a slow, desperate sigh. 'Then I'll stand before a magistrate myself,' he says resolutely. 'I may be only a shepherd, but I'm an honest subject of Her Majesty.'

'I can't let you do that, Master Aaron. If I'm right, they killed your son to stop 'im talkin'. They wouldn't think twice about killin' the father.'

'Are we to let this stand then? Do we turn our eyes away from such deceit, while other brave fellows are riskin' their lives in Ireland?'

'For the present, I think we 'ave no choice,' Ned says gravely. 'The friends I 'ave who might give me their wise counsel are far away. To keep us both safe, I think we must 'old our tongues until they return. The war in Ireland ain't goin' to last for ever. They'll be 'ome just as soon as the Earl of Essex 'as triumphed. They'll know what to do.'

Godwinson's eyes brim with impotent fury. 'I shall seek out this Vyves and smite him to death with this here staff,' he announces, wielding his shepherd's crook so alarmingly that Ned has to fold one hand around it to calm him.

'Swear to me, Master Aaron, that you will do nothin' so foolish.'

But instead of so swearing, Aaron Godwinson begins to sob. He lets his crook fall to the dry earth floor of the shelter. His weathered country stoicism dissolves before Ned's eyes.

For a moment Ned doesn't know what to do. But then he remembers his earlier days – days when his own frustrated rage and loneliness had turned him into a thing that other folks feared. And so he wraps his huge arms around the shepherd and lets him sob out his despair over the leather jerkin that Rose washed only the day before, murmuring soothing endearments in his gravelly voice, as though this old shepherd was the child that he and Rose have, so far, been denied.

31

Nicholas has never truly laid to rest the memory of his unravelling following the death of Eleanor, his first wife, and the child she was carrying. He has often wondered how he would respond if he were to lose Bianca. The fact that he can function at all, he thinks, is a testament to the strength she has given him. Even so, he goes about his work in a daze. His fingers seem to function without the need for any commanding thought. His mind is elsewhere. Where is she? Is she alive? Is she hurt? More than once he has feared that the worst of his black imaginings will take physical shape and drag him back to that time when self-destruction seemed to be the only way to end the pain. He has interrogated the survivors of the raid on the baggage train until they have become almost fearful of his relentless questioning. For all their sympathy, they cannot help him. *It was foggy... there was utter confusion... I was too busy trying to save myself to see what befell Mistress Bianca...*

Despite Nicholas's best efforts, Sir Henry Norris dies of his wounds without regaining consciousness. In another of Robert Devereux's wild swings of mood, Nicholas makes the instant transformation from a necessity for the army's continued effectiveness to being responsible for the death of its general of infantry.

'Ormonde told me you were a competent physician. Why do my officers lie to me?' Essex demands to know when Nicholas is brought before him in his tent. 'If you're so good, how is that one of my finest generals is now lying dead?'

In the corner Sir Oliver Henshawe stands casually picking the dirt from his fingers and twisting the expensive rings he wears, like a disreputable family retainer. He drops his gaze to the floor, as though to avoid the blast.

'Your Grace, Sir Henry came to me grievously hurt,' Nicholas protests. 'The chances of him recovering were always slim. At least I was giving him a prospect of life. I'm truly sorry that he did not survive.'

'*Sorry?*' echoes Essex contemptuously. 'You've done the rebels' work for them, sirrah. You're a traitor!'

The attack is not what Nicholas was expecting.

'Your Grace, this is most unjust. I did everything in my power to save him. Sir Oliver, here, will confirm it.'

But Henshawe merely gives him a sly, knowing smile. Nicholas's jaw tightens. He hadn't expected comradeship from Henshawe, but he would have settled for honesty. Instead the man seems to be enjoying Nicholas's humiliation.

'You're a charlatan – like every damn physician it's been my misfortune to meet,' Essex tells him with a contemptuous wave of his hand. 'What's more, you're a spy for Robert Cecil. I'd lay odds that all that time you spent in Padua turned you into an apologist for heretics.'

A spy for Cecil *and* an apologist for heretics? The contradiction seems not to trouble Essex in the slightest. Nicholas lets the accusation fall without comment. He has other worries on his mind.

'Your Grace, I beg to be allowed to search for my wife. She was taken during the raid on the baggage train. She could be lying hurt somewhere in the forest. I *must* look for her.'

'Are you a Catholic? Is that why you let Norris die?' Essex sneers, as though he hasn't heard what Nicholas has just told him. 'Henshawe tells me that wife of yours was one. I'd stake coin on her going with the rebels of her own free will. You've probably become infected with the same papist disease.'

The words land with such force that Nicholas wonders if Henshawe, at the earl's secret bidding, has crept over and punched him in the head while he wasn't looking. But there he is, still in the corner, still studying the gorgeous rings on his fingers.

'Your Grace, I will say it again. My wife, Bianca, has been taken by the rebels. I *beg* you: allow me to search for her.'

But Essex waves him away. 'I should have hanged you along with Harington's rogues,' he snarls. 'If another of my officers dies through your incompetence, I swear to Almighty God that I'll put an end to you myself.' He turns to Oliver Henshawe. 'Take this mountebank back to his tent. If he shows even the slightest inclination to leave camp, you have my permission to string him up from the nearest bough.'

✠

Later that afternoon Nicholas searches out Henshawe's tent. His hands are shaking with rage, his jaw set so tight it aches. He finds Sir Oliver sitting on the grass, chewing on a joint of chicken.

'When you brought Sir Henry to me, apparently I was the best surgeon in the army,' he says without preamble or courtesy. 'Back there in the earl's tent, I was infected by papistry and a traitor. What happened in between?'

Henshawe looks him up and down with lazy disregard. 'Always best to keep on His Grace's good side, don't you think?'

'But you know it's not true.'

'Do I?' He takes a bite of meat. 'More to the point, do you?'

Standing over him, Nicholas resists the urge to kick Henshawe in the face. 'I need permission to take a party of men in search of Bianca at first light.'

Henshawe gives him a sickly smile. 'That's a pity. You heard His Grace. "From the nearest bough".' He jabs the chicken joint at the darkening trees beyond the camp. 'Pick one you fancy. There's plenty to choose from.'

'What do you think I intend to do? Desert to the rebels? My wife is missing. I want to find her.'

'And His Grace has decreed that you are more important to him here – just as I decreed you were important to poor Henry Norris. *Temporarily*.'

'God's nails, Henshawe! Show some compassion, for once in your life.'

Sir Oliver regards him with mild amusement. 'Remember what I said to you in Dublin, when you rejected my offer to escort you both to Kilcolman?'

'No, my attention must have been elsewhere. I tend not to listen to bombast.'

Henshawe gnaws at the chicken bone as though the insult has not struck home. Then he waves it accusingly in Nicholas's direction. 'I said, "I would allow no wife of mine to go wandering off into the wilderness. I'd make sure she knew her station." Perhaps you should have listened to me.'

Nicholas considers taking the joint off Henshawe and stuffing it down his throat. But Henshawe is his only hope. 'For mercy's sake,' he says, trying not to shout, 'if you still have any feelings for my wife, lay aside your hurt pride and help me find her.'

But Henshawe is implacable. 'She could have enjoyed comfort and status as the wife of a gentleman. Instead she chose you. That was *her* mistake.'

'Is this to somehow punish us both?' Nicholas asks in astonishment. 'Is this a gentleman's sense of honour on show?'

Henshawe sneers. 'Don't flatter yourself, Shelby. If it were up to me, I'd willingly let you go blundering about out there until you got your throat cut and your head sent to Dublin as a present from Tyrone. As it is, His Grace has pressing need of a competent physician. Questions about your loyalty can wait.'

'My loyalty? That's rich! A loyal man wouldn't be holding back his English muster. Why are you doing that, Henshawe? Do you have another purpose for them? Don't think I have heard the tavern talk about going back to England and routing Devereux's enemies.'

Henshawe doesn't answer the question. He studies Nicholas for a moment. Then he tosses away the chicken bone, as though he expects him to scamper off and fetch it. When Nicholas declines, he adds, 'Look, His Grace knows you didn't let Norris die. So stop playing the maid with the hurt feelings and be gone with you. Back to your duties, Master Physician. And stay in camp, if you don't want to end up swinging from a tree.'

✠

In the soft light of evening the English camp looks like a faded fresco painted on ancient plaster. Through the tent flap Nicholas stares out at the misty silhouettes clustered around their cooking fires. The sounds of men boasting, complaining, gossiping, arguing and gambling carry easily on the still air. Nicholas dismisses the idea of joining them, of seeking out any human company. It would only make things worse. He hasn't eaten all day, yet hunger is the last thing on his mind. He wonders how long he can keep despair at bay.

When the Earl of Ormonde stoops to enter the tent, Nicholas remains sitting dejectedly on his straw pallet. He hasn't got the strength left in him to get up.

'I thought I'd come and see if I can raise your spirits, Physician,' Ormonde says, sitting beside him without invitation. His face is still streaked with the dirt and sweat of the morning's battle.

The white stubble lies flattened against his skull like harvested corn after a summer shower of hail, evidence that his helmet has scarcely been off his head all day.

'That is kind of you, my lord. But I fear it's one victory you will be denied.'

'Come, sirrah, things may not be as bad as you fear.'

Nicholas lets out a brief cynical laugh. 'My wife is missing – taken by rebels. Or worse. What could be more fearful to me than that?'

Ormonde looks around the tent. 'They took her medicines?'

'Most of them: her balms, her ointments, even her pestle and mortar. Fortunately most of what the army needs is still in the wagons.'

'That's a good sign, isn't it – that they emptied the tent?'

'I suppose so.'

'It shows they understood her worth.'

'More so than does His Grace the Earl of Essex, apparently,' Nicholas says despondently. 'He won't let me search for her. He blames me for letting Henry Norris die.'

'That's probably his wisest decision today. A good physician is more encouragement to our men than a battery of artillery. No point in letting you wander off and handing them another useful captive.'

'By the time I reached him, Sir Henry had lost too much blood. I would have had to work a miracle to save him,' Nicholas says, staring at his hands and noticing he hasn't even attempted to wash off the blood from his efforts.

Ormonde gives him a fatherly pat on the knee. 'His Grace has a habit of blaming his mistakes on others,' he says bluntly. 'Like marching his forces close to a forest when you can't see your hand in front of your face. It wasn't only your wife we lost today: a score of dead, including Norris; five slain with the baggage train; and a gentlemen adventurer of the noble earl's faction carried off as a prisoner. If you want my opinion, him we can afford to lose. But I imagine that His Grace will be keen to arrange his freedom.' He pulls at the points of his tunic, loosening the collar. Nicholas catches the pungent reek of hard effort and old leather. 'Is that possible?'

'Of course. We have some of Tyrone's people languishing in Dublin that I dare say will stand as surety. Severed heads are not the *only* coin of exchange in this benighted island.'

'If he can be released, then so perhaps might Bianca,' Nicholas suggests, feeling the hope course through him like the shock from a whiplash.

'Everything is possible, Nicholas – save, it seems, bringing Tyrone to a reckoning. But don't tell His Grace I said so.'

Ormonde rises to leave.

'I did all I could, in the circumstances – for Sir Henry Norris,' Nicholas tells the Lieutenant-General's departing shoulders.

'I know it,' Ormonde says, turning to face him. 'More importantly, the army knows it. Particularly those of us who saw the efforts you and Mistress Bianca made in Cork. I fear we must accept that men of such heightened qualities as His Grace tend to have temperaments to match. Put it out of your mind, if you can.'

'I believe His Grace is sick,' Nicholas says bluntly. 'He may not be wholly able to discharge his duties to Her Majesty. I think his reason may be impaired.'

'Sick? We're all sick in some regard, in this place. What in particular do you think ails him?'

'I think he may be suffering from the pox, my lord.'

Ormonde studies Nicholas for a while, the candlelight turning his features into a harsh mask set against the soft mauve of the evening sky.

'*That* is a diagnosis I would keep to myself, Physician – if I were you,' Ormonde says. 'You will not improve His Grace's humour by telling him.'

'And what if it's affecting his reason? What then? You said yourself he made an error today, taking us so close to the forest in fog, allowing us to be ambushed. He has shown himself prone to wild impulses and misjudgements. Look at his reaction when I asked to be allowed to search for Bianca. He ordered Sir Oliver Henshawe to hang me from the nearest branch if I attempt to leave the camp.'

Ormonde gives him a grim smile. 'Then I heartily suggest you comply. Sick or not, His Grace is appointed over us by Her Majesty. Acting against his express orders would be more than mutiny, Nicholas. It would be treason. There would be nothing to be gained by it, not if your wife were to return only to discover she was a widow.'

And with that, Ormonde turns away and disappears into the thickening mist.

✠

The depleted army returns to Dublin. For Nicholas, Ormonde's encouragement is short-lived. The days are even worse than the nights. The nightmare has forged chains from which he cannot escape, even with the arrival of the dawn. When he climbs off his pallet to attend to the sick and wounded, he drags the nightmare with him. The possibilities clamour in his head like bells rung to warn of danger. Bianca is dead. Her body lies as carrion somewhere in the forest. She's alive, but in the hands of the rebels. They use her for their sport whenever they choose. She is the Merrow. She has walked back into the sea, leaving him alone on the shore to grieve for ever.

He goes in search of Piers Gardener, hoping the scrivener's journeyings to the more remote English garrisons, and his contacts with the people of the countryside, might produce some rumour, some gossip, of a woman taken by the rebels – he is certain Bianca would make her presence known somehow. But Gardener is out of the city on one of his meanderings.

Nicholas senses he is walking on the edge of a high parapet. One misstep and he will plunge into the abyss. The only barrier to prevent him falling is the hope that Bianca is still alive, that the rebels have taken her – spared her – for her skills. He imagines her plotting her escape, enchanting her captors into carelessness, slipping away in the night. If anyone can do it, she can.

But even this thought brings Nicholas little comfort. How will she find her way back to him? What if her captors are attacked by English forces? In Ireland, giving quarter – it seems – has long since gone out of fashion. She might not be lucky a second time.

His dreams darken even more when news of another disaster arrives: a force under Sir Conyers Clifford, Governor of Connaught, is defeated in Roscommon and put to rout. The rebels cut the head off Clifford's corpse for a trophy. When the news reaches Dublin, Nicholas has cause to recall Ormonde's words with bitter irony: *Severed heads are not the only coin of exchange in this benighted island...*

For days, he cannot hear a cart rumble past without seeing in his mind Bianca's head lying on the tailboard, her amber eyes for ever dulled.

32

Like everyone else in the baggage train, Bianca had mistaken the men running out of the forest for returning English soldiers. In the fog it had been almost impossible to tell otherwise – until the throat-cutting had begun. She remembers emerging from her tent to be confronted by three bearded men dressed like characters from a Bible story. They wore simple knee-length gowns of wool that glistened with the tears of the fog. Each carried a small round shield buckled to the left arm. In their hands they wielded heavy, archaic swords. To Bianca's mind, they could have been soldiers of King David about to do battle with the Philistines. One of them shouted at her in a language she could not comprehend. *Gaeilge*, she had assumed. But she hadn't needed to understand their speech. Their intent was clear by the delirium of slaughter she could see in their eyes. Then they had noticed the jars, pots, bottles and mortars, the boxes of dried leaf and root, the weighing scales, the ladles, spoons and iron lancets.

'You serve a physician?' one of them asked in English.

'I serve no one,' Bianca had replied indignantly. 'I am Bianca Merton, mistress of the Jackdaw tavern on Bankside.'

'Then you are a camp whore?' he had suggested menacingly.

'Certainly not! I am wife to Dr Nicholas Shelby.'

'Are these his medicines?'

'Not all of them. Many are mine. I am also an apothecary – licensed by the Worshipful Company of Grocers, in London.'

While they discuss this information in their native *Gaeilge*, Bianca takes the opportunity to try to worm her way under the tent wall. But she only gets one arm through before they seize her by the ankles and haul her back.

She can tell by their agitation that they are expecting a counter-attack. One of them takes off his cloak and fills it with as much of the physic as it will hold. Then they drag her outside, where she averts her eyes from the five fog-shrouded corpses strewn about the now almost empty camp.

The one who had spoken to her in English sheathes his sword, draws a dagger and cuts a length of tent-rope and fashions a noose out of it. For a moment she thinks they intend to hang her. It is not the prospect of death that makes her begin to tremble; rather it's the image that springs into her head: a bereft Nicholas weeping as he kneels at her gently swinging feet.

In fact they have nothing more lethal in store for her than simple indignity. The noose makes an efficient leash. They slip it around her head, tighten it so that she can only just breathe and lead her into the forest like a pack-mule. So much as a whisper, they warn her, and she will join the dead whose blood is already pooling in the sodden grass.

After the initial violence of the capture they had shown her no further anger or hostility, but rather a studied indifference, as though she was nothing more than a package they had been ordered to transport from one place to another. During the first few days of her captivity the urge to escape had flowed through her body like the shock of ice-cold water on the skin. Her senses had trembled with expectation. She thought she might take any risk to find her way back to Nicholas, to return safely to Bruno. But her captors had never let go of the leash, not even when the call of nature forced her to beg them to stop. Then she had to endure the humiliation of relieving herself like a dog on a lead, though they had shown her the small civility of turning their backs while she crouched. At night, or when they were resting during the march, a guard was always appointed to keep hold of the leash. Besides, where would she go? she asked herself. She had no real idea of where she was, or in what direction Dublin lay.

Looking back, she can place a form of order on events. First, there is the period that she calls *Hoodman Blind*, after the child's game. The raiding party – now a dozen strong – makes little dashes through the landscape. These are interspersed with periods of hiding from English patrols. Then there is the *Strolling* period. It takes place in territory that Bianca assumes is firmly under rebel control, because the crops stand unburnt in the fields and cattle graze contentedly under the first proper sunshine in weeks. Were it not for the fact that she is a prisoner, and sick with worry that Nicholas might have been caught in the ambush, or what he must going through after her disappearance, she might even enjoy it.

But the pace never slackens. However, now it is driven not by the possibility of pursuit, but by some definite intent on the part of her captors. Where they are taking her, they will not say. What is to happen when they get there is a secret she is not permitted to learn. Eventually a numbing resignation takes hold of her. She becomes submissive, a condition previously alien to her. She no longer resists when they hurry her with a tug of the rope. She sleeps when they sleep. She eats what they eat: oatmeal and bread – never less than her equal share, which serves to confirm her growing view that she is important to them.

Finally comes the *Progress*. In this, the most recent period, Bianca becomes in her imagination very much like the queen, journeying through her realm and lodging by night in the houses of the nobility. In truth, these start off as the humblest of dwellings. But they show a definite improvement as each day passes. So much so that within a week she is sleeping in substantial stone tower houses, much like Kilcolman.

The Progress is her very own achievement, and Bianca is rightly proud of it. It begins on the night they spend in the company of the first host, who looks as though he might have some authority over her captors. He is a fidgety, bald little man but well dressed, and his house has real furniture: high-backed chairs, a table and a good collection of pewter. The sword he wears is a size too big for him, as – apparently – is his own self-regard. But by the deference her captors show him, Bianca assumes he is a minor chieftain of some sort. When she is brought before him, she decides that now is as good a moment as any to play her hand. Adopting the haughtiest pose possible on the end of a leash, she tosses her head to display her mane of dark tresses to best effect – ignoring the fact that she has only ever washed them in cold water from a pail or a stream since leaving Dublin.

She learned long ago in Italy that the lot of the captive common soldier was to languish and perhaps die in a dungeon, whereas a gentleman could expect to be swapped, or his freedom purchased with gold. And if not a ransom – for she cannot imagine either Robert Devereux or Robert Cecil dipping their hands in their purses on *her* account – then at least an exchange of prisoners. Adopting her proudest voice, she says, 'I don't know who *you* are, sirrah, but I am Bianca Shelby, wife to the physician to the Earl of Essex. My husband is also often called to attend Her Majesty, Queen Elizabeth, in London. I demand you release me at once.'

At first her stratagem seems to have failed. The little bald chieftain stares at her blankly. Bianca decides her plan needs a little embellishment. These men are surely Catholics, she thinks. Perhaps it might be wise to separate the Paduan Bianca Merton from the Bankside one.

'I am also a servant of the one true faith, of Holy Mother Church. I am half-Italian, and while living in the Veneto I was gainfully employed by His Eminence, Cardinal Santo Fiorzi.'

Then she repeats this in Italian, and recites the beginning of the Holy Mass in Latin, just to be sure. It is, after all, true – even if it was almost twenty years ago now.

The response takes her by surprise. Her host almost prostrates himself before her. It seems that he only needed a little time to take in the wonderful news. As for her captors, they proceed to jump around as though they have discovered they have taken Queen Elizabeth herself. From that moment on, Bianca makes the swift transition from parcel to prized possession. She is treated gently, almost with reverence, although, with much regret, they decline to let her off their improvised leash.

And so, after a week or more of peripatetic journeying, Bianca finds herself standing beside a pleasant little river that winds contentedly through stands of alder and oak, flanked by well-tended meadows. Encamped along the bank, almost as far as she can see, is an army that she judges to be twice the size of anything Essex might now field. And, watching over it, a small castle of dark-grey stone with a little portcullis. The river is the Blackwater, her guardians tell her in a rare moment of openness. We have reached our destination.

But quite where that destination is, Bianca cannot tell. In the English army, maps are as rare as griffon eggs and about as dependable. They carry little detail. All she can recall of the Blackwater is a meandering line that could be thirty leagues or more in length, for all she knows. And when she asks where upon that line she stands, or indeed who dwells within the castle walls, the old reticence returns.

✠

The portcullis drops behind Bianca with a menacing rumble. She is reminded of the many journeys she has made on the Thames, and the dark mouth of Traitors' Gate that she has always imagined might somehow suck her in like a leaf carried on the current, never to escape. Rough, ungallant hands sweep over her body, searching for hidden weapons. How could she possibly have contrived to secrete a knife about her person? Do these guards not know she has been roped to her captors for days?

At last she is permitted to step out of the gatehouse. She is led across a courtyard packed with all the appurtenances of rebellion: wagons piled high with hay for the horses; armourers hammering like demons at damaged plate; spinning whetstones that send showers of sparks into the air as they sharpen sword blades; blacksmiths pouring molten lead into moulds to make musket balls... She can tell, by the expensive gold accessories worn by some of the men she passes, that this is the headquarters of someone of high importance. She dares to hope that person is the Earl of Tyrone. Surely a man of his station will know his chivalrous duty and arrange her freedom. And if he demurs, well, a man is a man whether he's an earl or a potboy, and she hasn't met one yet that she could not bend to her will. Except – and only then on occasions – Nicholas Shelby.

But what if Tyrone is just as his enemies would portray him – a merciless butcher, bent on ripping the English out of Ireland by their admittedly shallow roots? What if he imprisons her in some foul dungeon while he tries to extort concessions out of the Earl of Essex? She cannot imagine *that* ending in her favour.

In fact Hugh O'Neill turns out to be neither of these extremes. The sternness of his appearance is countered by kindly, almost merry eyes. His voice has a pleasant, lazy current beneath the initial gruffness. He is dressed simply in woollen plaid, the gold fittings on his belt and the sheath of his dagger being the only clue to his rank.

'It is our joint good fortune that you were taken by fellows who owe their fealty to my trusty friend, James Fitzthomas,' he tells her after she has been given food and drink and her leash removed. 'They always have an eye for useful loot.'

Bianca remembers the little fellow to whom she had first admitted her identity. 'Well, you may tell Master Fitzthomas that I'm not *loot*. I'm Bianca Merton,' she says proudly, guessing that Tyrone is the sort of man to quickly tire of false pleasantries.

'Oh, I know who you are. Or at least I know who you claim to be. I just don't know whether to believe you. Some people will say anything when they think their lives are in danger.'

'Is *my* life in danger?'

'That rather depends.'

'Upon what?'

'Upon how good you are at the healing arts.'

'Why? Are you sick?' she asks.

'Only of English perfidy.'

'Then why have I been brought here?'

'I would like to think it's because God Almighty favours our cause,' Tyrone says, without smiling.

'If you're not in need of healing, then who is?' she asks. 'You can't have had me brought all this way to treat blistered feet or lame cattle.'

'A guest of mine.'

'Have you no healers of your own?'

'This isn't London, Mistress. We're at war, and Ulster is a wild place,' Tyrone points out. 'Most of our physicians are scattered with our bands. The few that I have close to hand, well, let us say this: Ireland is not exactly known as the wellspring of medical advancement. So when the wife of the physician to the Earl of

Essex, and a licensed apothecary to boot, falls like a ripe fruit into my hands, I'm not about to pass on the opportunity, am I?' He glowers at her, though his eyes still twinkle mischievously. 'You *are* these things, are you? Because if you're not, I have a very quick way of finding out.'

'I am,' Bianca says, feeling her resolve begin to crumble. 'You have my word for it.'

'Then come with me.'

Tyrone's castle seems to have been built for an ancient, smaller breed. There is not a passage down which Bianca is led that does not cause her to bend her head. She feels the cold, uneven stone brushing her shoulders, rasping her elbows. She wonders if Tyrone has changed his mind and decided to imprison her anyway. She has no option but to follow him, pressed from behind by three of his retinue.

At last Tyrone bounds energetically up a narrow, winding stone stairwell to a low door set into an archway. A guard stands before it. He dips his head at Tyrone's approach.

Another prisoner must lie within, Bianca thinks. She racks her memory, but she can think of no figure of importance that Nicholas has ever mentioned falling into rebel hands.

At Tyrone's command, the guard raps twice on the door. Not pejorative hammerings that would suggest an enemy imprisoned on the other side, but almost respectful, as though to give warning. She hears a woman answer in English, heavily accented.

A brief exchange follows, to determine if all is proper and decent within. Then the guard lifts the latch and opens the door. No rattle of chains, or keys turning in unbreachable locks. If there is a prisoner within, thinks Bianca, they have a remarkable degree of freedom. She follows Tyrone into the neat little chamber.

Poking out from a sheet of fine linen edged with Alençon lace is a plump, rather grey face, redeemed by a set of rosebud lips. The heavy black eyebrows guard a pair of closed lids. The linen rises and falls over the swell of the breasts in faltering steps, like an old man climbing steep stairs. A slow, whining whistle accompanies each exhalation.

But it is not the woman on the bed who seizes Bianca's attention. It is the one standing beside it. A tall, strongly built young woman with a wise face, a face as dark as any foreign merchant to be seen in Padua or Venice. She is dressed plainly in a cloth gown, her black hair roped back over her brow. Even to Bianca – no stranger to the whole palate of human colours, thanks to a childhood spent in close proximity to Venice – the presence of such a woman in this damp, wild place is startling. But what truly rocks her on her heels is her belated identification of the woman's accent.

Spanish.

'This is the young woman I need you to heal,' says Tyrone, indicating the figure whose face pokes out of the coverlet. 'Her name is Constanza. You need know nothing more of her than that.'

Oh, I know far more than you think, Bianca replies silently in her head as she struggles to impose some small control over her reeling mind. For instance, I know the likelihood of there being more than one Constanza of Spanish stock presently to be found in Ireland. I would consider it as likely as discovering that you were keeping a live cockatrice in your castle and feeding it on nectar.

But Tyrone has one last shock in store for her.

Bianca is too astounded by the realization that she has managed to achieve the one thing that both she and Nicholas, not to mention Robert Cecil and Edmund Spenser, had thought impossible – even if it was without her own active agency – that she doesn't hear the footsteps of someone else entering the chamber. And she only half-registers Tyrone saying, 'You're just in time. Is *this* the physician's wife? Has Fitzthomas hooked us a fine fresh salmon, or nothing but a wee pollan?'

But she hears the reply alright. She hears it because the voice is familiar.

'Oh yes, my lord,' says Piers Gardener. 'That's Mistress Bianca. I'd recognize that head of hair anywhere, even from behind.'

33

When two separate shocks of such magnitude strike at the same time, the only way to keep standing – or so Bianca thinks, as her head turns from Constanza to Piers Gardener, back to Constanza and then again to the scrivener, like a coney's swivelling as it searches for foxes – is to start with something you can handle. Force order upon the storm, even if it's only a temporary order. Break it down into fragments. Deal with each one in turn. Hope that in the meantime you don't drown in a flood of disbelief. Start with what you know. Start with Piers Gardener.

She sees at once how easy it must have been for him to pass between the two sides, constantly on the move, alone, under no one's supervision. What was it he had called himself when they'd met in the Tholsel at Dublin when she and Nicholas first arrived in Dublin: *grey merchants... It's the dust we pick up from always being out on the road...*

She knows she should despise him as a traitor, but looking at that child's face with its moon-calf eyes and its golden curls of hair, she wonders how Gardener found the courage. She can think of a score of questions to ask him, from: How long have you been spying for the rebels? to: Did you murder Edmund Spenser because he found out? But they have to form a mannerly queue in her mind, because at the front is the one question that bursts from her mouth without even the preamble of acknowledging his sudden appearance in the chamber.

'Please God, Master Piers, tell me if my husband is safe?'

He looks genuinely concerned to put her mind at rest. He opens his palms as though she were holding him responsible for any harm that might have befallen Nicholas. 'He *was*, when I left Dublin, Mistress. I have not been much in his company of late, but I have heard no ill report of him.'

'You must tell him you have seen me. He will be losing his mind with worry.'

Before he can answer, Tyrone puts a stop to the exchange. 'Madam, if you want to see your husband again, the fastest way is to bring this woman out of her malady. The sooner you begin, the sooner we can decide how it may be contrived – without jeopardizing Master Gardener's position.' He extends his hand in invitation towards the bed. 'Will you attend her – *please*?'

Bianca steps forward, her heart racing. A blizzard of possibilities, blind alleys, opportunities, missteps, potential triumphs and certain disasters swirls in her head. Gardener is the means of saving Nicholas from grief... but now that she knows Gardener is a rebel spy, Tyrone will never let her leave. If she cannot heal Constanza Calva de Sagrada, Tyrone will have no use for her. If she *can* heal Constanza, how will she contrive an escape? What if the woman on the bed isn't Constanza Calva de Sagrada at all, but some other stray Spaniard with a similarly given name?

Start with something you can handle... force order upon the storm, even if it's only a temporary order...

Taking a deep breath, Bianca looks the Earl of Tyrone squarely in the eye. 'There are too many men in this chamber for decency,' she says firmly, as though it were her castle, not his. 'We need privacy. Please, leave us.'

Tyrone shoos away his attendants. 'You, too, Master Gardener,' he adds. 'We may consider what is to be done later.' Then, from the doorway, he adds, 'Please work swiftly, Mistress. This woman is of great importance to me. I need her well again.'

When the door closes, Bianca hears a key turn in the lock. From the bed, Constanza lets out a low moan. The woman who stands beside her stares at Bianca with deep suspicion in her dark, distrusting eyes.

Bianca thinks back to the meeting with Robert Cecil in the Paris Garden lodgings. In her head, she hears again a fragment of the exchange between Cecil and Edmund Spenser: *Where was this meeting to happen, Master Spenser?*

At Kilcolman... the perfect place.

Addressing the woman she assumes is Constanza's servant – the woman she reasons *must* have been the one who spoke English, because the other is near enough unconscious – Bianca says, as though it were nothing more than a trivial observation, 'Mercy! This is a wild and desolate place in which to fall sick. I haven't seen the like since I was at Kilcolman Castle, with Master Edmund Spenser. Tell me – what ails your mistress?'

And there it is: the sudden gleam that enters the eyes of the extraordinary figure standing beside the sickbed of Constanza Calva de Sagrada. The suspicion has fled, replaced by a gleam of understanding. Of empathy. The budding of new-found hope. As if both women have found each other after a long and arduous trek across whole continents of obstacles.

✠

'Who *are* you?' the woman asks.

'You heard what Master Piers said. I am a physician's wife. My name is Bianca. I am also an apothecary.' She glances back to the locked door. 'They seem to believe I may be able to help your mistress. I don't know about saving *her* life, but I think she may have saved mine.'

'Can you help?' asks the other.

'I can try.'

Bianca approaches the bed. She lifts a finger to her lips to signify caution. Then she gestures to the woman to come closer. When they are shoulder-to-shoulder she whispers, 'Is this the daughter of Don Rodriquez Calva de Sagrada?'

The dark face beside her hardens. Bianca can see the battle between the desire to trust and the fear of betrayal playing out in the woman's eyes. She studies Bianca with a cautious but penetrating gaze, as though inspecting a treasure she thinks might be a fake.

'I fear the man her father came to Ireland to meet is dead,' Bianca whispers, deciding that blunt honesty is the best approach. 'I am a friend. But you must behave as if I know nothing at all of this matter.'

She waits a moment, fearing the servant will shout for help. *Take this person away! She is trying to entrap me. She seeks to entice me into conspiracy!*

'I was at the site of the wreck. I found your mistress's lace mantilla. I think I know how you came ashore,' she breathes, hoping that detail might convince. To her relief, the iron hardness goes out of the other woman's body.

'I am Cachorra,' she says. 'I am maid to Señora Constanza.'

Bianca grins at her. To her joy, she receives one in return, a grin bright enough to lighten anyone's mood – even one who, at this exact moment, has not the slightest idea how she is going to a cure a sick girl of a malady she has yet to diagnose, and then spirit them all out of a rebel castle.

Start with something you can handle... Start with what you know.

Bianca says loudly enough to be heard beyond the door, and in a tone that suggests competence, 'I need to observe the patient. I need to note the symptoms.'

'Stomach cramps and pains,' Cachorra explains. 'Sweating, nausea, periods of insensibility that have grown longer as the days pass.' She drops her eyes as she speaks, as though she holds herself guilty for not protecting her mistress well enough.

A bowl of water and a cloth lie beside the bed. Bianca wipes away the sweat gleaming on Constanza's brow. Another soft moan escapes her plump lips. Her eyes open, fill with vague, watery interest, then close again.

Bianca asks, 'What treatment has she received while you've been here? Who has attended her?'

A small procession of old men claiming a knowledge of ancient physic, Cachorra tells her. And women even older, including one who had rolled her eyes alarmingly at the ceiling until Cachorra thought she was more in need of relief than her patient, and had then called down spirits to assist her while she rubbed Constanza's body with the pelt of a dead mole. Constanza had complained bitterly, as was her habit – well or sick. *Where are your qualified men of medicine, like our fine Spanish physicians, who have studied at Zaragoza and Madrid?* It had been politely pointed out to her that Ireland did not possess such temples of learning, or the attractions to lure physicians who had studied in them. This news had served only to steepen Constanza's decline.

'When did your mistress first fall ill?' Bianca asks.

'Soon after we arrived here. First was pain in the belly. Then the sweating.'

'You have eaten the same food, drunk from the same jugs?'

'Always,' says Cachorra.

'Is there anything she has taken that you have not?'

Cachorra's brow furrows. 'Nothing. Only that she takes more of it.'

Bianca leans over and sniffs Constanza's laboured breath. 'When these people came to attend your mistress,' she asks, 'did they give her any liquids to revive her – decoctions perhaps?'

'What is decoctions, please?'

'Herbs crushed and boiled in water or wine.'

'Ah, *decocción*. Yes, several. But they make no difference. My mistress still ill.'

'When was the last time?'

'Many days ago. Now she has only the *remedio* I give her.'

'What is that?'

'Is to make stop her being angry all the time. Is same as what her *niñera* give her when she is little girl. I make for her the same here.'

'In Padua my mother made much the same thing,' Bianca says with a smile. 'Whenever I would grizzle, out would come the *acqua prezzemolo*. I suspect she put *grappa* in it. What do you put in yours?'

'I put in *perejil*,' says Cachorra proudly. 'Is growing beside river.' She takes a small bronze bowl from beside the bed and holds it out for Bianca to inspect. The bowl is empty. Bianca sniffs it. A musty smell rises into her nostrils. To be sure, she inspects the chamber for mouse droppings. But it has been kept spotlessly clean.

'You must show me where you find this *perejil*.'

'Now?'

'Now is as good a time as any. Are you allowed to leave this chamber? When I arrived, I noticed the door was not locked.'

'We are permitted to come and go as we please,' says Cachorra. 'But we wish to walk beyond wall, we must have guards – in case the heretic English come.' Peering at Bianca as if heresy might be determined by the colour of the eyes, she adds, 'Are *you* also heretic English?'

'Certainly not,' Bianca tells her indignantly. 'I'm half-Italian. And a Catholic.'

'*Una hermana en Cristo!*' gasps Cachorra, throwing her arms around Bianca. 'You are sister in Christ, yes?'

'I suppose I am,' Bianca says laughingly as she gently prises herself loose from Cachorra's crushing embrace. Still in a whisper, she adds, 'What's more important, I know why your master came to Ireland. And I can help you fulfil his wishes. But first we must find out if I'm right about what's ailing his daughter.'

And with that, she calls out to whoever has their ear to the keyhole, 'Fetch the Earl of Tyrone! I need to see what plants and herbs may be gathered, to replace the medicines his saucy fellows stole from my tent.'

✠

In a shady spot that slopes down to the river the two women begin to explore the wild plants growing amidst a stand of willows. Insects thrum in the dappled shade. Dragonflies skid over the gleaming water. The two guards that Tyrone has appointed to keep watch sit a little way off. Bored by their unsoldierly task, they throw stones into the water. Suddenly Cachorra drops to her knees. She runs her fingers through a thick mass of green leaves.

'Here,' she says. 'See? I notice very first time they let us walk here.'

Bianca reaches down beside her and plucks a leaf. She rubs it between her fingers. At once the musty tang from the chamber affronts her sense of smell. 'This is *perejil*?'

Cachorra nods proudly. 'Yes. I pick, to make *remedio* – in castle kitchen.'

'You think this is parsley, don't you?' replies Bianca. 'I can see why you might. The leaves are very similar.'

'Is not *perejil?*' asks Cachorra, her face suddenly full of doubt and fear.

'No. It's hemlock. In Italian, *cicuta*. I'm not sure about the Spanish.'

Cachorra leaps to her feet, her hands flying to her mouth in horror. '*Cicuta! Santa madre de Dios!*'

Shushing her to silence, Bianca glances at the guards. They are still engrossed in their stone-throwing.

'It's alright. No one but us need know you've been poisoning your mistress, not healing her.'

Cachorra's strong features crumble. 'But only I wish to stop her complaining. No poison her!'

'I won't tell anyone if you won't,' Bianca says, laying a comforting hand on the other's wrist. 'I come from a long line of poisoners myself. Didn't anyone in the castle kitchen notice?'

'They leave me to myself. They frightened of Carib woman. They think I make witchcraft.' She looks back towards the castle. 'What have I done? I have killed the daughter of Don Rodriquez!' Tears begin to run down her cheeks. They glint against her dark skin like beads of mercury flowing over polished teak. Bianca pulls her kerchief from her sleeve and offers it.

'I don't think you've given her a fatal dose. But it's certainly time to dispense with the *remedio*. We'll pretend she's suffering from a malady of the stomach,' she says. 'Fitzthomas's people stole most of my physic. But I think I still have some sow-fennel. And I saw some euphorbia growing over there. We'll get an egg and some wine from the kitchen and mix a purgative. Your mistress will have her dignity affronted for a while, but she should recover.'

Leading Cachorra down to the river's edge, she washes her hands in the glittering clear water to remove the smears of hemlock, instructing the Carib to do likewise.

'Death is most usual sentence for poisoning a mistress,' Cachorra says wretchedly. 'I should die.'

'Don't be silly. I suspect Constanza wouldn't be alive at all if it were not for you. How did you both manage to survive the wreck?'

In short, unadorned sentences, Cachorra tells of how she and Constanza were swept overboard from the *San Juan de Berrocal*, how they were found by a young lad who hid them until they could be passed into the household of a local chieftain, and hence into the care of the Earl of Tyrone himself.

'It was fortunate that you were swept into the sea,' Bianca says when she has told her tale. 'Had you remained on the ship—' She can barely bring herself to recall the scene of murder she witnessed with Nicholas and Edmund Spenser at the site of the wreck. 'Do you understand that Don Rodriquez is dead?' she says gently.

'How do you come to know all these things?' Cachorra asks.

'Because my husband works for the man who was to receive the information that Don Rodriquez was carrying. That man's name is Robert Cecil.'

It is a close enough approximation to the truth, thinks Bianca. She would not be here, were it not for Mr Secretary Cecil and his intrigues.

'I have heard Don Rodriquez speak of this *Say-sill*,' Cachorra says with a wise nod.

'Master Edmund Spenser was to be the intermediary, wasn't he? That is why your barque was in Irish waters, I think.'

'What is intermediary, please?'

'He was to be the go-between. The first safe harbour for this information that Don Rodriquez was carrying.'

'Yes,' Cachorra agrees. 'That is what he was, the between-going.'

'But I am afraid that Edmund Spenser too is dead. He died in London, after telling Robert Cecil about Don Rodriquez and his like-minded friends in Spain. The question I have to ask you is this: does your mistress know the names that Don Rodriquez was carrying in his head?'

Cachorra fixes Bianca with a look of great seriousness. 'My mistress might be the daughter of a good man, the daughter of a lord, but she has the brains of the *tábano*.' She makes a buzzing sound and flutters her fingers in imitation of an insect.

Bianca's face falls. All this effort, all this way – for nothing. She closes her eyes in disappointment.

And then she hears Cachorra laugh, a sweet trilling as merry as the babbling of the river flowing so close to where she kneels. Opening her eyes, Bianca sees the kneeling Cachorra tapping her own forehead. 'Here,' she says. 'Is all in here.'

'*You* have the list in your head?' Bianca asks in disbelief.

'With Padre Persons, with Don Rodriquez – my mistress is always the same: *la-la-la*...' Cachorra says. 'Always daydream! No thought of anything, only of the *danza*. Which is why her Cachorra must always be the one who pay the attention. Otherwise' – an explosive puff of breath to signify the ruin of everyone's dreams – 'nobody learn *nothing*.'

34

The healing of Constanza Calva de Sagrada is swift but insanitary. The purges Bianca spoon-feeds her flush the poison out of her body, but in a manner no Spanish noblewoman with even a passing regard for her dignity is likely to consider agreeable.

'I poisoned her,' says Cachorra. 'Therefore I should be the one who carries the buckets to the midden. It's only fair.'

'No,' says Bianca. 'I prescribed the purgative, so I will live with the consequences.'

In the end they leave the bucket in the corridor for the guard to dispose of.

Within days Constanza is back to her old cantankerous self. The chamber is too cold. The chamber is too hot. The servants who washed her soiled clothing have not soaked it in rosewater to make it pleasant to the nostrils. How is she to face her waiting husband in clothes borrowed from Irish serving maids?

For it is clear she is determined that the marriage is merely postponed, not cancelled. And, indeed, it appears that is Tyrone's intention, too.

'I have sent a messenger into the Spanish Netherlands,' he reveals one evening when he summons Constanza and Bianca to join him at supper in the castle's hall. 'In a few days, when Mistress Bianca considers you well enough, I shall send you to

Scotland. You will be safe there until your intended husband can recover you.' Then he makes clear his motive. 'I trust he will inform Madrid that I have done all I may do, in difficult circumstances, to aid a friend.'

Bianca wonders how he would react if he knew the true reason Don Rodriquez had come to Ireland. Best he never finds out, she thinks – at least until she is free.

'And now that I have done what you asked me to do, my lord,' she says, 'may I too be permitted to return to *my* husband?'

'I shall see if it is possible to send a message informing him that you are safe,' Tyrone says, which Bianca notes is not at all the same thing.

✠

'They're not going to let me go,' Bianca tells Cachorra on one of their visits to the riverbank.

'But you do what they ask you to do.'

'Yes, but I saw Master Piers Gardener here. They think I'll betray him.'

'Then you must come with us, to Scotland.'

'I don't think Tyrone will let me do that, either. I have only one other option. I shall escape.' She says it as though it were something simple, like choosing to take a wherry across the Thames rather than brave the throng on London Bridge. 'You must write down the list of names that Don Rodriquez wishes to pass on to Robert Cecil.'

Cachorra replies with a look of true regret in her eyes. 'I cannot do. I swear an oath to Don Rodriquez never to place these names on paper. Is too dangerous.'

'But you were going to let Edmund Spenser write them down.'

'But Spenser is dead. So, I cannot write.'

Bianca can see the despair in Cachorra's eyes. She reaches out to take her hand. 'Don Rodriquez gave his life to get that list into friendly hands.'

'This I know,' Cachorra whispers, bowing her head as though in confession. Through Cachorra's fingers, Bianca can almost feel the struggle going on inside her. After a while she raises her eyes again. There are tears gleaming on the dark skin of her cheeks. 'Is not possible,' she says, as though she is to blame. 'I cannot write these names. Is too dangerous.'

But Bianca senses the struggle is not quite lost. She tightens her grasp on Cachorra's hand. 'My husband and Robert Cecil write in code to each other. Nicholas could ensure the list reaches Cecil safely,' she says, almost pleadingly.

Cachorra's face crumples in despair. 'But you *cannot* ensure. And I make solemn promise to Don Rodriquez.'

'Then to keep that promise – to finish the brave task Don Rodriquez began – you must give those names directly to Robert Cecil himself,' Bianca says in a moment of inspiration.

Cachorra withdraws her hand and wipes the tears away. 'How is this possible?' she asks.

'We shall escape together.'

Cachorra stares at her as though she has just suggested they fly to the moon on winged horses.

'Listen to me, Cachorra,' Bianca says urgently. 'Don Rodriquez gave his life because he wanted the war between England and Spain to end. He wanted the death, the destruction, the suffering to end. That is a noble ambition. We cannot let his courage die with him.'

Cachorra climbs to her feet. Bianca watches as she walks to the riverbank, not proudly and erect, but like a small child weighed down by grown-up fears. She sits quietly in deep contemplation, staring at the river. Watching her, Bianca wonders what it must be like to believe you have no more control over your fate than a solitary leaf drifting on the current. After a while she walks over and sits down beside her.

'And when I give to Cecil this *información*? What then?' Cachorra asks. 'Where do I go?'

'Home,' suggests Bianca. The word is no sooner out of her mouth than she understands how foolish she must sound.

Cachorra gives her a guilty smile, as if the fault is her own. 'I do not even know where in the world *is* my home. Don Rodriquez shows me once, on a globe. But still I could not imagine where it was. So, I cannot go back. Even if I find it, how do I speak? My poor tongue – she remembers more English than the language I say when I am a child. I do not hear my Carib name spoken for so many years, I almost forget it.' She thinks for a moment, then says slowly and very carefully, '*Yaquilalco*.'

She repeats the name as if it belongs to someone else, someone she met long ago. Then she smiles. 'But I am Cachorra now. *Cachorra de Leopardo* – the leopard cub. This is the name Don Rodriquez gives me. I like it.'

On the understanding that, in the absence of a priest, confession should not be a one-sided affair, Bianca says, 'I know a little of what it is like to arrive in a strange land. That is how I felt when I fled from Padua to England, when the Inquisition imprisoned my father. But I was lucky; he had told me many things about England. It would be a greater shock for you than it was for me.' A grin of encouragement to show that a woman can overcome any obstacle, if she is brave enough. 'But Bankside is a fine place – once you understand it. We have a certain disregard for authority there. At least you would be free.'

'In England?' Cachorra says, to be sure of what Bianca is suggesting.

'Yes.'

'But how do I live? What do I do – sell myself to men so I can eat?'

'I have an apothecary shop and a tavern. I can find work for you. Of course you'd have to learn the difference between hemlock and parsley.'

Cachorra returns to staring at the river. Bianca can only imagine the turmoil her thoughts must be in. What right, she wonders, do I have to ask this woman to take even *one* step onto this rickety bridge that I am trying to throw across so deep a ravine?

'Is it Constanza who holds you back?' she asks. 'Is it loyalty to your mistress?'

For a while Cachorra's head does not move. Then her shoulders give a little lurch and a small cough of laughter escapes into the drowsy air.

'I was a child when Don Rodriquez bring me from Hispaniola,' she says in a far-away voice. 'He save me from bad men: Ciguayo raiders. They want to sell me to Conquistadores. But Don Rodriquez, he pay gold for me, to make me *compañera* to his daughter.'

'He bought you as a *toy*, for his daughter?'

'I do not think that is how he saw it. He was a good man, I know this.' A louder laugh, wistful yet resigned. 'So many years I have to listen to this *lloriqueo*, this whining. *All* the time.' She adopts an irritating sing-song voice. "Cachorra, why you no comb my hair properly? Cachorra, why you no clap when I play viola da gamba?" – badly, I may say. "Cachorra, why you not bring me my book of Herrera poems open at the proper page?" *Madre de Dios!* For more years than I count – *always* something wrong. Sometimes I think Don Rodriquez should have left me on that beach. Sometimes I think I should have given Constanza the *cicuta*—' A glance at Bianca for the right English.

'Hemlock.'

'Yes, I should have given her the hemlock years ago. But I do not do this, because of Don Rodriquez. I owe him my life.'

And then, suddenly, Cachorra stands up and throws back her broad shoulders. She claps her hands together as though she were dusting flour from her palms.

'Is decided,' she says resolutely, without looking down at Bianca. 'I go to Robert Say-sill. I escape with you.'

Bianca jumps up and puts her hands on Cachorra's shoulders, as though to stop her toppling, which – looking back – she will say there was never the slightest chance of, not with a woman of Cachorra's strength. 'Are you sure?' she asks. 'It will not be easy. It will be dangerous. I could just try to learn the names.'

But the resolve on Cachorra's face is unshakeable.

'What is future for me now?' she demands, apparently to the army encamped around Tyrone's castle. 'My mistress will have a husband. He will give her new maids. Spanish maids. Cachorra will be made slave, like when you and I were carrying bucket of her *mierda* all hours of night. Is enough. I go.'

35

Since the death of Sir Henry Norris, Nicholas has ridden the see-saw of Robert Devereux's favour as best he can. It swings wildly between accusation and grudging tolerance. One moment Nicholas is undermining the army's health. He is Cecil's spy and should be sent back to England – were it not for the inconvenient fact that the queen herself has appointed him. The next, Nicholas is the only man who can relieve Devereux of his pains and discomforts.

Nicholas has watched this deterioration with alarm. His money is still on the French pox, though he is sensible enough to keep his opinions to himself. And while the noble earl's symptoms might be eased by the *aqua vitae* that Nicholas prescribes, they are inflamed by the never-ending stream of letters from the queen – letters in which Her Majesty makes clear her deep and growing disapproval of her former champion's conduct of her war.

They come written in neat secretary-hand and bearing the royal seal. But each one is a fanfare of imperious command. Strike at once, she tells him from the comfort of Whitehall, or Richmond, or Greenwich, or wherever else she is fulminating. Make no treaty with the rebellious Tyrone. Do not dare to set foot in England again until you have triumphed.

Nicholas knows this not because Essex confides in him, but because all Dublin knows it. It is the talk of taprooms throughout the city. And the gallants that Essex has taken to Ireland for what was supposed to be a share of the glory now mutter sedition of their own. Why should our general face such insults, and from a woman – even if she is the queen? Perhaps it would better to abandon the bogs and rains of Ireland, take the army back to England and put an end to the nest of snakes that surround her and drip their poison into her ears. Snakes like Robert Cecil.

Observing this casual tavern-talk sedition, Nicholas has begun to wonder if he is witnessing the seeds of a different rebellion being sown, a rebellion not in Ireland but in England. He is starting to think he was right when he wondered if Henshawe was holding back his English soldiers for just such a purpose. Perhaps Sir Oliver – and other captains, too, for all he knows – has mustered, armed and paid his English recruits not to fight rebels in Ireland but to support a march by a disgruntled Essex on the earl's enemies at court. Perhaps the most dangerous rebel of all is not Tyrone, but Essex himself.

Nicholas would send an enciphered letter to Mr Secretary Cecil, were it not for a new humiliation that has been imposed upon him.

'His Grace has ordered me to censor any letter you may write, lest they contain foul libels destined for Cecil House,' Oliver Henshawe had told him barely an hour after another of Devereux's frequent accusations that Nicholas is Cecil's spy.

'Not *your* idea then?' Nicholas had countered. 'I thought perhaps you were concerned I might be asking Sir Robert if he could find out where your English levies had got to – the ones stuck in Chester.'

'Why should I care what you choose to write? His Grace has the fullest confidence in *me*. I am not the one whose loyalty he mistrusts. Oh, and by the way, you're not allowed anywhere near the harbour without an escort.'

Looking back, it had been foolish in the extreme to goad Henshawe. His stare had been so direct that Nicholas had wondered if his eyelids had forgotten how to blink. I'm looking straight into the soul of a man who thinks it sport to murder survivors of a shipwreck, he had thought at the time. But at least he now knows for certain that Henshawe is harbouring a second secret, one that even *he* keeps to himself while he's boasting in a Dublin tavern.

✠

As befits any great healer, Bianca has become a figure of renown. The prisoner who brought the Spanish envoy's daughter back from the brink of death is a wonder. Tyrone's household, even the servants, are united in their admiration. It is proof, they insist, that God bestows his greatest favours only upon good Catholics, even those who are part English. All Bianca has to do now in order to win certain beatification is to put the sugar on the dish by coming up with a cure for Constanza's restored ability to complain endlessly. The chamber is too draughty... the venison is not prepared to her liking... the soldiers in the camp are too rowdy...

'The arrangements are made,' Tyrone tells Bianca one day when he calls her to his chamber at the end of a council of war. His captains look at her with new-found admiration as she is shown in. They appear to be celebrating some good fortune or other. There is a flagon of wine on the table.

'Am I to be freed, my lord?' she asks. 'Has chivalry prevailed?'

His craggy face makes its best effort at a show of regret. 'Sadly not yet, Mistress. I mean the arrangements for the Lady Constanza.'

'Oh.'

'Now that she is restored to health, she and her Blackamoor will travel under escort into my lands at Clandeboye. A barque will await her on Belfast Lough, to take her to Scotland. The husband is sending men from the Spanish Netherlands to meet her there. It is good that even in these times of sadness, a happy marriage may be made, don't you think?'

Wonderful, Bianca agrees. 'And what of *my* marriage, my lord – now that I have done as you ask?'

Tyrone looks uncomfortable. 'I fear you have seen too much.'

'You mean I've seen Piers Gardener?'

'He's too valuable to have you betray his true identity to Robert Devereux.'

'I promise not to. I'll give you my word.'

Hugh O'Neill doesn't seem much like a man given to regret, but he does his best. 'I would trust the Catholic Mistress Bianca in that regard. I'd even trust the Italian Mistress Bianca. But I fear I cannot risk trusting the English one.'

'Am I to be a prisoner until the Earl of Essex defeats you?'

'He's not going to. We both know that.'

'But neither can you defeat the English Crown.'

'I don't want to defeat the English Crown, Mistress.'

'Then what is all this for?'

'I am an O'Neill,' he tells her proudly, as though that is the answer to everything. 'All I want is for Elizabeth to recognize me as *the* O'Neill, the leader of my clan, as much the rightful ruler of my people as she is of hers. It is our custom for a clan to choose its ruler; the gift does not flow from the father, like hers does. It is offered, based on merit and reputation. In addition, we want the right to abide by our laws, not hers. And I don't want avaricious men like Devereux taking *our* land for *their* profit. Do you know what his father did here?'

Bianca doesn't. But she suspects Tyrone is going to tell her.

'Twenty-five years ago, when I was a young man, he lured some of my clan to Belfast, under the pretence of negotiating an end to a dispute over lands in Antrim. He wanted the territory for the plantation of English settlers, and to make himself a lot of money. Well, his men fell upon his host, my kinsman, and slaughtered his household. He took my kinsman, his wife and son to Belfast Castle and hanged them. I wouldn't trust a Devereux if he wore sackcloth, sandals, had a shepherd's crook in his hand, carried a lamb tucked under his arm and had a shining halo around his head.'

The stern, warrior faces of some of Tyrone's captains soften in something approaching mirth. But O'Neill's expression is as cold as a pebble in a stream.

'So, I am your prisoner until this war ends. Is that what I am to understand?'

'You are treated well, and with courtesy and dignity, are you not?'

'Yes, but that's not the point.'

'The sooner the Lady Constanza reaches her husband, the sooner I may confidently hope that another envoy will be sent by the Spanish in the place of her father. When the Spanish come, not even a dozen Devereux will be able to stand against them.'

'When does Mistress Constanza leave?'

'Three days from now – the day after I take my army down to face the English on the River Lagan.'

'You mean to give Essex battle?'

'Heavens, no. I could, but there's no need. His army is weak. If I defeat him, his queen will send a stronger one, with a better general at its head. So I intend to *tease* His Grace the Earl of Essex. I shall make a sweet treaty with him. I shall give him my pretty face. I shall dance a measure with him. I shall agree to almost anything he asks. And his own vanity will stop him seeing the truth: that I am simply buying time – until the Spanish come.'

'And I am to remain your prisoner until then?'

'Call me ungallant, but necessity requires it.' Seeing the look of misery in Bianca's amber eyes, Tyrone looks affronted. 'And we shall continue to treat you well, just so long as you don't think of escaping. Try that, and I'll have you killed. Please don't say I failed to warn you.'

'That's how I am to be rewarded, after what I have done for you?'

'That's how much Piers Gardener is worth to me.'

'Then I ask but one thing.'

'Ask it.'

'Make sure my husband, Dr Nicholas Shelby, learns I am safe. You did promise to.'

'I've been a little busy.'

'I had not thought you so ungallant.'

Tyrone relents. 'I have one of Devereux's officers, captured at the Conna fight. My men wanted to cut his head off and send it to Essex as a salutation. But I'm going to exchange him, to show what a reasonable fellow I am at heart. I'll tell them you're with me. I won't say where, but I'll say you're in good health. It's the best I can do.'

'Then I suppose I must be grateful to you, my lord.'

'A toast,' he says, pushing a cup of wine across the table. 'To peace.'

From Tyrone's captains comes a muted, knowing laughter.

'To peace,' she responds, lifting the cup to her lips. But neither she nor her captors specify precisely whose.

An hour later, Bianca is walking beside the river with Cachorra. Their guards, she notices, while still bored, now carry loaded crossbows. Pretending to search for herbs, she tells Cachorra about the plan to send her mistress on the final stage of her journey.

'Then we must escape before they come for her,' Cachorra says, her wide eyes brimming with alarm. She casts a glance at the guards. 'But how?'

Bianca raises a finger to her lips. 'I think it's time your mistress suffered a small relapse. Only on this occasion, I'll do the mixing.'

✠

With an army less than a quarter of the size he began with, Essex orders a march to Navan, where the waters of the Boyne and the Blackwater meet. He is determined to meet Tyrone face-to-face. His Grace seems distracted, and Nicholas knows why. It is not the fear of defeat that unsettles him. He is suffering from the flux. In addition to all his other ills, England's new Caesar is soiling his toga.

'You're needed,' says Ormonde despondently when he thrusts his grizzled head through the tent flap one evening while the army is encamped. They walk together towards the Earl Marshal's pavilion, past campfires where men washed clean of colour by wood-smoke and the evening twilight play dice, grumble, argue and contemplate. 'His reason is quite out of balance,' Ormonde tells him. 'One moment he wants to throw our force boldly against the enemy, despite their strength; at another, he wants to speak with Tyrone like a brother, call him back to the family bosom. Last night at supper he said he would challenge O'Neill to single combat. What odds would you put on a fellow of thirty-three years with the shits against a fifty-year-old who's campaigned as cannily as Hugh O'Neill? I know which side my coin would fall.'

When Nicholas enters, Essex breaks off from his conference with Southampton and his other captains. He is clad in the padded arming doublet he wears beneath his plate, though he looks more like a man who hasn't slept for a week than England's champion. His eyes are hollowed and bloodshot. His height no longer serves to impress, merely to accentuate the weight he's lost.

'Dr Shelby, is there *any* possibility you may prevent the rest of my army sickening away before the end of the month?' he asks with a breathtaking lack of self-knowledge. 'My army seems made of men with weak constitutions. The first hint of rain or fog and they wilt like grandmothers at a bear-baiting. Am I to have none but camp-followers to array in the field when I meet Tyrone?'

Camp-followers.

Is it said to inflame the hurt that has haunted me every moment since Bianca was taken? Nicholas wonders. Has the earl fallen from nobility into petty spite?

'It is not I who cause your men to sicken,' he answers, struggling to remain calm. 'Their conditions, their food, the demands made upon them, and the Irish climate – that's what ails them. They have enough to bear, even without the attentions of the enemy.'

'I need every man fit to march. Work your physic, Doctor,' Essex says, as if he's not heard a word Nicholas has spoken. 'If you think they're feigning, tell Henshawe. He'll hang a few. That should cure the rest, even if you can't.'

The assembled commanders show no sign that their general is jesting. Only Ormonde gives an almost imperceptible roll of his eyes. Nicholas gives an assurance that he will do what he can, given the limited resources.

'I believe there was something else you wanted to see me for, Your Grace,' he says.

Essex gives a small reluctant nod, as though admitting a minor indiscretion. He dismisses his officers and leads Nicholas into the private part of his pavilion, separated from the rest by an embroidered cloth hanging. 'This is what you asked for,' he says, lifting an object wrapped in a cloth from beside his pallet. A nauseatingly sulphurous odour clings to it. Nicholas takes it from him, bows and promises to return before the earl makes his evening prayers.

Outside the pavilion, Ormonde is waiting for him. 'That's it, is it?'

'I fear it is.'

'Well, I don't envy you. Rather face a six-foot rebel who was cup-shot on potcheen, myself.'

Nicholas nods acknowledgement of his misfortune. 'Just part of a physician's lot, I'm afraid. One gets used to it eventually.'

Alone in his tent, Nicholas spends a few uncomfortable moments examining the contents of the pewter bowl in which His Grace has thoughtfully provided a sample of the offending extrusions. Bearing the stench as bravely as he can, he makes a determination based on the colour and consistency of the matter and the blood contained within. Is Essex suffering from lienteria, tenesmus or dysenteria?

Nicholas diagnoses the last. To help him, he has not only the earl's evidence to go by, but numerous similar cases steadily depleting his army. Hanging won't cure the outbreak, whatever Essex might think. So, taking the remedy from his knowledge of Galenic medicine – and knowing from experience that it's likely to be as efficacious as telling his patient to dance naked through the nearest wood at midnight wearing his chamber pot for a helmet – Nicholas prescribes a decoction of sorrel, dried rind of pomegranate and briar root. And rest. A lot of rest.

But His Grace cannot rest. Pricked by yet more letters from the queen deriding his performance at the head of her army, the next day Essex gives the order to strike camp. He will march into Louth, towards Ardee. News has reached him that Tyrone seeks a meeting there. The final reckoning – flux or no flux – is close at hand.

36

Tyrone slams his wine cup down. 'A relapse?' he says irritably. 'How bad?'

On the table, spilled red malmsey forms stigmata on the exquisite gold crucifix Bianca has been admiring. It is to be a wedding gift for the Lady Constanza. As slender as a dagger, and fashioned from the finest gold ever panned from an Irish river – or so Tyrone has just informed her – she suspects it's more of a down-payment on Spanish aid than a gift to the happy bride and groom.

'Oh, not nearly as bad as before, my lord,' she assures him as she contrives an expression of self-recrimination. 'But I was a little premature when I said she was cured.'

Tyrone lifts up the crucifix and points the shaft at her, almost as if he's thinking of plunging the point into her breast. 'I had intended to give her this, before she departs. I cannot delay my departure.' His eyes reveal a faint hint of smugness. 'I have an appointment to keep, with His Grace the Earl of Essex.'

'In my opinion, my lord, it will be a few days before Constanza will be well enough to travel. But when she is, I believe I should go with her – lest she sicken again on the journey.'

The smugness changes to suspicion. Tyrone studies her, scratching at his bushy beard while he tries to gauge her capacity for deceit. Then he makes a little stabbing motion with the crucifix. 'And no doubt when you get to Scotland you'll slip away in the night, cross into England. I can't have that.'

'I wasn't planning to, my lord,' Bianca assures him in her most earnest manner. 'I am sure Lady Constanza will be fully recovered by the time she takes ship. I need accompany her only that far. By then her servant will be quite capable of attending to her needs.'

'The Blackamoor?'

'The Carib – Cachorra.'

'Is *that* what she's called? A wild creature, to be sure.'

No wilder than many of your fellows, who look more like Scythian warriors of old than modern fighting men, thinks Bianca. But she says nothing, adopting what she hopes is her serious apothecary's face.

'Very well,' Tyrone says at last. 'But you'll be guarded. And the guards will know their instructions, should you attempt to slip away.'

'I would expect nothing less, my lord.'

As Bianca makes her way back to Constanza's chamber, she is gripped by a fear even greater than that of what would happen to her should her attempt to escape fail. It is fear for Nicholas. He must surely be with Essex and the English army. What if Tyrone, with his superior force, decides – after all – that Ardee is the place not for parley, but for attack?

Nicholas is in favour again, at least for the moment. His Grace has pronounced him the finest physician in Christendom. Nicholas does not take this as a sign that Essex has really changed his opinion. When a man is relieved of the flux – even if only temporarily – his mood is always likely to improve. Thus it is that Nicholas finds himself in Devereux's pavilion, listening attentively while

Southampton and the other commanders attempt to talk the earl out of meeting Tyrone face-to-face. Essex has just announced that he intends to do so, without any of them being present. A privy meeting – with no close witnesses.

Their objection is both simple and direct: the earl's enemies at court in England – by which they mean Robert Cecil – will use such a parley to his great disadvantage. *His Grace has entered into a secret deal with Tyrone against Your Majesty's express commands... who knows what traitorous pact he has made with the rebels?... Without witnesses, without secretaries present to record what was said, who is to say that your erstwhile favourite has not betrayed Your Majesty's trust?*

Nicholas recalls how fearful Edmund Spenser had been of even the merest suggestion that he had been in contact with Spain, regardless of his motives. For a man of Devereux's importance, such an accusation could mean an appointment with the executioner.

But Essex is adamant. Following an offer of parley from Tyrone, he will array his army at the place suggested: the ford on the River Lagan at Bellaclinthe. It will be a display of strength, though everyone but Essex seems to know on which side of the river the true strength lies. But there will be no battle. He will bring the rebel leader to heel by the force of his will alone..

✠

With Tyrone and his army absent, a strange air has fallen upon the little castle. The household suffers from the listlessness of children kept at home while the adults are out doing something interesting. Bianca's guards have changed, too. O'Neill needs every fighting man he can muster. Only three are left to escort the Lady Constanza to the coast to take ship for Scotland, and one of those is still lame from a wound sustained in the rout of the English at the battle of the Yellow Ford over a year ago. They are civil enough, but she doesn't doubt they would carry out their commander's orders if it came to it.

It is the morning after Tyrone's departure for Ardee. The dawn creeps up over the soft hills. Cockerels call forlornly to the still-smouldering campfires on the abandoned riverbank.

'I need to speak with the steward, if you please,' Bianca says when the change of guard outside the door to Constanza's chamber has had a few minutes to settle himself to his duties. 'I assume you will want to accompany me – lest I try to escape.'

On the way down to the steward's chamber, she goes to work. Her small talk is mildly flirtatious, and clearly well received. After all, what young lad assigned to a demeaning and stultifying post in an almost empty castle wouldn't be flattered by the attentions of a comely older woman, a woman whose dark waves of hair and amber eyes suggest – even if somewhat modestly – excitements long denied to a lowly foot soldier of the rebellion?

The castle's elderly steward is stooped and white-haired, as reedy as anything that grows in the shallows of the Blackwater. He looks to Bianca as though he might snap if she blew on him. 'I believe the Lady Constanza will be well enough to travel tomorrow,' she tells him. 'We shall need food. She is also demanding wine, for the journey.'

He rolls his eyes in the manner of the perpetually suffering. 'I'll have a skin made ready,' he says. 'You may have it when you leave.'

Bianca gives him a doubting frown. 'I really would prefer it now. I shall need to mix a restorative into it, lest she suffers another relapse on the ride. She refuses to drink it neat, and it will take a while to infuse the wine.'

'Can you not do that overnight?'

'I must do the mixing in daylight; I need to be careful with the balance. Too little and it will be ineffective, too much and it may harm her recovery. Can you show me what skins you have available?'

The steward leads her to the kitchens. He shows her a collection of empty leather bladders hanging by their carrying straps from a hook in the pantry. He says, 'The O'Neill always takes one of these when he goes out hawking.' Then, in a sarcastic tone, he adds, 'I trust one of these will be worthy enough for her gracious Spanish majesty?'

Bianca notes the wooden stopper has a screw thread turned into it, to ensure a tight fit. 'This will do perfectly,' she says, giving the steward a wink to show how she, too, has laboured under Constanza's relentless demands.

'Very well,' says the steward. 'I'll send a full skin up to the chamber.'

'And a jug for mixing the restorative.'

'*And* a jug.'

'One more thing...'

'With the Spanish lady, there is *always* one more thing.'

A conspiratorial laugh, shared.

'There was a wedding gift, or so I understand. Would you be good enough to wrap it in a strong cloth? There's no point in making a display of its presence. I'm sure you have thieves here, just as we do in England. I'll send the Lady Constanza's servant down to collect it.'

'I shall have it ready,' the steward says, won over entirely. 'I hope you bear the ride to Clandeboye without developing a chancre of the ear.'

Back in their chamber, Constanza is snoring noisily in her bed. 'I'm not sure about the wedding gift,' Cachorra whispers when Bianca has explained her plan. 'Is my mistress's. Cachorra is no thief.'

'Of course you aren't. But that's *why* we need it. They'll believe I've escaped, and you've run away with me because you've stolen your mistress's possession. Constanza is bound to think the same. It will take away any suspicion that she was complicit in our disappearance. Besides, she's not going to starve when she gets to Antwerp – whereas *you* could do with a little something to set yourself up on Bankside. Consider it recompense for all that moaning you've had to put up with over the years.'

An hour later they contrive another walk together along the riverbank, in search of herbs. The air feels heavy on Bianca's skin, adding to the weight of her thoughts. She has tugged at her plan to see which threads will unravel, which will stay fast. It is by no means a perfect plan, but it is the best she can come up with. Out of the guards' hearing she says, 'In all the time you've been here, has anyone ever told you where *here* is?'

'I know only the name of this river. Is *aguas negras* – Blackwater. Nothing else do they tell me.'

'It's in Ulster, I know that much. And Tyrone said he was taking his army *down* to meet Essex on the River Lagan. Down must surely mean south. So south is where we're going. South is where Nicholas will be.'

Bianca is shocked by the expression on Cachorra's face – a look of utter desolation, as though a loving husband to escape to is something so far beyond her reach that the very thought of it hurts like a physical pain.

'But when they find we have gone, they will come after us, yes?' Cachorra says.

Casting a quick glance at the guards to ensure they have not moved within earshot, Bianca says, 'They won't know if we're following Tyrone's army or taking a more easterly path, towards the English garrison at Drogheda. And there aren't enough men left behind to cover both possibilities in any strength.'

'But how to know where to go?' Cachorra asks plaintively.

'Easily,' Bianca says with a smile of reassurance. 'Tyrone's army is seven thousand strong. Unless they all went on tiptoe – including the horses – I suspect they will have left more than just a few traces to follow. All we have to do is to ensure we don't follow *too* closely.'

Cachorra ponders Bianca's words for a while, making a play of grubbing for herbs to reassure the guards. When she stands up again, her face is a picture of newborn, fragile hope. 'First we have to go from here,' she points out, as though she cannot quite believe the future could be hers for the taking. 'We are still watched.'

From where the guards are standing, the two women could be old friends swapping amusing tales of past dalliances. Bianca glances back at one of them, the lad who had escorted her to the steward's chamber. She gives a smile that is just a little more than merely friendly. Then she turns back to Cachorra. 'For that,' she whispers, 'we must rely upon the knowledge of the Caporetti.'

✠

The day passes languorously. The September air has a summer sultriness about it. The willows droop beside the river, untroubled by even the faintest breeze. Kingfishers hunt on the river, their rainbow wings flashing above the crystalline surface.

It is late afternoon. In her chamber Constanza Calva de Sagrada sleeps as deeply as only those who have drunk a soporific – knowingly or unknowingly – can sleep. In the meadow beside the river, two women are taking another amble through the trees in search for herbs and plants. When Bianca had been asked why two visits in one day were necessary, she had said there must be enough physic to ensure the daughter of the Spanish envoy – who so bravely lost his life coming to Ireland's aid – might be assured of speedy relief, should she fall ill again.

Their guards follow a little way behind the two women, crossbows still loaded but held casually enough. They have changed their minds about the duty that O'Neill has given them. Instead of bemoaning their exclusion from his army – surely about to bring the hated Earl of Essex to his gartered knees – now they are like soldiers anywhere who have found themselves an undemanding post well away from danger. After all, what could possibly be more pleasurable than strolling along a riverbank in the company of two comely women? 'Let us pray the apothecary doesn't attempt to slip away,' says one guard to his companion. 'It would be a terrible tragedy to have to shoot such a beauty with this crossbow.'

'I can think of better uses for my bolt,' says the other.

And what is this – a coy invitation to come closer and join them? Look: they've brought manchet bread and cheese from the kitchens. Why, they've even managed to prise a skin of wine out of the miserly kitchen steward! What a turn of events. Who'd want to be on the march when a fellow can sit beside such beauties, making flirtatious small-talk in the warmth of the afternoon, lulled by the humming of the bees and the flowing river? Who'd want to risk life and limb when you can drink wine on a flowery bank in such attractive company?

And the wine *is* very good.

And the company *is* very pleasant.

And it *is* very warm. Soporific in fact.

'How long have we got?' Cachorra asks when she's sure the guards are safely asleep.

'What?'

Bianca has been thinking how proud her mother would be that the line of Caporetti poisoners is maintained, even if this particular example is merely a harmless sleeping draught made from some of the ingredients the rebels forgot to steal from her apothecary's collection.

'I said, "How long have we got?" Before they wake?'

'Two hours at least.'

Across the pebbled ford, in the trampled empty meadow and around the ashes of abandoned campfires, only the crows move, grubbing for scraps of food left by the departed army. Bianca glances back at the castle. With Tyrone's household stripped of fighting men, there is no one left to keep watch from the walls. She and Cachorra are unobserved. It is time.

37

It is a performance as good as any at the Rose playhouse on Bankside. But it is an illusion, a pretence in which everyone knows the scenery is fake and the man at the centre of the stage is playing a part. Everyone, that is, except Robert Devereux, Earl of Essex, Earl Marshal of England and Lord Lieutenant of Ireland.

Clad in his black field armour like the last of the medieval knights – and dosed with all the physic Nicholas can give him – he rides his magnificent charger down to the bank of the Lagan. Behind him, drawn up on the grassy slope, is the tired, dispirited English army.

Nicholas remains in his tent in the baggage train. He has no interest in watching this vainglorious display. It is all he and his little band of barber-surgeons can do to treat the cases of sickness amongst the ranks. And sickness is not the only drain on the earl's depleted force. Desertions too are on the rise. Several of Henshawe's company have slipped away on the march, making Sir Oliver's own temper even more unpredictable. He shares Devereux's inclination to hang anyone who cites a malady as an excuse to fall behind.

A fine drizzle mists the Lagan valley. It drifts through the trees like cannon smoke, as though a battle has already been fought and lost. The river meanders like a flow of cooling pewter melted in a fire. On the far bank a small contingent of men in fur pelts and broadcloth gowns sit upon shaggy ponies. Matched against the armour of the English commanders, made into mirrors by the rain, they look like a band of ancient Celts come to parley with a Roman legion.

Southampton and the other commanders sit astride their chargers in front of the English lines. They know the score well enough. Their skirmishers have told them that while the far bank might seem almost empty, out of sight beyond the rising ground waits the mass of Tyrone's rebels. And while they are confident their shot and artillery might defeat an attack, there's not a hope in Hades of launching one of their own and having it end in anything other than a slaughter.

In the centre of the river, a stocky, bushy-bearded man sits in the saddle of his horse. He has no stirrups. The legs hang loosely as though the body is suspended from a gibbet. The water is almost up to his heels. His head is bowed, the drizzle streaming down his broad brow. He looks the very picture of a supplicant who knows he can no longer summon the strength to fight against impossible odds. So he has come to make a deal.

And Essex has fallen for it.

✠

For three days they have followed the trail of Tyrone's forces. Now, tired, hungry, but filled with a growing conviction that they have evaded any search party, Bianca and Cachorra huddle in the undergrowth of a wood barely a mile from the river. They have made the landscape their accomplice, keeping to the trees as best they can, avoiding open ground where a pursuer might spot them from a distance. Bianca's judgement about the effect of the soporific she had put in the wine proved accurate. It wasn't until darkness fell on the first day that the sound of a horse at full gallop had given them just enough warning to slip into hiding, before what they assumed was a messenger came flying past. The next morning they had spotted small bands of riders well off to their left. Burrowing into the bracken like frightened hares, their hearts racing, they had waited to be discovered. But when Bianca dared cautiously to raise her head again, they had disappeared from view.

Their hiding place now is a spinney of silver birch, set on a small hill overlooking what Bianca assumes must be the Lagan itself. Tyrone's army is halted a good mile away to their left and hasn't moved for hours. Since first light, she and Cachorra have cautiously skirted around its right flank to reach their present position. A thin drizzle has fallen for hours, and from this distance there is no sign of either army. But a short way off, the river's far bank folds around a heathered hill. Beyond it, the smoke from many campfires rises forlornly. If those fires are burning on the opposite bank, Bianca reasons, then it must be English smoke from English campfires.

They have eaten the last of the bread and cheese, though it has done little to assuage their hunger. They are wet and cold, weary and footsore. But Bianca's heart is vaulting inside her chest. The thought that Nicholas might be on the other side of that hill, warming himself by one of those fires, is enough to warm her body, were it frozen solid. It is all she can do to stop herself running down to the river.

'Can you swim?' she asks Cachorra.

'What is swim?'

Bianca flails her arms purposefully.

'Ah, *natación*,' says Cachorra, restraining a squeal of laughter. 'Yes, I do all the time in Hispaniola, when I am young.'

'Then tonight we *natación* – all the way to freedom.'

✠

Nicholas wakes from a half-sleep. He has been daydreaming, fighting his way through ranks of rebels. Each one wears Oliver Henshawe's face. Each one is more determined to prevent him reaching Bianca than the one in front. He yawns, rubs his eyes and sits up on his straw pallet.

The light from the campfires outside sends lurid shapes flitting across the interior of the tent. He sees a dark shape squatting in the entrance. 'Nicholas, I've come for His Grace's... *comfort*,' says the Earl of Ormonde.

It has become a ritual. Each evening, around this time, Ormonde comes to his tent on the pretext of learning how many new cases of sickness there have been. What he does with this information, Nicholas is uncertain. He suspects Ormonde keeps it to himself. And each evening Ormonde takes with him when he departs an *aqua mulsa* of rose petals, myrtle and powdered comfrey root to ease the Lord Lieutenant's current indisposition. It could be considered strange for one earl to send another earl to fetch his medicine, but Essex has decided that no one but his most trusted lieutenants must know of his malady. If the common soldiery were to learn of it, His Grace would have to make laughing a capital crime, and then he would have no army left at all.

'Please God, don't tell me he had an attack while he was talking to Tyrone,' Nicholas says as Ormonde enters. 'I made the syrup as powerful as I dared.'

Ormonde gives a grim laugh. 'If he had, it might have cleared his mind as well as his bowels. He might have seen the foolishness of what he was doing.'

'Was it that bad?'

'Bad enough. Tyrone has wound him around his traitorous little finger like a ribbon.'

'But is to it be peace?'

'For six weeks. But Tyrone keeps all the land he has taken, and *we* are to place no new garrisons. His Grace is calling it the greatest treaty since Athens and Sparta agreed to stop bickering. When Her Majesty finds out what he's given away, I can see us all on our knees with our necks stretched out on a block, like so many chickens awaiting the butcher's cleaver.'

'But surely these are good tidings. Essex can't win. Tyrone can't win. Half the island is laid waste, no one has enough food, the living suffer and the dead go unburied...'

'Her Majesty will not countenance a peace that does not first bring the rebellious Earl of Tyrone to his knees,' Ormonde says wearily. 'She is queen of this island by God's grace and her father's gift. She has expressly commanded Essex not to make a treaty that allows a *traitor* to dictate the terms.'

'Then this is only temporary?'

'There can be no true peace on this isle until its people are brought to an understanding of their duty to God and their sovereign.'

'You sound like Edmund Spenser.'

'He was right, Nicholas.'

'He recommended starving them into submission. How does *that* sit with a duty to God?'

'A quick, firm hand is often the kindest, Nicholas. Better a harsh storm that is soon over than a cold wind that blows for years to come.'

'That's easy to say if you're the one with the hearth, the thick walls and the solid roof,' says Nicholas, handing Ormonde the clay flask containing Essex's physic.

'I'm merely a humble soldier,' Ormonde tells him. 'I do as God, my queen and His Grace the Lord Deputy command.' Turning to leave, he pauses. 'I almost forgot,' he says archly. 'I've some good news for you.'

'That this is all just a dream, brought on by too much malmsey?'

'I wish it were,' Ormonde says, laughing. His face softens. 'It's about your wife.'

Nicholas is on his feet in an instant, forgetting the proximity of the canvas above his head, which turns purposeful movement into an ungainly stoop.

'You have news of her?'

'There was an exchange – one of His Grace's fine young gallants who got himself taken at Conna, swapped for one of Tyrone's men we captured.'

'He's seen her? She's alive?'

'He was told only that a woman, an apothecary, was taken in the same engagement. But it sounds as though it's her.'

'Is she safe? Is she well?'

'Apparently. She's in Tyrone's custody. The fellow doesn't know where.'

'Thank Jesu!' Nicholas whispers. A surge of relief sweeps through his body, forcing him back down onto the straw pallet. 'Is she to be freed?'

'That was not stated. But with this new accord, we can hope she will soon be returned to you.'

It is only when Ormonde has departed that Nicholas realizes his hands are trembling. Finding the tent unbearably stuffy, he goes out into the dusk. The drizzle has stopped. Patches of purple sky peep between the clouds. The stars are emerging to see how the day has gone, crystalline eyes observing him with indifference as he wanders amongst the campfires and the huddled groups of soldiers.

What shall I tell Bianca when she returns? he wonders. When we have held each other long enough, what shall I say to her? *Robert Cecil has had my soul too long. I want it back. Now that I've seen the true results of the conspiracies his kind deals in, it's time to throw down my cards and leave the game. And look at what we were playing for: severed heads and blackened fields... earls in fine plate armour who rot from the inside with ambition and disease... starving villagers who should be grateful for the mercy of a firm hand... God's name invoked as an excuse for savage butchery...*

He remembers Cecil's promise that Bruno could one day enter his household. He allows himself a glimpse into an imagined future. He sees his boy at twenty, no longer heir to a Suffolk yeoman's son but to privilege and position, just another glory-hungry gallant with no conscience, like the ones who buzz around Robert Devereux the way flies buzz around the earl's pewter pots of stinking flux.

You've done the rebels' work for them, sirrah, he can hear Essex shouting, the day Henry Norris died of his wounds. *You're a traitor!*

Perhaps I am, Nicholas thinks. And perhaps there are worse things to be in life than a traitor to a tainted cause.

✠

When Tyrone had told her that he was taking his army to meet the English on the Lagan, Bianca had known she would likely have to cross the river. The rebels would no doubt choose a ford for the meeting. But she had decided from the start that it would be far too risky to attempt to cross anywhere within view of their flank scouts. That would mean the distinct possibility of having to swim across. And a heavy woollen gown, once waterlogged, would take her to the bottom as efficiently as an iron anchor.

'Now I understand why you bring this,' Cachorra says with a smile as Bianca blows as many breaths into the empty wineskin as her bursting lungs can manage. Red-faced, she screws the wooden stopper down tightly into the neck.

'Everything off, down to our under-smocks,' she gasps as she stoops to unlace her boots.

When they have assembled their clothes in a pile, Bianca stuffs everything into her own kirtle. Only Constanza's gold crucifix remains.

'I should not have taken it; is stealing,' says Cachorra regretfully, staring down at the dull gold, robbed of its lustre by the twilight.

'Not really,' Bianca tells her. 'You've earned it through forbearance. If I'd had to live in your shoes, I would have belted her over the head with it.' She bends down, retrieves the wedding gift and pushes it deep inside the clothes. She binds the bundle to the inflated wineskin, tying the sleeves tightly around its leather carrying-strap. Then she hoists the improvised float over one shoulder. 'Leave the boots,' she says. 'They'll only fill up with water and impede us. The English must have *some* to spare that haven't fallen to pieces.'

Leaving the shelter of the birch wood, they make their way down towards the river. In the aftermath of the drizzle, the grassy slope is as slippery underfoot as the Thames when it freezes over.

A sudden crack, like an angry slap across a cheek. Bianca turns her head sharply. Her heart tries to hurl itself from her breast. Close behind her, Cachorra gives a guilty grin and lifts a palm away from her left wrist. 'Mosquitoes,' she whispers. Bianca shushes her to silence. They move on at a crouch.

At the water's edge the bank has slipped away. It takes some stumbling about in the gloom to find an easy way down. With a brief hug for good luck, the two women slip down into the dark river. Two simultaneous gasps of shock, quickly stifled. Then, with no more sound than a pair of wading herons might make stalking a plump fish, they strike out in a measured breaststroke, making as little disturbance in the water as they can.

✠

The Lagan is not particularly wide at Bellaclinthe. Nor is the current overpowering, certainly not for two young women with more than enough reason and determination to reach the far side. But the light has almost gone. The rising ground ahead is rapidly dissolving, the land mixing with the water to make a blackness that Bianca fears is stealing away her hopes of safety, of finding Nicholas. She has an alarming impression that she is swimming not to a nearby riverbank, but out into a boundless ocean.

The first stabs of panic make themselves felt in the tips of her fingers as they explore the cold liquid. The measured stroke of her arms takes on a faster, desperate action. Her feet fail. She forgets the need for silence. Now she has lost her bearings. She glances ahead, searching for the bank. Surely it must be almost within reach. It *has* to be. She thinks she has been swimming for an age. But when she lifts her head, she sees nothing but darkness.

Where is Cachorra?

Frantically Bianca twists in the water. *There!* Barely a yard behind her. She would have missed her completely, a gleam of breaking water the only sign she hasn't drowned. She treads water, offering the float to her companion. But Cachorra has no need of it. She looks as though she could swim all the way back to Hispaniola if she chose.

Then another fear strikes Bianca: what if she has lost her bearings? What if her makeshift float, looped around one arm, has caused her to swim in an arc, taking poor faithful Cachorra back to the rebel bank? She hadn't thought of that.

Bianca lets her legs sink a little, thinking she might touch bottom. Nothing. She pushes out again, gaining strength from the fear growing inside her. She feels something scrape across her belly. Convinced that a great fish with needle-sharp teeth has just passed beneath her, she opens her mouth to scream. Water rushes in and suddenly there is no air in her lungs. I'm going to drown, she thinks. I'm going to die almost within sight of Nicholas. Her arms begin to flail as if they had a will of their own.

But instead of beating against the river, she is hammering at a shelving bed of mud and gravel. Her fingers and knees scrape themselves raw, though she will not even notice the damage until long after she and Cachorra have clambered up the grassy incline, laughing and splashing water from their soaking clothes over each other like children playing in a rockpool.

'We've done it! We're safe,' she gasps, wiping the grit from her mouth with the hem of a wet sleeve.

'*No más idiota Constanza,*' says Cachorra in wonderment, looking around as if she cannot quite believe it. '*No más quejas! Aleluya!*'

It is only then that Bianca sees a pair of horsemen a little further up the slope, reined in by a clump of trees. In the twilight she cannot determine their expressions. But they look like stone monuments in an abandoned temple, hinting at an ancient power once held over the vanished congregation. One of them calls out – in a tone familiar to any spy who has just been caught in the act of stealing across the lines. And not in English, but in native Irish.

38

The valley of the Lagan is in darkness. On either side of the river the campfires of the opposing armies glow like stars in a looking glass held towards the night sky. In the English camp a sense of weary acceptance reigns. The day that has passed cannot be called a victory. But neither can it be called a defeat; not while His Grace the Earl of Essex is in such an ebullient mood.

He has single-handedly brought the rebellion to an end. He has done what no general, past or present, could do. He has tamed Tyrone. The queen will restore him to the boundless generosity of her favour, along with all who had faith in him. As for the doubters, to the Devil with them. Tomorrow he will retire the army to Drogheda, thence to England to claim his real prize: the overthrow of his enemies.

In this dangerous delusion, Devereux is encouraged by Southampton, Henshawe and his closest captains. Ormonde and the others, including Nicholas, are of a very different mind. They have not so easily forgotten Her Majesty's express command to her Lord Lieutenant not to enter into any unworthy treaty, and not to show his face in her presence until all the fires of rebellion have been smothered. For Nicholas, these great affairs are little more than a secondary discomfort when set against the far greater pain of retreating to Drogheda without further word of Bianca.

He has just finished treating one of Southampton's cavalrymen. The man presented a short while ago with a corrupted blister on the inner thigh. Once Nicholas had expelled the pus, he'd been forced to rely only on plantain and lentils to make the cataplasm, because his supply of arnoglossum is almost exhausted. There's little chance of getting more from England because the main source of the plant is in the Spanish territories in the Americas. The merchants in France and Italy charge an arm and a leg, and even if he could send word that he needed a fresh supply, the chances of it arriving before his patient dies of old age are slim. So much for a victorious army, he thinks. Horsemen with boils, a general with dysenteria and the pox, and an enemy that rides away with the better deal. Could anyone have a finer metaphor for Her Majesty's present enterprise in Ireland?

Exhausted, he leans back against the wall of his tent. If the past is anything to go by, Essex will call for the camp to be struck even before first light. The army will be on its way to Drogheda by sunrise. Away from Bianca – wherever she is.

'Master Physician... Master Physician...'

Someone is calling to him in a low voice made all the more urgent by its Irish lilt. Probably one of the locally raised levies, he decides, come to seek treatment for the flux, or the bog fever, or the tertian ague, or any of the other debilitating maladies this isle seems to harbour specifically for English armies. My first task, he thinks, will be to convince the poor fellow that he's not going to hang for seeking help.

'Yes, I'm Dr Shelby. Come in. How may I help?' He looks up.

Holy Jesu, there's three of them. They're falling sick in batches now. At this rate, Essex will be going to Drogheda all by himself.

With the tent lit only by a single lantern to work by, the three figures are mere shadows against the night beyond. Even the campfires lend them nothing but fragments of outline where the firelight touches. Then one ducks down and enters.

It's a phantasm, Nicholas thinks, rubbing his sore eyes. It's brought on by exhaustion. Because how else could Bianca herself appear before my eyes, her usually unruly hair plastered around her face, dripping water as though she's swum across an ocean and smelling faintly of river mud?

'Good morrow, Husband,' the phantasm says, a strand of river weed in her hair and a grin barely under control. 'Have you missed me? I've brought you not just one Merrow, but *two*.'

✠

The moment for rapturous reunion must wait. Nicholas is nothing if not a practical man. The night is not overly warm, and both Bianca and the woman she has brought with her – almost as much a shock to him as seeing his wife again – are shivering from the swim. He enlists the help of the two lads who found them: lancers in Captain Bellingham's company of native Leinster men, who had been patrolling the riverbank when Bianca and her companion clambered out of the water. Together, they build a fire behind the tent. It takes a little juggling, some back-turning and a makeshift screen of gaberdines, sleeping pelts and sacking, but soon Bianca and Cachorra are warming themselves beside the flames, with pelts around their naked shoulders. A change of kirtles is begged from the women camp-followers who, learning that Bianca has returned, must be restrained from rushing to her side like maids of honour at a wedding. With the dry clothes, they provide two bowls of weak but hot pottage, a generous gift given the paucity of their rations.

True to her name, Cachorra observes this industry with the wariness of a hungry cat. There is resignation in her eyes, as though to swap one estate for another is something that simply has to be borne. But there is hope and anticipation there, too. Bianca admires her ability to make the best of the world in which she finds herself. Perhaps she has learned it as an antidote to her former mistress's endless dissatisfaction with her own world.

'I have the suspicion you'll fit into Bankside as easily as a hand into a fine, doeskin glove,' she tells her, while the firelight plays on Cachorra's skin.

A hasty rearranging of the pots, hemp bags, boxes and jars that contain his physic, and Nicholas contrives two extra sleeping places in the already cramped tent, adding the scrounged sleeping pelts for comfort. Like the survivor of a catastrophe, Cachorra is soon fast asleep, though what dreams she may have are beyond even Bianca's comprehension. What does a prisoner dream of on her first night of freedom, if she can barely remember anything but imprisonment?

'Who is she? Where did you find her?' Nicholas asks Bianca as they stand outside the tent, watching the campfires burn down. Neither is ready for sleep, despite the exertions of the day and the fact that the army will move at dawn.

'Her speech – I can't quite place it. Her English is spoken with an accent that sounds almost... almost—'

Bianca tries not to laugh as she watches Nicholas's thoughts play out on his face. She's always believed his yeoman's honesty the one major obstacle to his work for Robert Cecil.

'*Spanish?*' she says teasingly.

'No! She can't *possibly* be—'

Even though he's become accustomed to Bianca's ability to confound him, he struggles to get the words out.

'No, Nicholas, she isn't,' Bianca says, trying not to laugh at his obvious confusion. 'But she is – or rather she was – Constanza Calva de Sagrada's personal maid.'

She relays to him the story Cachorra has told her of how she and her mistress survived the shipwreck. She recounts how they were passed from hiding place to hiding place because Tyrone believed that Don Rodriquez had been an emissary from Spain, come to offer assistance in his rebellion against the English. She explains how she herself proved the saving of Constanza, though she diplomatically omits Cachorra's inadvertent role in her mistress's illness.

'Where is Constanza now?'

'On her way to Scotland, I hope. Then to Antwerp – to what her husband probably anticipates will be a life of wifely duty and devotion. I really do hope he's a patient man. Failing that, that he has a palace with a *lot* of rooms.'

He stares at her, all pretence at comprehension abandoned. 'Then has Constanza given *you* the list of names?'

'No. But Cachorra has it.'

'Wrapped in sailcloth,' he ventures, recalling the small package Cachorra had been carrying when she arrived, and which now lies beside his rearranged stock of physic.

'Oh no. That's Cachorra's dowry, for her future.'

'Then *where* is it?'

'Where we women keep all our most priceless attractions,' she says sweetly, kissing him chastely on the cheek. 'In her head.'

✠

The sultry drizzle has passed. Dawn brings a clear early-autumn sky, laced with wisps of cloud the colour of poached Lagan salmon. The Lord Lieutenant gives the order to depart the valley, convinced that a great victory has been won. Only the less servile of his captains eschew the congratulatory mood. They know the dangers to which Robert Devereux has made himself a hostage.

And what of the latest addition to the train of camp-followers? How to pass off this tall, imposing-looking young woman whose appearance is, to say the least, uncommon?

Although she may be noteworthy, Cachorra is not exactly a rarity. There are others amongst the camp-followers who, judged by the colour of their skins, are clearly not descended from Brutus of Troy, or Joseph of Arimathea, or King Arthur, or any other of England's ancient forebears. Three of Sir Henry Bartlett's musketeers – a company only recently transferred from the Low Countries – have married native women from the Dutch settlements in the Indies. One of Captain Mackworth's pikemen has a Moor for a wife, taken as bounty at Lisbon, during Essex's somewhat more successful expedition there three years ago. One of Nicholas's own barber-surgeons, when serving aboard *The Dolphin*, took an African wife while in port in the Azores.

Even so, Cachorra will still need a story, a background, an explanation. Bianca has one readily to hand, dreamed up while waiting in the birch wood for dusk to fall before she swam the river. She had remembered Edmund Spenser's recounting of the foreign ships that traded with the honest merchants of Cork. Thus Cachorra now becomes a Carib servant taken from Hispaniola by a foreign ship's master – which in itself is an approximation of the truth – who ran away when her ship docked at the Watergate. Entering into a marriage of convenience with a Munster settler who abandoned her when the rebels stormed out of Limerick, she was taken captive.

When Bianca rouses her from a deep sleep – more than a little envious, for she and Nicholas have managed no more than a few hours – she explains the importance of speaking only English or her native Carib. Spanish must be avoided at all costs.

'What shall I do about Piers Gardener?' Bianca asks Nicholas as they strike down the tent and load the supplies of physic into a waiting wagon.

'He's a spy. It will be our duty to report the fact.'

'If we tell anyone, and Master Piers is taken, I imagine his end will take a long while to come and the journey will be hard on him. Very hard,' Bianca says, hoisting a small sack of powdered ragwort into the wagon. 'Hasn't there been enough pain and suffering already?'

Nicholas shrugs. 'He will have been responsible, even if only at a distance, for the deaths of who knows how many people: soldiers, settlers attacked by the rebels... Yet I can only see him on the journey to Kilcolman, sitting with us at the *Seanchaí*'s house, listening to those magical tales.'

'Who are we to sit in judgement on a man's conscience,' Bianca asks, 'if he truly believes that what he is doing is in a just cause?'

'That rather depends upon *what* he's doing. Still, there's a sort of peace in place, so perhaps you should forget you ever saw him. Now that you've escaped, I doubt very much if he'll risk returning to any town with an English garrison.'

An agreement is reached. For the sake of conciliation – domestic as much as political – the name of Piers Gardener is quietly consigned to a faulty memory.

And just as well, because the discussion has barely ended when Sir Oliver Henshawe arrives. His field armour bears no more than a light coating of dirt on the sabatons, where his feet have had to encounter the rebellious Irish mud. The rest looks as though some hapless groom has been up all night with the cleaning oil and the rags.

'Well, I didn't dare believe it true,' he says, looking Bianca up and down as though she were an unveiled painting set before him to be admired. 'They say you swam across the Lagan with a Blackamoor in tow.'

'What did you expect her to do – sit in Tyrone's chamber

working at her sewing and improving her soul by reading a psalter?' Nicholas asks hotly.

'It's alright, Nicholas,' she says. 'Oliver should be used to women escaping a tedious confinement by now. You're still unwed, I think, Oliver?'

Henshawe ignores the riposte. 'This Blackamoor I heard you brought with you – where is she?'

'Returning the clothes that we borrowed,' Bianca tells him. 'And she's not a Blackamoor, she a Carib – from Hispaniola. Nor is she mine. In fact she's not anyone's. Not any longer.'

'Hispaniola – New Spain,' Henshawe says with a slight lift of an eyebrow.

'Being conquered doesn't make you the conqueror, Oliver. It makes you a slave.'

She tells him the story she has concocted for Cachorra. It seems to satisfy him.

'It's you I'm more interested in,' he says airily.

'Me? I thought your interest in me ended long ago.'

A smile like a wince. 'We shall need to know exactly what you saw and what you heard during your captivity,' he says, a smirk crawling its way across his pretty mouth. 'And whether or not it undermined your loyalties in any way.'

The insinuation could not be plainer.

'And why would it do that?' Bianca asks.

'Captivity can do strange things to a person's judgement, especially if that person is half-Italian and is known for her heretical tendencies.'

Not for the first time Nicholas restrains himself from planting his fist squarely in the centre of those supercilious features. 'Are you suggesting my wife is a spy?'

'If the husband is prepared to spy on His Grace for Robert Cecil, who is to say the wife would not spy for the heretic rebels?'

Bianca lays a restraining hand on Nicholas's arm. 'He's trying to bait you, Husband. It's what weak men do when they can't have their way.'

'Have I discomforted you, Nicholas?' Henshawe asks, his voice oily with provocation.

'Only by your continued existence,' Nicholas replies. 'Now carry away your pretty carcass before I tell someone with real authority around here about the game you're playing.'

It lands as well as any punch Nicholas could have thrown. But the unshockable courtier's mask slips for only a moment.

'And what game, *precisely*, is that?'

'Keeping your English levies back, so that you can use them for a purpose other than fighting Irish rebels.'

With the eyes narrowed so, the symmetry of Henshawe's face breaks down. He looks like a petulant child trying to peer through a keyhole.

'What do you imply, Shelby?'

'You're the one whose ensign did the mustering, Henshawe – the mustering of English levies. Still in Chester, are they? Why aren't they here? It's not as if His Grace doesn't need the replacements. Do you bother to count the men you have under your command? How many have you lost to sickness this week alone? Don't you need to fill the holes in your company's ranks?'

With a glare of unfettered malice, Henshawe draws a length of steel from his scabbard. The heavy, bejewelled rings on his fingers flash like a warning.

'I've killed men for speaking to me with more civility than that, Shelby. What say I run you through here and now?'

Out of the corner of his eye, Nicholas catches a movement. Without turning his head, some unfathomed sense tells him that Bianca has just slipped her hand into his box of instruments and has pulled out an iron lancet. Against a sword, it will be useless.

But then Henshawe won't be expecting an attack from that quarter, and even a lancet blade can ruin a gallant's swordplay if it's thrust into his neck when he's least expecting it. He raises his right hand a fraction, spreading the fingers towards her, warning her not to be precipitate.

'But you won't, will you?' he says, holding Henshawe's gaze. 'Your master needs me alive to mix his potions – potions to stop up the other shit he keeps company with.'

For a moment no one moves. Then Henshawe gives a grunt of sour amusement. He lets his sword slip back into its scabbard. 'There will be a reckoning between you and me, Master Physician,' he says in a matter-of-fact voice that – judged against the rage in his eyes – comes from another man's mouth entirely. 'You may count upon it.'

Bianca moves closer to Nicholas's side. She folds her arm around his, as if to say that a threat to one is a threat to both. She smiles at Henshawe with cold eyes. 'Be careful what you drink tonight, Oliver,' she says, giving him the icy look she reserves for customers at the Jackdaw who've outstayed their welcome and overspent their credit. 'How do you think I got past the men Tyrone set to guard me? Could you tell if there was hemlock in your malmsey?'

There can be few more entertaining experiences, Nicholas thinks, than watching a man you loathe wondering if your wife is a competent poisoner.

After a moment's silence, during which he seems unable to decide whether Bianca has spoken in jest or deadly earnest, Henshawe turns on his heels and stalks away.

'Are you *so* determined to get yourself skewered, Husband?' Bianca asks.

'Your old paramour is up to something, Wife,' Nicholas replies. 'And now *he* knows that I know it. I should have kept my peace.'

'That's why you'll never make a courtier.'

'Odd that you should say that. While you were away – doing what I told Robert Cecil was impossible – I came to the same conclusion.'

'I always trusted that you would.'

'Little Bruno will grow to a far better manhood as the son of an honest physician than as an appendage to the Cecil household,' he says, looking into Bianca's eyes with a weary resignation. 'Even if his mother *is* the match of Lucrezia Borgia and Locusta put together.'

Bianca kisses his ear. 'It is a goodly thing in a marriage,' she says, 'for a husband to have the measure of his wife's abilities. It prevents any possible misunderstanding.'

✠

To Drogheda, thence to Dublin. The earl's entrance into the city is made with much display and loud hosannahs. Yet if His Grace expects unalloyed praise for his new treaty with Tyrone, he is soon disabused. Within days, more stinging letters from Her Majesty and the Privy Council arrive. He has betrayed her by his inept handling of her army... he has disobeyed her instruction not to conclude a peace with her enemies... he has made a fool of himself and – worse – his queen.

The real culprit is Robert Cecil, Southampton tells Essex in Nicholas's hearing. He's poisoning Her Majesty against you. Take the best of us and go into England – stamp out this nest of vipers that infects the court and turns Her Majesty's heart against her former favourite. Henshawe agrees. So does Christopher Blount, the earl's stepfather.

'Her Majesty has expressly forbidden Your Grace's early return,' Nicholas warns in a moment of something approaching pity for this ruined jewel of a man.

'Hold your tongue,' Henshawe snaps.

'Look only to your physic, sirrah,' snarls Southampton. 'His Grace has no need of *your* counsel.'

'Christ's nails, Shelby!' groans Robert Devereux as a sudden spasm of the gut heralds a return of his dysenteria. 'Get me that syrup of yours, and hurry!'

✠

Early in the morning of the twenty-fourth day of September, Nicholas is summoned to the earl's chambers. Essex is not there. He waits patiently until Robert Devereux returns from chapel. Quiet prayer and impulsive action; unbounded optimism followed by deep despair; everything to gain, everything to lose. Such are the arcs marked out by the Essex pendulum. Today we get impulsive action, though not without a measure of self-serving apologia.

'You called for me, Your Grace. How is your... your... *inconvenience* today?'

'No man could have done more than I, in the circumstances,' Essex asserts, as though Nicholas was his judge rather than his physician.

'Are we speaking of the dysenteria, Your Grace?' Nicholas asks as tactfully as he can.

'I'm talking of this Irish enterprise,' Essex snaps. 'This isle is cursed. It ruins even the very best of men.' He stalks to his desk and sets down the personal Bible he has brought from chapel. He turns to Nicholas, his face full of hurt, like a child wrongly chastised. 'But I could have tamed it. I *could* have – had it not been for a Brutus, a Cassius, a deformed traitor who would sooner stab me in the back than face me like a man.'

Robert Cecil, thinks Nicholas.

'I hope my physic eased your discomfort, Your Grace,' he says tentatively, waiting for the next swing of the pendulum.

'I know that Cecil sent you here, Shelby,' Essex says, though strangely with no malice in his voice. 'I know he was behind your appointment. But you've *seen* it. You've seen how this island is like a living creature, purging itself of an infected wound. Spenser was wrong. A heavy hand will not bring peace. We could slaughter half the population and still make no lasting gains here. We, too, will be purged. Ireland will form a pustule around us, and in the end it will expel us like corrupt matter.'

Nicholas is used to patients baring their innermost thoughts to him. He offers Essex no opinion. Staying silent, he has found, can often bring forth secrets a man might otherwise reveal not even to himself. But what Essex says next lands like a blow.

'We are going to England, you and I – today.'

'England? Today?'

The earl's hand slams down on the leather cover of the Bible. 'Decisiveness, Shelby – that is how battles are won.'

'But, my lord, as I ventured to remind you a few days ago, the queen has expressly forbidden it.'

'Because she doesn't know the truth!'

'But, my lord, why me? I can give you physic to take with you.'

'It's not about the physic,' the earl announces, as though he's just discovered the answer to all his problems. 'You, sirrah, will be my witness at court.'

'Me? But I'm merely a physician. What do I know of great matters of state?'

'You will back everything I say to Her Majesty,' Essex announces confidently. 'After all, it was her signature on your letter of commission. Even if she won't listen to me, she *has* to listen to you.'

Before Nicholas can begin to picture in his mind the full extent of the dire consequences of disobeying a direct order from the queen, Essex shouts for his attendants.

In an instant the chamber is full of men lauding their commander's decision. Southampton and stepfather Blount embrace him as though he's been miraculously cured of a fatal disease. His gallants – Sir Thomas Gerard, Sir Christopher St Lawrence, Sir Henry Danvers, Sir Oliver Henshawe, half a dozen more – fidget like hounds who've caught a scent and are straining to be unleashed. To Nicholas, they all appear to be indulging in a communal delusion, like simple milkmaids who've seen Christ's face in the random folds of a cloud.

And then, for one of them at least, the Essex pendulum swings the other way.

'Sir Oliver, be so good as to remain here in Dublin,' Essex says. 'Bring some order to the army. I don't want it dissolving into a rabble behind my back. I may have need of it, if Cecil and the other traitors seek to do me down, once Her Majesty has heard the truth from my own lips.'

Henshawe looks like the child excluded from the party. His pretty features sour. 'Your Grace, I was with you at Cádiz. Surely you cannot mean to deny me the joy of seeing you vindicated now.'

Essex cuts him off with a wave of his hand. 'I've enough traitors to my front, Oliver. I need a reliable man to guard against them when my back is turned.'

'Are you sure you're well enough for so taxing an enterprise, my lord?' Nicholas asks quietly. It's as near as he dares come to telling Essex he's an impetuous, deluded fool.

'Well? Of course I'm well, Dr Shelby. Why would I not be? I have the best physician in all the realm to attend me.'

God help us all, Nicholas thinks, as he meets Henshawe's stare and sees his expression turn from petulant resentment to outright loathing. We're on thin ice now.

✠

Take Cachorra and sail for England, Nicholas tells Bianca while he snatches a few precious moments at their cramped Dublin lodgings. We'll meet again at the Jackdaw.

When she asks how she is supposed to achieve this feat, he has an answer already to hand. The master of a pinnace, the *Joan Bonaventure*, currently under contract to the royal post, is one of Cecil's trusted men. Indeed, Amos Errington has carried enciphered letters from Nicholas to Mr Secretary Cecil in the past – before Oliver Henshawe imposed himself as Essex's censor. 'You'll be safe enough with Errington,' he says, handing her a sheet of paper. 'Here – I've written a note of passage, saying you're on Privy Council business. That way, when you land at Bristol, you can demand a post-horse to get you to London.' He glances at Cachorra, who – though she has caught only a little of their rapid exchange – understands that a crisis is at hand. 'Can you ride a horse?'

'Of course Cachorra rides. What woman who lives beside a Spanish nobleman's daughter since she was six years old cannot ride a horse?'

'This is madness, Nicholas,' Bianca says, close to losing her temper, yet terrified of what Nicholas is getting himself into. 'Can't you refuse him?'

'How can I? He's commander of the queen's army. I am the queen's subject. I have no choice.'

'But what if your fears that Essex is planning some rash act against Her Majesty are real? If you're at his side, that makes you a traitor. You could go to the scaffold with him!'

'Or I could be the one to talk him out of it.'

As she helps him gather up a few necessities for the journey, she says, 'I hope, when this is over, you'll present him with a proper physician's reckoning.'

'What would be the point?' Nicholas replies dejectedly. 'He's an earl. He'll expect credit. I'd have to wait until he was dead before trying to prise payment from his executors.'

Bianca hands him his saddle pack. Giving him a look of weary resignation, she says, 'You might not be waiting as long as you think, Husband. If what you've told me is true, Her Majesty's temper is even shorter than a Caporetti's.'

39

In the two days since the Earl of Essex sailed so precipitously for England, Sir Oliver Henshawe has found a pleasurable consolation. Indeed, he now considers himself fortunate not to have been included in the earl's party. Who would want to spend two days at sea and another two in the saddle when there is such sport to be had here in Ireland?

Word has reached him from the hamlets within the Pale to the north of Dublin that a band of some half-dozen rebels have taken advantage of the current truce to sneak into the country around St Mary's Abbey, on the north side of the River Liffey. From their hiding place they can watch English shipping entering and leaving Dublin Bay.

Strictly speaking, it is against the terms of the present agreement to hunt them down. But spying is a deceitful, dishonourable occupation. Sir Oliver is sure His Grace would approve.

Hunting rebels, Sir Oliver believes, is best achieved by traditional methods. In his opinion, your rebel is a cunning quarry. He possesses none of the nobility of the red deer, like those to be found on the Henshawe lands at Walworth in the fair county of Surrey. Rather, he exhibits the bestial instincts of the fox. He is lower in God's order even than a Spaniard – and that's saying something. To soothe his disappointment at being forced to stay behind, Henshawe now embarks upon the destruction of this nest of inquisitive traitors. He organizes their destruction much as he would a hunt at Walworth.

On the afternoon of the earl's departure, still smarting from his exclusion, Sir Oliver has his company practise its drills on the land below the abbey. Make a show, he instructs his officers. Give the seditious vermin something to look at. Keep their eyes fixed firmly to the south. Make no sign that we are aware of their presence. And on no account make a move northwards. We've signed an accord, after all.

Two days later he changes his orders. Start moving, he commands. Not aggressively, just enough to force the rebels to pull back towards Navan. Act the spaniel. Flush the game.

His plan is simple. He will drive the quarry onto the waiting line of light horse that he has slipped around the western side of the abbey the previous night under cover of darkness. He will cut off the rebel line of retreat. *Two* can play the game of ambush.

✠

The *Joan Bonaventure* is a small, speedy little craft. But the only shelter for her passengers is a cramped space below the main deck where Bianca must stoop if she is to walk at all, and Cachorra must bend almost double. Neither is relishing the voyage to Bristol. As a consequence they are on deck as she clears Blind Quay, with the mudflats of Hoggen Green lying ahead to starboard like the grey, glistening backs of basking sea monsters.

As they stand beside the port rail, watching the seagulls rise and dive over the water, a ragged volley of musketry drifts on the wind from the direction of St Mary's Abbey on the rising ground across the estuary.

'What's that?' Cachorra asks, turning towards the sound. 'Has the fighting started again? Has the truce collapsed?'

'Probably some of His Grace's fine gallants shooting woodcock,' Bianca says, her thoughts firmly on the journey to London. 'There'll be little else for them to do, now that a truce has been agreed. They're still living off the Essex coin, so they probably consider it their duty to slaughter at least *something* while he's gone.'

✠

By nightfall, the sole survivor of the rebel party is brought, bound and bloodied, to a cold, damp, windowless chamber beneath Dublin Castle. Oliver Henshawe takes charge of the inquisition. He enjoys putting a man to the hard press as much as he enjoys hunting the red deer. Killing is in Henshawe's blood. And tonight his blood is hot.

By chance, he has caught himself the son of a minor O'Connor chieftain.

At first the rebel is proud and uncooperative, taunting his captors with contemptuous silence. But unlike the rebel captive that Robert Cecil had asked Nicholas to treat in the cellars at Cecil House, this man has no river to hurl himself into.

To induce a willingness to cooperate, Henshawe chooses the *strappado.* With the prisoner's arms chained behind his back, a rope is attached to the manacles and passed over a hook set into the ceiling. His arms are then hoisted up and back until his body is suspended, its entire weight taken by the shoulder joints. Muscles and tendon cannot bear the strain. The shoulders dislocate.

Oliver Henshawe is a man who believes in putting the proper amount of effort into a task. He takes up a long ribbon of chainmail, the end of which is set with fish hooks, and which he has fashioned especially for occasions such as this. He begins vigorously to apply it to his subject's already ruined shoulders, as though he were the high priest of some stern religious order of flagellants. Or perhaps he is simply expunging his anger at being left behind in Dublin.

By midnight the screams have turned to weeping. And flowing freely with the tears comes the information: information about Hugh O'Neill, Earl of Tyrone... information about a grey merchant who is, in reality, a spy for the rebels... information about a Spanish woman, survivor of an embassy to Ireland to aid Tyrone in his fight against the English queen... information about her Blackamoor servant... information about the English woman who was brought in to cure the Spanish maid when she fell ill... information about whatever subject his tormentor would care to hear about, no matter how important or how trivial. Just so long as he makes the pain stop.

40

A more leisurely ride might have afforded Nicholas a better appreciation of an English autumn. But time is in Devereux's gift now. The pace has been relentless. As the mud flies up from the country lanes and the late-September mist parts to the crashing progress of steaming horseflesh, there have been moments when even Nicholas could almost believe Essex might succeed in his wild attempt to regain the queen's favour. It is hard not to get swept away by the mood of euphoria. The riders – save for Nicholas himself – encourage each other by shouting ever wilder fantasies over the drumming of their horses' hooves. *We'll make His Grace Secretary of State... we'll clean the Augean Stables until the flagstones shine like silver... we'll hang the Privy Council from the arches of London Bridge... we'll make a new Jerusalem in Whitehall, and our leader will sit as close to God's right hand as Jesus will allow...*

But in his more reflective moments, to Nicholas they sound like doomed men fortifying themselves for a last, hopeless charge against the enemy. Do they truly believe they can do this? he wonders. And how is *he* to avoid the almost inevitable end that must await them, if they try?

He is with them, but not one of them. When they notice his presence, they are friendly enough. But he is not from their world. He is no gallant. They know the sword he wears would be as much a danger to himself as to any opponent, were he to draw it. He is reminded of the gentlemen scholars at Cambridge, who treated the unmannered yeoman's son as though he were one of their servants. Indeed, when they pause for rest, he is expected to look after the horses. He thinks of slipping away, warning Robert Cecil of the approaching fiery comet of sedition heading his way. But his horse would have to sprout wings and fly in order to outpace these driven men.

At dawn on the twenty-eighth day of September the small band clatters into the precincts of Whitehall, exhausted, muddy, throats parched and limbs aching. Imperiously Essex brushes aside the guard at the gatehouse at the end of King's Street.

And then the whole airy edifice that his supporters have constructed threatens to collapse.

Whitehall seems almost deserted. A few bleary-eyed clerks and retainers go about their business in the cool morning air, but the usual bustle is absent. Nicholas is ordered to wait with the horses in the orchard between the King's Street gatehouse and the Privy Gallery where the bedchambers are, while Essex and his gallants go in search of Her Majesty and the hated nest of vipers who deceive her.

Left alone, Nicholas prays that his assumption is correct, and that the court is not in residence. Perhaps that will take the wind out of Devereux's sails. Perhaps reason may be restored. He throws his gaberdine cloak down over the wet grass and sits. The black outline of the buildings is stark against a sickly yellow dawn sky. He thinks that if he were to close his eyes now, he would sleep for a week.

'Dr Shelby? Is that you? What in the name of Christ's sweet wounds are you doing here?'

Startled out of his thoughts, Nicholas looks up to see a dark shape approaching. The stride is brisk and youthful, though the triangle of grey beard cutting the fur collar of his gown marks him as a man of some age and importance. As he draws closer, Nicholas recognizes him: Lord Grey, one of the Cecil faction, a man who has had more than his share of run-ins with Robert Devereux.

'My lord, thank Jesu you are here,' Nicholas says, jumping to his feet and almost crying out as the cramp burns the muscles in his legs and thighs.

'I've just seen armed men near the queen's chambers,' Grey says in astonishment and no small alarm. 'Whatever is this commotion? And at such an ungodly hour, too.'

'Where is Her Majesty? Is she here?'

Grey looks puzzled, rather than alarmed. 'Why, at Nonsuch, of course – with the court. But I had thought you to be in Ireland, sirrah.'

Nicholas almost laughs. 'No longer, my lord.' He points in the general direction of the privy chambers. 'And nor is His Grace the Earl of Essex.'

'Essex? But he was expressly ordered—'

'His Grace has a wild scheme in his head. He intends to confront Her Majesty, to redress her grievances against him.'

'With armed men?'

'Southampton, Danvers, Blount...'

'God's nails! That's treason.' Grey puts a gloved hand to his mouth. 'And *you*? You're with him?'

'Unwillingly, my lord. *Very* unwillingly. His Grace ordered it. He seems to think I may help his cause. But I fear for his health *and* his reason. Someone must ride at once to Nonsuch and warn Her Majesty.'

'Delay them, Dr Shelby,' Grey commands, as though it is an easy thing for one man to stand against the passions of twenty. 'I will ride for Nonsuch with all speed.'

As Grey hurries away, Nicholas goes to the horse that Essex

has been riding. He loosens the saddle-girth strap. He thinks of cutting it, but that would be obvious sabotage. But removing the saddle? He *might* convince the earl that he'd merely been resting a hard-ridden mount. He is about to unbuckle the strap when he hears loud voices coming from the direction of the river. Angry voices. Bitter voices. The voices of men who've been thwarted and are looking for someone upon whom to vent their frustration. Black shapes appear, moving through the orchard towards him.

The coldly languorous Southampton is the first to reach him. 'What are you doing?' he asks, seeing the loose-hanging girth strap.

'Giving His Grace's mount a little respite,' Nicholas says.

Southampton pushes him aside and rebuckles the strap. 'I could swear an oath I saw you talking to someone, sirrah. Who was it?'

'Just a clerk, my lord,' Nicholas says. 'He wanted to know who we were.'

'And what did you tell him?'

'I told him to mind his own business.'

It takes some fifteen minutes, according to the chapel bell, for everyone to muster in the orchard. Essex is the last to arrive, moving through the dawn with brisk, agitated strides.

'Where are we going, Your Grace?' Nicholas asks, wondering if he might contrive a delay by sending Essex on a wild goose chase.

But if Essex hasn't found his queen, he's discovered where she is.

'Why, to Nonsuch, Dr Shelby,' he says, as if his ambition was burning him up from the inside. 'We're going to Nonsuch.'

✠

Essex has lost himself in a lover's longing. In the strengthening light he stares fixedly ahead, as if to catch a glimpse of his paramour. Nicholas wonders if Devereux, in his mind, is now living in the days when he was the queen's young favourite, remembering the nights they sat together at dice, or cards, or poetry, until the birds began to sing in the morning. Does he really believc he can turn back time? Does he truly think bravado will win her round?

Their mounts are on their last legs. A change of horses is needed for the last twelve miles of the journey or else they'll be crawling to Nonsuch on their knees. Essex decrees it will take place when they cross the River Thames at the Lambeth horse-ferry. There will be fresh beasts to hire on the other side. In the meantime the pace must be maintained. There is only a short window – what the ferrymen call 'dead low water' – when the great wooden raft may be safely steered across the current. Miss it, and they must wait half a day for the next low tide. Nicholas prays they do. It will give Lord Grey all the time he needs, and more. It is a small rebellion, but all that he can think of at present.

A feeble sun, jaundiced in the morning mist, is rising over the Lambeth marshes when they reach the crossing. To Nicholas's joy, the ferry is on its way back from a previous journey, inching across the water, the pole-men labouring at their shafts in the pale morning light. It offers only a small delay, but perhaps Lord Grey is already across and on his way. If he is, he can't have more than fifteen minutes' head-start.

While he waits impotently on the Westminster side for the ferry to come to him, Essex becomes almost apoplectic. Nicholas wonders if he's going to call upon God to part the waters. But not even God, let alone England's Earl Marshal – for however much longer Her Majesty intends to leave him in the office – can make a Lambeth ferryman hurry. The St Mary's bell chimes the halfway mark of the morning's seventh hour before they wade through the stinking mud to stand helplessly – almost comically so, to

Nicholas's mind – amidst the farm carts and country passengers as the great contraption makes its snail-like progress once more towards the Lambeth side.

From the stables close to the church, new mounts are brought out. As Essex swings up into the saddle, one of his gallants – Sir Christopher St Lawrence – announces loudly that he's spoken to the head ferryman. A rider from Westminster has gone before them – by the ferryman's account, a man even more impatient than Essex.

'We are betrayed!' shouts one of the earl's party.

Southampton glares at Nicholas. 'A clerk, you said. Mind your own business, you said. *Who* was it?'

There seems to be no point in denial. 'It was my Lord Grey,' Nicholas says. 'And he didn't need me to tell him anything.'

'I'll ride ahead like the wind, Your Grace,' says St Lawrence theatrically, though Nicholas can see he is in deadly earnest. 'I'll slay the bastard before he reaches Nonsuch. Better yet, let me go on. I'll cut off Robert Cecil's scabrous head. I'll have it ready for you, as a present.'

For one awful moment Nicholas thinks Devereux is going to give St Lawrence his blessing. He stares as the earl's mud-splattered face, trying to read his mood, trying to fathom where on the arc the pendulum lies. Armed and bloody rebellion in the presence of the queen – whether it fails or succeeds, the executioners will be busy for months.

And then Essex slowly shakes his head. It is the first restrained gesture Nicholas has seen him make in hours.

'No,' he says, the lover's longing returning to his eyes. 'I will not seek her favour with blood on my hands.' And then, with a yell of determination and resolve as though he is leading his party into battle, he drives his fresh horse forward. Setting their spurs to their horses' flanks, his gallants follow. The morning air is split with the whinnying of stung, surprised animals and the shouts of their riders.

Southampton and two others manoeuvre their horses to box Nicholas in, giving him no option but to go forward.

'Lag behind' – Southampton snarls as he slaps one hand on the guard of his sword – 'and I'll run you through, myself.'

✠

In Nonsuch park the grazing deer scatter like terrified survivors of a catastrophe as the riders plunge over the puddles on the London road. The mist has thinned a little, revealing ahead the pale ashlar walls that King Henry raised around his love-nest for Jane Seymour – a love-nest she would never live to enjoy, but which the king's daughter, Elizabeth, by the Grace of God, Queen of England, France and Ireland, now enjoys as her inheritance.

Nonsuch looks to Nicholas like the country seat of a mythical eastern potentate set down in the soft fields of Surrey. Its towers stand like minarets, their gilded onion-domes gleaming gold in the weak autumn sunlight. From the white stucco panels on her walls the gods and heroes of antiquity observe the approaching horsemen like a phalanx of protectors, frozen for all time by some magician's spell. If Nicholas were not in such uncertain company, he would feel a sense of homecoming.

Nonsuch has been part of his life for almost a decade. It was to this palace that he had come on his first mission for Robert Cecil, sent to entrap its then-owner Lord Lumley, a known Catholic. The Cecils had wanted Lumley destroyed, and Nonsuch – sold out of the Tudor family more than forty years past – returned to Elizabeth. It had not ended as the Cecils had planned. Nicholas had saved John Lumley from their ambitions, giving him time to negotiate an arrangement with the queen that gave her back Nonsuch, but allowed him and his wife to remain in the home they loved. Nicholas had become something of a son to the dour Northumberland baron. It was in the private chapel at Nonsuch that Nicholas had married Bianca Merton.

These thoughts and memories fill his head now, as the party races across the wide bowling green in front of the outer gatehouse, divots of grass flying from the pounding hooves.

The doors to the outer gatehouse are wide open. Has Grey been waylaid? Nicholas wonders. Has he only just arrived? Why aren't the doors shut and barred? Are the white walls of Nonsuch about to be stained with blood?

He can see the guards scurrying in the archway. He waits for them to slam the doors closed or at least cross halberds, blocking the way inside. But they don't.

And Essex intends to stop for no one. He slows the pace only a little, from a full gallop to a canter. Wisely the guards throw themselves out of the path of the oncoming horses. Recognizing several of the riders' faces, they can do little but stare. Then the party is through the arch, the sound of hooves echoing like the frantic hammering of a crazed drummer.

In the outer courtyard startled servants flee to the safety of the kitchen wall. A ham joint rolls in the mud like a severed head.

The last barrier lies directly ahead: the inner gatehouse that gives onto the secret heart of Nonsuch, the inner courtyard. Through it, Nicholas can see the grand fountain with its statue of a rearing horse – one of John Lumley's most prized works of art – and beyond it the wide steps leading to the royal chambers.

Surely now there must be guards hurrying to block the way? Where are the halberdiers with their axe blades, guarding Her Majesty's privy chambers? An awful thought occurs to Nicholas: Essex has conspirators within the royal household. Perhaps Lord Grey is one of them.

He can see John Lumley standing on the steps to the royal apartments, looking on with calm puzzlement in his eyes. His mournful face, scholar's gown and grey beard make him look older than his sixty-six years, a wintry man, no matter what the season. As the riders come to a halt in a spray of gravel, Lumley descends a couple of steps, unconcerned, as though mud-caked madmen on horseback are common fare at Nonsuch and of only passing interest.

'My lord of Essex, you should have sent us earlier warning. I would have had your usual chamber made up,' he says, his soft Northumberland burr robbing his words of even the faintest accusation.

Essex is already down, Southampton and the others in the process of dismounting. Only Nicholas stays in the saddle.

'Stand aside, sirrah,' the earl says, brushing past Lumley as he strides up the steps towards the entrance to the privy lodgings. 'This is not your house now.'

Being the only man still mounted, Nicholas realizes his face is clearly visible from where Lumley is standing. When their eyes meet, Lumley gives him a look of disbelief, as if to say, *Surely not you, too?* There is time only for a brief shake of the head to show that he is not party to this madness, before Southampton seizes Nicholas by one leg and hauls him to the ground.

From this moment on, Nicholas is little more than a passive witness, swept along in the tight press of Essex's gallants. Southampton is at his back, ensuring he doesn't entertain any foolish thoughts of making a break for it.

Once through the door and into the south wing of the palace, Nicholas catches a brief glimpse of startled white faces: servants in royal livery, clerks and secretaries in legal black, courtiers there for the food and the reputation that closeness to the sovereign brings, even a few members of the Privy Council flapping like hens at the sight of a fox.

Up the stairs to the presence chamber Essex runs, his gallants swept along in the fervour of his cause. Nicholas is still too hemmed in even to think of bolting. The familiar interior of Nonsuch flies past him: the expensive oak wainscoting from floor to ceiling; the fine Flemish tapestries; the paintings and the statues that John Lumley has collected over the years of his fluctuating favour with his monarch; the countless chamber doors that seem to sprout a harvest of inquisitive heads as the party hurries past... Nicholas even catches sight of Lumley's wife, lady Elizabeth, standing open-mouthed by the door to the private chapel where he and Bianca married. She's come from her morning prayers, he thinks. Catholic prayers. A small act of defiance, even in the queen's proximity. The realization gives him comfort: no matter how great the power of an Essex or a Cecil – even of the queen herself – the secret heart remains one's own, untouchable.

The queen's presence chamber is empty, save for a clutch of women chamberers going about their business of dusting, plumping and arranging, in preparation for the audiences scheduled in the Lord Chamberlain's diary. They pause, looking up in alarm. We must look like brigands, Nicholas thinks.

Of the queen herself there is no sign. They've whisked her away to somewhere safe, he decides. Grey must have arrived in time.

But Essex is a hound with a good scent in his nostrils. The party barely breaks stride. Onwards, like the last charge on a disputed battlefield.

In the privy gallery a coterie of attendants stands idly awaiting the emergence of the queen from her bedchamber: ladies-in-waiting, ladies of the privy chamber, maids of honour, gentleman ushers, grooms. Male or female, their rank may be judged by the same measures: looks, languor and finery. Nicholas wonders what they all do. How many people are needed to shore up the edifice of majesty? Their eyes turn towards Essex as he approaches. One or two even make a bow.

Now, so close to their quarry, with one last door ahead of them – closed – the little band fragments, loses its pace, loses its determination. Loses its courage.

All except Robert Devereux.

He is a man reduced in appearance from an earl of England to a mud-splattered cut-purse fleeing from the night-watch, but he strides towards the great carved door set into the panelled wall as though it is he, not the queen, who owns Nonsuch. The courtiers make no attempt to challenge him, perhaps because even at this late moment no one can really believe his intention. Without bothering to knock, he lifts the latch, throws open the doors and strides inside.

At first there is silence, save for a few gasps of disbelief from the courtiers in the privy chamber. For a fleeting instant, Nicholas fears Essex is going to draw his sword. If he does, his very worst fears will have been realized. There will be no way back.

But the sword remains in its scabbard. Instead, England's Earl Marshal – though for how much longer is anyone's guess – sinks to his knees. He prostrates himself before his sovereign.

From where Nicholas is standing he can see only snatches of the tableau: the back of Devereux's riding cape, the muddy heels of his boots as he kneels, the alarmed faces of the ladies of the bedchamber as they turn towards him... and, in the moment before the door slams shut, a whey-faced woman with a look of astonishment burnedinto the deep hollows of her eyes. A woman whose grey hair is as sparse as a moorland knoll blasted by a winter wind. An unpainted woman, bereft of powder or ceruse, of pearls or jewels. Bereft of majesty. Just a tired, elderly woman well on her way to the same common end as the very lowest of her subjects.

41

Without their blazing comet to guide them, Southampton and the others seem unsure of what to do next. All impetus has been lost. All their brazen words, their promises to stamp out the nest of vipers at court, are revealed as nothing more than bluster. The immensity of what they might have done, had Essex given them proper orders, has begun to dawn upon them – along with the price of failure.

And then Nicholas sees Robert Cecil scuttling towards them, Grey at his side, John Lumley two paces back. With them is a squad of halberdiers, poleaxes held at the port position – lest any of these unruly intruders think they are purely for ceremonial display.

If Southampton, or any other member of the Essex faction, is foolish enough to draw steel now, Nicholas thinks, there will be no way back. It will be taken as clear evidence of treason.

But the pendulum has swung again. Stepfather Blount, the oldest – and perhaps most astute – of the Devereux faction has seen which way the wind is blowing. He begins to protest loudly that they have never, not even for a moment, intended Her Majesty the slightest harm.

Even Southampton looks relieved when Nicholas steps out of the little band and addresses Mr Secretary Cecil as he comes to a lopsided halt at the entrance of the privy chamber.

'Sir Robert, please don't mistake the ardour of these gentlemen for anything but an eagerness to assure Her Majesty of their love and obedience,' he says, wondering whose words these are, because he's never thought of himself as being skilled in diplomacy.

But it does the trick, because Cecil raises a gloved hand to stay the halberdiers. He looks up at Southampton, who towers over him, and whose elegance – even in this muddied condition – serves only to highlight Cecil's ill-made form. 'Would you care to explain the reason for this insult to Her Majesty's peace, my lord of Southampton?' he asks, his voice so crisp that the words spilling from his mouth land like shards of ice.

'There is no insult intended, Mr Secretary,' Southampton says earnestly. 'His Grace has come only to assure Her Majesty of his enduring devotion, and to slay the malicious falsehoods that *some* have laid before her on the matter of his Irish enterprise.'

'Then perhaps it would be best if you all removed your muddy boots and cloaks, gentlemen,' Cecil says, offering the party a bridge back to sanity. 'Her Majesty will not care to see her privy chamber treated like a hostelry for common travellers.'

Blount unbuckles his cloak. Southampton considers his options a little longer – and then follows suit. Nicholas lets the breath out of his lungs in a slow exhalation of relief.

But what of His Grace the Earl of Essex? In the confusion, he has been quite forgotten. Now that the moment of crisis has passed, and bloodshed averted, all eyes turn towards the closed door to the queen's bedchamber. To Nicholas, the figures in the privy chamber are like a troupe of players who have simultaneously forgotten their lines. No one knows what to do next. Should someone enter, to ensure Her Majesty is safe from the earl's wild eccentricities? Should we all pretend nothing has happened? Even Mr Secretary Cecil seems, for once, to have been robbed of his energy.

And then the door opens. His Grace stands in the frame, a beatific look on his face as he smiles at his followers, while behind him the ladies of the royal bedchamber form a guard against impertinent eyes. Essex has been transformed, reborn, raised once more to his former, happy estate. Forgiven.

'Our Irish storms are over,' he announces, as though bringing God's word down from the mountain top. 'We have found a glorious calm at home. God save Her Majesty!'

And although everyone in the chamber – Cecil, Southampton, Blount and all the others – echoes the earl's prayer for the queen, Nicholas can see in their eyes that none of them, save perhaps Essex himself, believes a single word of it.

✠

And neither, it seems, does Elizabeth. Over the next two days Essex is summoned on several occasions to her presence to make a fuller account of himself. It does not go well. Nicholas can tell this, not because he is party to any of the conversations, but because the Essex and Cecil factions remain resolutely separate. They avoid each other. They take their meals at separate tables. And Devereux's seems much the more subdued. Even more so after the arrival of more privy councillors, who have come to join their colleagues in a full and frank appraisal of His Grace's actions in Ireland. The sole remaining joy for Essex seems to be that his flux has cleared up.

Nicholas waits for the summons to give his account of Essex's actions in Ireland – the very reason the earl has dragged him here. It does not come. This is a relief for Nicholas, because he hasn't the faintest idea what to say in Devereux's defence.

It has not escaped his attention that despite comfortable quarters being provided, no one in Devereux's party is permitted to leave Nonsuch. In the afternoon of the day after the earl's precipitous arrival, Nicholas is summoned to meet Robert Cecil in the privy garden below the royal apartments.

'How, in the name of Jesu, did you manage to become caught up in the mess?' Cecil asks to the tinkling accompaniment of a fountain.

'I thought that's what I was sent there for – to keep watch on him for you.'

'I haven't had a dispatch from you for weeks.'

'Strangely enough, Sir Robert, His Grace considered my presence suspicious. He had Sir Oliver Henshawe censor every letter I attempted to send to England. At the end I wasn't allowed anywhere near the quayside, lest I attempted to smuggle something onto the postal pinnace.'

'Do you believe it was his intent to harm Her Majesty?'

Is it this easy to send a man to the scaffold? Nicholas wonders. Just one word?

'I don't believe so, Sir Robert,' he says. 'His Grace is a much-conflicted man. But I don't believe he ever wished harm to Her Majesty. Besides, he is not well.'

A quizzical look from Cecil.

'His Grace is ill? From what?'

Again it would be so easy to damn Essex with a single word. But Nicholas is not a vindictive man.

'Ambition,' he says. 'And pride. They can be the making of a man, if he can constrain them. Unfettered, they are as injurious to him as any other serious malady. I fear that His Grace's symptoms are beyond *my* treatment.'

Cecil laughs. 'If that's a measure of your diplomatic skills, we should make you an ambassador.' He gives Nicholas a fatherly pat on the arm, though there are barely two years between them. 'I am sure you did your best. Now, I fear I can spare you no more time. I am due at a conference of the Privy

Council. We are to consider this present matter and put our findings to Her Majesty.'

As Cecil turns to leave, his little heels grinding on the gravel path, Nicholas says, 'We found Constanza Calva de Sagrada. Well, Bianca found her.'

Robert Cecil stops. His narrow lips part in disbelief. But no words come out. It is the first time Nicholas has seen him lost for words.

'She's alive?' he manages eventually.

'Yes.'

'How extraordinary. Where is she now?'

'Probably in Scotland, on her way to a marriage.'

'Did she reveal to you the names of the Spanish peace faction before she left?'

'No.'

'That is a pity.'

'But her servant did.'

Cecil gives him a doubting laugh. 'A servant? And how much will *that* cost me?'

'Nothing, Sir Robert – save what you think is due to a brave and remarkable woman.'

Cecil considers this a moment. A thrush lands on the rim of the fountain to drink. His gaze lingers on it, as though it might assist him in his deliberations.

'Are you sure this person is trustworthy?'

'Completely.

'Where is this list? It is secured?'

'It's in her head. And she will not reveal the names until she can stand in your presence.'

'And where is this servant now?'

'With Bianca. Somewhere between Bristol and London, if all has gone well, as I hope.'

Cecil lifts his brow in grudging admiration. 'Well, I don't know what to say. When all this is over, bring her to me at Cecil House. She shall be rewarded.'

And with that, he flies away. And the thrush with him, leaving Nicholas to wonder if Sir Robert does that with every living creature that strays within his orbit – captures it.

✠

Then comes the brief encounter with the queen. It happens later that day, in the presence chamber. Only her ladies-in-waiting remain in attendance, and they are shooed away to a distance that permits Elizabeth and Nicholas to converse without being overheard. The evening sunlight paints bright bars on the stone casements of the windows. Whose prison? he wonders.

She is not the same woman whose mortal state he had observed so briefly the day before. The paint of monarchy has been reapplied, the natural blemishes on the canvas hidden. She does not speak to him of Essex. He assumes it is because he is a commoner and Devereux is an earl. She speaks to him of Ireland.

'Was Master Spenser right, sirrah?' she enquires. 'Does his view upon the present condition of that isle remain sound?'

Nicholas thinks of what Bianca has told him about Tyrone. He thinks of Piers Gardener, and the death of Henry Norris. He thinks of the old *Seanchaí* and her husband, of the fall of Kilcolman, of heads lying on the tailboard of a cart trundling through the streets of Dublin.

'I am just a physician, Majesty,' he replies. 'But I live on Bankside, close to the bear-pit. I've learned a thing or two about bears. You may feed them treats to make them dance for your amusement. You may chain and whip them to teach them obedience. You may bait them with dogs for your entertainment. But whatever you do, they will still be bears. And in their hearts

– while they may fear their master – they will never love him. Perhaps it might be better to leave them in the forest.'

✠

On the first day of October – the Privy Council having deliberated, and the queen having pondered its charges against her Earl of Essex – Robert Devereux is handed into the custody of the Keeper of the Great Seal of England, Sir Thomas Egerton. He leaves Nonsuch for confinement at York House. None of his gallants is permitted to accompany him. His grand Irish enterprise is over.

As he watches the coach roll out of Nonsuch, Nicholas wonders if – had things gone the other way for Robert Devereux – he might have attempted Edmund Spenser's grim solution to Tyrone's rebellion. He has to conclude that, while he can raise a measure of pity for England's fallen Caesar, on balance he's mightily glad Essex didn't.

He recalls again the accusation Essex had hurled against him on the day Henry Norris died of his wounds. *You've done the rebels' work for them, sirrah. You're a traitor!*

And he remembers, too, his unspoken response: that there are worse things in life than to be a traitor to a tainted cause.

42

From Nonsuch, Nicholas returns to Bankside. The journey is far less frenetic than the one made only a few days before, almost leisurely. He makes it alone, on a chestnut palfrey borrowed from the Nonsuch stables. As he rides, he watches the labourers in the fields sowing the winter wheat. They'll be doing that now at Barnthorpe, he thinks. Perhaps that is where I should be, when the dust has settled: helping my father and my brother Jack, earning my living from the land. What is the point of practising medicine that I don't trust to people I don't respect? I've seen enough of court life now to last me a lifetime. I'm done with it. When Cachorra is safely delivered to Robert Cecil, perhaps it is to Barnthorpe that I should go. He manages to make the notion last almost until he reaches the first houses at the bottom of Long Southwark. In his heart he knows he won't leave Bankside. Bianca's life is too firmly rooted here. She has the Jackdaw, and her apothecary's shop on Dice Lane. She would droop like sodden corn in the wilds of Suffolk.

Take Cachorra and sail for England, he had told her in the snatched moments before his departure with Essex and his faction. *We'll meet again at the Jackdaw.*

He had chosen the tavern, rather than their house at Paris Garden, because it is minutes nearer the road in from the country. And Ned is there. If Cecil or the Privy Council were to suddenly summon him back to Nonsuch, having Ned around when Bianca arrives might ease the underlying sense of anxiety that has refused to leave his mind, even though Robert Devereux has been taken into custody. So it is directly to the Jackdaw that he goes.

He arrives as the St Saviour's bell tolls eight in the evening. By the time he has stabled the palfrey at the Tabard and walked to the Jackdaw, sunset has made dark caverns of the Bankside lanes. A mist is rising from the river, lapping through the streets as if the Thames is starting to flood. He sees dark figures ahead of him, customers dropping by for a jug of knock-down, stitch-back or bishop's-folly after a hard day's work. The firelight gleaming through the new glass tiles in the windows dabs their silhouettes with orange, but not enough for him to recognize anyone.

And perhaps twenty paces further on, and almost lost to him in the darkness of the lane, the figure of a man watching the tavern's entrance.

A prickle of disquiet puckers the flesh on Nicholas's arms. He recalls the animosity of Southampton and the others during the ride to Nonsuch, and the hard glances they had cast his way as their champion's insane enterprise had crumbled around them. Men like that feast on revenge, he thinks. And they don't forget.

But when he looks again, the figure has gone.

✠

Little Bruno is asleep on the truckle of the bed in Rose and Ned's chamber. Nicholas refuses Rose's offer to wake him. There will be time enough for a proper reunion in the morning. He tiptoes into the room to feast his eyes on his son, grinning at the sight of the boy curled up with Buffle, the Jackdaw's dog. He wonders where Bianca and Cachorra are. They should be approaching London. Perhaps in a day or so they will be here. He turns his back on the sleeping pair and softly closes the door behind him.

Down in the taproom, when he has cleaned himself from the ride and fed himself on Rose's coney pie, Nicholas sits down for a jug of small-beer with Ned.

'Is it true – 'bout the Earl of Essex?' Ned asks. 'All Southwark's talkin' about it. Did 'e really burst in on 'Er Majesty while she was wearin' naught but her night-shift?'

'Yes, he did, Ned. I was there.'

'Christ's nails! And so 'e's confined at York House – for seein' 'Er 'Ighness as God made 'er?'

'I'm sure there are many women who would wish to have detained at their pleasure those who catch them unpainted, Ned. But not in this case.'

Ned announces proudly, 'I know about Barnabas Vyves. I worked it out, while you was away.'

'I did too, Ned. He's holding back men for Oliver Henshawe, to support the Earl of Essex in a planned strike against his enemies at court. Mercifully – for *all* – that cannot happen now.'

Ned stares at him. 'No, 'e's not,' he says. As he shakes his head, his great auburn beard sways back and forth like a thicket in a high wind.

'Isn't he?'

And then Ned tells him about the fraud Vyves and Strollot are playing on the Exchequer, mustering companies of ghosts who fade away as soon as the money is paid over. Nicholas shakes his head in disbelief.

'I really did think it impossible to find the bottom of that man's well of wickedness. But the deeper you go, the deeper it gets. There was I, thinking that even in sedition Henshawe might be acting at least from a *measure* of principle – when all along it was nothing but a grubby little deceit to steal money from the Treasury.'

'I would 'ave denounced them to the magistrates myself, but they said if I did, they'd swear it was me what slew poor Lemuel.'

Ned raises his branded thumb. 'An' with my 'istory, I couldn't take the chance.'

'I'll tell Sir Robert Cecil when next I see him,' Nicholas promises. 'Young Master Godwinson will have his justice.'

Then he remembers the figure he glimpsed watching the Jackdaw from the lane. He asks, 'Before I arrived, did you have cause to throw anyone out – a troublemaker perhaps?'

'Not tonight. Why?'

'I thought I saw someone watching the door. I wondered if he was thinking of coming back inside to argue the toss.'

Ned laughs and shakes his great head. 'Most peaceable tavern on Bankside, the Jackdaw is, these days. 'Alf our customers is convinced Mistress Bianca knows exactly what they're about, even if she's not 'ere to see it; the other 'alf is 'fraid of my Rose. I don't 'ave to lift a finger these days. Maybe it was a cut-purse.'

'Maybe it was,' says Nicholas, though in his heart he knows that local cut-purses are no more inclined to target Bianca Merton's Jackdaw than troublesome drinkers are.

✠

Next morning at sunrise Bruno bursts into Nicholas's chamber, prompted by Rose to discover who might possibly be sleeping behind the door. His four-year-old legs are no match for Buffle, and so – with both being equally determined to greet him – Nicholas is soon laughing uncontrollably under a squirming mass of dog-boy-dog-boy-dog.

'Where is my lady mother?' Bruno asks, when a measure of calm has been restored.

'Your lady mother? Who's been teaching you court manners?'

'I've taught 'im proper, Master Nicholas,' says Rose proudly from the doorway. 'For when 'e grows up to be a young gallant at court.'

'Kind of you, Rose,' Nicholas says. 'But wasted, I fear. After what I've seen of court life, I'd be happier if he was a potboy in a Bankside bawdy-house.'

At noon Bianca and Cachorra arrive, mud-stained and weary, but safe. They have made good time from Bristol. It is some while before Bianca will relinquish Bruno long enough to listen in astonishment to Nicholas's recounting of his experiences at Nonsuch.

'So we are free of Robert Devereux, Husband?' she says at last.

'I trust so,' he replies, fearing she won't detect the hollowness in his voice. 'And we shall be free of Robert Cecil, too, once we have brought Cachorra before him.'

That night the Jackdaw rings again with companionable laughter. Nicholas loses track of the times he's asked to recite his account of the impetuous earl and his encounter with unrobed monarchy. 'I honestly didn't see very much' is his stock answer to questions like *Is her royal body made of flesh like ordinary folk?* and *Is she really a man underneath? – because surely no woman could be possessed of such puissance as our Gloriana.*

But the true fascination of the night is Cachorra.

Bankside is no stranger to the remarkable. Her taverns, dice-houses, stews, cock-fighting pits, bear-rings and playhouses are a daily – and nightly – lure for mariners from the ships moored on the river, ships from lands that most Londoners could not place with any accuracy on a terrestrial globe. Some of them have even settled here. But a tall, stately Carib woman from Hispaniola is enough of an attraction to lure customers from the nearby Turk's Head and the Good Husband. When they learn she has escaped from Spain, they assume she was once a slave. Their loud condemnations of Spanish perfidy are received with polite reserve. A servant I may have been, Cachorra thinks. And one whose patience has been sorely tested by her mistress. But a slave? She finds that a hard judgement on Don Rodriquez Calva de Sagrada.

'Why do you keep looking out of the window?' Bianca asks Nicholas later, as they help Ned, Rose and Timothy clean up.

Nicholas wonders if he should tell her of the figure he saw watching from the street on the evening of his return. But then Bianca would only worry that the Privy Council has reconsidered their view on whether or not her husband was party to Devereux's mad scheme, or that Southampton is having him watched for some dark reason.

'It's nothing,' he says. 'I'm just amazed at how clean Ned has kept the windows since we went away.'

✠

It is two days before a brief meeting with Robert Cecil can be arranged. Mr Secretary Cecil has been kept busy in the aftermath of His Grace's fall. There are formal accusations to prepare for the Star Chamber. The full extent of the ill-advised agreement with Tyrone must be considered, as must the ease of breaking it. Then there is the cost of the whole calamitous enterprise to be weighed. The Lord Treasurer, Lord Buckhurst, is of the firm opinion that England could have launched an outright attack on Spain, for all the money Robert Devereux has poured into the bogs and marshes of Ireland.

Nicholas cannot help but feel a measure of pity for his former patient. Are physicians allowed entry to York House? he wonders. Is anyone prepared to treat a man so publicly shamed? The answer to both questions appears to be no.

The trio – Nicholas, Bianca and Cachorra – are finally granted a few minutes with Sir Robert in his study at Cecil House. Beyond the windows, the leaves are beginning to fall from the trees in Covent Garden. Autumn seems the wrong time to bring hopes of peace. Such a gift as Cachorra brings is better suited to spring.

'Don Rodriquez was a most excellent and brave man, Mistress,' Cecil says expansively as he cranes his neck to meet her proud gaze. 'Would that we had his like in England.'

'You are safe now, Cachorra,' Bianca assures her friend. 'You may be further than ever from one home, but you are far closer to a new one. It is time to complete what Don Rodriquez gave his life trying to achieve.'

And so Cachorra – once, a long time ago, *Yaquilalco* – begins to give up her secrets in a clear and commanding voice:

'Juan Fernández de Velasco, Lord of Castile... Count Villamediana... Señor Alessandro Robid—'

'Wait just one moment, Mistress,' interjects Robert Cecil. 'I shall need paper, ink and a pen.'

✠

Bianca has broken out the best glasses for the occasion. She raises one, the firelight making the measure of sack gleam like liquid gold. 'To the memory of a brave man, Senõr Don Rodriquez Calva de Sagrada,' she intones. 'And to his even braver leopard cub.'

The little group in the corner of the Jackdaw's taproom acknowledge her toast and lift their glasses to their lips. Cachorra lowers her eyes. She is still unaccustomed to the notion that she is beyond Constanza's beck and call – a person in her own right, with her own life to make. She allows herself a slight smile. 'And to my old mistress. May her husband be granted patience everlasting.'

It is the evening of their return from Cecil House. Outside in the lanes the same cold mist is spreading, as it has done for several nights in a row. Nicholas has joked more than once that the river is sulking at the fall of the Earl of Essex. But inside the tavern there is nothing but warm good-fellowship. News that Dr Shelby and Mistress Bianca have returned safely from Ireland has spread. The Jackdaw is busy. Rose works her usual miracles in the kitchen. Timothy marshals the other serving staff more efficiently than the Earl of Essex ever marshalled his army, carrying stacks of brimming tankards around with the panache of a performer at a country fair. The atmosphere cannot be soured even when Constable Osborne arrives with news that the watch has spotted a suspected cut-purse skulking by the Winchester water-stairs.

'If you're planning on walking back to Paris Garden, we'll escort you,' Osborne tells Bianca. 'Would the eleven-o'clock bell suit?'

'That's a kind offer, Constable Osborne. But there's no need. We're lodging at the Jackdaw for a few days. There is much for us to catch up on with Ned and Rose, and it's going to take a while to prise my son away from their affections. Besides, I want to introduce Mistress Cachorra to my shop on Dice Lane tomorrow. She's going to be my apprentice.'

One of the watchmen – a new recruit – mutters, 'So they're making women apprentices now?'

Constable Osborne gives the man a poke in the ribs with his official cudgel. 'Now that you've come across the river from Cripplegate Ward, Master Barnaby, it would be wise to remember whose tavern you drink in.'

'Just the one man?' Nicholas asks.

Osborne turns back to him. 'Aye, just the one, Dr Shelby. But he could be a watcher, spotting for his fellows.'

'Did you manage to get a look at him?'

'No. Afore we could gain on him, we lost the rogue in the mist.'

Bianca says, 'I'll pass the word around, so folks can go home in numbers.'

One man, thinks Nicholas. Keeping watch. But keeping watch on who? And why?

✠

By the time the St Saviour's bell strikes eleven the watermen and the labourers, the artisans and the tellers of long tales have all departed. Most of them will rise with the dawn for an honest day's work, though being Banksiders that honesty will depend somewhat upon their own individual interpretation.

Bianca and Cachorra are helping Rose tidy the kitchen, Nicholas is assisting Ned and Timothy to gather up the soiled rushes on the taproom floor. When the street door shudders to four distinct and imperious blows they pause in their work almost in unison.

'In the name of Her Majesty's Privy Council, I order this door unlocked!' comes a shout from outside.

But the door isn't yet locked. Securing the Jackdaw is Timothy's final duty before he goes to his pallet in the pantry to sleep. He has more work to do before he turns the key. But, being the queen's obedient subject – and by chance nearest the door – he has unlatched it before anyone even thinks of stopping him.

The taproom fire flares for a moment, then dies, as a blast of night air sweeps in from the street, and with it a spray of autumn rain. It is a cold, ill wind. It carries with it a faint smell of decay and corruption from the river.

And five cloaked men.

Two of them are lean, hollow-cheeked fellows that Nicholas recalls seeing hanging around Robert Devereux's pavilion in Ireland. Two others have more familiar faces: the one-eyed Barnabas Vyves and the porcine Gideon Strollot. But it is the fifth intruder who holds Nicholas's attention the tightest. He holds his sword poised as though it were a talon – a part of him, a limb perfected for death. His slack gaze confirms what Nicholas has known ever since he looked down upon the survivors of the *St Juan de Berrocal* lying slaughtered on an Irish beach: Oliver Henshawe enjoys his killing.

43

No screams. No protestations. No burst of street Italian from Bianca, as she is liable to do when faced with unexpected insult. Barely, even, an overly sharp intake of breath from Rose. Just mute surprise from everyone in the taproom.

And then Ned says, in that low rumble of his that manages to sound polite even while it warns, 'We're closed.'

Henshawe seems to appreciate the defiance, laughing even as he reaches out with his free hand to seize the astonished Timothy by the shoulder and force him to his knees. Vyves lays the tip of his sword against the lad's neck.

Henshawe says, 'And *closed* will be this boy's life – if any here so much as moves.'

Timothy looks at his mistress, his eyes full of guilt for letting the Jackdaw fall so easily. Ned glowers at the intruders. His fighter's instinct would have him act, but he knows Timothy will be dead before he has taken his first stride. His huge fists ball with frustration. He can do nothing as Henshawe's two lieutenants close on him, their blades holding him at bay.

'What is this about, Oliver?' Bianca asks calmly. 'Put away the swords and let us talk peaceably. There is no call for this.'

But Henshawe gives her no answer. He advances into the taproom, his sword pointed at Nicholas's chest. 'I should have killed you in Ireland when I had the chance,' he snarls, the firelight glinting on the jewelled rings he wears on his fingers. 'But I truly believed he had need of you. Jesu! How wrong I was.'

'I take it you're speaking of Robert Devereux,' Nicholas replies. 'You won't find him here. Have you tried York House? I hear that's his home these days.'

Even in the half-light of the taproom the hatred is clear on Henshawe's face. 'Don't mock me, Shelby. I know where His Grace is held. And I know you're behind the treachery that has brought him there.'

'Shouldn't you be in Ireland?' Nicholas asks, ignoring Henshawe's accusation. 'Or is it now customary in His Grace's faction to desert your post?'

Henshawe's reply is covered with a rime of icy loathing. 'I came into England because I have news to bring him. I came to tell him that you and your whore wife are traitors, agents of Spain.'

'You've lost your reason, Oliver,' Bianca says, as though bitter rage was an illness demanding sympathy.

'Oh, my reason is sound enough,' Henshawe says, lowering the blade of his sword a little. 'I have proof.'

'What you have, Oliver, is a heart full of anger,' Bianca says. 'It would be best if you were to put away your sword. It will be a little difficult to speak reasonably otherwise.'

Henshawe answers her with a slack smile of triumph. 'While you were on your way to England, madam, we captured a rebel. We put him to the hard press. And mercy, how he sang!'

'What madness is this, Oliver?' Bianca says.

'Not madness – truth. I know all about that treacherous rogue, Piers Gardener. I know who the Blackamoor is.' A jab of his sword in Cachorra's direction. 'I know of her mistress. I know that they escaped me on that beach when their ship came ashore. I know they have been whispering sweet succour into the ear of that dog, O'Neill, ever since.' The sword blade swings unerringly towards Bianca. 'And you, my sweet mistress – who once disdained me so – *you* have been consorting with our enemies.'

Bianca wonders how such a pretty vessel can hold so much spiteful resentment for the failure of a courtship that lasted barely a month. What weakness of the soul can account for such long-harboured bitterness? But there is no doubting the menace beneath his words.

'Oliver,' she says, 'you've invented a whole forest of nonsense out of a single sapling of half-truth. Now put up your sword, take your' – a doubting glance at Strollot, Vyves and the two others – 'your *gentlemen* and depart, before I call for the watch.'

But Henshawe is too far into his warren of conspiracy to turn back now.

'I wouldn't be surprised to learn that your husband was putting poison in the physic he gave to my lord of Essex,' he says, his pretty mouth as tight as a crack in a porcelain plate. 'I'll warrant he's behind His Grace's sickness. You're in this together, in the pay of Spain.'

Nicholas wonders if Henshawe might be drunk. But there is no tremor or uncertainty in the way he holds his sword. The tip barely moves.

Then Bianca says calmly, 'You're wrong, Oliver. Cachorra and her mistress came to Ireland for a very different reason from the one you think. She's an ally, not an enemy.'

'It's true,' Nicholas says. 'Mr Secretary Cecil will confirm it, if you dare to go to Cecil House and ask him.'

Henshawe's mouth twists as though he's swallowed a fly. 'Robert Cecil? He's the greatest traitor of all,' he proclaims. 'But I will set things right.' He nods in Cachorra's direction. 'When I bring that Spanish bitch before His Grace, the Privy Council will have no choice but to open their eyes. They will see then who are the real enemies: the ones who would sell this realm – and the immortal souls of every true Christian in it – to Spain, for nothing but a worthless promise of peace.'

'And how exactly do you intend to do that?' Nicholas asks. 'By marching on York House and freeing Essex? After all, it's not as if you have a *real* company of mustered men waiting to follow you, is it?'

If he had just called Henshawe's mother a whore there would be less malice in his stare. Nicholas wonders if he were to goad Henshawe further, whether he might be able to create enough of a reaction to give Ned Monkton a chance to break away from his guards.

'We know all about your squalid little scheme,' Nicholas says contemptuously. 'I suppose I might have seen a scrap of honour in a man who raised a force to overthrow a court he believed to be corrupt, but to gull the Exchequer for your own private gain, when braver men than you are dying in Ireland because there aren't enough of their fellows to fight beside them – that is true treachery, Oliver.'

The reaction comes not from Henshawe, but from Vyves. The muster ensign turns his lean, cadaverous face away from the kneeling Timothy. His one eye fixes expectantly upon his master, but the tip of his blade remains laid unerringly against Timothy's neck. He seems to be seeking permission to make the lad pay for Nicholas's insult.

'Don't hurt him!' Nicholas shouts in horror. As the lad looks in his direction, his eyes pleading for help, a cold, jagged knot of fear – and guilt – forms in Nicholas's stomach. 'You have no quarrel with him, Oliver,' he pleads desperately.

To his relief, Henshawe lifts a hand to keep Vyves in check. He raises his sword until the blade is pointing at Nicholas's mouth. 'Hold your tongue, or I'll cut out your filthy heart,' he growls.

How far dare I push him? Nicholas wonders. It's like baiting a wild beast. One more insult and Henshawe might strike. One more goad and Vyves could kill Timothy. Yet somehow he must take the initiative from Henshawe or they may *all* die.

He considers his chances of dodging Henshawe's blade. If he could reach Strollot, whose confidence with a sword appears the weakest, he might be able to disarm him, take up his blade. But before the idea is even half-formed in his mind he remembers the advice that sword-master Silver had given him before he left for Ireland: *I suggest a backsword, rather than a rapier... With only one edge to the blade, you're likely to do less harm – to yourself.* No, he thinks; the only chance they have is if he can give Ned the opportunity to act. And to do that, he must risk baiting Oliver Henshawe further.

'So where *is* your company?' he asks, glancing around at Henshawe's companions. 'Surely this can't be it. Does the Privy Council know what they got for their money? A coward with one eye, a corrupt alderman's clerk, two hired swordsmen and a cheap trickster to lead them?'

Timothy stares at him in disbelief, as if he's just been handed a death sentence.

The movement is fast and horribly accurate. For an instant Nicholas thinks Henshawe has punched him on the right clavicle. Then he feels the icy burn of steel twisting on bone – and a warm release flowing down over his breast. Finally the pain. Hot and dizzying.

'Nicholas!' Bianca screams. But as she tries to run to him, Henshawe holds her back with a jab of his now-bloodied sword. With a smile of professional satisfaction, he observes the tear in Nicholas's shirt and the blood flowing freely down over the linen.

'Shall I kill the lad now?' asks Vyves, a sickening eagerness in his voice.

But again Henshawe lifts one hand. And, like an obedient hound, Vyves lowers his head.

Sensing that Henshawe has a reason for keeping Timothy alive – at least for the present – Nicholas finds the courage to risk another push at his opponent's one weakness: his brittle self-regard.

'Tell us the truth, Oliver,' he says through gritted teeth. 'The Privy Council have bought themselves nothing but a company of ghosts.'

Henshawe moves the point of his sword slowly across Nicholas's throat till it rests on the opposite collarbone. He makes a play of gauging whether his next thrust will balance the first. Nicholas forces himself not to step back. All his instincts tell him to run. But that would be a humiliation he could not bear. Better to take what's coming. Better to hope. He glances at Ned Monkton. Ned's face is twisted with impotent fury. And his two guards know their business well enough not to take their eyes off him for even an instant.

'Prove it,' Henshawe sneers. 'I mustered one hundred fellows in England. I had one hundred fellows on the company's roll in Ireland.'

'But they weren't the same fellows, were they? You paid off your English recruits and mustered Irish ones at, what, half the price? You've been keeping the coin for their pay and supply ever since. Lemuel Godwinson was the only man whose conscience got the better of him. And for that, Vyves there had him murdered.'

The second strike lands before Nicholas even notices Henshawe's arm move. As accurate as the first, it twists a small gobbet of flesh out of his shoulder, spattering more blood across the front of his shirt. This time he cannot stop himself crying out.

'Oliver, for mercy's sake, stop it!' Bianca shouts in anguish.

'I know of no Lemuel Godwinson,' Henshawe says dismissively.

'But Vyves and Strollot do,' Nicholas says through teeth gritted by pain. 'Together, they lured him to Bankside and killed him before he could go to a magistrate.'

The sword tip hovers at the centre of Nicholas's throat. But Henshawe does not strike. Instead he looks at Barnabas Vyves.

'Do you know of this Lemuel Godwinson, Master Vyves?' he asks.

'I do not, Sir Oliver. Never heard of him.'

'And you, Master Strollot?'

'Nor me, neither.'

'Do you see?' Henshawe enquires pleasantly. 'We know naught of Master Godwinson. His name is unknown to us.'

Sow discord, Nicholas thinks. Foster distrust. Cause friction. Buy time.

'That's not what Strollot admitted to the coroner's jury,' he says. He turns to Vyves. The ensign has moved his sword tip an inch or two away from Timothy's neck. 'You even helped him to remember, didn't you, Master Vyves?' The pain from the twin holes that Henshawe has carved into his shoulders feels, to Nicholas, like a burning brand thrust deep into his body. But he keeps going, almost daring Henshawe to strike again, praying that he can survive another thrust, that Ned's guards will reward his pain with a moment's inattention.

'How many dead men did you have still serving in your company in Ireland, Oliver, still being fed and sheltered on Her Majesty's coin? I'd wager my own money that Lemuel Godwinson's name is on the muster roll, still earning his pay.'

'There *are* no names on the muster rolls, Shelby,' Henshawe says sneeringly. 'Only numbers. And the Privy Council won't have the time, or the inclination, to chase their tails investigating the allegations of a man who conspired with his wife to aid the Spanish and the rebellious Earl of Tyrone.'

'Or a brute who bears the brand of a killer on his thumb,' says Vyves, safely removed by several feet – and the length of his own sword blade – from Ned Monkton's response.

Timothy looks around as though he still cannot bring himself to believe what is happening. Nicholas's only satisfaction is that Vyves's blade is no longer as close to the lad's neck as it was.

'We're wasting time,' says Henshawe. 'You, your wife and the Blackamoor are to come with us, now.'

'Where?' Nicholas asks.

'Somewhere secure, until morning.'

'As secure as Lemuel Godwinson is?' Nicholas asks, certain now of Henshawe's intentions.

A knowing gleam flashes in Henshawe's eyes. 'More secure even than Edmund Spenser,' he says with a slack grin.

Nicholas forces himself to stay calm. He breathes slowly. Henshawe must not see his fear. Bianca must not see that he has no notion how to stop Henshawe killing them all. Because it has occurred to Nicholas that Henshawe doesn't need them to be alive when he presents them as evidence of Cecil's secret communication with Spain. Indeed, it might be better all round for him if their tongues were stilled. Dead, there is no one left to disprove a claim from the Essex faction that Cecil has been plotting to capitulate to Spain. Dead, there is no one to expose Henshawe's fraud.

I'm thinking too hard, he tells himself. Since when did Oliver Henshawe need an excuse to kill?

And then, seemingly out of nowhere, he remembers a fragment of his conversation with Edmund Spenser at the Whitehall revels in December, while Bianca had been dancing with Robert Devereux. He had enquired whether Spenser knew anything about Henshawe's Irish recruits. *I seem to recall Sir Robert telling me that you were once in charge of the muster in Munster. Is that true?* he had asked. Now he understands.

'Spenser was once a commissioner of the muster for his country in Ireland, wasn't he?' he says. 'He must have realized what you were up to. Is that why you killed him? What did you do: smother him with a pillow? Poison him?'

This time Nicholas has a moment's warning. He sees Henshawe's hand tighten on the grip of his sword. He turns his head up and away, closing his eyes – waiting for the pain.

It starts just beneath his jaw. A blaze of cold fire that seems to flow up through his skull and pool behind his eyes. Fire that screams in his ears for an instant, until it dawns on him that it is his own cry of agony that he can hear. He feels the blood course over his stretched throat and wonders if Henshawe has deliberately cut through a jugular vein. He grasps his chin – and feels the most extraordinary relief when his fingers encounter only a flap of hanging flesh and blood that merely flows over his hand, not pumps out in a fatal gush.

Ignoring Henshawe's bloodied sword, Bianca rushes to Nicholas's side. She rips the pleated collar from her gown and holds it against his chin.

'You should learn to keep hold of your tongue, Shelby,' Henshawe says. 'Like Spenser, you ask too many questions. It would have been wiser for him to remember he was no longer commissioner for the Cork muster. If he hadn't gone poking his nose where it wasn't wanted, he might still be scratching out his God-awful verse.'

'We'll be no use to you dead, Oliver,' Bianca says, glaring at Henshawe. She, too, has understood. 'If you kill us to hide your dirty little crimes, you won't be able to use us to Robert Devereux's benefit. Have you thought of that?'

'They say you can't slander the dead,' Henshawe tells her with a smile. 'It's not true. It's just a matter of what people are prepared to believe.'

'And if we refuse to come with you?' she asks.

'Were you at the cove with your husband?'

'Yes.'

'Then close your eyes awhile. Remember what you saw on the bluffs above the wreck of the *San Juan*. Remember the eyes pecked out by the gulls. Remember the smell. Then ask yourself if I am a man overly concerned with mercy.' He looks at the kneeling Timothy. 'And when you have reached a conclusion – be sure to tell *him*.'

'This is not the Oliver Henshawe who paid court to me,' Bianca says, appealing to whatever scrap of humanity might still lie gasping at the bottom of his deep well of bitterness.

'You never got to know me properly.'

His eyes are blank, almost fish-like, as though he were a creature of deep, dark water, hunting the minnows that swim where the sunlight still penetrates.

'Then thanks be to Almighty God that I didn't,' she says, admitting defeat. 'Given the choice, I would rather have taken the Devil to my bed.'

Ned Monkton calls out, 'We'll summon the watch, the moment you've gone.' He looks as though he's struggling to restrain himself from springing upon the two men guarding him, swords or no swords. Nicholas gives him a pleading look. For all Ned's size and strength, it would be a suicidal act.

'Then your friends' deaths will be on your conscience, not mine,' says Henshawe.

Bianca glances at the stairs to the chambers above the taproom. Nicholas knows at once that she is thinking of little Bruno, asleep. Her pain hurts him even more than his own wounds. Bruno will wake to find his mother and his father gone – probably for ever. Yet if either of them begs Henshawe to allow Bruno to accompany them, he will probably die too. For Nicholas is certain now that Henshawe would happily kill them all to keep his secret.

'Are you coming?' Henshawe asks, as though he's inviting them for a pleasant stroll along the river. He looks contemptuously at Timothy. 'Or must we begin with this weak sapling?' The tip of his blade swings in the direction of Rose Monkton. 'Or maybe with this woman?'

Defeat – together with pain – brings a rasping tone to Nicholas's voice. 'We have no choice,' he tells Bianca. 'If we don't go with him, he'll do as he threatens. We have ample evidence of that. We know what he's capable of.'

Henshawe lets out a bark of laughter. 'At last! The physician has learned how to make a proper diagnosis.'

Nicholas feels his mind begin to topple. This is my own fault, he thinks. We are here because of me. When Robert Cecil called, I should have had the courage to turn my back... Holding Bianca's blood-soaked scrap of linen against his jaw, he turns towards the street door. It is all he can do to make his legs function. Helplessness – like shame – is a poison that saps the will.

Henshawe sheathes his sword. In the dying firelight his face is infused with harsh satisfaction. 'Come,' he says quietly. 'Come.'

And then, for the first time since the door flew open, Cachorra speaks.

'We go with this man,' she says simply. 'I trust him.'

Standing in the shadows by the hearth, she has a powerful stillness about her. She could be a stone guardian in the doorway to a temple. Or a priestess deep in supplication to some ancient deity. Immutable. Ageless.

'Oh, that *all* Spaniards were so biddable,' Henshawe says sneeringly, stretching out the words like a song.

Cachorra steps forward. One arm hangs loosely at her side, the other held across her body. She moves with grace and nobility, as if she hasn't understood Henshawe's intentions at all. Bianca wonders if it might not be best to allow her a few more moments of ignorance.

And then – with Henshawe partly blocking her way – Cachorra speaks again.

'Are you English really so ill-mannered?' she enquires, her head tilted upwards slightly in a manner Bianca suspects she has learned from Constanza. 'I was informed Englishmen know what is *galantería* – what is correct.'

Henshawe laughs brightly. He could be indulging in a bout of flirtatious dinner-table repartee. He gives Cachorra a mocking frown of self-recrimination. Then he makes an elaborate courtesy to her, an exaggerated flourish of a bow, slowly sweeping one hand from his temple down across his body in a theatrical arc, bending from the waist as he does so.

'*Please*,' he oozes. 'Your *Imperial Majesty* of Spain...'

He straightens as she passes, stepping back to make way for her. The small retreat brings him up against one of the Jackdaw's oak pillars that support the ceiling beams.

And that is when the leopard strikes.

Afterwards, Nicholas and Bianca, Rose and Ned, even Timothy, will offer differing accounts of what actually happened. Each will note, or fail to note, minor differences in time and movement, in sound and action. But all will agree that it happened almost too swiftly for the human eye to catch.

It was like a spider pouncing on a fly, Bianca will say. Ned will prefer the image of a hawk taking a sparrow on the wing. Rose, being of a romantic inclination, will liken it to a sudden, stolen last embrace between doomed lovers. Nicholas will not describe it at all, as his back was turned slightly and his eyes were on Barnabas Vyves, wondering how much brief agony he would endure if he threw himself on the man's sword in a last attempt to give Ned the opportunity he needed.

Bianca will also say that she caught a brief flash of gold in the dying firelight. And so will the others, though their recollections vary. But all will agree they heard a sound like the last choking breaths of a man drowning.

As Cachorra steps back, Oliver Henshawe falls to his knees, a marionette whose strings have been cut. He twists slightly, his body rotating so that he lands on the flagstones, head back with a sickening *crack*, eyes staring at the ceiling. Embedded beneath his jaw – right up to the crossbar – is Constanza's gold wedding present. The firelight gleams on what remains visible of the sharp little crucifix, rammed upwards with almost superhuman strength through Henshawe's chin, through the roof of his mouth and into his brain.

Instinctively Henshawe's two swordsmen turn towards their master. It is the moment both Ned and Nicholas have been praying for, as though privy to each other's thoughts.

Ned moves with all the speed and dexterity of a Bankside street-trickster playing a sleight of hand. One blow to the side of the head sends the nearest man reeling into the other. He falls, already senseless, across his companion's blade, opening up one arm from the shoulder to the elbow, before hitting the floor. The second man has only half-turned back towards the threat when Ned's fist fells him as efficiently as a good slaughterman fells cattle.

The fight goes out of Vyves like air from an uncorked wineskin. As he stares at Henshawe's body, his captive nimbly dodges away from his blade. Seizing an empty tankard from an uncleared table, Timothy redeems himself with one swinging blow into the lank curtain of hair on the back of Vyves's head. Strollot, never a swordsman, simply lets go of his rapier.

And then all eyes – at least those still undimmed – turn towards Cachorra.

She is kneeling on Henshawe's chest. Whether or not he still has the capacity to hear her voice is anyone's guess, for although his eyes are open, they do not move. But Cachorra seems to think he can, because she is speaking to him as she lifts each of his hands in turn and removes the heavy jewelled rings from his fingers.

'These rings are not yours,' she is saying. 'You stole them from my dear friend, Don Rodriquez Calva de Sagrada. He was my past.'

Bracing her knees against Henshawe's unmoving shoulders, she grasps the crossbar of the crucifix. 'And *this* is my payment for many years of insult from his daughter. It is my future. My freedom. By an act of kindness, it belongs to me now.'

Then, leaning close to Oliver Henshawe's half-open mouth, she says softly, almost as if she were whispering an endearment to a lover, 'And you, Senõr, *you* now belong in hell.'

And with that, she slowly draws the now-gory shaft of the crucifix from the depths of his skull.

44

Bianca has washed Nicholas's wounds with a distillation of wild campion, agrimony and fluellin and has applied a cataplasm to halt the bleeding. His injuries are painful but superficial. Even the slash beneath his jaw has not penetrated his mouth. But it will be a while before he can speak much above a croak.

Save for Henshawe, the only other serious hurt is to the arm of the guard Ned felled with his first punch. Bianca has done her best to treat and bind the deep gash, and now he sits against the taproom wall, ashen-faced and wary. His companion and Strollot and Vyves are under Ned's care, which – given the circumstances – is surprisingly benevolent. But then no one without a sword is likely to give Ned Monkton any trouble. Henshawe himself lies where he fell, his face covered with a hemp sack fetched from the brew house in the Jackdaw's yard.

Whatever courage Vyves and the others entered with has flown away into the autumn night, now that they are disarmed and without their leader. But there is still defiance. Barnabas Vyves seems to think he retains the upper hand.

'The Blackamoor will surely hang for murder,' he says confidently, from his place on one of the Jackdaw's benches

Timothy makes to strike him again with the tankard, but Nicholas raises a hand to stop him.

'Do you think so?' he croaks, wincing as the movement of his mouth tugs at the torn flesh below his jaw.

'You haven't the stomach to kill us,' Vyves says, his single eye fixed on the body lying on the floor. Whether he is mourning Henshawe's demise or the ending of a lucrative income, Nicholas cannot be sure. 'You ain't the sort – none of you.'

'Oliver Henshawe came here with violence in his heart,' Bianca tells him, inspecting the extent of the blood on her gown and wondering how she's going to wash it clean. 'He was killed in self-defence. There's none here who can claim otherwise.'

Vyves gives a petulant little laugh. 'A Spaniard slaying an English gentleman? There's not a judge in the realm what wouldn't help to rig the gallows.'

Rose, back from checking on the still-sleeping Bruno, hands Nicholas the clean shirt she has fetched. As he pulls it on, he says, 'But you have to ask yourself, Master Vyves, who is more likely to swing from those gallows – a woman who acted to protect the lives of others, or a man who has been cheating the Treasury these last several months? And we haven't even begun to consider Henshawe's confession regarding the death of Edmund Spenser, or any part *you* may have played in it. Then, of course, there's Lemuel Godwinson—'

'There's no evidence that would convince any magistrate,' says Strollot. 'You have nothing.'

'But a confession would.'

'And why would we make one of those?' Vyves sneers.

'There's a chamber under Cecil House,' Nicholas says. 'I've been there, so I can describe it to you, if you'd like.'

'A chamber?' enquires Strollot. 'What manner of chamber?'

'Let us simply say it's not a storeroom,' Nicholas tells him, recalling the dying rebel whom Robert Cecil had asked him to treat there. 'And the only man I saw keep his tongue silent in it was a lot braver than either of you.'

'What are you proposing?' asks Strollot, his plump red jowls quivering as he sniffs the scent of a deal.

'Two things, as a matter of fact. The first is that you all carry *that* out of here.' A glance at Henshawe's body. 'I suggest you leave him for the night-watch to find. You already know how to do that. You've done it before. In return, *we* will forget you were ever here.'

'Nicholas, what are you proposing?' Bianca interjects, her face clouding.

'Peace, sweet,' he says with a smile that starts the blood trickling again over the new shirt. 'I think Masters Vyves and Strollot will want to hear what I have to say.'

'Go on,' Vyves invites.

'We will all agree that Oliver Henshawe was a little rash in coming to Bankside tonight – whatever his motive – given the known presence of cut-purses.'

'Cut-purses?' says Vyves.

'Constable Osborne saw what he thought was a cut-purse earlier. We'll pretend it wasn't one of you. We'll pretend you were never here.'

'And the second?' asks Strollot.

'That, Master Strollot,' says Nicholas, dabbing at his chin with the back of his hand, 'will depend upon your willingness to be frank with me over how much of the stolen Treasury's money you have left.'

✠

The low afternoon sun tugs spidery shadows from the trees along the Strand. It sharpens the outlines of the fine mansions lying in the countryside west of Temple Bar. In Robert Cecil's study the panelled walls glow with reflected golden light.

'I would be lying to you if I said that the Privy Council has been diligent in stamping out this corruption,' Cecil tells Nicholas as they stand together looking out across the sculptured gardens. 'But this is the most egregious case I've heard of so far.'

'You knew?' Nicholas asks in disbelief.

'Of this specific crime, no. But defrauding the muster commissioners is not unheard of. I have tried to draw the attention of my honourable colleagues to the problem, but there are too many other pressing issues weighing on the attention of the Privy Council. Perhaps Henshawe's wickedness will make them pay attention. We can ill afford to have our efforts in Ireland hampered so.'

'I have been led to understand that what remains of the money he stole may be retrieved from the grounds of his house at Walworth, hidden in a dovecote,' Nicholas says. 'I would imagine it is a considerable sum.'

Cecil turns away from the window. As the sunlight leaves his face, the old paleness returns, as though the well of intrigue has been recharged. 'You show remarkably detailed knowledge of where the money is, Nicholas, and yet you tell me you have none at all of how Henshawe's body came to be found on the riverbank by Battle Creek. How can that be?'

Nicholas contrives to appear the simple yeoman's son fresh from the wilds of Suffolk. He says, 'I have only Bankside gossip to rely upon, Sir Robert: fragments overheard, scraps picked up here and there. Sir Oliver Henshawe will not be the last gentleman to disregard the dangers of wandering alone south of the river at night.'

'And what of accomplices?' Cecil asks. 'It's most unlikely he could have perpetrated this fraud alone.'

'If I hear anything, I'll tell you.'

As Cecil takes his seat behind his desk, he gives Nicholas a bland smile. 'I shall look forward to it.'

Trying to steer the subject away from Oliver Henshawe, Nicholas says, 'How are the peace negotiations to progress? Will there be emissaries? A conference?'

Mr Secretary Cecil looks at him blankly. 'Peace negotiations?'

'Now that you have the list of names that Don Rodriquez sent.'

'Oh, *that*,' says Cecil, as though he has just remembered where he left some unimportant trinket. He taps the desk drawer. 'That's safe in here. No need to worry for the present.'

'But aren't you going to—'

'All in good time, Nicholas,' Cecil interrupts. 'The greatest threat to the safety of the realm was Robert Devereux, and he has now been gelded. Lord Mountjoy is to be sent to Ireland in his place. I'm sure *he* will soon bring the Irish to obedience and all this disquiet and expense may be dispensed with. Then we shall have time for the luxury of sounding out the gentlemen on Senõr Calva de Sagrada's list.'

Do they teach that smile to the young lawyers studying at the Temple? Nicholas wonders – the sort of smile that tells you how little you understand the world, and how better it would be if you didn't trouble yourself trying.

But it tells Nicholas all he needs to know. Cecil's response to Edmund Spenser's approach was nothing to do with advancing peace, it was all to do with the humbling of his rival, Robert Devereux.

Nicholas thinks of Cachorra's bravery and determination, of the courage of Don Rodriquez to extend the hand of peace to an enemy, of Piers Gardener's willingness to risk his life for a cause he believed in. Their example makes what he has to say next all the easier.

'There is something else I came to tell you, Sir Robert,' he begins, feeling a great weight lifting from his shoulders. 'It is with regret that I must inform you that I can no longer serve as your physician – or your intelligencer.'

He looks at Cecil and waits for an answer. Will it be rage? Cold anger? Threatening?

But Mr Secretary Cecil is a busy man. He is attending to the many important documents on his desk. The crooked shoulders hunch like a hawk pecking at the carcass of its prey. He doesn't look up. In fact, as far as Nicholas can tell, he seems not to have heard him.

✠

Ned remembers the directions from his first visit.

'Follow that line of beech trees along Alleyne's Meadow to the brook,' the steward at Milkwell Manor had told him then. 'Once across – it's not much of a jump – you'll find old Godwinson's hut on the far side of the pasture. He's bound to be there. He can't have left more than twice since his son was murdered.'

'Was it *really* necessary to 'ave Vyves and Strollot leave behind *quite* so much of the money left over from what 'Enshawe gulled from the Treasury?' he asks Nicholas as they walk together in the cool of an October morning.

'It was part of the bargain, Ned,' Nicholas says, admiring the dewy cobwebs glinting like lace against the hedgerows. 'That money was no more ours than it was his.'

'Pity,' says Ned.

'But right.'

'S'pose so,' admits Ned. 'What I shan't never understand is why a fellow who 'as everything – a pleasing front, manners, position, reputation – why does that man turn out so bad? Why does 'e turn so cruel?'

'I can't answer that, Ned. I'm a physician, not a confessor.'

At the brook Ned Monkton needs do little more than step across. He puts out his hand to help Nicholas follow. 'Aye, well, it was a shame to see it go,' he says. 'We could 'ave 'ad ourselves a right old revel with that much coin.'

Nicholas jumps across the stream, his free hand holding tight to the heavy purse at his belt. As he lands, a stab of fiery pain bursts through his still-healing wounds. Recovering his balance and his composure, he says, 'This won't cure Aaron Godwinson of the grief of losing his son, but it will buy him a flock of his own, and enough to live on for a good while. I know it's rightly the Exchequer's money, but if they are so determined to be careless with it, then it's only right that we put at least *some* of it to good use.'

'I can see the right in that,' says Ned, his auburn beard and hair merging with the autumn leaves so that he looks like a creature born of the wildwood.

'And what better use for it than that a father gets some recompense for his son's service – even if that son didn't make it all the way to Ireland?'

Ned lets out a laugh that rolls like summer thunder. 'Playin' fast and loose with government money – why, I do believe we've made a Banksider of you at last, Dr Shelby.'

And then he turns his back on Nicholas and starts to climb the bank.

Nicholas follows. Up through the bracken he goes, the silvery spiders' webs clinging to his sleeves like the dried trails of a lover's tears, and into the meadow – where an old, white-haired man is sitting on the dewy grass, singing a mournful song to a small huddle of studiously indifferent sheep.

Historical Note

Robert Devereux, Earl of Essex, did not give up on his plan to restore – by force – his reputation and rid England of the courtiers he still believed to be the queen's enemies. In February 1601 he would embark on the brief rebellion that would lead to his execution a few days later.

Spain made one last attempt at an invasion of Ireland, landing a large force in the same year. It was soundly defeated at Kinsale, along with Tyrone's army. Hugh O'Neill himself continued his struggle against the English Crown. In 1607 he was forced to flee Ireland. He died in exile in Rome nine years later.

Did Essex really suffer from syphilis? In his excellent account of the earl's life, *An Elizabethan Icarus*, the historian Robert Lacey certainly thinks so.

The muster fraud was a significant drain on England's efforts to quell the Tyrone rebellion. Lax official control meant it was easy for captains to pay men to join the muster, then send them home and recruit far more cheaply in Ireland, pocketing the difference. Robert Cecil and Essex's successor, Lord Mountjoy, made strenuous efforts to stamp out the practice.

The severing of heads as trophies was common on both sides during Tyrone's rebellion. Which side began the custom is unclear. The journal of Sir William Russell contains several instances:

Captain Street sent in five of the traitors' heads... Garrald McShaan Begg's head sent in... Captain Willis brought in two traitors' heads...

Quarter was in short supply:

The foragers took a prisoner in a house, wherein they found a bag of bullets newly molten for the enemy. He was executed.

Edmund Spenser's views on how Ireland could be quickly brought under control were not unusually harsh for the time, though it is noteworthy that his pamphlet *A View of the Present State of Ireland* did not find a publisher until 1633.

The list of the peace faction that the fictitious Don Rodriquez brought to England must have languished in Mr Secretary Cecil's desk drawer for quite some time. It was not until 1604, the year after Elizabeth's death, that envoys from King Philip III sat down with the English Privy Council to agree a peace treaty between the two realms. A contemporary depiction of the event – *The Somerset House Conference* – hangs today in London's National Portrait Gallery. Save for the gowns and the ruffs, it could almost be a photograph of any modern-day international political gathering. On the left of the table are the delegates from Spain and the Spanish Netherlands. On the right sit the representatives of James I. Amongst them – nearest to the viewer, and the only one who appears to have notes in front of him – is a rather enigmatic-looking Robert Cecil.

The Merrow remains just one of Ireland's many enticing myths. Unless, of course, you know otherwise.

Acknowledgements

When I was growing up, no one in my family had ever known my paternal great-grandfather. His very identity was a mystery, though a proper Y-DNA search has now established beyond much doubt that he was a Donovan from County Cork, who must have come to the East End of London sometime in the late nineteenth century. Thus I can reliably claim possession of at least a modicum of Irish blood in my veins.

But I am undeniably English, and it would be foolish of me to profess great authority when writing about the millennia-old relationship between England and Ireland. There is no doubt that the Elizabethan enterprise in Ireland was at times brutal. Starvation and massacre were commonplace. The shockwaves caused by the Tudor plantation of Protestant landowners still reverberate to this day. But I am not a historian, and I have therefore set the story you have just read firmly in the experiences of Nicholas and Bianca. I must also confess to having taken a few minor liberties with the timescale of some events, purely in the interests of a fictional narrative.

For those interested in finding out more about this relatively unfamiliar period of English-Irish history, some fifty years before Oliver Cromwell ever set foot on Irish soil, I recommend the following: *Tyrone's Rebellion* by Hiram Morgan and *Elizabeth's Irish Wars* by Cyril Falls are fine accounts told from each side of the divide.

I am also indebted to Robert Lacey, having made much use of his superb *Robert, Earl of Essex: An Elizabethan Icarus*, and to Andrew Hadfield for his excellent *Edmund Spenser: A Life*.

Heartfelt thanks are due to Susannah Hamilton for her belief in the Jackdaw series. Likewise, to my agent Jane Judd, Emma Coode, and the great crew at Corvus. To Mandy Greenfield I owe an equal debt, for once again saving me from far too many self-induced embarrassments.

And finally I must express my boundless appreciation for the support and encouragement of Jane, my wife, who bears being married to a time traveller with extraordinary forbearance.

S. W. Perry
Worcestershire, September 2021

Read on for an extract from . . .

1

London, Summer 1600

His plan is to slip into the city unobserved and unremarked. He has chosen the place carefully. The gatehouse guarding the road from the east is bound to be busy at this time of day, a chokepoint for Londoners hurrying home for the shelter of the hencoop before the light fades and the foxes begin to prowl.

A group of gentlemen on horseback, returning from a day's hawking in the fields beyond St Botolph's, provides the perfect cover. He falls in between them and a gaggle of servant women bringing in bundles of washing that has dried on the hedgerows in the uncertain June sunshine. A procession of the damned, he thinks, looking up at the raised portcullis hanging above his head like a row of teeth in a dragon's jaw.

In appearance he is forgettable. The only flesh he carries is in his face, as though God hadn't allowed enough clay from which to make the rest of him. What remains of his hair is as sparse and wiry as dune grass after a North Sea gale. It is as white as a cold Waddenzee mist. All he possesses are the clothes on his back, the boots that trouble his raw feet, a set of keys, and the ghosts he carries in his pack.

Only in name is he rich.

Petrus Euesebius Schenk.

Petrus after St Peter, long dead. Euesebius in honour of the great Christian theologian from Caesarea, also dead.

And Schenk?

What is there to say about the Schenks? Little enough, other than that they are an honest if unremarkable family from Sulzbach, a one-spire little place astride a crossroads of no note, barely two leagues to the west of Frankfurt.

But this is not Frankfurt. This is London. Aldgate, to be precise, of the four original towered gatehouses in the ancient wall that the exiled Trojan, Brutus, raised when he founded the city a thousand years ago. A city he named New Troy. Or so it goes.

After all, what are we if not the sum of the myths we tell ourselves?

The short tunnel stinks of horse-dung. From the narrow ledge where the walls reach the domed ceiling an accretion of pigeon-shit hangs like clusters of pale grapes. Slipping out of the crowd as easily as he entered, Schenk drops to his haunches, wincing. It has taken him five days to walk from the place he came ashore –Woodbridge in the county of Suffolk. As he wiggles his feet to ease the cramp in his calves, the sole of his right boot flaps like a wagging tongue. A rivulet of grit trickles down under the inset, adding to the torment. He sits down on the trampled earth and unlaces the boot to inspect the damage. The glue holding the sole in place has split and a few nails have worked loose. It's nothing a cobbler couldn't put right in a moment, although Schenk's coin is all but spent. He won't receive more until he finds the man he has come to see. Turning side-on to the wall, he hammers the boot against the indifferent stone, silently chanting words from a verse in the Old Testament with each strike: *Enticers... to... idolatry... must... be... slain...*

Biting against the pain of his blisters, Schenk squeezes his foot back inside the leather and reties the laces. A temporary fix, but it should last until he reaches the Steelyard.

In Schenk's mind it is always the *Stalhof*, from the archaic German. His English friends have told him that 'Steelyard' is a corruption of an old term for a measuring balance, or a distortion of the name of the ancient fellow who once owned that stretch of land on the north bank of the Thames close to where the Walbrook empties into the river. One thing alone is indisputable: no steel is sold there now, not since the queen's Privy Council expelled the Hansa merchants from Lübeck, Stade and Cologne.

Schenk knows the story well. For more than three centuries – since the time of England's third Henry – generations of Hansa merchants have made the little self-contained enclave beside the Thames their home. They have built their houses and their businesses, paid their taxes and worshipped God in their own churches. But they are not wanted in England now. The English can make their own trade in pitch, sailcloth, rope and tar. England has no need of the Hansa merchants any more.

It might be empty, its houses boarded up, but the Steelyard offers Petrus Euesebius Schenk something he craves: undisturbed shelter. Now almost deserted, the warren of warehouses, storage sheds and private homes is the perfect place for a man to hide.

But the echoes of his boot striking the wall have attracted one of the gate-guards, set there to raise and lower the portcullis and to watch for vagrants, papists and other undesirables attempting to enter the city. He walks over. Schenk watches him approach, alarm spiking in his veins.

'God give you a good evening, friend,' the man says, smiling without merriment. 'Do we have a name, perchance?'

A name? Why yes, we a have a name fit for a Bohemian prince, thinks Petrus Euesebius Schenk. But these days we must be careful about proclaiming it, in case we linger in the memory of a man such as this. Schenk's English is good enough to pass muster, though a little too guttural for general taste. As he answers, he prays his accent won't prick the guard's suspicion.

'Shelby,' he says. 'My name is Nicholas Shelby, of Bankside.'

✠

William Baronsdale, the queen's senior physician, breaks his stride halfway down the long, panelled gallery. His gown – a sinister corvine black – flaps around a frame as angular as a sculptor's armature. The sudden halt releases a faint scent of rosewater from the rushes underfoot, anointed by the grooms to keep the coarser smells from the royal nostrils. In his long professional life, Baronsdale has held every major office the College of Physicians has in its gift to bestow: censor, treasurer, consiliarius, even president. Clad in his formal robe and in the grip of a fearsome indignation, he reminds Nicholas Shelby of nothing so much as a man caught by the sudden urge to burst the swelling head of a particularly uncomfortable boil. Baronsdale's usually placid Gloucestershire tones tighten in concert with his features.

'I can remain silent no longer, sirrah. She *will* die one day, sirrah. And when she does, who will abide your... your... your *heresies* then?'

There was a time – and not so long ago, Nicholas recalls – when to give voice to the very thought of Elizabeth's demise was treason. In the taverns, the dice-dens, the playhouses and the bear-gardens, suggesting that the queen might be anything other than immortal would draw the unwelcome attention of the secret listeners placed there by the Privy Council. But today we need stay silent no longer. Now even the unspeakable may be imagined, made corporeal. Faced. Accepted. Not even those anointed by God can live for ever. At least, not on this earth. Mercy, thinks Nicholas, how times have changed.

Through the open windows the spring sunshine dances an energetic volta on the brown face of the Thames, racing the breeze upriver towards Windsor. The priceless Flemish hangings fidget gently against the wainscoting, caught by the waft from the open windows. And at the end of the corridor: two yeomen ushers in full harness, barring the way. Nicholas can make out the Tudor rose woven in red and white thread into the breasts of each tunic, and in the polished blades of their axes the reflections of himself and Baronsdale, two tiny curvaceous gargoyles with enormous heads. He waits for Baronsdale to resume his march. But Baronsdale seems reluctant to move, glancing at the yeoman ushers to gauge how long he can delay. I understand, thinks Nicholas – there is still a little pus left to squeeze from the boil.

'I confess it willingly, before my maker,' Baronsdale announces as if it were a last testament. 'I have *never* liked you, Mister Shelby. *Never.* Your arrogant rejection of the discipline you took an oath to uphold... your contempt for tradition, precedence and custom... Who are *you*, sirrah, to scoff at the writings of the learned ancients?'

The thin lips fold in on themselves as though sucking water through a reed. The jowls wobble. They have grown pendulous over the years, the only weight Baronsdale carries. They're where he keeps his store of vitriol, Nicholas decides.

If Baronsdale is expecting an answer, Nicholas is not of a mind to provide one.

'To my mind, sirrah, you are no better than a mountebank,' the senior physician continues petulantly. 'If men of your ilk represent the future of medicine, I see little hope for the continuing survival of Adam's progeny. I prophesy that within a generation it will be an easier thing in England to find the fabled basilisk than an honest doctor. You could at least have worn your physician's gown. You look like a... like a...'

Baronsdale has a lexicon that would stretch around Richmond Palace twice over, most of it medical, much of it Latin. But he seems at a loss to find the right words for the hardy-framed man of middling height with the wiry black hair who stands beside him, a look of weary sufferance on his face.

'An actor from the playhouse?' Nicholas suggests. 'A cashiered pistoleer?'

'Are you mocking me, Shelby?'

'Not at all. I'm merely repeating what Her Majesty has said to me on more than one occasion. Anyway, I wouldn't worry. She's in rude health. She hunts, she dances—'

Yes, and she also ages, Nicholas tells himself. In a few months she'll be sixty-seven. It could happen at any time. But he's damned if he's going to give Baronsdale the slightest satisfaction.

'If she tires of me, I'll live with it.'

Baronsdale wags an accusing finger at him. 'You revel in this, don't you? Despising your betters, laughing at us, as though you have some superior right to question all we hold to be the truth – a truth revealed to us by the Almighty.'

Nicholas responds with a casual shrug. He's growing tired of the lecture. 'I hear you prescribed a freshly killed pigeon to be lain across the ankles of the Countess of Warwick last week, to relieve the swelling,' he says.

'Meat that is still warm draws to it the heat of inflammation,' Baronsdale says defensively. 'I would have thought you'd have learned that at... Where was it you studied medicine: the butcher's shambles on Bankside?'

'Cambridge. And Padua. But the best of it I learned in the Low Countries, on the field of battle. Couldn't get a pigeon for love nor money: the Spanish had eaten them all.'

Nicholas sets off again towards the yeomen ushers guarding the privy chamber. He wishes to God he hadn't bumped into

Baronsdale in his hurry to answer the summons. He has no stomach for this fight. His wife Bianca, being half Italian, would blaze with anger, were she here. But Nicholas is made of calmer clay. Acting the firebrand will only confirm Baronsdale in his prejudice. And besides, there's bound to be a prohibition against brawling within the royal verge.

But Baronsdale is right about the queen's favour. The mercurial nature of her interest in young men with good calves and passable looks is legendary. Soldiers, poets, physicians... if you last long enough to receive a nickname, you're doing well. As far as Nicholas is aware, he has not yet been honoured with one. He knows that the time will come when her interest in him wanes. The calls to discuss advances in physic and the natural philosophies will become more infrequent. Then they will cease altogether, and Baronsdale – along with all the other elderly worthies of the College of Physicians – will be ready for his revenge. Their spite will be as sharp as any scalpel. They'll probably drag him before the Censors and have him struck off on some trumped-up accusation that he's practised witchcraft.

'I cannot keep Her Majesty waiting,' he says, laying just enough emphasis on the *I* to remind Baronsdale that he is not invited. 'Is there anything you wish me to ask her – while we're speaking?'

✠

Safely past the first obstacle, Petrus Euesebius Schenk hoists his heavy pack over his shoulder and sets off towards the Aldgate pump. Looking back, he sees the guard trying to settle an altercation between two waggoners over who has right of way through the arch. A cold trickle of sweat makes its way down his spine as he considers how close he had come to disaster.

'And where are you bound, Master Shelby?' the guard had asked.

'The Dutch church at Austin Friars, to give thanks to God for seeing me safely home.'

'And why would an Englishman named Shelby pray in a church for aliens? Besides, you don't sound English.'

'Because I was Dutch before I was English,' Schenk had explained, struggling to keep his nerve and trusting the man couldn't tell the difference between a Dutch accent and a Hessian one. 'I became an Englishman by letters patent from the Privy Council. Cost me more money than I shall likely see again this side of heaven. And I have friends amongst the Calvinist refugee families who live in the Broad Street Ward. It's good to catch up with old friends after a sermon.'

'Where have you been, then, to get so dusty and travel-worn?' the guard had asked, still not entirely convinced.

'Does it matter?'

'It might. We've been told to keep an eye open for fellows carrying pamphlets.'

'Pamphlets? What manner of pamphlets?'

The guard had lowered his voice, leaning towards Schenk as though to impart a great secret. 'Seditious tracts. Puritan tracts. Tracts that denounce the queen's bishops as corruptors of God's word.'

'Mercy,' Schenk had replied, fearing the guard was about to demand that he open his pack to see if he was carrying such incendiary items. 'Things *have* taken a turn for the worse while I've been gone.'

And then God had sent a brace of angels to save him – in the shape of two particularly stubborn waggoners, whose irate voices are even now echoing around the interior of the Aldgate arch, to the annoyance of the gate-guard.

Schenk's thirst is raging now. Once he would have stopped at the sign of the King's Head on Fenchurch Street for ale and a bed, but no longer. Too many questioning eyes. Besides, ale is a sinful intoxicant that allows the Devil a way into your soul. Schenk will take honest, God-given water at the Aldgate pump. Then he will walk south along Gracechurch Street towards the river, cut west into Candlewick Street before making his way through the narrow lanes of Dowgate Ward to the Steelyard. How far must he walk before he spots another of his secret companions?

They are always with him. He has seen two on the road from Woodbridge, where he came ashore. The first was a pretty fair-haired youth, the second a woman of around fifty who carried a goose in a wooden cage. He hadn't spoken to either. He knows it is improper to speak to the dead unless they invite you. Schenk is nothing if not polite, an English habit he is proud to have adopted.

After quenching his thirst at the pump, he encounters the next one between the church of St Gabriel and the junction with Lime Street. She cannot be more than seven years old. She walks with a swaying, merry gait. Her arm is raised so that she may hold the hand of the woman beside her. The child's dark hair is tucked up in a French coif, a miniature version of the one favoured by the adult – her mother, Schenk assumes.

There was a time when he would have slowed his pace, held back, perhaps even dived down a lane if there was one to hand – anything but face what he knew was about to happen. But no longer. Now he has learned to embrace the inevitable. It is his way of testing himself against the punishment he knows will one day come.

As the woman senses his presence behind her, she turns. Not caring much for what she sees, her grasp on the child's hand tightens. She steps out across Fenchurch Street, the child stumbling along after her, confused by the sudden change in direction. Just before the woman steers her charge around two apprentice tanners bent under a canopy of hides, the child glances back at him.

Her eyes are exactly what he was expecting: blank, filled with dirt, a worm twining its way out of the corner of one bleached socket. The child smiles up at him, her gums studded not with teeth but with gravel. The tongue lolls – a devil's tongue, the maggots writhing upwards towards the dark safety of the throat. The dead, Petrus Euesebius Schenk knows, enjoy nothing better than to play their little games with the living.

That was probably me, he thinks.

I did that.

✠

In size, the room Nicholas Shelby is standing in is modest. Barely fifteen paces square, he reckons, with painted panelling and a row of windows looking out over an orchard. Save for a pair of heavy, overly carved sideboards, it is furnished with satin and damask in the style of the Turk, fashionable amongst the quality these days, now that there are exciting new markets in Barbary and the Orient to explore, and an alliance against Spain with the King of Morocco. Instead of chairs or benches to sit upon, a profusion of cushions covers the floor. Nesting amongst them, propped languorously on one elbow, is the majesty of England personified, a potentate in flowing cloth-of-gold, pearls gleaming like the dew on a spider's web. Her white face tilts thoughtfully towards her breast as one of the ladies grouped around her reads in a soft voice from a leather-bound book.

After what seems like half an hour, but is probably only a minute or two, she looks up.

'Marry,' she says, observing the waiting Nicholas and waving away her coterie with the merest spreading of the fingers of her right hand, 'I see my Heretic has arrived.'

She saw me enter, Nicholas thinks, but I did not exist until she had need of me. In this chamber, time itself is at Elizabeth's command. She beckons to him to join her. He kneels beside her, a pose he will have to maintain for as long as it pleases her, regardless of the limitations of his commoner's knees.

'God give you good morrow, Dr Shelby.'

Nicholas bows his head. 'Majesty, I came the moment I was summoned. I feared perhaps you might—'

'Have no concern, sirrah, England is well.'

By 'England', she means, of course, herself. And indeed, she looks well enough. But then she always does. The Venetian ceruse is laid on like mortar, the hair as authentic as the mock-Turkish cushions she reclines upon.

'Then how may I serve, Majesty?'

'Lady Sarah was reading to me from a new translation of *De Rerum Natura*. Did you study Lucretius, when you were in... where was it now?'

'Padua, Majesty.'

'Yes, Padua. Do you know his work?'

'I do, Majesty.'

'And do you believe his claim?'

'Which claim in particular?'

'That everything in the world – rocks, trees, animals,' she gives a regal frown of distaste, '*ourselves* – is in truth made from tiny particles so small that our eyes cannot see them.'

'I am familiar with the opinion, Your Majesty,' Nicholas says. 'Master Shakespeare, in his work *The Tragedy of Romeo and Juliet*, has one of his players speak of tiny *atomi*, creatures so small that they can draw Queen Mab's fairy chariot up men's noses and into their brains whilst they sleep, to make them dream.'

'And Master Shakespeare is naught but a saucy rogue,' the queen tells him firmly. 'It is a blasphemous suggestion. We are made in God's image, not Queen Mab's. Besides, if it were true that we are no more than piles of dust, we would each blow away at the first breeze.'

'Only a week ago I heard the Bishop of London giving a sermon, Majesty,' Nicholas says, without adding that he had been forced to attend because the service had been to inaugurate a new president of the College of Physicians. 'He quoted from Genesis, about us being from dust, and to dust returning.'

'That's not the point, Dr Shelby. While I concede Bishop Bancroft may at times be a little dry, I refuse to believe he is made of soil. More to the point, God is most certainly not made of dust and *therefore*' – a pause to makes sure there can be no debate – 'neither is His anointed, the Queen of England.'

'I'm sure you are right, Majesty,' Nicholas says. He is accustomed now to the inevitable consequence of these conversations: there is only ever one opinion that prevails.

'I recall you did us some small service with the Moors a while back,' Elizabeth says, changing the subject now that victory is hers.

'That was some seven or so years ago, Majesty – Morocco.'

'Sir Robert Cecil told me you made a goodly impression on our behalf, with the sultan and his vizier, Master Anoun.'

'Abd el-Ouahed ben Massaoud ben Muhammed Anoun,' Nicholas says, giving the man he remembers the courtesy of his full appellation. 'I believe it is also acceptable to call him by the shorter style: Muhammed al-Annuri.'

Given the Moorish nature of the furnishings, this chamber would well suit al-Annuri well, Nicholas thinks. He can picture the tall, imposing figure lying back on the cushions, his stern features relieved only by the merest twinkle in the hawkish eyes, like the sultan waiting for Scheherazade to tell him another story.

'You are familiar with Master Anoun?' the queen asks, as if renaming him by royal decree.

'I have met him, Your Grace.'

'You are friends?'

'I wouldn't say that. We did each other some useful service.'

At once Nicholas is back standing in the shade of the red walls of Marrakech, parched and dusty after the camel journey from Safi. *The* sharif's *most trusted minister*, he is being told in a reverent tone, as he watches the stately man in the simple white *djellaba* stalk away. Not that al-Annuri had needed identifying. Nicholas would have known him at once, from the warning he'd received before he'd even set foot on the Barbary shore: *Cold bugger... Eyes like a peregrine's... Not the sort of Moor you'd care to cross...* It had never occurred to him at that moment that in a matter of days he would owe al-Annuri his life.

'Sir Robert told me you wouldn't be here now, were it not for Master Anoun,' the queen says, breaking into his thoughts.

'That is so, Majesty. But nor might he be living in peace and comfort in Marrakech.'

'So, you understand each other?'

'Not in our native tongues, Majesty. But we both speak Italian to some degree, though not with the competency I understand Your Majesty possesses. He also has some Spanish.'

Elizabeth eases her position on the cushions. Nicholas thinks he detects the slightest wince of discomfort. He would ask if she was well, but that is not the kind of question a man asks his queen, even if he is one of her physicians. If she is ailing, he will have to wait for her to tell him so.

He remembers the day last year when he caught his one and only sight of the truth behind the royal mask. He had been just behind Robert Devereux, the Earl of Essex, when Devereux had committed the unpardonable insult of throwing open the doors to the queen's privy chamber at Nonsuch Palace and bursting in upon her. Before the ladies-in-waiting had slammed those doors shut again, Nicholas had caught a glimpse of an elderly woman with taut, pockmarked skin and thinning hair, as unroyal as the humblest Bankside washerwoman. Fortunate, he thinks, that the queen hadn't caught sight of *him*, or else he'd probably be under house-arrest like the unhappy earl.

'Master Anoun is to be received at our court, as the Moroccan king's ambassador. I want you, Dr Shelby, to be my ears and my eyes in his entourage.'

'Me, Majesty?'

'Is there a problem?'

'No, of course not. When does he arrive?'

'Not for a while. I am told he is yet to leave the Barbary shore. With fair winds and God's grace, sometime in August, I would hazard.'

Nicholas mumbles something about how honoured he is to be entrusted with Her Majesty's commission. In his heart, it is not a task he relishes. Until he had met Muhammed al-Annuri, he had never fully appreciated how much menace one man can exude from beneath an otherwise humble white robe.

'It will require a display of humility on your part, I think.'

Nicholas eases himself on his haunches. How can Elizabeth be so perceptive when his last encounter with the Moor took place more than five years past and more than four hundred leagues away? Then he realizes she is not speaking of al-Annuri at all. She fixes him with a cold gaze.

'If you are to please us in this matter,' the queen says, staring at him with a look that is even more unnerving for the false whiteness of her complexion, 'you must lay aside this petty quarrel you appear to have with Sir Robert Cecil.'

✠

It is raining when Schenk reaches the Steelyard, a sudden hard summer shower. Overhead the clouds are as black as coal, a halo of dying sunlight edging the rooftops and the spires and the darkness of the river where it turns at Westminster. The cobbles shine like polished tin. Now it's not rainwater but grit that torments Schenk's right foot; he is walking as though lame.

To his relief, he finds the Lord Mayor's men failed to put a lock on the Steelyard gate when they expelled the foreign merchants the year before last. The omission saves him having to scale the outer wall that was once the frontier between English London and the mysteries of the foreign Hansa. Pushing through, Schenk heads directly towards his destination. The way is familiar to him. Some of the storehouses and dwellings he passes show signs of recent occupancy. He spots an overturned stool-pot outside one door, a broom propped beside another. One or two have doors forced open, where some of the city's vagrants have sought shelter, regardless of who once lived here. But most of the properties are just as he expects: dark, empty and abandoned, their occupants banished for ever by royal decree.

On the wharf, wheeling gulls shriek at him, though whether in welcome or in warning he cannot be certain. A skeletal wooden crane still stands forlornly on the quayside, waiting to unload cargoes from the Baltic that will never arrive.

Schenk stops before a modest but neatly timbered house that looks out over the empty wharf and across the water to Bankside. The shadows are lengthening towards night. To his left, stretching across the river like a barrier planted to prevent tomorrow's dawn from coming too soon, he can make out the mass of buildings on London Bridge and the massive stone piers they stand upon. He has arrived in the nick of time. Any later and there would be no light to see what he was doing.

Dropping his pack, he takes the heavy key from his purse. In the gloom, with the rain now streaming down his face, it takes a while to find the keyhole in the square iron lock-plate. But when he does, the key turns with ease. Count on old Aksel Leezen to oil the lock regularly. Who did he think was likely to come here again when he'd gone? Certainly not the fellow presently standing at his door, one foot tilted to let the rainwater drain out of his boot.

Schenk tugs at the door. But it does not open.

He tries again. The solid Baltic birch planks remain firmly in the frame.

He tries the key again. Once more it turns without resistance. But still the door does not open.

Then Schenk notices a second lock-plate, set a foot or so below the first. He had missed it in the shadows. Someone – either Axel Leezen himself, or a locksmith sent by the Lord Mayor's men – has installed another lock. A lock for which he has no key.

Schenk looks up. The little window in the overhanging upper floor is latched shut. Through glass that hasn't been cleaned in some while, he can make out the interior shutters. He remembers the solid wooden beam that bars them from within – Leezen trusted his fellow merchants even less than he trusted his English customers. It would require a battering ram to break through.

The light is fading fast. Soaked by the shower, Schenk begins to shiver. He fortifies himself by recalling that he has known worse discomforts in his time than a summer shower. Abandoning the house, he searches for an alternative place to hide.

It doesn't take him long to find one: an empty storehouse near that part of the Steelyard wall that borders All Hallows Lane to the east. Inside, the air is stagnant, oily with the smell of pitch. The barrels themselves have gone, either sold before the enclave closed or stolen afterwards. The place has no windows, but that suits him. If he keeps the door shut, he will be invisible, and invisibility is what Schenk needs as much as he needs food and rest.

He retrieves a tinder box from his pack and a stub of tallow candle. Its meagre flame shows him a glimpse of brickwork with mould sprouting from the mortar. He makes a slow progress around his new realm, holding the candle before him like a priest's censer, oblivious to the stink of burning animal fat that make a rancid incense of the smoke. He finds nothing of use; the storehouse has been stripped bare. He will have to look elsewhere, when the rain stops.

The only other illumination is a grey splash of light on the earthen floor. It leads his eyes upwards to a small hole in the roof where a tile or two has blown away. He considers searching some of the other buildings to find enough dry detritus to get a fire going; the hole will make a vent to stop him choking in the smoke. He could do with the warmth, and he doesn't care to sleep in the dark. That is when his secret companions are more likely to visit him. There are nights when they cluster around him like desperate beggars.

But there are dangers to consider. The Steelyard is not entirely abandoned. Smoke rising from the roof might attract unwelcome attention. When the sun rises, the vagrants sheltering here might come calling. He has nothing of value for them to steal, and though he might once have looked like a diffident chorister, now his plump cheeks have hollowed somewhat, giving him a harder, tougher look. If they are merely curious, he'll tell them he's a masterless labourer thrown off the fields for lack of work. Should they come with evil intent, he knows how to use the knife he carries.

Schenk sits down for a while to rest his feet and wait for the rain to ease. He pulls his pack towards him, folding it to his exhausted body as a miser might hug his hoard of gold. From a pouch on the side, he retrieves the remains of the hunk of bread he stole from an unguarded saddle-pack outside an inn at

Chelmsford. The bread is coarse-grained and hard, but it goes a little way towards easing his hunger. He begins to plan.

Tomorrow he will go to see the Banker. He won't ask for much. If he has coin, he will be tempted to spend it. Profligacy will only get him noticed. He can wait for his reward. It will be enough just to be dry, less hungry and a few more steps closer to forgiveness.

Returning the last of the bread to the pouch, he starts to unlace the pack's leather flap. His fingers work cautiously, like those of a man about to open the door upon a scene he dreads but knows he cannot escape witnessing. When the flap is at last free, Petrus Euesebius Schenk draws it back and waits for his secret companions – the little girl with the earthen eyes and the maggots in her mouth... the old woman with the goose in a cage... and all the others – to come crawling out to keep him company.

To be continued...